The Quebec
Anthology

THE QUEBEC ANTHOLOGY
1830–1990

CANADIAN
SHORT
STORY
LIBRARY
No. 19

Edited by Matt Cohen
and Wayne Grady

University of Ottawa Press

University of Ottawa Press gratefully acknowledges the support extended to its publishing programme by the Canada Council, the Department of Canadian Heritage, and the University of Ottawa.

Most of the translations in this anthology were made possible with the assistance of the Canada Council.

© University of Ottawa Press, 1996
  Printed and bound in Canada
  ISBN 0-7766-0433-3 (cloth)
  ISBN 0-7766-0347-7 (paper)

Canadian Cataloguing in Publication Data
Main entry under title:
  The Quebec Anthology, 1830–1990

(The Canadian short story library; no. 19)
Short stories translated from French.
ISBN 0-7766-0433-3 (cloth)
ISBN 0-7766-0347-7 (paper)

1. Short stories, Canadian (French)—Quebec (Province).
2. Canadian fiction (French)—19th century. 3. Canadian fiction (French)—20th century. I. Cohen, Matt, 1942– II. Grady, Wayne III. Series.

PS8329.5.Q4Q43 1996   C843'.01089714   C96-900483-4
PR9198.2.Q42Q42 1996

"All rights reserved. No part of this publication may be reproduced or transmitted in any form or by any means, electronic or mechanical, including photocopy, recording, or any information storage and retrieval system, without permission in writing from the publisher."

Series design concept: Miriam Bloom
Cover illustration by Edmond-J. Massicotte for the cover of *Contes vrais* by Pamphile LeMay (courtesy of the Bibliothèque nationale du Québec and the LeMay estate).
Book design: Marie Tappin

Distributed in the U.K. by Cardiff Academic Press Ltd., St. Fagans Road, Fairwater, Cardiff CF5 3AE.

The University of Ottawa Press has made every possible effort to gather permissions for each of the selected stories from the authors or their estate as well as from their publisher. We ask that those we could not reach contact us directly.

Contents

Introduction	vii
Philippe Aubert de Gaspé, the Younger: "The Legend of Rose Latulipe" 1837	1
Paul Stevens: "The Three Devils, or, All's Well That Ends Well" 1867	8
Narcisse-Henri-Édouard Faucher de Saint-Maurice: "The Roussis' Fire" 1872	22
Philippe Aubert de Gaspé, the Elder: "Yellow-Wolf, Malecite Chieftain of Old" 1893	38
Robertine Barry: "La Gothe and Her Husband" 1895	53
Louis Fréchette: "How I Learned to Speak English" 1900	64
Sylva Clapin: "Hay Fever" 1917	69
Jean-Aubert Loranger: "The Ferryman" 1920	89
Harry Bernard: "The Italian Teacher" 1927	99
Louis Dantin: "The Mass of Florent Létourneau" 1930	111
Marie le Franc: "Foreign Souls" 1934	122
Albert Laberge: "Mrs. Filly" 1942	139
Yves Thériault: "Mother Soubert's Pig" 1944	152
Alain Grandbois: "Fleur-de-Mai" 1945	161
Ringuet: "Happiness" 1946	172
Anne Hébert: "The Torrent" 1947	183
Gérard Bessette: "Last Rites" 1960	219
Adrien Thério: "A Case of Sorcery" 1963	231

Jacques Ferron: "The Chronicles of l'Anse Saint-Roch" 1968	240
Hubert Aquin: "Back on April Eleventh" 1969	255
Roch Carrier: "The Goldfish" 1970	268
André Langevin: "A Blue Rose Perfume" 1974	284
Gabrielle Roy: "Part II of Children of My Heart" 1979	298
André Major: "The Good Old Days" 1981	326
Gaétan Brulotte: "The Secret Voice" 1982	340
Monique Proulx: "Beach Blues" 1983	346
Suzanne Jacob: "Pomme Douly and the Instant of Eternity" 1988	374
Anne Dandurand: "To Console Myself. I Imagine That the Bombs Have Fallen" 1989	382
Gilles Pellerin: "In My Condition" 1989	385
Claude-Emmanuelle Yance: "The Love of Lies" 1989	390
André Carpentier: "Tragedy Houses My Wound" 1990	395
Claire Dé: "Consuming Love" 1990	409
Marie José Thériault: "Portraits of Elsa" 1990	413

INTRODUCTION

The literature of French Canada has always been difficult to summarize and encapsulate, which may be why there are so few anthologies of it, and why the critical histories that exist have been so controversial. Although Québécois literature flourished during the first half of the nineteenth century, its principal genre was the *conte*, an oral not a written form—which presents a distinct problem for the anthologist. French Canada did not really have a written literature until the publication of François-Xavier Garneau's *Histoire du Canada*, the first volumes of which began appearing in 1845. One needn't go as far as Gérard Tougas, in his *Histoire de la littérature canadienne-française*, in condemning "the numerous versifiers, storytellers and memorists" who preceded Garneau for churning out works distinguished mainly by their "mediocrity of thought and invention," but it is nonetheless true that Garneau's rich collection of historical sketches instilled in his many readers a sense of their own past, and created an intellectual fervour capable of leading to a more mature literary output. The literary group Les Soirées canadiennes, founded by Garneau's followers in 1860, published the review *Les Soirées canadiennes* the following year; it included many of the early works of this *naissance* of Quebec writing. As Camille Roy, who has been called Quebec's first literary critic, has put it, "with [Garneau's] work the second period of French-Canadian literature opens—the period of its development."

Perhaps ironically, this development began by looking back to earlier days, a theme that still echoes throughout the literature of Quebec. The motto of Les Soirées canadiennes was taken from the words of the critic Charles Nodier: "Let us make haste to write down the stories and traditions of the people, before they are forgotten." Such was the spirit that moved Philippe Aubert de Gaspé, the Elder, to write *Les Anciens canadiens*, for as he stated, his purpose was merely "to note down some episodes of the good old times." At least, he did note them down so they could be read and even translated (as *Canadians of Old*, by Sir Charles G.D. Roberts), and thus reach a wider audience. De Gaspé and those who followed him had not yet created "*une littérature en ébullition*," a literature in ferment, as Gérard Bessette was to call the work of a later period, but theirs was definitely a literature in the throes of birth. During this second period, a whole school of writers began to make contributions to the national oeuvre: Paul Stevens, whose twists on older themes created a new kind of folktale; Faucher de Saint-Maurice, who tried to unite fact and fiction to forge a kind of historical ethos; Robertine Barry, the fiery female journalist and writer of closely observed short stories; and of course Louis Fréchette, perhaps Quebec's best-known writer of the nineteenth century, whose forward-looking evocation of the past seemed the perfect vehicle for easing Quebec into the brave new world of the future.

There followed, however, a period of relative obscurity in the literature of Quebec. As the indefatigable critic and anthologist Adrien Thério observed (in his *Conteurs québécois 1900-1940*), "It is no exaggeration to say that the period 1900 to 1940 is the least known in our literature, even though the teaching of Quebec literature has taken a considerable upward swing in our colleges and universities." The literary lights that did shine during those four decades shone primarily through the novel—Thério cited especially Louis Hémon's *Maria Chapdelaine* (1914), Albert Laberge's *La Scouine* (1918), and Marie le Franc's *Grand Louis l'innocent* (1927). But even those important works were problematic, since both Hémon and le Franc were born outside of Canada, and *La Scouine* was not published until nearly twenty years after it was written, and then in a small, private edition of only sixty copies!

But if novels were not thick on the ground, the short story seemed to fare somewhat better. Perhaps the Depression, coming as it did after a cataclysmic world war, instilled in writers a sense of the desperation inherent in everyday life, a desperation that can be caught so much more subtly in the short story than in the novel. Whatever the cause, it is in the short stories of such writers as Laberge, Jean-Aubert Loranger, and Harry Bernard that the social realist writing of the epoch first appeared: theirs were short, concise, unromanticized portraits of the reality of Quebec life cut off from its cultural roots.

The full consequences of that severance began to appear in the literature of the late 1940s and 1950s, with the work of writers such as Anne Hébert, Yves Thériault, Gabrielle Roy, and Alain Grandbois. The first modern Québécois writers—just how modern they were then is marked by the fact that they are all well known and widely read today—made almost a virtue of their alienation from the rural past, shrugging off the oppression of their history, and squarely facing the chaos of the life that remained. Anne Hébert's "Le Torrent," published in 1947, symbolizes not only the dark vision of the future held by Hébert and her contemporaries, but also the slowness of the Quebec public to accept that vision. Yves Thériault was seen almost as a madman when his *Contes pour un homme seul* appeared in 1944. But these writers, whose vision was unblurred and unwavering, were at the forefront of Quebec's cultural renaissance, its largely literary Quiet Revolution.

One of the remarkable things about Thériault's first collection was its revival of the *conte*, a form that was avidly picked up by many writers who had been searching for a definitive Québécois art form, one not borrowed from either English Canada or France. Jacques Ferron's *Contes du pays incertain* (1962) and *Contes anglais et autres* (1964), along with many other short-story collections published during the 1960s, revealed the *conte* to be an eminently suitable symbol of a truly Québécois literature. That the *conte* could be at once a subject for revival and a manifesto for the future was suggested by Ferron himself, who in 1966 declared that to write *contes* was another way of writing self: "I write *contes* not because I have a special calling for it, but because of grammar. Among all the pronouns, only one is personal: the 'I' (along with its adjuncts). The others are representatives: when I speak or write in the second person singular, or third person plural, I am a fabulist. This way, I am a writer of *contes* like everybody else."

Since 1960, many of Quebec's short-story writers have called their work *contes*: it was no accident that Adrien Thério, in publishing in 1965 the first anthology of modern short fiction from Quebec, called it *Conteurs canadiens-français*. His collection included, among others, the writers Thériault, Grandbois, Ringuet, Gérard Bessette, and Roch Carrier, and in his introduction Thério distinguished between the short story and the *conte* by citing the dictionary definition of the short story as "a sort of short novel," whereas the *conte* was "a short account of imaginary adventures." By not including in his collection stories that seemed to be novelistic, Thério was reflecting the increasingly fractured nature of contemporary Quebec society, a society that seemed more readily represented by short, conversational tales than by long, discursive, developmental novels. "Storytellers today," he wrote, "have more or less completely abandoned the nineteenth-century concept of the *conte* as a vehicle for legends, fables and the supernatural, and have adapted it to the presentation of facts that belong to reality, even as they transform that reality to their own ends."

Quebec's contemporary writers, the generation that followed the writers of the Quiet Revolution of the 1960s and 1970s, seemed to reject the *conte* again (to reject the personal for collective pronouns, perhaps), although many embraced what might be called a magic-realist style: prose that blends realism and fantasy to achieve its effect—which is not, after all, so removed from the style of the *conte*. Some still refer to their work as *contes*—Marie José Thériault, for example, called the stories in her first collection, *La Cérémonie* (1979), *contes*, and so they are—but the nature of the form has changed once again.

This may be because contemporary Quebec short stories take place within an urban environment. The narrative strategies of these short stories still owe a lot to the past, but stories such as Claire Dé's "Consuming Love," Suzanne Jacob's "Pomme Douly and the Instant of Eternity," or

André Carpentier's "Tragedy Houses My Wound" are decidedly urban in tone and effect. Despite its self-referential nature, contemporary Quebec short fiction is—like most short fiction everywhere—about people living their lives in the midst of urban, technologically determined environments that have reduced non-urban environments to faceless, characterless suburbs. And most writers feel uncomfortable in the suburbs, as is made abundantly clear by the stories mentioned above, as well as by André Major's "The Good Old Days," the title of which ironically recalls de Gaspé's *Les Anciens canadiens*.

This interplay with its own past is an element that distinguishes Quebec short fiction from that produced in other parts of Canada—which seems almost unconscious of its historical antecedents and instead eagerly claims kinship with British, American, and even South American writing.

In selecting the stories for *The Quebec Anthology*, we have attempted to give as representative a picture as possible of the Quebec short story from its beginnings to the present, while trying to keep an already large book from becoming immense. Some of the early stories, such as those by the Auberts de Gaspé, were chosen not only because they were written during the dawn of Quebec fiction, but also because they were also among the first stories to impose themselves both on readers of the day and those who have followed. By the 1920s and 1930s, an enormous number of short stories were being published in Quebec newspapers and magazines as well as in books. The stories in this collection have established themselves as historically important and are often by writers who—though perhaps less known today—were both critically praised and widely read during their lifetimes. At the same time, these selected stories had to meet the most necessary literary criterion: that they be engaging and interesting to a reader of today.

The writers who represent the 1960s and 1970s, such as Gabrielle Roy, Jacques Ferron, and Hubert Aquin, belong to the generation of Quebec writers best known to

English-Canadian readers. Their work appeared at a time when English Canada had great interest in French-Canadian writing, both for its literary merit and for the window it provided on the attitudes and aspirations of the society from which it sprang, and during this period many writers from Quebec became as important to English Canada as writers writing in English.

Since the 1980s, this has changed. It is fair to say that Quebec literature no longer enjoys the immense interest among English-Canadian readers that it held during the heady days of the Quiet Revolution. Part of the reason for this may be that many Quebec writers seem to have lost interest in English Canada, preferring to find new ways of writing for their own community. It is also true that writers of this period experimented heavily with narrative techniques. Perhaps because the main forum for short stories has once again become literary magazines, stories have become increasingly private, fragmented, and in many ways inaccessible to wide audiences. They have, in effect, become *contes*.

One of the unique and legitimate attractions of the contemporary short story is that the reader is not only offered "plot"—a delineation of what happens to a certain character—but is also entertained by the story's innovative, even playful, use of language and narrative form. It has become an unspoken assumption that great short fiction, like great paintings or great films, must constantly re-invent its own form.

The stories we have chosen from the 1980s and 1990s are those therefore that are engaging and inventive at every level. It is not the anthologist's job to predict the future, but rather to present a snapshot of the present. We do, however, feel that the contemporary authors included here represent the best and most solidly based of the many significant writers working in Quebec today. They are not old enough to have become classics, and some of them are just now establishing themselves in Quebec literary circles. Nonetheless, we feel these are the stories and writers who will find an enduring place in the future of the short story in Quebec.

Matt Cohen and Wayne Grady

Philippe Aubert de Gaspé, the Younger
Translated by Yves Brunelle

THE LEGEND OF ROSE LATULIPE

Born in Quebec in 1814, Philippe-Ignace-François was the second of Philippe-Joseph Aubert de Gaspé's thirteen children; he was named after his ancestor, the seigneur Philippe-Ignace Aubert de Gaspé, Chevalier of the Royal and Military Order of Saint-Louis. Unlike his illustrious forebear, however, the young Philippe-Ignace-François was destined for a brief and somewhat scurrilous life. Raised during the early days of Quebec nationalism, in 1835 he became a journalist and parliamentary reporter for the *Quebec Mercury* and *Le Canadien*. Two years later he founded *Le Télégraphe* and became an editor of the literary journal *Le Fantasque*. In 1840, he moved to Halifax to become parliamentary reporter for Nova Scotia's Legislative Assembly; less than a year later, on May 7, 1841—a few months before his father's release from debtor's prison in Quebec—he died, "ruined," according to the Abbé Casgrain, "by the abuse of alcohol."

In 1836, upon being accused of false reporting by Dr. Edmund Bailey O'Callaghan, a member of the Quebec legislature, de Gaspé demanded a retraction and threatened the politician with physical violence, whereupon he was sent to jail for a month. By way of revenge, de Gaspé poured a fulsome liquid onto the hot stove in the Legislature, causing the building to be evacuated. To escape a second jail term, he hid out at his father's seigneury in Saint-Jean-Port-Joli. There he wrote what is now regarded as the first Québécois novel, *L'Influence d'un livre* . . . (*The Influence of a Book*).

The novel is a work of fantasy and folklore, a blend of the surreal and the macabre that relates the story of Charles Amand, a native of Saint-Jean-Port-Joli who becomes obsessed by the desire to be an alchemist. Much of the book is taken up by Amand's attempt to secure a

"Main-de-Gloire," the severed hand of a hanged man. Equally important to the book are the two *contes* related by the village story-teller, the story of Rodrigue Bras de Fer, and "The Legend of Rose Latulipe," the tale of a village maiden who inadvertently dances with Satan—perhaps the most popular Québécois folktale ever recorded. De Gaspé's version was almost certainly written for the most part by his father, Philippe Aubert de Gaspé, the Elder. Included here in a lively translation by Yves Brunelle, it is arguably the best of the many forms given this traditional *conte* over the years.

∽

"The Legend of Rose Latulipe" is reproduced from *French Canadian Prose Masters: The Nineteenth Century* (Montreal: Harvest House Ltd., 1978) and was originally published under the title "L'Étranger" in *L'Influence d'un livre* (Quebec City: W. Cowan et fils, 1837).

There was once a man by the name of Latulipe, who had a daughter whom he loved madly. Rose Latulipe was a pretty brunette; but she was daring by nature, not to say indiscreet. She had a friend by the name of Gabriel Lepard, whom she loved like the pupil of her eye. However, it is said that when others made advances she played him false. She liked parties, so on a Shrove Tuesday there were some fifty people gathered at Latulipe's. Contrary to her usual practice, Rose spent the whole evening with her fiancé; it was natural enough: they were to be married at Easter. It must have been about eleven that evening when, all of a sudden, as a lively dance was going on, a sleigh was heard stopping at the door. Several people ran to the windows to knock the snow off to be able to see the new arrival. "It must be a big shot," someone said; "you see, Jean, the beautiful black horse, how its eyes are blazing! The devil take me! You'd say that it'd jump over the house!" As these comments were made, the gentleman entered the house and asked permission of the master to rest a while. "We'll be honored," Latulipe said. "Please take off your coat; I'll have the horse unharnessed." The stranger absolutely refused, claiming that he would stay only half an hour, being in a hurry. Still, he took off his superb wildcat overcoat; he had on a black velvet suit trimmed all over with braid. He kept his gloves on, and asked permission to keep his cap on, claiming a headache.

"The gentleman will take a shot of brandy," Latulipe said, proffering him a glass.

The stranger made a devilish face as he swallowed it, because Latulipe, having run out of bottles, had emptied the holy water from the one he was holding in his hand and had filled it with the alcohol.

He was handsome, this stranger, except that he was very dark and had something sneaky about the eyes. He moved up to Rose, took her two hands and said:

"I hope, my pretty miss, that you will be mine this evening and that we will dance together always."

"Certainly," Rose said in a low voice, looking timidly at poor Lepard, who bit his lip until the blood flowed.

The stranger did not leave Rose's side for the rest of the evening, so that poor Gabriel, scowling in a corner, was unhappily playing second fiddle.

In a little room adjoining the one where the party was going on, there was an old and saintly woman who, seated on a chest at the foot of the bed, was praying fervently; in one hand she held a rosary and with the other she frequently struck her breast. She stopped suddenly, and motioned to Rose that she wanted to speak to her.

"Listen, my girl," she said to her; "it's wrong of you to leave Gabriel, your fiancé, for this gentleman. There is something amiss here; every time I say the holy names of Jesus and Mary, he looks at me furiously. See how he just looked at us with eyes aflame with anger."

"Come on, aunty," Rose said, "tell your beads and let the worldly people have fun."

"What was that old dotard saying to you?" the stranger asked.

"Bah!" Rose said, "you know that old folks are always preaching to the young."

Midnight rang out, and the master of the house wanted the dancing to stop, saying that it was hardly proper to dance on Ash Wednesday.

"One more dance," the stranger said.

"Yes, yes, dear father," Rose said, and the dancing went on.

"You promised me, pretty Rose," the stranger said, "to be mine all evening; why wouldn't you be mine forever?"

"Stop it, sir; it's not right for you to laugh at a poor farmer's daughter like me," Rose answered.

"I swear," the stranger went on, "that there is nothing more serious than what I am proposing. Only say: yes . . . and nothing will ever part us."

"But, sir . . . ," and she looked at unhappy Lepard.

"I see," the stranger said haughtily, "you love this Gabriel? That settles that!"

"Oh, yes . . . I love him . . . I have loved him . . . but, see here, you fine gentlemen, you cajole girls so that they can't trust in what you say."

"What! pretty Rose, you believe me capable of deceiving you," the stranger exclaimed; "I swear by what I hold most sacred . . . by . . ."

"Oh, no! don't swear; I believe you," the poor girl said, "but perhaps my father won't consent."

"Your father!" the stranger said with a bitter smile; "say you're mine and I'll look after the rest."

"Well . . . yes," she answered.

"Give me your hand as a pledge of your promise."

The hapless Rose gave him her hand, which she pulled back immediately, uttering a faint cry of pain, because she had felt a sting. She turned as pale as a corpse, and feigning a sudden illness she left the dance.

At that moment, two young horse-handlers came in, aghast, and drawing Latulipe aside, they said:

"We went outside to look at that gentleman's horse; would you believe that all the snow around it is melted away and that it is standing on bare ground?"

Latulipe checked for himself, and appeared all the more horrified, since having noticed his daughter's pallor he received from her a half confession of what had happened between her and the stranger. Consternation soon spread through the crowd; there were whispers, and only Latulipe's pleas prevented the guests from leaving.

The stranger, seeming indifferent to what was going on around him, continued to pay compliments to Rose, and said to her as he offered her a beautiful necklace of pearls and gold: "Take off your glass necklace, pretty Rose, and accept, for my sake, this necklace of real pearls." But, to her glass necklace was attached a small cross, and the girl refused to take it off.

Meanwhile, another scene was taking place in the parish rectory, where the old curé, kneeling since nine o'clock, had not ceased praying to God, asking Him to forgive the sins his parishioners were committing on this night of dissipation, Shrove Tuesday. The saintly old man had fallen asleep, as he prayed fervently, and for an hour had been sunk in a deep slumber. Awaking suddenly, he called for his servant: "Ambroise, my good Ambroise, get up, and harness my mare, quickly. In the name of God, hurry. I'll make you a present of a month's, of two months', of six months' wages."

"What's the matter, sir?" cried Ambroise, who knew well the charitable zeal of the priest; "is there someone dying?"

"Dying!" the curé repeated, "worse than that, my dear Ambroise, a soul is endangering its eternal salvation. Quick, harness up."

In five minutes, the curé was on the road to Latulipe's, and in spite of the horrible weather he was moving with unbelievable speed. You see, it was Saint Rose who was smoothing the way.

He got there just in time. The stranger by pulling on the necklace string had broken it and was about to seize poor Rose, when the curé, quick as lightning, forestalled him by placing his stole around the girl's neck, and gathering her to his breast, where that morning he had received his God, he thundered:

"Miscreant! what are you doing among these Christians?"

The spectators had fallen to their knees at this terrible spectacle, and were sobbing to see their venerable pastor, who had always seemed to them so timid and weak, so strong and courageous now in the face of the enemy of God and of men.

"I don't recognize as Christians," Lucifer answered, rolling his blood-shot eyes, "those who, contemptuous of your religion, spend those days designated by your damned precepts for penance, dancing, drinking and cavorting. Besides, this young woman gave herself to me, and the blood that flowed from her hand is the seal that binds her to me forever."

"Begone Satan!" shouted the priest striking him in the face with his stole and repeating Latin words no one understood. The devil disappeared immediately with a frightful noise, leaving behind a suffocating smell of sulphur. The good curé, dropping to his knees, said a fervent prayer, all the while holding the hapless Rose, who had swooned, and all answered with renewed sighs and groans.

"Where is he? where is he?" the poor girl said as she regained consciousness.

"He has disappeared," came from all sides.

"Oh, father, father!" Rose cried, falling at the venerable pastor's feet; "take me with you . . . you alone can protect me . . . I gave myself to him . . . I fear he will return. . . . A convent! a convent!"

"Well, poor sheep that was lost and is now repenting," the good priest said, "come to my house. I will watch over you; I will surround you with holy relics, and if your vocation is sincere, as no doubt it is after this terrible trial, you will renounce this world which has been so baneful to you."

Five years later, the bell of the Convent of — had been announcing for two days that a nun, professed for only three years, had joined her celestial bridegroom, and, early in the morning, a crowd of inquisitive spectators had gathered in the church to attend her funeral. Although most attended this gloomy ceremony with the flightiness of people of the world, three persons were broken-hearted; an old priest kneeling in the sanctuary, praying fervently; an old man in the nave who bemoaned the death of an only daughter; and a young man in mourning clothes who was saying his last farewell to the one who had once been his betrothed, hapless Rose Latulipe.

Paul Stevens
Translated by Wayne Grady

THE THREE DEVILS
OR, ALL'S WELL THAT ENDS WELL

Paul-Jules-Joseph Stevens was born in Brussels, Belgium, in 1830, and emigrated to Canada in 1854 to become a school teacher in Berthier-en-Haut, now called Berthierville. He married Marie Valier in 1855 and the next year began publishing in such popular journals of the day as *Le Pays*, *La Patrie*, and *L'Avenir*. Upon moving to Montreal in 1858, he gave private lessons in French and drawing, and began giving lectures at the Cabinet de lecture paroissial; his lectures were published in the journal *L'Écho du cabinet de lecture paroissial* from 1859 to 1866. Ostensibly on such highly moral precepts as "The Effects of Making Bad Friends," or "The Disastrous Consequences of Intemperance," these "lectures" were often retellings of traditional folktales, but were exceptionally literary and quite well written. They thus represented a kind of transition from the oral *conte* to the literary short story.

    Some of the stories were eventually published as *Contes populaires (Popular Tales)* in Ottawa in 1867, the year Stevens moved to Coteau-du-Lac to become a private tutor to several wealthy families. He also wrote dozens of studies of popular figures in Canadian history, including Dollard des Ormeaux and Jean de Lauson, as well as a series of essays outlining the "principal events in Canada from its discovery by Jacques Cartier to the death of Champlain," which appeared in various newspapers in 1864 and 1865. Perhaps because he remained fiercely and vocally loyal to Belgium, he was never very popular as a Quebec writer, but, as Aurélien Boivin has remarked, "he remains an intellectual story-teller shaped by the 17th-century tradition." "Les trois diables," translated by Wayne Grady as "The Three Devils," first appeared in *Contes populaires* and was one of

Stevens's more successful stories. It is typical of his use of the mannerisms of the folktale to shed light on contemporary morals—on the one hand, it is a caution against alcoholism (or at least against marrying an alcoholic wife); on the other, it is a romping celebration of the triumph of the meek over the machinations of the devil.

Stevens died in Coteau-du-Lac on October 29, 1881.

⁐

"The Three Devils" is a translation of "Les trois diables" published in *Contes populaires* (Ottawa: C.-E. Desbarats, 1867); first appeared in *L'Écho du cabinet de lecture paroissial*, September 1, 1862.

There was once a shoemaker whose name was Rich, though he himself was far from it. Had he been consulted at his baptism he would probably have chosen a different name, but as we all know we can no more choose our names than we can our fates. The wisest among us accept both as they come to us, and make the best of them.

It is also true, by the way, that a person's name and character are not always perfectly matched. I once knew a boy who answered to the name Goodchild and who, without a word of a lie, was one of the worst brats ever to walk the face of the earth. I also knew a man named Armstrong who couldn't punch his way out of a wet paper bag. So there you have it.

But getting back to Rich. If it were absolutely necessary I could draw you a pretty detailed portrait of him, but since that would drag my story out too long I'll just say that he was neither tall nor short, somewhere between fat and thin, and though he wasn't handsome he wasn't what you would call ugly, either. In a word, he was very much like you and me. As for how old he was, he didn't know his exact age, and could only give it to the nearest decade. At the time my story begins, he would have said he was in his fifties.

In those days there wasn't a worker within ten miles who toiled as hard as Mr. Rich, or who did such fine work. Up at dawn, he hammered away at soles and stitched on uppers until sunset, hardly taking time off for meals. And yet, for all his industry, he was still as poor as a churchmouse.

Surprised? Well, you shouldn't be. And if you read the rest of this story, you'll understand why.

You see, Mr. Rich was married. Nothing odd about that, as you'd no doubt be the first to point out, and you'd be right. A shoemaker in his fifties certainly has the right to a wife, and having one doesn't automatically mean that he also has to be as poor as a churchmouse.

Maybe he has a house full of children and grandchildren, you say to yourself.

He never had any children.

Well, then, you say, maybe his customers didn't pay him on time.

Not a bit of it; everyone who had shoes made by Rich paid for them promptly, and paid a fair price for them, too.

But if he had no children, and if everyone paid him handsomely and on time for his work, then the man must have lived like a king. Unless he didn't get much work: maybe he was idle three-quarters of the time?

Sorry, but didn't I just say that he worked hard every day, from sunup to sunset, Sundays and holidays excepted? Eight hours a day in winter, thirteen and fourteen hours a day in summer. But even if he had worked ten times harder and sold ten times as many shoes as he did, he'd still be penniless. Why? Because he had the misfortune to have married a woman who drank.

For every dollar he earned, his wife drank two. She soaked it up as fast as a bagful of sponges. There was no end to her, or rather, no bottom: what more can I say? Throughout the area she was known by the unflattering sobriquet: the Fish.

Sure, Rich could hide his money when people came in to pay their bills, but the Fish knew every nook and cranny of the house so well that she always found it, and when she did I don't need to tell you that Rich's hard-earned cash didn't exactly find its way into the poorbox at church.

Well, it so happened that one day the Fish became so tired of always having to hunt for the money that her husband so obstinately insisted on hiding from her that she conceived of a horribly brilliant idea—the kind of plan that seems perfectly diabolical to us, but appears positively inspired to a drunkard. She decided to call up the Devil!

Dear readers, we all know the proverb that goes: "Speak of the Devil and he shall appear." Well, Madame Rich had hardly got the word Devil out of her mouth when there he was, standing in front of her. These things happen.

"What's on your mind, my good woman?" the Devil said to her in his oiliest voice. "There isn't a thing I wouldn't give you in exchange for your soul."

"G-good!" replied the Fish, between hiccups. "Gimme enough m-money to keep me in booze for a year, all the rum I can d-drink, an' you can have my soul."

"Sounds like a bargain to me," laughed the Devil, and he reached into his pocket and pulled out a bag brimming with gold coins. "Here you are, my lovely. Take this and drink away to your heart's content, and then some. But remember: in exactly one year and one day, you'll belong to me. Have a nice day!"

And he disappeared in a puff of smoke.

⌒

Two days after the Fish had sold her body and soul to the Devil, a beggar happened to pass the door to Rich's shop, and he stopped to ask for a handout.

Sitting on his bench and hammering away at his last, the shoemaker didn't hear the beggar come in.

"You wouldn't have any spare change, would you, my good man?" asked the beggar.

"Spare change?" said the shoemaker, looking up. "You can rest assured that nothing would give me greater pleasure than to have some spare change. I'd give it to you willingly if I had some," he added, wiping a tear from his eye with the corner of his leather apron. "As God is my witness, I ask for nothing more than to be able to help out the poor. But the fact is I don't have a penny to my name, not a cent. My wife drinks every nickel I earn. It's been going on for thirty years now, and I'm beginning to think she's a woman possessed."

Hearing these words, a change came over the features of the beggar; you might say he was transfigured.

"Your heart's in the right place," he said to Rich, casting upon the poor shoemaker a look of profound sympathy. "I would like to repay you for the good intentions you've expressed on my behalf. What can I do for you? What would you like most? Speak up. You can have anything you want, all you have to do is ask."

Master Rich, as you can well imagine, was struck speechless by these words; he simply stared at the man who had spoken them with a look of astonishment mixed with apprehension. He didn't know what to think.

"Come, come, speak up, my good man," said the beggar. "Look, I'll make it easier for you. I'll give you three wishes. There, now you can have an embarrassment of riches."

But the shoemaker continued to gape at the man in silence; it seemed he would be forced to take the beggar's admittedly unusual proposition seriously. Perhaps he thought the man was one of those practical jokers he had run across from time to time in the course of his rounds.

"Are you telling me the truth?" he finally asked, pronouncing each syllable carefully and staring fixedly at the beggar, as though he wanted to read what was written on the old man's heart.

"As true as there's a God in Heaven and you on your bench, Master Rich," said the other.

"Well, then," replied the shoemaker, having come to a decision. "Since you are being so kind to me, even though I've never laid eyes on you before in my life, I would like to have a bench that if someone sits on it they can't get up until I tell them to."

"That's one," said the beggar. "Here is your bench."

"And I also want a violin that, when I play it, everyone who hears it has to dance whether they want to or not."

"That's two," the beggar said. "Here's your violin, with a bow and a few extra strings to go with it."

"And I want a bag that keeps everything that goes into it until I let it out."

"That's three," said the beggar. "Here's your bag. Now good night, Master Rich, and may God bless."

⌁

There is nothing in the world that we place so little value on as time, and so there is nothing in the world that disappears so quickly.

At the end of a year and a day, the Devil—who had not forgotten about his deal with the shoemaker's wife—showed up at the Rich residence.

Well, said the shoemaker to himself. Here's a new face.

"Who the devil are you?" he asked aloud, and in a brusque manner, since the stranger had taken to pacing back and forth in the room as if he owned the place.

"Got it in one," said the Devil, still pacing.

"What do you want with me?"

"I've come to fetch your wife."

"My wife! You've come to fetch my wife? Great! Take her away! You'll be doing me a real service, believe me. She's sleeping at the moment—actually, that's about all she does these days. I don't think she's been sober for an hour in the past year. Why don't you sit down and wait for her."

Without waiting to be asked twice, the Devil sat down on the bench I told you about before.

When the Devil was sitting comfortably, Richard said to him:

"There . . . that was my wife coughing. She'll be waking up any minute—you may as well go get her now."

But, try as he might, the Devil couldn't stand up. He wriggled and threw himself about like a fish out of water, but he was stuck to the bench.

Seeing the Devil's contortions and the frightful grimaces he was making, Rich laughed. When his wife appeared at the half-open door to her bedroom, however, she cried to her husband in a terrified, tearful voice:

"Keep him there! Don't let him get me! Oh my darling, sweet husband, keep him away from me and I swear I'll never touch another drop of the hard stuff as long as I live!"

Rich kept the Devil sitting like that for nine days, at the end of which time the poor devil had worn off the cheeks of his behind from struggling so much. Finally, the pain was too much for him: "Listen, Rich," he said to the shoemaker, "let me go and I'll leave your wife alone for another year and a day."

"Very well," said Rich. "You may get up. Good day to you, sir, and I hope we won't meet again."

I should have mentioned before, probably, that this Devil who bartered for the soul of Rich's wife had two brothers. He and his two brothers made three brothers, or three devils, a sort of triumvirate or whatever you want to call them.

When he arrived back in hell, limping because he had suffered so much at the hands of the shoemaker, his two brothers hurried over to find out what he'd been up to during his long absence.

"What have I been up to?" whined the first devil in a piteous tone. "Ever since leaving here I've been sitting on a bench." And he told them about his dolorous misadventures.

"Never mind, little brother," said one of the brothers upon hearing the tale. "Go get yourself looked after—you won't have any trouble finding a doctor down here—and next time, I'll go fetch Madame Rich myself. The devil take me, I promise you she won't get away from me.

⁓

A second year and a day went by, and the second devil presented himself at the house of the shoemaker. I should mention here that Rich's wife had not stopped drinking—far from it: after her fright with the Devil, she drank harder than ever. You can't teach an old fish new tricks, as the saying goes. In fact it would have been astonishing if she had quit: she would have had the devil of a time of it.

Well, said the shoemaker to himself when he saw the Devil standing defiantly in his living room: another new face. "Who are you?" he asked aloud.

"I'm the Devil," said the Devil.

"What do you want?"

"I've come to fetch your wife."

"You're very welcome to her," said the shoemaker, "she can certainly go to hell as far as I'm concerned. But why don't you have a seat for a moment? You look tired."

"Have a seat, he says," laughed the Devil. "Hoo-oo, that's a good one. What kind of fool do you take me for? My brother's butt still hasn't healed."

"You don't want to sit, that's fine," said Rich. "You can stand up like a horse."

So saying, Richard took the violin down from its hook on the wall, placed it delicately under his chin, and took the bow in his right hand. The Devil watched without breathing a word, standing as still and straight as a post.

"Have it your way," thought the shoemaker, watching his strange guest out of the corner of his eye. "You don't want to sit down and you don't want to walk... All right, then, let's see you dance. I'll make you hop about like you've never hopped before."

And he drew a tentative note on the violin.

The Devil raised one leg off the ground, with his toe pointed inward.

The shoemaker played a second note, and the Devil tapped his foot.

Then the shoemaker plunged resolutely into a spirited reel, and the Devil began to dance, turn about, jump up and down, and fall into a furious, disorderly polka—for the polka, as is well known, is a favourite dance of the Devil's.

Rich kept him dancing for twelve days.

On the evening of the twelfth day, just as the sun was going down, the Devil was so hot that his skin had turned red, his eyes were popping out of his head, and his tongue was as dry as chalk.

"Stop, Rich!" he cried from time to time in a breathless voice. "Stop! You're killing me!"

But Richard played all the merrier, and the Devil danced all the harder.

At last the Devil could take it no more, and said to the shoemaker:

"If you'll stop playing your fiddle, I'll let you have your wife for another year and a day."

"It's a deal," said Rich, and he hung up his violin while the devil, completely out of breath, wiped his brow.

When his brothers saw him returning to hell empty-handed, the youngest one—the one with the pain in his butt—cried out to him: "I'll bet you sat on that bench, didn't you!"

"No, it wasn't that."

"Well, what then?" asked the eldest brother. "What kept you away for so long?"

"I don't want to talk about it," said the Devil. "I've been dancing for twelve days, that's what! That Rich is a real devil himself."

"Well," said the eldest, making a disdainful gesture, "it's clear to me that you two aren't. The next time, I'll go up to fetch Madame Rich myself, and we'll see who'll read the riot act to whom!"

⌇

A year and a day later, the eldest devil brother turned up at the shoemaker's house.

"Well, well, another new face," said Richard. "And who might you be?"

"I'm the Devil, as you well know," said the Devil.

"Glad to meet you. My wife is drinking down at the barracks, but she'll be back soon. She won't give you any trouble. Won't you have a seat?"

"No, no thank you. I'll just stand."

"Do you like music? I could play you a few songs on my fiddle?"

"Never mind the fiddle," said the Devil sternly. "Go get your wife and bring her here, that's all I came for."

"Just a second," said Rich, taking out the bag I told you about earlier. "I'll bring her back in this, but only if you'll do me a favour first."

"A favour?" said the Devil. "What kind of favour?"

"I've been told that the Devil is no fool . . ."

"So?"

"And that he can turn himself into anything he wants, any time he wants . . ."

"That's true," said the Devil, puffing out his chest.

"Well, I don't believe it," said Rich. "I'd be very interested in seeing a demonstration."

"Very well, what would you like—a lion?"

"No, no, not a lion. You could mangle me. Something smaller, a little animal that I can hold in my arms and pet—how about a rat?"

"No problem," said the devil. "Watch this—" and he turned himself into a rat. Quick as a wink, the shoemaker jumped on him and tossed him into the bag, tied the bag up, threw it over his shoulder, and headed out the door.

He went straight to the blacksmith's shop.

"Busy, neighbour?" he asked pleasantly.

"Not too bad."

"What about your apprentice?"

"About the same."

"Good, then let's 'forge' ahead: I've brought you enough work for two weeks," and he dumped his bag on the blacksmith's anvil. The two men watched it jump around a bit as the Devil struggled to get free. "I want you and your apprentice to take your heaviest hammers," said the shoemaker, "and pound this bag as hard as you can, until it's as thin as a piece of rice paper. Hit it with all your might."

So the blacksmith and his apprentice stood facing each other with the anvil between them and brought their hammers down on it as hard as they could.

Bim! Bam! Boom! They made the devil jump, they made sparks fly from the hammers.

And they kept it up for fifteen days.

As night fell on the fifteenth day, the Devil—who was beaten to a pulp—said to Rich: "Call off your thugs and I'll give you back your wife, no strings attached. If she keeps drinking the way she does now, she'll come to us eventually anyway; if she mends her ways, well, more power to her."

"It's a deal," said Rich, opening the bag. The Devil disappeared in a puff of smoke.

⌇

Not long after that, Rich's wife died.

As she had not mended her ways, she was turned back when she arrived at the gates of Paradise. In hell, though, the three devils seized her gleefully and threw her in the furnace, as was only right and proper.

When it was Rich's turn to die, he, too, knocked first at the gates of Paradise. When Saint Peter looked out and saw who it was, he said:

"Aren't you Rich, the shoemaker?"

"That's me," said Richard.

"Wasn't it you whose wife drank every cent he earned?"

"Yes sir."

"Do you remember the beggar who came to your shop and gave you three wishes?"

"Oh yes, I remember it as if it happened yesterday, although a lot of water has flowed down the St. Lawrence since then."

"Well," said Saint Peter. "That beggar was me, and since you didn't have the good sense to ask to go to heaven then, you can jolly well go to hell now. Good day to you, sir."

"Whatever you say," said the shoemaker, making a deep bow.

When he arrived at the gates of hell, he knocked again.

"Who is it?" called the devils.

"It's Rich," he called.

"Rich the shoemaker?" they exclaimed, tossing another log into the furnace that contained his wife.

"Yes, that's me. Rich the shoemaker."

"Do you have your bench with you?" asked the first devil.

"And your fiddle? And your bag?" asked the second and third devils.

"Yes, I've got them all here," replied Rich.

"Then go away," they all shouted. "We don't want you here."

So Rich climbed the long road back to heaven, where Saint Peter, perhaps wanting to test the shoemaker, sent him packing again. Rich returned to hell and knocked on the gates once more.

"Who's that knocking?" shouted the three devils.

"It's me again. Rich."

"We told you to get lost. Shoo!"

"I don't care what you told me," shouted Rich, "I'm coming in. Do you think I want to spend the rest of eternity walking back and forth between heaven and hell like this? Open up, I say, and right this minute, or I'll break the door down and put one of you on my bench, make one of you dance with my fiddle, and pound the hell out of the third one with a hammer until the end of time!"

The three devils opened the gate a crack and tried to reason with him.

"What'll it take to make you leave us alone?" they asked.

"I want you to return my wife's soul to me," he said.

"Your wife's soul?" they said. "But that's not possible. She died a drunkard; she belonged to us all her life, man, and now she'll belong to us forever. We don't give pardons here any more than they do upstairs. But tell you what: open your bag and we'll give you a hundred other souls in exchange. How's that? Look, here's a dozen merchants who kept their thumbs on their scales."

"Thank you," said Rich, shaking his bag to make the merchants' souls settle down to the bottom.

"And here's another two dozen souls—lawyers and doctors who killed their patients and then bilked the widows and orphans into the bargain. And here, take an armload of bankers, too, and a few of their clients who died without paying off their debts. How many are there?"

"Thirty," said Rich. "That makes sixty-five. Keep them coming."

"Okay, catch," said the devils, tossing another dozen souls into the bag. "These belonged to innkeepers who watered their beer. How many do we owe you now?"

"Twenty-three."

"Right. Here you go," they grunted, dragging out a fresh ovenful. "Twenty-three bus drivers, and surly buggers they were, too. Make 'em run for it. Now get the hell out of here, and don't come back!"

"Just as soon as you give me my wife's soul," insisted Rich.

"Your wife's soul bedamned! We've already told you you can't have that!"

"Oh I can't, eh?" said Rich, putting his violin under his chin.

"All right! Stop! Take the damn thing. Here she is. Now, get out!"

This time Rich threw his bag over his shoulder and lit out of hell like a bat. Arriving once again at the gates of heaven, he found them partly open. Without waiting around for the porter, he slipped between them and into Paradise, where he created quite a stir with his entourage.

And where we will find him ourselves one day, dear readers, as long as we live good, clean lives in the meantime. And I have no doubt that when we get there, he will sit us down on his bench and tell us his astonishing true story, point by point, very much as I have related it to you today. Only it'll seem to take longer.

Narcisse-Henri-Édouard Faucher de Saint-Maurice
Translated by Yves Brunelle

THE ROUSSIS' FIRE

Faucher de Saint-Maurice was born in Quebec City on April 18, 1844, and baptized Narcisse-Henri-Édouard Faucher. He attended the Petit Séminaire and the college Sainte-Anne-de-la-Pocatière, becoming a clerk in the law firm of Henri Taschereau and Ulric-Joseph Tessier in 1860. His heart was evidently more with the armed forces than with the law; in 1862 he published his first work, *Organisation militaire des Canadas: L'ennemi! l'ennemi!*, a military pamphlet signed "Un Carabinier." The next year he wrote another pamphlet, *Cours de tactique*, and enlisted in the French Expeditionary Corps, which at the time was fighting in Mexico against the revolutionary Benito Pablo Juárez. By 1867, however, he was back in Quebec, working as a clerk in the new Legislative Council—a position he maintained for the next fourteen years.

Faucher de Saint-Maurice (he took the name from his military ancestor and author, Léonard Faucher *dit* Saint-Maurice, because he thought it sounded more refined) was a prolific writer; in 1874 he published *À la brunante*, a collection of short stories and legends; *Choses et autres*, a collection of literary criticism and essays; and a two-volume military memoir entitled *De Québec à Mexico*. In 1881 he left his position as legislative council clerk to run for parliament, and was elected Conservative MP for Bellechasse. He helped found the Royal Society of Canada, and from 1883 to 1885 was the editor-in-chief of *Le Journal de Québec*.

"Le Feu des Roussi," translated here by Yves Brunelle as "The Roussis' Fire," first appeared in two instalments in the journal *L'Opinion publique* in 1872 under the title "À la veillée," which means "at twilight." It was later included in the 1874 collection under its present title. A fairly traditional tale involving werewolves, alcoholism, marital bliss and watery death, it is nonetheless a fine example of the way in which the literary and journalistic renaissance of Quebec in the 1870s and 1880s was reinventing the traditions of the past.

Faucher de Saint-Maurice died on April Fool's Day, 1897, in Quebec City.

∽

"The Roussis' Fire" is reproduced from *French Canadian Prose Masters: The Nineteenth Century* (Montreal: Harvest House Ltd., 1978) and was originally published under the title "Le Feu des Roussi" in *L'Opinion publique* 3, no. 7 (1872); no. 8 (1872).

1. Little Cyprien

At the outset it must be said that Little Cyprien Roussi had not performed his Easter duties for six years and eleven months.

The seventh year was near at hand, and, since it was the age when people in that sad condition were turned into werewolves or such creatures, the busybodies of the village of Good-St-Anne-of-the-North gabbed to their heart's content about the wretched man.

"He who laughs last, laughs longest," Widow Demers was saying. "When he has to roam the fields, all night long, without being able to rest, he'll have time to mull over the remorse which always follows partying and godlessness."

"Roam the fields! That would be good enough for him," Miss Angélique Dessaint, forty-eight-year-old spinster, added no less righteously; "but do we know what he'll turn into, poor Cyprien? I've heard it said that a bogeyman can be a bear, a cat, a dog, a horse, an ox, or a toad. It depends, it seems, on what evil spirit has gotten into his body. And, if you promised not to say a word, I could say something...."

"Ah! for God's sake, me gossip? not on your life," asserted Old Lady Gariépy forthrightly, who was knitting in her corner. "That's all right for the merchant's wife: she's rich and has nothing else to do. Come on, speak up, Miss Angélique."

"Well! since you want me to, I'll tell you that I have in my coop a little black hen that gives me a lot of trouble. It never roosts with the others, seldom cackles, and wouldn't lay for all the wheat Old Man Pierriche harvests on Sunday. Sometimes I feel like bleeding her; there's something suspicious about it."

"Well, bleed her!" Widow Demers interjected. "Who knows? maybe in pricking her you'll free a poor bogeyman; because, to cut their punishment short, a Christian has to draw a drop of blood from them; that's what the ancients say."

"Well, I won't be the one to bleed Cyprien Roussi; I'd be too afraid to touch his atheist's skin!"

It was young Victorine who ventured this timid observation, and perhaps she would have said more about Cyprien, but a drunken voice was heard coming from the King's Way.

It was singing:

> On dit que je suis fier,
> Ivrogne et paresseux.
> Du vin dans ma bouteille
> J'en ai ben quand je veux

(They say I'm proud, drunken and lazy. I have wine in my bottle whenever I want it.)

"Well, Well! there goes the bum," charitable Angélique whispered modestly, muttering a few more sweet words.

The voice was very close; and, with the continuity that characterizes knights of the bottle, a new song was shaking the windows of the joyful lair where these ladies gossip at leisure.

> Ell' n'est pas plus belle que toi,
> Mais elle est plus savante:
> Ell' fait neiger, ell' fait grêler,
> Ell' fait le vent qui vente
> Sur la feuille ron . . . don . . . don don,
> Sur la jolie feuille ronde.
> Ell' fait neiger, ell' fait grêler,
> Ell' fait le vent qui vente,
> Ell' fait reluire le soleil
> A minuit, dans ma chambre,
> Sur la feuille, etc.

(She's not prettier than you, But she's more knowing: She makes it snow, she makes it hail, She makes the wind blow On the leaf ron . . . don . . . don, On the pretty round leaf. She makes it snow, she makes it hail, she makes the wind blow, She makes the sun shine At midnight in my room, On the leaf, etc.)

"Ah! saints in Heaven! it makes my hair stand on end," Old Lady Gariépy twittered under her breath. "Did you hear that?"

> Il fait reluire le soleil
> A minuit, dans sa chambre!

(He makes the sun shine At midnight in his room!)

"Yes, it's sad, very sad, all that," sweet Angélique went on; "and yet, that sun which shines in his room at midnight, that's only the beginning. The poor boy will suffer a lot worse yet!"

The ladies went back to their gossip with a vengeance, because the voice was fading in the distance. And yet, it couldn't be said that its owner deserved such a bad reputation.

Cyprien Roussi was not born at Good-St-Anne-of-the-North; but he was very young when he lost his parents, and chance placed him in the care of an uncle, a bachelor somewhat Voltairian in his ideas, who had let Cyprien grow up on his own, without ever paying much attention to him except to scold him severely if he was late for meals.

As for the rest, absolute freedom.

So, at twenty, Cyprien had managed to gather around himself the most fun-loving gang of scamps that ever got together, from Chateau-Richer up to the back of St. Ferréol. He was by right of conquest the king of the band of revellers, king by virtue of his verve, of his dexterity, of his physical strength, for no one could tell a joke, punch somebody in the mouth, uncork a bottle with one shot, and empty pints, even quarts, of rum in an hour better that Little Cyprien.

A hangover could no more overtake him than a Bostonian a resident of Good-St-Anne-of-the-North.

Nature had spared nothing to fashion a good sturdy frame for Little Cyprien.

Forehead high and smooth, eyes proud and steady, mouth provocative and full of promises, head resting solidly on a neck strongly set between two broad shoulders, chest muscular and bulging, everything in Cyprien Roussi was cut to make him live to be a hundred.

Whenever reference was made to rheumatism, to mysterious illnesses, to sudden deaths, or to pain of hell, he would strike his chest with a hairy fist and say mockingly:

"Does one fear the cold, illness, old age, or the devil with a chest like this? Hot and cold touch it without leaving a trace. Stop intoning dirges on my account, dear friends; bemoan the fate of others. Seeing me come into the world, good St Anne said to her husband: 'Look, I see a strong fellow sprouting there who won't have to say many prayers through life.'"

Everybody would then make the sign of the cross. He was recommended to the prayers of the faithful, and good people in the parish told their beads on his behalf and devoutly attended Vespers, while with a merry crew Little Cyprien was cursing and drinking in the woods near Grande-Rivière.

There, huddled in the shadows, he would review the whole village for them and never find a trace of grace:

The old women had too sharp a tongue, which was true;

The young women wanted to allure the boys with charms imported from England and by a very artificial virtue;

The publican made a tributary of the St. Lawrence flow through his rum and his gin;

The curé drank hard, but secretly, which made it a distressing case of alcoholism;

There were not enough prayers said to good St Anne for her to work her miracles;

The crutches hanging from the ceiling and walls of the church were all the same length, which proved the limited ability of the workman hired to make them;

Votive offerings were made with the object of encouraging colonisation, at the expense of navigation, for which Little Cyprien had a strong affinity.

And the merry band would laugh heartily, toast every sally, and chorus the atheist's words.

They liked to shock everybody; but, one Sunday it was his evil friends' turn to be shocked. During High Mass,

Little Cyprien, who had not been seen around for three weeks, devoutly approached the altar rail and in sight of the whole dumbfounded congregation he received Holy Communion from the curé's hand.

2. Marie the Seamstress

Yet, the reason for all this was quite simple.

If on the Sunday following the party in the woods, the bumpkins of Château-Richer and of St. Ferréol had, while riding around, showing off their horses, chanced to go by Old Man Couture's modest house, at the foot of one of the pretty hills that cross the village of St Anne, they would have noticed Cyprien's buggy unharnessed in the shed.

At loose ends, tired of gadding and loafing about, Cyprien had heard about the return of Marie the Seamstress.

Marie the Seamstress was a tall, dark-haired girl, neither pretty nor homely, who with the work of her ten fingers was earning good wages in the city where she had made a reputation as a dressmaker. She had come to her uncle's for a few days of rest. Little Cyprien had gotten up that morning with the idea that he would go and court her; after lunch he had harnessed up and, all dressed up and with a new pipe between his teeth, had come along at a good pace to have a chat with her.

Old Man Couture was a sly old fellow, who had also sown his wild oats in his youth. So it was with a jaundiced eye that he saw the callow youth stop in front of his door, make his mare rear, and then nimbly jump on the verandah, all the while cracking his whip. But his niece Marie had shown him such a beautiful row of teeth, she had called to him, "Uncle!" with such an uncommon intonation, that he found himself pushing aside his ill humour as one pushes aside an evil thought, and not knowing why or how he had quietly put the horse in the stable and the buggy in the shed.

While this good deed was being performed, Little Cyprien, hair combed fashionably, handkerchief artistically sticking out of his breast pocket, had made his triumphant entrance, with his whip in one hand and his new pipe in the other.

Marie was a proper girl. This air of importance did not draw even a trace of a smile from her pink lips. She cheerfully held out her hand to him, saying:

"How are things with you, Cyprien?"

"So-so, Miss Marie; Uncle Roussi is not well, but as for me, this is made of iron," he added, rubbing his hand on his chest.

"You're lucky, Cyprien, to have such good health; at least that's a comfort to you who rely on things of this earth for your happiness, since I'm told you don't much believe in the next world."

"On that score they told you the truth; I go along with the adage: better one in the hand than two in the bush."

"That's false, Cyprien; we can't always hold the one in the hand, but comes a day when another hand irrevocably holds us; then it's too late to be sorry. Since we're talking about those things, tell me frankly what pleasure you find in being disliked by the whole parish and in continually making fun of everything your mother venerated during her life?"

"What pleasure? Well, Marie, we have to kill time, and I frankly admit, since you ask, that I would have much more fun in Quebec. There is a city! There one can do anything without being noticed; but here it's impossible to say anything without its taking the proportion of a sacrilege. You've known me a long time, Marie, and you know that all in all I'm a good fellow, but I don't like to be provoked, and when I'm provoked, I . . ."

"Well, I . . . what?"

"Darn it! I laugh."

"You laugh, poor Cyprien! But do you know what you're doing? You're laughing at sacred things. God, who from all eternity knows what you've been and what you'll become begins to reconsider this dust which He has drawn from nothingness and which now attempts to dirty Him, and then, that mouth that laughingly blasphemes, he sees it at the end twisted, purple, decomposing and eaten by the vermin of the cemetery."

"You read, Marie, you read too much; your reading goes to your head, and sometimes that brings bad luck."

"Don't worry about me, Cyprien; and your jokes won't stop me from saying it all, because I mean to reprimand you as I please. You deserve it, and I demand that you listen!"

She pouted almost childishly, and Cyprien, astonished to find himself so solidly caught in those pink claws, started to sway on his chair, remaining bravely quiet.

Marie went on softly:

"You were saying, Cyprien, that you're sorry not to be living in the city; life is so gay there, you think! You want to know what life is like in Quebec? Well, listen to me closely."

"Shoot, Marie! I'll borrow the beadle's long ears and I'll listen to your pleasant instruction."

"Pleasant, no. Frank, yes. Look at me, Cyprien. I'm only a poor girl, who went to school for a while, but who, having become an orphan before getting through, had to learn and understand a lot of things that affliction teaches better than the Ursulines. Left on my own, I thought that work was the safeguard of everything, and I wasn't wrong. I have worked, and in working I have seen and retained what the lazy don't see and the rich don't feel.

"I have seen poor shop girls, weak and trusting, fall, and get up again, hands filled with the kind of money only a portion of which can be earned by honest work.

"I have rubbed shoulders with men, respectable and deemed honourable, who, kindness on their faces and the smile of virtue on their lips, were spending in orgies and vice the earnings which their families woefully needed.

"I have seen women come to my shop covered with silk and fine lace, while their children, left with a servant, wallowed in ignorance.

"I have seen good reputations torn to shreds by god-fearing churchwardens who, piously and without remorse, snored in the official pew.

"I have seen many good minds go numb in contact with a full glass.

"I have seen well-brought-up young men use their intelligence to lead into debauchery poor children who until then had known no other sorrow but that brought about by a scarcity of bread.

"I have seen . . . but why should I tell you all those things, Cyprien? You know them better than I do, because if Quebec City abounds in these horrors, St Anne also has people to rival them, and what they do there in broad daylight and with lordly airs, is done here surreptitiously and untidily. Ah! Cyprien, it's not to hurt your feelings that I say those things; but it's distressing to see you, a farmer's son, drink away your farm instead of tilling it.

"Great God! what times do we live in? where is mankind going?"

Cyprien was not laughing any more; head down, cheeks flushed, he was pondering quietly.

Rascal, but kind-hearted, he could find nothing to reply, and since Uncle Couture was just returning from his chores, he said quite simply, in a low voice:

"Thanks! thanks for the sermon! it'll be turned to good account. Now I have to go; no ill feeling, Marie. So long."

He went away as in a dream and got home without having noticed the short ride.

From that day on there was a noticeable change in his behaviour. His friends could never lay hold of him; he was always out, and tongues began to wag: Cyprien's buggy was often seen at Old Man Couture's door.

Marie was not well for a few days; hard work had somewhat undermined her frail constitution. Under the pretext of going to inquire about her health, Little Cyprien spent his afternoons at the seamstress's house.

So, one fine morning, as Marie was sipping a cordial and Cyprien was drumming his fingers on the window, he suddenly blurted out:

"I feel like getting married, Marie!"

"Yea, one day the devil will become a monk!" the sick girl whispered softly, putting her cup down on a small table near her rocking-chair.

"I'm no longer a devil, Marie dear; I've been behaving for a month. Already my reputation as a gay dog is in shreds, and now I need a good girl to steady me on the straight and narrow. You know . . . the habit of straying is not easily broken," he added, laughing.

Then serious again, he went on:

"Will you be my wife, Marie?"

"You make quick work of it, M. Cyprien," the girl replied; "and you take advantage of the interest I have taken in you to make fun of me. Will you ever get out of your waggish ways?"

"God knows I'm telling you the truth, Marie!"

"God? the whole village knows that you've said a hundred times that you don't believe in Him."

"Ah! dear friend, those were foolish words that I'll spend a lifetime atoning for. I believe in Him now. In fact, I've always believed in Him, really."

"And how am I to know, Master Cyprien? With rakes like you, we poor girls must always take our precautions."

"Miss Marie, Cyprien Roussi has just been to Confession, and he'll receive Communion tomorrow," he answered slowly.

Marie was silent; a tear rose to her black eyes, then, doing her best to turn the conversation to a gayer plane, she went on:

"Good, Cyprien; that's fine! After scandal, atonement; that's reasonable enough, but I can't see why the curé has made me your penance."

"Oh! Marie, now it's your turn to joke! But listen to me; it's so easy for you to be good that I'll be good too. Look here, if you say yes, if you accept being Mme Roussi, well, I'm not rich, but I'll give you a beautiful wedding gift."

"And what might that be?"

"I swear that never again will a drop of liquor pass my lips."

Marie remained silent for a moment, then stretching her hand to Cyprien, said:

"Since you're speaking the truth, I'll be frank with you, too: I love you, Cyprien."

And that's how it came about that two months after receiving Communion, Little Cyprien, to the great astonishment of the village, married Marie the Seamstress.

3. The Roussis' Fire

Fifteen years had gone by since that happy day, fifteen years of peace, such as Cyprien had never dared wish for himself even in his most selfish dreams.

The little family had grown with the coming of a big, healthy boy, and, since Cyprien had soon gotten used to the idea of work, modest affluence had rewarded his labour.

Finding it difficult to stay in Good-St-Anne-of-the-North, which only reminded him of his past escapades, he had moved and now lived in Paspebiac. Here he had found a job with the Robin Company, which appreciated this sober, alert and steady man, and little by little he had built up savings, for Marie helped too. Everything was going wonderfully well.

Every week more coins found their way into the linen chest, there to accumulate silently, awaiting the following September when Jeannot was to go to college in Quebec City.

Cyprien had made up his mind that his son would get a college education, and Jeannot had had a good start by listening attentively to the wise principles his mother taught him, love of religion and the sad knowledge of the world with which she had once inculcated Little Cyprien's soul.

Earthly happiness seemed to be made for this humble home; peace of soul reigned there. Then one night a sudden catastrophe brought sorrow and tears.

It was winter, in January.

Marie was alone preparing the supper by the red-hot stove; Cyprien and Jean had gone over to talk business with some other employees of Robin's.

What happened during their absence no one could really tell. But, when Cyprien and his son came near their door, they heard groans. They rushed into the kitchen, and the father tripped over the body of his poor wife, who was lying on the floor in a pool of boiling water. At her side, an upset kettle showed only too well how this dreadful state of affairs had come about.

Marie lived on courageously for two hours; she offered her unspeakable suffering to God, in exchange for the absolution she could not get on earth—because this was in 1801, and the coast was served only by a saintly missionary who lived too far from Paspebiac to be fetched.

Kneeling by this calvary of pain, Cyprien and Jean wept bitterly. Already the heart-gripping calm that descends on the dying had betokened the last agony, and Marie seemed to be resting, eyes half closed, when suddenly she opened them wide. Cyprien saw that she was sinking; he bent over her, saw her hand moving feebly on the edge of the bed, and heard her whisper:

"Your promise, Cyprien, never to drink again...."

"I have never forgotten it, and I'll stick to it; set your mind at ease; sleep, child!"

So Marie went to sleep.

The silence of eternity had invaded poor Cyprien's little house, and with it tears and forlornness.

It was a hard blow; it took Cyprien a while to recover. This departure had upset everything, and like many other projects, that of sending Jean to college was abandoned. During those sorrowful days, his father had aged ten years; premature old age weakened his strength as well as his courage, and Jean himself had asked to stay to help in his father's work.

Days went by, drab and joyless, until one morning Daniel Gendron made a noisy entrance into their mournful house.

Gendron had come directly from St. Ferréol. There he had heard that fishing was good down river.

If Master Daniel did not care for poverty, he was not too keen on steadiness either, and, driven off every farm in County Montmorency, he had sought a job at Robin's. They needed hands, so he was taken on. His first outing was to go and see Cyprien, with whom he had been on more than one good drunk, in the endless days of idling along the Grande-Rivière in St Anne.

Cyprien did not like to encounter those who had known him in his wild youth, so he gave him a cold welcome.

Gendron could not help but notice it:

"You look cross today, Master Cyprien; is it that you're not too pleased to see me?"

"Well, Daniel, I'd like it any other time; but today is a fishing day, and since you're a novice, I have to tell you that you don't get ready to put out to sea in a minute."

"Good! I'd like to go with you, to see what it's like; you can give me my first lesson."

"I'm willing; but if you want my advice, you'd be better off enjoying your last day of freedom: we work hard here."

"Bah! it'll be fun to go drop a line; and then, we'll talk about the good times."

"No way!" Cyprien said energetically; "I don't like to be reminded of them."

"Why not? We drank hard and sang loud then! Wasn't it really fun, Cyprien?"

"Daniel, what's dead is dead: let's drop it."

"As you wish, sir; you sure have become dull! You used to joke so heartily about our curé, but you've made up for lost time, and now you're more devout than the Pope!"

Without answering Cyprien made for the beach, followed by Jean and Daniel; there, they pushed the boat into the water and started to row toward the open sea.

It was a bit cloudy; there was a light breeze; everything pointed to a good catch. Daniel was singing an oarsman's song, while Cyprien and Jean rowed silently. This went on until they reached the fishing grounds, and then they dropped their lines.

For two hours they worked hard, and the boat was filling with cod. Then Daniel stopped, saying:

"Cyprien, don't you think the wind is getting stronger? Wouldn't it be safer to go ashore?"

Cyprien seemed to snap out of a day-dream; he looked up at the sky; then speaking sharply he ordered Jean: "Raise anchor!"

Turning to Daniel, he said: "Unfurl the sail! I'll take the tiller! Quickly with the sail; we don't have a minute to lose, Daniel!"

In a moment the boat was tilting in the wind and sailing swiftly toward Paspebiac Point.

It was the middle of May; it was still cold, particularly in the wind, and it was not surprising that hands were cold. Daniel was well aware of it; he had been blowing on his hands for a while, when he suddenly reached in his pocket and pulled out a bottle of rum.

He held it out to Cyprien:

"Take a drink; it'll warm you up, and this is sure the time to do it! Blazes! who got the idea of calling this Bay des Chaleurs?"

"Keep it for yourself, Daniel; I don't touch the stuff, thank you! Keep alert!" And he knocked his pipe over the side with the air of a man who is uneasy.

The wind was getting stronger; the weather was souring. The grey clouds had become as black as ink, and the sea augured nothing good for the night. Suddenly the boat rolled, and a wave, higher than the others, hitting just then, covered Cyprien from head to foot.

Roussi held on; his hand had not let go the tiller; his clothes were dripping; it was getting colder, and Daniel, who had partially dodged the wave, took comfort in another drink.

"Now, really Cyprien, won't you take some? It's great when you're all wet!"

Cyprien shivered; he could no longer feel his hand on the tiller; his fingers ached; finally reaching out towards Daniel, he took the bottle and drank deep.

He had cheated his dead wife!

What happened to them afterwards? No one knows.

The next morning, an upturned boat was found on the shore, and near it Daniel Gendron, who was unconscious.

Since this disaster, a bluish flame can be seen running across the bay on the eve of a storm.

"According to those who have watched it," Abbé Ferland says, "it rises sometimes out of the sea, half-way between Caraquet and Paspebiac. Sometimes small as a flare, sometimes wide and spread out like a conflagration, it moves forward, moves back, rises. When a traveller thinks he has come to where he had seen it, it disappears, but it reappears when he has moved off. Fishermen assert that these fires mark the spot where a boat manned by hardy sailors by the name of Roussi sank in a storm; the light according to popular belief, is there to ask passers-by to pray for the drowned men."

That is the honest truth.

So, travellers and fishermen, when you see a light flickering on the Bay des Chaleurs, kneel down and say a *De Profundis* for the two dead men, because you will be looking at the "Roussis' Fire."

Philippe Aubert de Gaspé, the Elder
Translated by Jane Brierley

YELLOW-WOLF, MALECITE CHIEFTAIN OF OLD

"On the 30th of October in the year 1786," Philippe Aubert de Gaspé wrote in his *Mémoires*, "in a house within the walls of Quebec where the archbishop's palace now stands, a puny little thing first opened his eyes to the light." Shortly after, the de Gaspé family moved to Saint-Jean-Port-Joli, a village on the St. Lawrence with which Philippe-Joseph was to be associated for the rest of his life. He studied law and in 1816 was named sheriff of Quebec, but in 1822 he began to get hopelessly into debt and was relieved of his office. The following year, he was committed to the Quebec penitentiary. Upon his release in 1841, he retired to Port-Joli and began to write. The result was a novel, *Les Anciens canadiens* (1864), and the *Mémoires* (1866), both of which were resounding popular successes. Among de Gaspé's admirers were the influential Abbé Casgrain and the historian François-Xavier Garneau, who were working to initiate a cultural revolution in Quebec.

After de Gaspé's death in 1871, one of his sons, Alfred-Patrice, found a manuscript of stories among his father's papers. This was published in 1893 as *Divers*. Jane Brierley, whose translation of *Divers* (as *Yellow-Wolf and Other Tales of the Saint Lawrence*) appeared in 1990, notes a parallel between the proud chieftain Yellow-Wolf and de Gaspé himself, "the last seigneur of Saint-Jean-Port-Joli." The determination to preserve the old order is certainly one of the main themes of *Les Anciens canadiens*, and there is no doubt that the aging, exiled de Gaspé sympathized with Yellow-Wolf's desire to maintain contact with his own heritage.

De Gaspé died in 1871 at his seigneury in Saint-Jean-Port-Joli, which can still be visited today.

∽

"Yellow-Wolf: Malecite Chieftain of Old" is reproduced from
Yellow-Wolf and Other Tales of the St. Lawrence (Montreal: Vehicule
Press, 1990) and was originally published under the title "Le loup-
jaune, ancien chef Maléchite" in *Divers* (Montreal: C.O.
Beauchemin & Fils, Lib.-Imprimeurs, 1893).

Among the Indians who camped each year on our beach during my childhood was an old Malecite by the name of Yellow-Wolf. According to my father's calculations, taking into account this Indian's acquaintance with the men of yesteryear and the events he had witnessed, he must have been a hundred years old at the time. Yellow-Wolf was a great favourite with my family, and my father loved to get him talking about the adventures of his long career.

The old Indian was in the habit of pitching his wigwam at some distance from his fellows. He seemed to have little in common with them, exchanging but a few brief words with those he met. For their part, they seemed to feel more fear than friendship for him. He led a solitary life in their midst, his only companion being a small, distinctly foxy-looking dog.

Ever sombre and meditative, Yellow-Wolf treated my childish advances with discouraging reserve. Witnessing my mischievous antics, he no doubt considered me a frivolous being, incapable of conducting a serious conversation. It wasn't until I reached the age of eighteen that I succeeded in overcoming his distaste for my company and gaining his friendship.

Yellow-Wolf presented a most imposing ruin—what was left of him after days of captivity and hours of horrible suffering at the stake, at the hands of enemies as versed in the art of torture as the Iroquois. He had lost none of his tall stature, and still walked, shoulders thrown back, with the fine bearing of a man of forty. True, he had one blind eye, but the eagle orb that remained still blazed forth when he became animated. He might have been a disciple of Molière's Toinette, who propounded the philosophy that having one eye plucked out only made you see more clearly with the other. His left hand had just the index finger and thumb left, but these two digits, separated though they might be from their brothers, were no less prompt in their unfailing obedience to his behests.

As for Yellow-Wolf's lower regions, I had no way of assessing the damage. He tended to limp, despite efforts to hide it, and I am obliged to conclude that this infirmity was the result of his Iroquois enemies eating a few of his toes, after first smoking the nails in their *calumets* to pass the time.

The joys of indolence were dear to this savage of ancient lineage and noble race, and the rich gifts of the Crown to a great chief allowed him to indulge himself at will. One day I remarked how surprised I was that he didn't drink rum like his fellow Indians, and he told me that until the age of thirty he had been a drunkard. After he had gone on a two-week binge, his ancestor, the first Yellow-Wolf, had appeared to him in his sleep and forbidden him to taste firewater, which was poison to Redskins.

"The time had come," said the old chief. "I'd drunk up a hundred francs' worth of pelts, my gun, my canoe, and even my wife. I sold her to a Frenchman for a bottle of rum."

"You sold your wife, my brother? What a low thing to do!"

"It was the best deal I ever made," retorted the Indian. "She was a no-good thief and an even bigger drunkard than myself. Ha! That Frenchman got more than he bargained for!"

"*Ma foi*, in that case I think you did well to let your friend the Paleface have her, my brother," said I. "But you married again to console yourself."

"Yes, and this time I was lucky. I married a good woman who gave me two fine boys, brave warriors. They were both killed at my side in a great battle against the English and their allies the Foxes. I revenged their deaths, but not enough. I still hear the voices of my children in the still of the night, in the raging storm and the waves lapping on the shore. Always I hear, 'Vengeance! Vengeance, my father!'"

There was a long pause, the old man added, "*Hoa*! My heart is very heavy. To think I will never see my children again! Their mother made them Christians and they are with her in her heaven. I will hunt without them in my grandfather's paradise. He has never abandoned his grandson. When those dogs of Iroquois were torturing me, I called on him and he always came to my aid. But come and sit with me this evening and I'll tell you all about it."

A magnificent night greeted my arrival. Moon and stars seemed to dance in the waters of the Saint Lawrence, and I could hear the waves faintly breaking on the sandy beach only a few feet from the old Indian's wigwam. Some larks, disturbed in their sleep, stretched their wings and hopped about, uttering little cries as the water invaded the shore.

Yellow-Wolf was smoking meditatively at the door of his wigwam. At my approach his dog started up and barked, ears perked like steel blades. "*Que ci! Céna*—Come here, hound!" shouted the Indian without turning his head. The dog lay down obediently a few yards from his master, keeping a wild and malevolent eye firmly fixed on me. I sat down beside my aged friend. He said nothing for a few minutes, then commenced the story that follows. "Long, long ago, before the Paleface had passed over the great lake in his giant ship to visit the Redskins, my grandfather Areskoueh took the form of a yellow wolf. As he passed by a Malecite village he saw a young Indian girl, daughter of the voice of the woodlands, lakes, and mountains, and carried her off to a cave far, far away. He made her his wife, and she gave him a fine boy whom he named Yellow-Wolf. By the time the boy was six, he was stronger than the men of our day and those who will come after us.

"Areskoueh said to his wife, 'Show our son how to make the voice of the woodlands, lakes, and mountains speak, and I will make him a great hunter and warrior.' And the child learned to make the voice of the woods, lakes, and mountains speak, and his father taught him to be a great hunter and a fearsome warrior.

"When Yellow-Wolf became a man, Areskoueh said to his wife, 'Go and take your son to the Malecites and he will become a great chief. When he digs up the hatchet, the earth and trees of the forest will tremble beneath the feet of the warriors who run to answer his call! At each new moon he will drink from the skull of one of the twelve enemy chiefs to die by his hand and whose scalps hang in his wigwam. But before going on the warpath he will pray to his father, and Areskoueh will come to him in his sleep and say, "Go!" Yellow-Wolf will then set forth, and enemies will fall beneath his hatchet like dry leaves before the storm! My son Yellow-Wolf will burn many prisoners to thank Areskoueh.'"

What did he mean, said I, interrupting the narrator, by the voice of the woodlands, lakes, and mountains?

"When you speak aloud on a calm evening, standing in front of your house, what do you hear?" was his reply.

"*Parbleu!*" I exclaimed. "I hear the echo of the cape."

"Good!" retorted the old man: "Well, all the descendants of Yellow-Wolf know how to make the echo speak whenever they wish, day or night."

"Then make it speak now," was my rejoinder.

"No, no, Areskoueh would be angry. He has forbidden his children to make the echo speak except in moments of great peril."

Yellow-Wolf was a ventriloquist, as will be borne out by what follows.

"But it seems to me," I started to say, "you were in considerable peril when your enemies . . ."

"Let me speak," said the Indian. "Yellow-Wolf is very old, and clouds pass through his head. Things suddenly go dark, and he has difficulty finding the trail of his memories." I had to be content with this. Yellow-Wolf passed a hand over his brow two or three times, and continued his story.

"The sun was sinking when Yellow-Wolf and his mother came to a large Malecite village after a week of walking. In the old days, the wigwam of the Malecite was always open to the stranger, as it is today. The men of old used to say, 'Come, my brother, rest from your labours in my wigwam, and my squaw will make a fine stew to satisfy your hunger.' But today the poor Malecite often has nothing to offer travellers but the shelter of his wigwam. In order to sell pelts, the Palefaces have seized our forests and destroyed the game that the Great Spirit put there to feed his children.

"Several Malecites offered the strangers the hospitality of their wigwams," continued the old man after this digression, "but mother and son thanked them and asked first to speak to the chiefs, warriors, and old men of the village.

"The council fire was lit, and the chiefs, warriors, and old men took their places, waiting silently for the strangers to deliver their message.

"Yellow-Wolf stayed by the entrance while his mother, being the one to speak, went in alone. 'Let the heart of the Malecite rejoice, for your sister brings you good news,' said she. 'Let the old men search their memories, and they will recall that a young Malecite girl, the orphan of a great chief, was carried off by a wolf near this village.'

"'My sister has spoken truly,' replied several old men of the council.

"'My brothers remember well,' said the woman. 'Their sister who now speaks to them was the one carried off by the wolf.'

"The wise men of the council shook their heads at this and a great chief spoke these words: 'Wolves carry off young girls to eat them. My sister is lying.'

"'My brother Malecites are easily amazed,' retorted the woman. 'Let them listen and then judge whether they are right in disbelieving the words of their sister.' The chiefs, old men, and warriors remained silent.

"'The wolf carried the young squaw in his jaws a long way off,' continued the woman, pointing to the north. 'He said to the squaw, "Yellow-Wolf is Areskoueh, god of war. He has kidnapped you to be his wife, for you are the daughter of a great chief whom he loved, and you will be the mother of a race of formidable warriors!"'

"Then spoke Porcupine, a young Malecite and a great chief. 'My sister has fine words, but the words of a woman are as light as a feather on the wind.'

"'Your sister will speak to Areskoueh,' replied Yellow-Wolf's mother, 'and he will answer her beneath the earth, in the sky, and under the water. Porpucine will open his ears and then he will believe his sister's words.' She stretched a hand toward the council fire, and a voice came forth crying, 'The wife of Areskoueh has spoken truly!' Then she lifted her hand toward heaven, and a voice descended crying, 'The wife of Areskoueh has spoken truly!' And she lowered her hand toward the river, where a voice arose crying, 'The wife of Areskoueh has spoken truly!' And all the chiefs, the old men, and the warriors cried, '*Hoa!* My sister has not lied.'

"'Now that the chiefs, the old men, and the warriors believe their sister's word, will they let her bring in her son?' asked the woman. The men bowed their heads in assent.

"When Yellow-Wolf entered the council wigwam, the warriors cried out, '*Hoa!* Our brother is indeed the son of Areskoueh. Let him take his place in the council with his brother Malecites.'

"'My brothers have spoken well and Yellow-Wolf thanks them,' replied the young man, 'but he will not sit in the Malecite council except as their great chief. When Areskoueh bade his son farewell, he said, "Go, tell the Malecites, 'I am Yellow-Wolf, son of Areskoueh and grandson on my mother's side of Arena, great chief of the Malecites. By this double heritage I am your great chief.'

"'My brother speaks as though to command, but Porcupine will not give up his place to any warrior,' retorted the great Malecite chief. 'Let Yellow-Wolf take second place, and he will still be a great chief.'

"'My brother Porcupine has a great heart and has spoken like a warrior,' replied the young man. 'Yellow-Wolf would have scorned him had he given up his place like a coward. But Yellow-Wolf, too, has a great heart. He loves the Malecites and asks only to pitch his wigwam near his brothers and live in peace with them.'

"And so Yellow-Wolf set up his wigwam in the village of his brothers. The Malecites had never seen such a formidable hunter. His arrow could pierce the eagle in the clouds. He could crush the black bear's skull with his hatchet and carry the animal back to the village on his shoulder as though it were a young badger.

"Six moons did Yellow-Wolf live among the Malecites. Then early one morning he rose and said to Porcupine, 'Let the great chief light the council fire, for his brother has solemn words.'

"The council assembled. 'Let my brother speak,' said the great chief.

"'Areskoueh has visited his sleeping son,' said Yellow-Wolf, 'and has told him, "The Iroquois are advancing at great speed and their warriors are so many that the forest trembles beneath their feet! Before the sun has set three times, their war cry will be heard in the village of the Malecites."'

"The warriors smoked in silence, their hearts filled with sadness, for they knew the weakness of their tribe.

"'Let my brothers open their ears and listen to the words of Yellow-Wolf, that their hearts may rejoice. Areskoueh has said to his son, "Go, and the dogs of Iroquois will fall beneath Yellow-Wolf's hatchet like dry leaves before the tempest!" Let the great chief strike the stake, call his warriors, and await the enemy a day's march from the Malecite village.'

"A great battle took place. The Iroquois, although taken by surprise, were so numerous that one would have thought the earth, trees, and rocks were spewing them forth like waves breaking upon the shore when the Great Spirit is angry and makes the storm blow. Porcupine was soon killed, and the Malecites, losing heart after the death of their great chief, were about to flee when Yellow-Wolf revived their courage with a terrible shout that shook the forest. He fell upon the enemy, splitting their skulls with a crunch that could be heard above the ghastly yells on both sides. The old people named this battle the feast of the Iroquois dogs' split skulls.

"After the enemy's defeat, Yellow-Wolf was named great chief of the Malecite tribe. His children and grandchildren succeeded him, and the old man who now speaks to you is the last chief of this family of fearsome warriors, and also the last of his line."

"When you cut me off just now, my brother," I interposed at this juncture, "I was about to ask why you didn't make the echo speak when your enemies tortured you so cruelly."

"When moon and stars shine in the night," the old man retorted, "they light the steps of the wanderer. The blood runs fast in the veins of the young man and clears his mind, but in the head of the old man who has seen a hundred winters it is often dark, and he needs rest. Let my brother come back tomorrow when Yellow-Wolf can speak once more."

I arrived punctually at our rendez-vous the next day.

"Yesterday evening," said the old man, "you asked me why I had not made the echo speak when my enemies tortured me. But Yellow-Wolf is a great warrior, you see, and he wanted to show those dogs of Iroquois that he cared nothing for their tortures. Listen, and I shall tell you of all this.

"For two weeks I had been hunting in the forest, and after a long tramp was very tired. Having seen no trace of the enemy, I went to sleep at the foot of a tree. I felt a blow and opened my eyes to find nearly a dozen Iroquois standing around me. They had taken my gun, hatchet, and knife.

"'The Iroquois are great warriors!' I said, smiling scornfully. 'They are ten against one, yet they tremble at the sight of a sleeping Malecite and quickly seize his weapons. The Iroquois deserves the name "Fox," for he has its cunning and cowardice!'

"'Yellow-Wolf would do well to call upon his grandfather Areskoueh before his enemies scalp him, burn him at the stake, and throw his bones to their village dogs,' replied Timakai, the Iroquois chief.

"'Yellow-Wolf has no need of his grandfather's aid,' I retorted. 'The knife that will scalp him is still in the Paleface's stores, and the wood that will burn him at the stake has not yet come out of the earth.'

"The Iroquois enemies shrugged and bound my hands. We set off and walked until nightfall, when they tied me to a tree and built a campfire. While they prepared supper

Timakai lit his pipe and smoked the little fingernail of my left hand, biting the finger off at the knuckle and spitting it in my face. A second Indian did the same to the next finger and put it in my mouth."

"That must have been very painful, by brother," said I. "Your face must have twisted in agony. Why didn't you make the echo speak?"

The old man drew himself up with great dignity. "Yellow-Wolf is a great warrior! If he had grimaced as much as a Paleface with a finger-scratch, his enemy would have been delighted."

Hoist on your own petard, Paleface! thought I.

"We set out again next day and walked until nightfall without stopping. They built a fire near a little spring while I sat on the ground. While the meat cooked, another Iroquois smoked my third finger, chopped it up and laughed as he threw it to his dog. Now I had only two fingers on my left hand, and I needed them to support my gun. It was time to put an end to their games."

"I should think so, my brother," I remarked. "I admire your patience, but I swear I'd have put an end to their games from the moment they began smoking my first fingernail."

The old man looked at me pityingly. There was a moment of silence. "The Great Spirit created both Redskins and Palefaces, but he gave them different ideas," he said at last, and continued his account.

"I behaved just like a man about to fall sick—struggling to get up, heaving sighs, gasping and rolling on the ground, then lying perfectly still as though I'd lost consciousness. The Iroquois threw water in my face and I sighed like a man coming out of a fainting spell. 'Where am I?' I cried. My enemies burst out laughing. '*Hoa!* Yellow-Wolf boasted of being a man, yet he fainted like a young girl with a finger-bite.'

"I looked about me with a dazed expression and replied weakly, 'Yellow-Wolf was sick when the enemy ambushed him. He had not eaten for three days, being unable to hunt, and he has had no food since being taken prisoner two days ago. His enemies have allowed him no water to quench his fever. If Yellow-Wolf dies, his only regret will be his failure to show the Iroquois they were nothing but women who didn't know how to torture a warrior.' And I pretended to faint again.

"The Iroquois threw water in my face once more, then untied me and gave me something to eat and drink. When I had finished, I imitated the sound of indistinct voices on the trail behind us, calling, 'Iroquois! Malecites! Iroquois!' As my captors reached for their weapons in fear of an enemy attack, I let out a Malecite warwhoop, grabbed the tomahawk hanging from Timakai's belt, and split his skull with a shout of triumph before disappearing in the direction of the voices. The night was dark, and I quickly hid behind a tree until the Iroquois had fled in the opposite direction. Then I went back for the weapons Timakai had taken. But before bidding him farewell, I also took his scalp. *Hoa!* Yellow-Wolf is a great warrior."

"Indeed you are, my brother," said I, "and a warrior with little regard for his own skin."

"In time of war we must always be on the watch for ambush when hunting in the forest," the old man went on. "Each nation has war parties continually on the prowl. During the day the hunters spread out but they agree on a meeting place for the evening. I had been hunting for several days with four young braves. One morning, as we separated, I told them not to light a fire at our camp that evening, for I had just seen a wounded deer go by. But when I joined them at nightfall, they had started a fire to cook supper. 'My brothers have done wrong,' said I, 'for I have seen signs of the Iroquois. I climbed a tree and thought I saw a puff of smoke rising beyond the nearby hillside to the south.' We ate our supper and I cautioned them. 'Keep watch, my brothers. Yellow-Wolf senses the enemy's presence and is going on the warpath. If he yells, let my brothers be ready to flee or to fight.'

"It was very dark. Fearing an ambush I took a great many precautions, sometimes walking on all fours or slithering along on my stomach like a snake and frequently putting my ear to the ground. I heard nothing and kept moving forward. As I rounded a small rock five men jumped on me, but I let out a terrible yell before they could gag me. Although I was their prisoner, my heart rejoiced at having warned my brothers. They made the most of it, too. A dozen Iroquois ran in their direction and we heard four gunshots. The Malecites had wounded two and killed a third before getting away. My captors returned bearing the body of the Iroquois dog.

"Although I was a prisoner, my heart was glad because my young braves were safe. The Iroquois led me off to their camp and tied me to a tree. Karakoua said to me, 'Let Yellow-Wolf call upon his Malecite brothers, who run away like cowards, to rescue him. Before the sun has set three times he will be burned.'

"'When Yellow-Wolf is tied to the stake he will sing his death-song like a warrior,' I retorted. 'He will not shed tears as did the father of Karakoua when Yellow-Wolf, after tearing the skin from his skull, threw red-hot cinders on his head. Let Karakoua go to the wigwam of Yellow-Wolf and there he will find his father's scalp in the bed of Yellow-Wolf's dog.'

"After five days' walk we came to their village on the edge of a river. Next day they bound me to the stake and I sang my death-song like a warrior. My torturers began by tearing off three of my toenails and sticking thorns and burning brands into my toes. That explains why I limp a little with my left foot. They branded my thighs with red-hot irons. 'My eyes look everywhere for men, but I see only *matchiotes*,' said I. *Hoa!* This last insult cost me dear, for that dog Karakoua drank one of my eyes."

"Drank one of your eyes?" said I. "How does an Indian manage that, my brother?"

The old man snorted. "You are not very bright. Karakoua said to me, 'Your eye looks good, Malecite!' Then he gouged it out with his knife and swallowed it. 'Karakoua does well to drink the eyes of Yellow-Wolf,' I told him, 'since he is too cowardly to meet the gaze of a Malecite warrior, even when tied to a stake.'"

I froze with horror at this account. "My brother," said I, "it seems to me that it was more than time to make the echo speak while there was still something left of you."

A little smile appeared on the old man's lips. "You are right, my brother. I thought so too, for if Karakoua had drunk my other eye, I could not have escaped. I made a voice come out of the sky, crying 'Untie the prisoner. He has the smallpox. If he dies in your village none of you will survive, from the old man who cannot leave his wigwam to the new born *baboujine!*'

"The whole village fled in panic. I believe I would still be tied to the stake if they had not sent back an old slave to cut my bonds, beating her soundly by way of encouragement. Once freed, I had no trouble finding weapons in the deserted village. I crossed the river in one of their birchbark canoes and camped on the opposite shore to taunt them. After two weeks I was well enough to return to my village, where my Malecite brothers received me with great joy, for they had never expected to see me again.

"A hundred winters have passed over the head of Yellow-Wolf," concluded the old man. "Now he lives alone in the midst of his tribe, for his brothers enter their wigwams at the sight of him, like little animals of the forest who hide beneath the ground when they hear the owl's mournful hooting. Micmacs and Malecites forget that when the enemy digs up the hatchet, Yellow-Wolf will strike the stake with his tomahawk and their fathers will hasten to answer the voice of the grandson of Areskoueh, who led them to victory!" And the centenarian's head fell on his breast.

"Listen, my brother," said I. "If I have understood your words aright, you do not worship the same God as your brother Micmacs and Malecites. They are Christians, but you worship heathen gods and that is why they shun you."

"When the eagle falls upon the marten that is about to devour the timid and defenceless hare, the hare—when he is safe in his burrow—will shout to the eagle, 'Go away! I owe you nothing. You worship the sun, and I the earth that feeds me!" The old Indian paused for a moment, then added, "When Yellow-Wolf's hooded coat is old and worn, he throws it away and puts on another. But he cannot say to his beliefs, 'You are old and worn. I shall now toss you to the back of my wigwam for my dog to sleep on.'

"Good night, young man. Remember my words well."

Robertine Barry
Translated by Patricia Sillers

LA GOTHE AND HER HUSBAND

Robertine Barry was born on Isle-Verte on February 28, 1863, and studied in Trois-Pistoles and Quebec City. A pioneering woman journalist, her work was championed by her contemporaries, including Louis Fréchette. Under the pseudonym Françoise, she published *Fleurs champêtres* (*Rural Flowers*), her first collection of stories, in 1895. Light, semi-instructional tales written for Christmas, New Year's, and Easter, all but one of them had been serialized in the magazine *La Patrie*. A second, darker collection, *Chroniques du lundi* (*Monday's Chronicles*) appeared in 1900, the title story of which had appeared in *La Patrie* in 1893. Though still highly romantic and predominantly historical, the chronicles displayed more sinister undertones: one of them, for example, was about a certain Madeleine de Repentigny who, in 1717, helped her young lover escape from prison and, when he was killed by a guard, entered the Ursuline convent. Another took place in a rather bizarre morgue in Montreal's Hôtel-Dieu hospital, where the corpses seemed to howl and whisper to one another until it was discovered that one of the hospital's patients was a ventriloquist.

"Le mari de la Gothe," translated here by Patricia Sillers as "La Gothe and Her Husband," first appeared in *Fleurs champêtres*. Closer in character to the gothic tales of Barry's later period, the story obviously represents a transitional phase in her creative imagination. It is about two women, Louise Bresolles and Madeleine Renaud, who seek shelter from a storm in the house of Mère Madeloche, and whose servant La Gothe entertains them with an embittered account of the atrocities committed by her deceased husband. This is the one story from the collection *Fleurs champêtres* that was not printed in *La Patrie*, and it was not published separately until 1916, six years after Barry's death, when it appeared in *Le Réveil* under the title "Pages canadiennes oubliées."

The fiercely independent, determinedly romantic Robertine Barry is believed to have inspired two poems by Émile Nelligan, "À une femme détestée" (To a Woman Scorned) and "Rêve d'Artiste" (The Artist's Dream), and there is perhaps a glimpse of her in that troubled poet's longing, in the latter poem, for "a good and gentle sister" who would "softly teach me the secret / of how properly to pray, hope and wait."

Barry died in Montreal's Hôtel-Dieu hospital on November 17, 1910.

∽

"La Gothe and Her Husband" is reproduced from *Stories by Canadian Women* (Toronto: Oxford University Press, 1984) and was originally published under the title "Le mari de la Gothe" in *Fleurs champêtres* (Montreal: La Cie d'imprimerie Desaulniers, 1895).

Many weddings have I seen; not one did I find tempting;
Yet everywhere the human race seems bound to undertake
The step that runs the greatest risk of ending in mistake:
And everywhere the human race is also now repenting.

> Fable of La Fontaine

"Such stifling weather! We're sure to have rain."
"No sooner said than done. A great drop just fell on my nose. Heaven knows how drenched we're going to be!"
"Excellent reason to make haste and find shelter. This little path leads to the home of Mère Madeloche, the nearest neighbour. Follow me—if we go quickly we can be there before the storm."

This was during one July hot spell. The sun's scorching rays had been beating down so intensely, it seemed like the days of Phaeton, when he grazed the earth, venturing to set it ablaze. Oppressive and suffocating, the atmosphere made breathing a laborious effort. The very ground was feverish, thirsting for water, for refreshment, for dew; the plants, thickly coated with dust, had lost the green of spring and seemed to be withering before their time.

Suddenly the sky darkened and menacing clouds rose on the horizon. The cricket silenced his chirp in the grass, as did the bird his song in the wood. In the meadows the animals roused themselves from their torpor, and with their rough tongues lolling, panted—as if waiting anxiously for some strange occurrence. Out in the countryside, where the voices of animals are more commonly heard than the sounds of men, the hour before a storm is a solemn time. And when everything is hushed, insects, birds, when the breeze no longer murmurs in the leaves, a great silence falls, majestic and unsettling, like the reverent lull preceding creation's end, the disintegration of the elements.

All at once the storm broke, violent and terrible, like anger long-suppressed. The wind recovered its voice, but not a soft whisper of leaves in the boughs. Rising in long whistling sounds, it scourged those same shrubs that only moments before had been caressed by it: the grand master loves no more. The frail willows plead for mercy, bowed down and weeping, then submit, while the indomitable poplar arrogantly thrusts defiance at the clouds.

The storm was raging in all its fury by the time the two young girls, who had exchanged the few words above, managed to make their way, running, to a long, low, whitewashed house with a pointed roof and heavy shutters neatly fastened to the walls with leather hinges. An elderly woman, still erect despite her years, came to answer the urgent knocking of the two young strollers. She wore a dress of coarse fabric and sombre hue, and a white cap, with wide trimmings that only partially concealed her grey hair; an apron of blue and white chequered cotton completed her costume.

Mère Madeloche showed a broad smile of welcome upon recognizing Louise Bressoles, the daughter of a wealthy landowner from the village, whom she had known from infancy.

"Come in, come in, 'demoiselles," said the good old woman. "What a weather for Christen folks to be out in, when it's pouring like this!"

"It's tremendously beautiful," said Madeline, pausing on the doorstep to observe the havoc being created by the storm. "Who could have forseen such an upheaval a few moments ago? It has often been compared to the winds of passion..."

"Do come inside quickly," cried Louise. "You may philosophize at your leisure when you are safely under the hospitable roof of good Mère Madeloche!"

"Come in, come in, 'demoiselle, you're going to get your pretty dress all spoilt, an' you'll be as doused as a dinghy. This here's a storm that'll be real good for the crops and make barrels o' *patates*, for sure! Sit you down. We don't often have the pleasure of your company."

"Thank you, Mère Madeloche. You seem to be enjoying your usual good health. This is my cousin Madeline, whose mother—my aunt Renaud—you used to know before she went to live in Quebec City."

"What's that you say—Madame Renaud? Such a nice little lady—so pleasant! She's one that had many kind ways, an' I rocked her in her cradle when she was ever so little. *Mon Dieu*—can it be that this here grown-up 'demoiselle is her daughter? That makes you feel old, for sure!"

"Nevertheless, Mère, you are still hale and hearty, like a young woman of twenty."

"These city 'demoiselles love to make their little jokes," said the old woman, secretly flattered by the compliment. "I'll be seventy years old come harvest time, an' since the deceased passed on, I'm not like before—my strength is going."

While she spoke, the good woman had taken up her spindle full of flax and tucked the end of it into the waistband of her apron, whereupon the thread began to fly between her nimble fingers.

"What a lovely little spinning wheel! Oh, I would so much rather spin than drudge away at our everlasting embroidery," exclaimed Madeline. "But what is that you are doing now, Mère Madeloche?" she added, as the old woman ran her thread over small steel pins with pointed ends that were bent back at the top.

"I'm filling up the bobbin so's it's even from top to bottom; if I didn't wind the thread around the teeth of the blades, the bobbin, d'you see, would only fill up on one side."

"And this big screw on the end of the spinning wheel?"

"That there, 'demoiselle, is the prop that makes sure the thread don't get too thick or too thin; when the spinning wheel gobbles too much, I tighten her or loosen her, just as I need. The loop—that little wheel there at the end of the bobbin—it's where you take the thread so it turns the big wheel. An' this here, where I put my foot, that's the treadle that makes everything go. An' this little wooden bowl 'tached to the pin here, that's called the dish; see there, it's still got some water in it, for wetting down the warp from time to time."

"Most interesting, Mère Madeloche. And what do you call the little rest there at your side?"

"Why, a winder my dear, a winder for the spindleful, after it's all spun out. Hey, *mon Sauveur*, how times change, eh! In my day a girl—let alone grown-up 'demoiselles—wouldn't have no chance to get married if she didn't know nothing about how to spin proper."

The room in which the young girls found themselves renewing their acquaintance with Mère Madeloche was a spacious chamber that made up the main body of the dwelling and served as sitting-room, dining-room, bedroom, and kitchen, all at the same time. Picture, if you will, white-washed walls, and a ceiling with broad cross-beams; long poles attached crosswise to the beams for drying laundry; a long table of white pine; a bed in one corner, covered with a brightly-coloured patchwork quilt and surrounded by snow-white curtains, and at its head a phial of holy water attached to a woollen cord that hung from a nail. Near the bed, a large chest—a favourite seat for lovers—a few rustic chairs, and you have before you, almost without exception, the standard interior of our farmers' homes.

Holding the place of honour, in plain view, on a square of painted paper or a coloured page from a magazine, hangs the cross, black, simple, as severe as the event it commemorates. Beside the cross, a huge palm branch, still draped with the red, white, and blue paper flowers that adorned it on Palm Sunday.

On the smouldering coals of the soot-covered hearth a pot of potatoes simmered for the evening meal. The hutch displayed rows of blue earthenware crockery, gleaming like fine china. By the door, on a low bench, two oblong pails—frequent visitors to the well near the vegetable garden behind the house. The room was filled with the aroma of hearth-baked bread, and of the pine boughs used for sweeping the floor, whose balmy forest fragrance still lingered in the air...

Here everything has an air of homely simplicity, in keeping with the rough ways and naive ingenuousness of our country *habitants*.

Rain continued to beat furiously against the panes; through the ill-fitting windows, water seeped onto the floor.

"Do you think the storm will last long, Mère?"

"No, young 'demoiselle, it's brightening up a bit over towards the sou' west; but we'll get some tricky weather this week, 'cause Sunday past, the gospel-side of the altar was shut. Hey there—la Gothe! Come bring these 'demoiselles some milk an' cream. It's all I can offer you, but I give it with an open heart."

At Mère Madeloche's call, a heavy tread could be heard as the woman called la Gothe began to descend the ladder from the loft. A strapping young woman of about thirty years of age, she was plump and jolly-looking. She approached, greeting them in an awkward manner, but laughing good-naturedly at the friendly questions put to her by Louise, whose servant she had been for many years.

"So, you are staying here with your grandmother now, la Gothe? I imagine it is much less tiring for you than being out in service?"

"Oh—I'm pledged again, only this time it'll be for a good long spell," replied la Gothe, exhibiting a row of great broad teeth.

Madeline threw a questioning glance at her friend, as if to say, 'What does she mean?'

"Are you going to marry again?" asked Louise, thus translating La Gothe's quaint expression for the benefit of the city girl.

"Yes, an' more fool her!" muttered the old grandmother, "as if she didn't get beatings aplenty with her old one."

"Ah well, it's wrote all over a woman that she's always for getting married."

"Were you not very happy with your first husband, my poor woman?"

The old woman took it upon herself to reply: "Well, he sure never hid from her what he was, 'demoiselle. Père Duque, her dead husband, he'd already put two other women into their graves with his cruelties and miseries; we told her time an' again, but she wouldn't listen to nobody an' married him anyway, despite God and the saints."

"Hey, old lady—if not me, it would of been another!"

"But surely," exclaimed Madeline, "you were not obliged to sacrifice yourself for someone else?"

"It was my fate," replied la Gothe, with a shrug of her shoulders.

The last word had been spoken.

Why is it that fatalism is so deeply engrained in our country folk? Destiny—that is the great answer to everything. It terminates all discussion and is the consolation of everyone. Misfortune befalls? The means of preventing it are never spoken of, nor is thought taken to avoid it in future. Everything is simply accounted for by saying, 'It was fated.' Fruitless to oppose any dangerous endeavour; if fate permits, the person involved will emerge unscathed; otherwise, nothing can rescue him from peril—his destiny needs must be accomplished.

And who is to say that they are entirely mistaken? Regardless of the conflict between fatalism and our innate sense that we have total freedom in all our actions, who can declare that the latter is always victorious? Some events occur quite apart from our will, foreseen throughout eternity, and their outcome can never be thwarted by vain human precautions.

While the young widow talked, she covered the table with a linen cloth, the pride of the French-Canadian housewife, of a coarse fabric it is true, but sparkling white. Then, shuffling out to the dairy, she soon returned with two large bowls of fine fresh milk, topped with tempting rich cream; and lifting the lid of the bread bin, she brought forth an enormous loaf, crusty and golden, which she sliced into thick chunks for the young girls.

"Eat your bit of lunch, pretty 'demoiselles," and taking up her knitting, she settled herself in her chair.

"Yes," she continued, as if this stormy hour had revived all her memories of turbulent times, "there are some terrible wicked men! An' I'm sure one that knows it! Many's the time mine gave me black and blue arms—an' every other part of me. He slaughtered me with his beatings; many's the time he'd pound my head against the wall an' lock me up in a big chest, an' wouldn't give me nothing to eat. *Sainte bénite!* A woman can take a heap of suffering without it kills her. I can tell about it now, when it's all over an' done with . . ."

"Besides that, he was jealous like a pigeon-cock," added the grandmother.

"I sure got him going—I sure did!" replied la Gothe, and a wild gleam flashed in her pale eyes.

Her whole being trembled with mute rage as she recalled her past sufferings. This creature, so placid a moment before, now assumed a vicious expression; her nostrils quivered, as if she were in the grip of a powerful emotion; the lips that had smiled so sweetly now curled, and her long knitting needles clacked furiously in her tense fingers. Not the years, not even death had made her forget, so cruel had been her trials. The wounds rankled still from having been under the yoke of that harsh durance.

"Might he have been under the influence of strong drink, and not always responsible for his actions?" asked Louise, who felt a vague need to excuse such vile brutality.

"No," came the firm reply from la Gothe. "I'd of gladly given him every penny I could lay hands on, if he'd only stayed drunk, 'cause he was always better with me when he had a skinful. But, y'know, I think meanness and the pleasure of tormenting me kep' him away from the drink, seeing that I could always get clear of him at such times— an' he never wanted me to be farther away that the end of his arm."

"How many years did this ill-treatment last?"

"Eight years, 'demoiselle, eight years of all the time waiting on him, working for him, an' taking every kind of cruelty from him. A long time of it, mother of God, a long time of it! Well—you don't die from it, that's all you can say. He's the one that died first, eh, all of a sudden an' without no time to ask God's blessing—or anyone else's. He was sitting in the big chair by the hearth an' he bent down for a coal to light his pipe—an' he never got up again. By the time Toinette, his daughter from his first marriage, spied him there, his hands an' feet—with all respect—were just like lumps of ice, an' not so much as an eyelid moving. They sent quick, quick for the priest. An' then, when the good father came to give the extra-munction, that old busybody Jacques Bonsens had to go to the door an' say that the deceased was dead an' gone. An' M. l'curé, he said, 'Poor wretch, why did you tell me that?'—an' turned 'round an' went back the way he came. He might at least have confessed him."

"How could he have confessed him, if he was dead?"

"But 'demoiselle, you're so educated, don't you know that as soon as the priest leaves his vestry to see a man that's just died, he has power to bring him to life, so's he can hear his confession? Only, you mustn't tell the priest he's dead, 'cause then he can't do nothing about it."

"Have you ever been afraid of your dead husband?" enquired Madeline, whose curiosity and interest had been aroused by this strange tale.

"No!" she replied with passion. "Whoever was keeping him there—where he was on the other side—was hangin' on to him good, I can tell you . . . M. l'curé wanted me to have masses said for him, but I knew him better than he did, an' I knew that the deceased was so pig-headed he'd serve his time without help from nobody, 'specially from me."

The rain had ceased to fall. A few clouds, chased by the wind, scurried here and there across the sky, but the sun, now radiant and refreshed from her bath, gaily sent a last kiss to earth from the end of the horizon, before retiring for the night.

Madeline had another question. "Were you at home when your husband died?"

"No, I was down scrubbing clothes by the little stream. When they came an' told me, it was quite a blow, for sure! But—I can tell you," added la Gothe, suddenly recovering her great foolish grin, "it was the last one he ever gave me!"

Louis Fréchette
Translated by Wayne Grady

HOW I LEARNED TO SPEAK ENGLISH

Born in Pointe-Lévis on November 16, 1839, Louis Fréchette attended the Petit Séminaire, the Collège Sainte-Anne-de-la-Pocatière, and the Séminaire de Nicolet before becoming a clerk in the law firm of Francois-Xavier Lemieux in 1860. For the next three years he studied law at Université Laval, worked as a reporter for *Le Journal de Québec*, wrote his first play, *Félix Poutré*, and published his first book of poems, *Mes Loisirs*.

Then began his difficult years. Called to the bar in 1864, he opened an office in Lévis and founded the controversial newspaper *Le Drapeau de Lévis*, in which he voiced his opposition to Confederation. The paper ceased publishing after four issues, and Fréchette left the country—settling eventually in Chicago, where, as editor of *L'Amérique*, he proposed the annexation of Canada and the United States. He soon quit the newspaper over a disagreement about the Franco-Prussian War (he took the side of France); returning to Quebec in 1871, he set up a law firm, wrote a scathing diatribe, *Lettres à Basile*, attacking Adolphe-Basile Routhier, a popular Quebec lawyer, and ran for Parliament. He lost. He was elected, however, in 1874, and served one term before losing again.

Moving to Montreal in 1880, he contributed to the controversial *La Patrie* (owned by Honoré Beaugrand, a friend of Faucher de Saint-Maurice and the future mayor of Montreal), and that year won the Prix Montyon, awarded by the Académie française. From then on his reputation as a writer of international stature was secure. He spent a year in France, then returned to Quebec City to accept a sinecure as clerk of the Legislative Council; for *La Patrie* and *Le Canada artistique*, he wrote a series of portraits of typical Québécois characters later published as *Originaux et détraqués*. He was named president of the Royal Society of Canada in 1900, the year he wrote his *Mémoires intimes*—a work of gentle charm and biting wit—and died of a stroke on May 31, 1908, in Montreal.

Fréchette was in love with language. His *Originaux et détraqués* is full of wild descriptions and untranslatable puns, and his later work also explores the limits of conventional speech. "Comment j'ai appris l'anglais," translated by Wayne Grady as "How I Learned to Speak English," from *Mémoires intimes*, is an excellent example of Fréchette's wry and irreverent humour, very modern in its style and approach. It is not surprising that the *Mémoires* remained unpublished for more than fifty years after Fréchette's death.

∽

"How I Learned to Speak English" is a translation of "Comment j'ai appris l'anglais" published in *Mémoires intimes* (Montreal: Fides, 1961).

Our closest neighbours were an English family named Houghton. They had two sons, Bonnie and Dozzie. There was a daughter, too, but never mind her for now—I was too young for the more interesting half of humanity, what we call the fair sex, to hold any interest for me. Quite the reverse, in fact: I was more disposed to pity girls, small, fragile creatures that they were, with no wind for running, who had to wear skirts that prevented them from having all kinds of fun, especially climbing trees, turning somersaults, or rolling head over heels down hills.

My brother Edmond and I and the two Houghton boys, though, we were a pretty good foursome, the oldest Houghton being exactly my age, and the youngest the same age as my brother. And in spite of my prejudice against the English, and the fierce arguments that would flare up between us at even the mention of the name Papineau, we were two pairs of buddies even more assiduous in our relationships than our parents encouraged us to be.

"Playing every day with those Houghton youngsters can't help but teach our boys to speak English," my father would say, "and at their age there's a good chance they'll acquire a decent accent."

"Hanging around all the time with those Fréchette kids," Mr. Houghton, on his part, would reflect, "Bonnie and Dozzie will be speaking French in no time, and learning another language so young, why, they'll grow up with a real accent!"

So it was that our father would often say to us: "Go play with the Houghtons, they're proper little gentlemen, and you'll learn English."

And their father would say to them: "Go play with the Fréchettes, they're well-mannered boys, and you'll learn French."

We didn't have to be told twice, of course: we'd play with our tops, we'd play hopscotch together, fly kites, play hide-and-go-seek, shoot marbles, play patty-cake—you name it, we played it. My father'd hear us running around shouting, "Tag, you're hit!" or "High spy with my little high," or playing games with names like "Jack-in-the-Hay" or "Puss-in-the-Corner" or "Hoppy-Go-Kicky," and he'd congratulate himself and us on how quickly we were learning to speak English.

"Very good, my boys," he would say to us. "I see you're picking it up just fine. Do you always speak English like that when you play together?"

"Always, papa."

"Perfect, boys, keep it up."

"Well, well," Mr. Houghton would say to his two sons. "French coming along all right, then?"

"Oh, yes, papa."

"You always speak it when you're together, do you?"

"Oh, yes, father."

"All right, boys, carry on!"

Now, you've probably noticed a certain inconsistency in our several responses to these questions, but in fact neither we nor the Houghtons were lying. By saying that we always spoke English together, my brother and I were replying in the best of faith; and our friends were just as sincere in saying that they spoke French. How could that be, you ask? Well, here's how it worked. Without knowing it, we had invented a kind of Esperanto, a sort of jargon that two of us thought was English and the other two thought was French. This jargon was made up of expressions borrowed from both languages, with the English words pronounced with a French accent, and the French words flattened out into English.

Our township being almost exclusively French, of course, the Houghtons were much more familiar with our language than we were with theirs; it followed that French was the basis for this hybridized amalgamation. A few simple variations here and there, and Bob's your uncle. Very simple variations, I should say. For instance, the negation *non* in French translates as "no" in English, so we'd take the possessive adjectives *mon*, *son*, and *ton* in French and turn them into *mow*, *so*, and *toe* in English. Simple, eh? So that if we said *mon père* and *ton frère* with a sort of slurry English pronunciation, we'd get *moper* and *toe fur*. Sounded English to us. And when Bonnie or Dozzie did the same thing, it came out sounding (to them) like perfectly good French.

If we wanted to say, for example, what in good French would be *Mon père est plus grand que ton père*, or *Ton frère est plus p'tit que c'ty-là de moé*, it would come out sounding like, "Mopers blue gronka toper," and "Toe furs bloop Sitka steal Adam way."

And we sincerely thought we were speaking English. I was personally extremely proud of myself for having become so fluent in a language that everyone else seemed to think was a bugger to learn and a bitch to pronounce. And what really turned my crank was the fact that the whole thing took place without my having to lift a finger.

"There's nothing to it, Mom, really," I told her over and over again. "You just have to let yourself go."

Well, we couldn't let ourselves go for long, as you've probably already figured out. A discovery like that couldn't be kept quiet indefinitely. Such a beautiful light wasn't meant to shine under a bushel basket. Here's how our linguistic talents were finally dragged into the open.

One fine morning, in front of my father, my brother said to me:

"Would you lend me your top?"

"Take it if you want," I replied.

"Hey, you guys," my father said. "Why don't you say that in English for me?"

Oh, boy . . . If only we could have!

"Set way pretty toe to pee, Amway," my brother said, with nerveless sangfroid.

To which I replied, equally unperturbed, "Prawn lassy tofu!"

My father thought we were pulling his leg at first, but after a serious and prolonged interrogation the true depth of our ignorance was revealed, and he had to give up any notion he may have had about our linguistic prowess. To paraphrase the critic Brunetière, all our science was a fraud. We were paw blue foreign on clay Connor Tog Raffy, a lass! My vanity sea-changed on humiliation, and the satisfaction de moper on day courage meant.

Sylva Clapin
Translated by Wayne Grady

HAY FEVER

Sylva Clapin was born in Saint-Hyacinthe, Quebec, on July 15, 1853, and studied at the Séminaire de Saint-Hyacinthe until 1873, when he joined the United States Navy and served aboard the *Kansas*. He returned to Saint-Hyacinthe to become the village librarian, to run a bookshop and a music store, and to edit the *Courrier de St-Hyacinthe*. Before long, however, he was off again: to London and Paris in 1879, and to Montreal in 1880, where he began writing for *Le Monde*, *Le Canadien*, and *L'Électeur*. He published his first short story, "Victor et Marie," in *L'Album des familles* in October 1882, then returned to Saint-Hyacinthe, married his second-cousin, Marie-Archange Clapin, and moved with her to Paris, where he spent the next six years as a correspondent for *Le Monde*.

Clapin returned to Montreal in 1888 and edited *L'Opinion publique* for a year, then once again found himself serving as a gunner in the U.S. Navy. Following the decisive Battle of Santiago, he was decorated for bravery but discovered that he was becoming deaf, a condition that somehow did not prevent him from accepting the post of translator in the House of Commons in Ottawa, which he held from 1902 until his retirement in 1921. He wrote continually: one acquaintance noted that Clapin wrote the way some people play cards. He wrote dozens of short stories, a sequel to *Maria Chapdelaine* (entitled *Alma-Rose*, never published), and a history of the United States for Quebec schools. He even compiled a *Dictionnaire canadien-français* (1894), a *New Dictionary of Americanisms* (1902), and, the year before his death in 1928, edited the Canadian edition of the *Dictionnaire Larousse complet*.

"La fièvre des foins," translated by Wayne Grady as "Hay Fever," was first published in 1917, and is taken here from Clapin's *Contes et nouvelles*, a collection of his short fiction that appeared in 1980. It is an extremely humorous story, with the kind of gentle, rural charm that is nonetheless sly and somewhat satirical: consider, for example, that the story was first published in the 52nd edition of the Montreal annual *Almanach Rolland*, and that its plot turns, in part, on the unreliability of almanacs.

∽

"Hay Fever" is a translation of "La fièvre des foins" published in *Contes et nouvelles* (Montreal: Fides, 1980).

One afternoon in February, while the snow outside was blowing to beat the devil, Ambroise Latourelle, justice of the peace and postmaster of the little village of X in the region of Lac Saint-Pierre, was dozing beside his woodstove when the door was suddenly flung open and in walked a stranger, bringing with him a gust of cold air. Old Ambroise (as he was known thereabouts), roused from his reveries, recognized the newcomer as the man who had come in the day before to ask if there had been any mail for him, saying he was a salesman for a large farm-equipment company in Ontario.

"Not very good weather for selling farm machinery," muttered Old Ambroise.

The young man didn't reply at first, but busied himself with brushing the snow off his clothes, and then went over to the stove to warm his hands. "It could be better, that's the truth," he said after a moment, "but I can't complain. I've sold a few threshing machines and a couple of separators. But I can't sell a hay-baler to save my life, and I'm damned if I can figure out why."

Old Ambroise knew why. "Hay-balers," he said. "We used to buy a lot of them back when we could grow hay. But for the past few years it hasn't been worth our while even to think about hay in these parts, on account of the rain we've been getting every year just at haying time. Last year, for example, it came down and didn't stop for four days, never mind what it said in all those worthless almanacs, that there'd be sunny skies for the whole month of July. Sunny skies. Ha! And here you are trying to sell us balers! I'm not surprised if balers are a hard sell around here."

At the mention of almanacs, the stranger pricked up his ears and, when Ambroise finished speaking he walked over to the chair where he had deposited his suitcase and began rummaging about in it. At length, he brought out a small book bound in brown cloth with the front-cover title printed in gold lettering: *Doctor Wiggins' Almanac, Encyclopedia and Weather Prognosticator*.

"There's the tragedy in not being able to read English," he said, waving the book under Old Ambroise's nose. "I've not been able to find a single soul in this whole region who knew enough English to read this little book, which is nothing short of an absolute must for farmers."

"What's that book got to do with us?" queried Old Ambroise.

"Well, sir," replied the salesman, "since you ask, I'll tell you. It just so happens," he said, tapping the book with his forefinger, "that this little book is the only one of its kind—the one and only one, mind you—that gives accurate, one-hundred percent, bona fide predictions of the weather for every day of the entire year. For the insignificant sum of seventy-five cents, which is all I'm asking for it, anyone who can read English would be able to plan his harvest weeks and even months in advance."

Now, Ambroise Latourelle was no book-lover, as anyone could tell you, and any salesman trying to sell him an ordinary almanac for seventy-five cents—or even a hefty tome with colourful illustrations, for that matter—would normally have a tough time of it. But when this fellow mentioned weather predictions, he touched a sensitive nerve in Old Ambroise, who, as everyone also knew, prided himself on being unequalled in the parish for his ability to say, on any given afternoon or evening, what the weather was going to be like the next day and even the day after that. Whenever anyone came in to visit, the conversation would inevitably come around to the weather, and Old Ambroise was bound to wink his eye at some point and say, "It's going to rain like hell tomorrow," or, "Looks like it'll be clearing up overnight," in a manner that would annoy the most sceptical of his neighbours. And annoy them all the more because, perhaps due to a kind of sixth sense he had developed, he was hardly ever wrong. Just the same, he thought now, being able to predict the weather days and weeks in advance—no, he couldn't credit it. There was no way on earth this young whippersnapper could convince an old codger like himself, who had seen a bit of the world in his time and had even lived in the United States as a young lad, that such a thing was possible.

So he simply relit his pipe, took a few tentative draws on it, and looked up at the salesman with a crafty eye. "Oh, aye," he said. "And how many of those lies in there ever turn out to be true, eh?"

"Eighty-five percent," replied the salesman promptly, "according to the Royal Dominion Observatory in Toronto. And I am willing to bet you twenty-five dollars that I am not here to pull the wool over your eyes. Look, there's an easy way to find out, if you're willing to try a little experiment." And rummaging in his suitcase again, he produced a second volume, similar to the first, which he brandished with redoubled enthusiasm.

"Here's Wiggins's almanac from last year," he said. "You tell me what the weather was like up here during last year's haying season, and I'll tell you what the almanac predicted it would be."

"What the weather was like?" exclaimed Old Ambroise. "Why, it came down like horse piss for ten full days!"

The salesman flipped through the pages of the book until he found the section dealing with weather forecasts, and stopped at the page for July. Then, folding the book back almost in half, he held it up to Ambroise with an eloquent flourish and said: "Here, read it for yourself."

Old Ambroise read with an astonished expression on his face, his eyes widening more and more as he read:

July 1-7: Cloudy, wet, frequent storms.

July 7-14: Wet weather continues; clouds become more frequent.

"Well, I'll be damned," said Old Ambroise. "That's exactly what it was like." And he went back to smoking his pipe with short, rapid puffs, all the while casting covetous glances at the little book. His mind was working no less rapidly. How grand it would be to be recognized as a prophet of such magnitude, and what a pleasure to put that Toussaint Grenon, his rival from the other side of the village, in his place once and for all. These long-term forecasts might not be such nonsense after all. Hadn't he heard about scholars who were able to read the future in the stars as if they were open books? No doubt this Professor Wiggins was one of those learned men.

"I might take the book off your hands," he said to the salesman. "But only if you'll take fifty cents for it."

After a brief discussion, they settled on a price of sixty cents.

"But remember, now, not a word to anyone hereabouts about this," he cautioned the salesman. "I'd be the laughingstock of the parish if word got out that the justice of the peace was spending good money on almanacs!"

Since it was already late in the evening, Old Ambroise postponed perusal of his purchase until the next day. But the first thing in the morning, after making sure no one would disturb him, he placed his best kerosene lamp on his desk, lit it, leaned back in his chair, and began to read.

The first thing he did was satisfy himself that his English was good enough to enable him to form an opinion about the book; and, in his opinion, there wasn't much in it of particular interest to himself. It had obviously been written for the English in the neighbouring province, and he began to regret wasting his sixty cents. But, when he came to the section in which Astrologer Wiggins explained the system on which he had based his prognostications, Old Ambroise's attention began to perk up. It all had to do, apparently, with the relative positions of the earth, the sun, the moon, and the stars; with certain vibrations within the bowels of the earth, with the Aurora Borealis, the tides of the oceans, and a few other things of that nature. If a man could only get all those factors arranged in his head, it seemed that predicting the weather for such-and-such a day in any particular small corner of the country, which Lac Saint-Pierre certainly was, was as easy as poking yourself in the eye with a sharp stick.

Still, it wasn't until he reached the actual meteorological forecasts, as they were properly called, and in particular those for the month of July, that he realized what a veritable gold mine he was holding in his hands. So surprised was he that he let fly with an oath that he usually reserved only for great occasions—"By the Holy Mary of the Pine Trees!"—and slammed his fist down on the top of his desk.

For this is what he had read:

July 1-7: Hot and dry, with perhaps a few occasional showers

July 7-14: Continuing hot and dry, no chance of rain, excellent weather for haying.

He couldn't for the life of him see why he shouldn't use such information to make a bit of money for himself, and in a very few minutes he had devised his plan. He knew that no one in the area had planted hay last year, despite the high price hay had been fetching since the beginning of the war. All he had to do to put his scheme in motion was to convince a few farmers to forget about the past and try hay again this year. That wouldn't be easy, he knew, but after all it was still only February. There was plenty of time, and once he put his mind to a thing, he reminded himself, the devil take him if the thing wasn't as good as done.

Looking at the almanac for the current month, that is to say for February, he noticed that some of the forecasts were somewhat ambiguously worded, which gave him pause to think. The book foretold a series of thaws, cold spells, rain squalls, and so on, without being too specific about the exact days on which these events would transpire. Generally speaking, however, if he took a particular day and worked backward and forward from it, the coincidences of accurate predictions were frequent enough to be encouraging. Allowing for liberal interpretations of some of the predictions, and keeping an open mind, it was usually possible to give Dr. Wiggins the benefit of the doubt. His mind was soon made up, and for the first time in his life, Old Ambroise, whose frugality of habit was legendary in the region, and who had never once gambled with so much as a single dollar, resolved to throw himself body and soul into the heady arena of financial speculation.

As one rode out of the village, the first farm one came to was owned by a family of Scottish origin. Their name had been McIntyre, but they had lived in the region for so many generations that their name had become Frenchified, and they had forgotten that they had ever spoken English. They now called themselves MacEnterre, and bore the name as proudly as if they had come over with the Sieur de Champlain himself.

They retained only one hold-over from their ancestry: they were as parsimonious and proverbially pig-headed as any clansman who ever chipped a tooth on a penny. Joe MacEnterre, the current head of the family, subjected even the most insignificant deal to such close scrutiny and went over each detail with such a fine-toothed comb that anyone having business relations with him could count himself lucky if he came away without leaving behind a pound or two of flesh.

So it was to Joe MacEnterre that Old Ambroise resolved to direct his first salvo. "If I can get that old leather-headed penny-pincher on my side," he said to himself, "my plan is assured, for the rest of the parish will follow like lambs to the fold."

To give himself the best possible chance, he waited another whole month. Then, on a fine day toward the end of March, when the air was still just brisk enough to make you want to warm your hands by the stove for a few minutes when you came in from outside, Old Ambroise intercepted his man as he came into the post office for his mail.

"Nice day, eh Joe?" he said while the farmer was looking through his newspaper. "If it stays like this we'll have an early spring."

"Hmmph, early spring, oh aye," said Joe without looking up from his paper. "Everything's so turned on its arse these days you hardly know where to put your hat."

"Have a pipe before you go, why don't you?" said Old Ambroise. "You're not in any hurry, I hope?"

So they dragged two chairs closer to the stove, lit their pipes, and sat in silence for a moment or two. After a few puffs, however, Old Ambroise decided to take the bull by the horns.

"You planning on putting in much hay this year, Joe?" he asked.

To which Joe expostulated: "Hay! Now, what in tarnation would I be doing growing hay? I've had enough of growing hay to last me a lifetime, and then some. Hay! No, I'll put it all into oats, so I will. Oats, oats, and more oats. Oats is the only thing that pays these days."

"Why," said Old Ambroise innocently, "what makes you say so?"

"What makes me say so? You know damned well what makes me say so. I say so because it's God's own truth. Don't tell me you don't remember what the weather's been like for the past two or three years at haying time."

"No, I won't tell you that," replied Old Ambroise. "But things could be different this year, you know."

They sucked thoughtfully on their pipes for a few minutes, and then the postmaster drew his chair conspiratorially closer to that of his friend. "Listen, Joe," he said, "you know what I'm thinking? You know that piece of land I have across the river, the one I've been renting out to that fellow for the past few years, and that I've been getting the same rent for year in and year out, fair weather or foul? Well, I'm thinking that that's a bad bargain, you know? Even in a good year, it's hardly worth it for me. No risk to it, if you know what I mean. I'd rather strike a deal with you here and now. You put half of your forty acres into hay this year, and I'll pay you twelve dollars an acre for the hay whether you get any off it or not. What do you say to that, eh?"

Joe MacEnterre didn't say anything to it for quite some time. Instead, he puffed on his pipe so furiously that his whole head became enveloped in smoke, which hid the gleam of astonishment that had crept into his eyes. He hunkered down lower in his chair, drew his neck into his shoulders like a turtle, buried his chin in his beard, and closed his eyes. For a moment Old Ambroise thought he had gone to sleep, but in fact he had merely descended into a state of profound contemplation. "If Old Ambroise is willing to take a gamble like this," he was thinking, "then the whole world really is going to hell in a manure spreader." After a while, he opened one eye and said:

"If those twenty acres yield two tons of hay apiece, you'll make yourself a piss-pot full of money, Ambroise."

"That's true," said Old Ambroise. "On the other hand, if they bring in half a ton or less, as they have for the past three years, then I'll lose my shirt."

"What makes you so sure the weather'll hold for haying this year?" asked Joe.

"I didn't say it would," evaded Ambroise. "I only said it could be different this year, is all."

"Hmm," said Joe. "Well, shoot me for a lame heifer, but I'll take you up on it, provided you put down in writing what we've agreed to. And make sure it says just the twenty acres, too."

As soon as Joe MacEnterre left the post office, his piece of paper tucked into the bib of his overalls, Old Ambroise summoned his clerk. "Now listen here, Zéphirin, my lad," he said, "I don't suppose you missed much of what just went on, eh? Well, I've just one thing to say to you. If I ever hear tell that you've been spreading rumours about my being a gambler, I'll fire you so fast you'll think your arse has turned into a firecracker. Do I make myself clear? I can't have the village thinking they've got a card shark for a justice of the peace. And if you lose your position here, there'll be no marrying that young daughter of Toussaint Grenon you've been courting for a good little while now. So I hope we understand each other!"

Well, it was true that young Zéphirin Piquebois had no desire to lose his job. He had put up with Old Ambroise for too long to give it up now, after four years of trying to save enough money out of his measly five dollars a week to even think about running a household. No sir, he'd keep his lip buttoned as tight as Old Ambroise's coin purse and no mistake—although he did resolve to keep his ears open. And damned if the very next day he didn't overhear the old man make the same deal that he'd just made with Joe

MacEnterre with another farmer. Twelve dollars an acre for hay! And another the day after that! And another, until it was clear as the nose on his face that Old Ambroise was out to buy up every last bale of hay he could lay his hands on.

Old Ambroise, gambling with money. Zéphirin didn't like the looks of it at all. What on earth could have caused such a change in the old man? Now, Zéphirin wasn't the world's sharpest observer by a long shot, but even he couldn't help noticing that the old man had been doing something different for the past few days. Old Ambroise, who ordinarily never so much as opened a book, who rarely read anything more complicated than the evening newspaper, was now spending almost every waking hour with his nose buried in a small, brown volume that he kept under lock and key when he wasn't in the office, and that he only took out of its hiding place when he thought no one was looking. Zéphirin would bet his bottom dollar that the little book contained the explanation to this whole mystifying business.

He tried several times to find out what the book was. If he could just catch a glimpse of the cover he might be able to tell, but the old man was on his guard, and never left it lying in the open. Every time he left his desk, even just to go to the outhouse, he opened his desk drawer, dropped the book into it, and "click"—the tiny sound of the key turning in the lock told Zéphirin that once again his hopes had been dashed.

Then, one afternoon near the beginning of April, the chance he'd been waiting for finally presented itself. Someone came into the post office to fetch the justice of the peace to preside over an inquest into the drowning death of a man found floating in the lake. Ambroise departed in such haste that he forgot to lock the drawer that contained the little book. Zéphirin the Eagle-Eyed noticed right away, but was careful not to betray the slightest awareness of the fact for fear of reminding the old man. Not until he'd seen Old Ambroise's horse and buggy disappear out of the village did he even hazard a glance in the direction of the desk.

At first, he could make nothing of the book at all, even though he knew enough English to make out what it was that his boss had been guarding so assiduously. A simple almanac. What the hell? Why would Old Ambroise be spending the better part of his days reading an almanac? Then suddenly it dawned on him, as though someone had reached in through his ear and lit a tiny candle inside his head. It happened when he flipped to the section dealing with weather prognosticating, and came to a page that was dog-eared, smudged, and covered with Old Ambroise's chicken scratches: the famous forecast for the first two weeks in July.

"Why that cunning old bastard!" cried Zéphirin, and he instantly fell into an agitation of mind that grew more and more uncomfortable the longer he thought. The source of this agitation was the fact that Toussaint Grenon, Zéphirin's future father-in-law, was one of those who had signed a contract with Old Ambroise, in his case for thirty of the sixty acres he owned. Zéphirin clearly had to warn Toussaint about the trap he had blundered into, and prevent him by all means from planting the other thirty acres in oats. (It never occurred to Zéphirin to doubt the accuracy of the almanac—after all, he had seen the predictions printed right there in black and white, in a book that came from Ontario, and was probably written by learned men, and in which his boss, who was no slouch himself when it came to deep thinking, had obviously put a lot of stock.)

But what about his promise to keep his mouth shut about his boss's affairs? Well, he thought, Old Ambroise would never find out. And since he was sure the old man would be away from the office until well into the evening, he knew he had plenty of time to run over to the Grenon farm, a mere half-mile away, show Toussaint the almanac, and get back in time to return the book to its hiding place before Old Ambroise arrived back from the inquest. Immediately, he put this plan into effect. He closed up the office as quickly as he could, advised Old Ambroise's wife not to expect him for dinner, and ran as fast as his legs would carry him to the farmhouse of his prospective father-in-law, the little brown book safely in the inside pocket of his overcoat. Just before reaching the house he had to slow down for a moment, as one of those sudden downpours, accompanied by thunder and lightning that we sometimes get in these parts at the beginning of spring, passed by.

Imagine Grenon's surprise when, hearing a frantic knocking at his door, he opened it to see his future son-in-law standing on the doorstep looking like a drowned rat and displaying all the signs of having lost what little mind he had had to begin with. His daughter Élodie, who had come up behind her father, gave a little gasp of pity, and the two of them led the shivering lad to the stove, all the while asking the reason for this unexpected visit.

Zéphirin explained as quickly as possible, given his breathless state, and took the almanac from his pocket to show them what he was talking about. Grenon let him finish his exposition without saying a word, then lit his pipe with a stick of kindling from the stove, rocked back in his chair for a few moments, and said: "Well, there's one way to find out if all this is true or just a bunch of malarky. Look in the book for today, and see what it says about the weather."

Zéphirin hurriedly turned to the appropriate page and read the entry aloud, his voice now even more breathless:

"*April 6-12: Unusually warm for the time of year, wind from the south bringing storms, possibility of thunder and lightning.*"

At that very moment, as if to underscore the prophecy, a great flash of lightning lit up the windows, and a violent clap of thunder shook the walls. All three were struck dumb, while from the room above their heads they heard a loud wail from Élodie's mother, who came bounding down the stairs an instant later in a state of complete terror. Grenon, who had let his pipe go out, sat with his gaze fixed on a maple log burning in the stove. Finally, taking another taper from the fire, he relit his pipe, gave a few sighs, and said: "This is the very devil, Zéphirin. Read me that bit again about the weather during haying season."

Zéphirin again read the forecast for the first two weeks in July.

"That crafty old bugger," Grenon exclaimed. "What a horse's arse I was to sign that piece of paper!"

"If you want my advice, sir," said Zéphirin, "maybe you should try to buy your way out of that contract while there's still time."

"That's just what I was thinking," said Grenon. "But that old fox would never go for it, I'm sure. He's got me over a barrel, and that's the truth."

"There's still a chance, I think," Zéphirin continued. "The reason I say that is because Old Ambroise turned down an offer just yesterday, from someone who said he'd take only ten dollars an acre. Maybe the old man's in a bit over his head, eh? Maybe he wouldn't mind getting out of a contract. Holy cow!" he said suddenly. "Look at the time— I've got to get this book in the old man's desk before he gets back."

Toussaint Grenon's first thought was to go over to the post office the next day and strike while the iron was hot. But the more he thought about it, and being the old slyboots he was, the more he realized that it might be better not to tackle the postmaster so soon after last night's thunderstorm, which had demonstrated how accurate that cursed almanac really was. Such proof of the value of its forecasts would only cement Old Ambroise in his determination to hang on to his contracts.

So he waited two more weeks. Then, on a fine, bright morning, he walked into the village and, after chatting with Old Ambroise about this and that, remarked in as off-hand a tone as he could muster: "By the way, Ambroise, I've been having second thoughts about that piece of paper we signed."

Old Ambroise said nothing, so Grenon cleared his throat and barged ahead: "I'm not easy in my mind about it, and the wife, well, she kicked my arse all around the barn when she heard tell of it. I've always worked my land for myself, you know what I mean, and it just doesn't seem right to be selling off my hay before it's even up out of the ground. Makes me feel like I'm growing it second-hand or something."

"Twelve dollars an acre is a fair price, Toussaint," said Old Ambroise.

"Oh, 'tis," said Grenon. "It's a darn fair price. And probably a lot more'n I'd get for it on the open market. I'm not saying that. It's just that, well, I wish to hell I'd never gotten into this contract thing. What I'm going to ask you, Ambroise, as a friend, is if there isn't some way you and I can work it so I get back that gol-darned piece of paper."

"How much did you have in mind?" asked Old Ambroise, getting right to the point. "I mean, per acre."

At this point, Zéphirin, who just happened to be passing by, pricked up his ears. He certainly hadn't expected the old man to give in so easily. Even Grenon was taken aback, although he was too smart to let on.

"I was thinking a dollar an acre," he said.

Old Ambroise gave a snort of laughter. "Sorry, Toussaint," he said, "but I thought you were joking. One dollar? You think I'm that eager to break off our agreement?"

"Well, two dollars, then. How would that suit?"

"Toussaint, Toussaint," said Old Ambroise, "you know I'd really like to help you out of your jam, eh? But a deal's a deal. For two dollars an acre I'd just as soon take my chances on the weather, thank you very much."

"All right, you old son of a birch tree, I'll give you three dollars an acre and not a cent more. Take it or leave it!" And so saying he stood up as if to leave the post office.

"Now hold your horses, Toussaint," said Old Ambroise. "Three dollars, you say? Good enough, I'll take your three dollars. But I want the money right now, in advance, and I'm only doing it at all because you're a friend."

It took a great effort of will for Grenon, who was reputed to have one of the tightest fists in the parish, to write a cheque for ninety dollars in return for a piece of paper. But after all, he must have thought to himself, he was lucky to get out of the contract at all, and at such a price—in his own mind, he had been prepared to go as high as four dollars an acre.

Zéphirin, too, never dreamed that his boss would be so accommodating. Such a good deal, and for hay practically guaranteed to come in at two tons an acre! But if Zéphirin had had the presence of mind to sneak a glance at Dr. Wiggins's almanac again, he might not have been so mystified by Old Ambroise's willingness to get out of his contract with Grenon. It was a beautiful spring day, buds bursting open on the trees, brooks gurgling merrily in their beds, the sun streaming though the windows, and a warm, south wind gently pushing away the last lingering chill of winter. But what did the almanac call for?

Sudden cold snap: snow flurries, turning into a full-scale blizzard followed by freezing rain.

There were still three days before this sudden cold snap was due, and Old Ambroise spent them curled up beside the woodstove, puffing on his pipe like a steam engine, his feet feeling as cold as if the expected blizzard were already raging, and shivering as if there weren't a single stick of firewood to put in the stove. For the first time since February he had begun to worry that he had stepped into a hornet's nest with that blessed almanac, signing all those contracts. He was now wondering whether there wasn't some way he could get out of the mess he was in. Obviously his precious Dr. Wiggins was not exactly infallible; what if his predictions for the month of July were as wide of the mark as they seemed to be for this week in April? What then? Just thinking about it sent a river of icewater running down his spine all the way to his ankles. No, Old Ambroise wasn't surprised at all by his eagerness to accept Grenon's offer to get out of his contract.

In fact, Grenon had no sooner left the post office when Zéphirin saw his master behave in a manner he was accustomed to seeing only on very rare occasions. Instead of remaining quietly behind the ramparts of his desk, the old man took to pacing up and down the length of the office, his forehead wrinkled like an old shirt, and his hands clasped behind his back, proof positive that his mind was working at maximum capacity. What could be going on inside that infernal combustion engine? Zéphirin wondered. But he never learned—not even when, the next day, a line of farmers who had signed a contract with Old Ambroise formed all the way from the old man's desk, out the door of the post office and through the village half-way to Repentigny. It made him wonder whether the old man hadn't committed some sort of crime. For a whole week the postmaster took back contracts in exchange for hard, cold cash, until he had broken the agreements he had made with all the farmers in the district. There were grumbles and complaints here and there, to be sure, and occasional weeping and wailing and gnashing of teeth, but in the end every contract was handed over, and by the time Joe MacEnterre came in—the last to pay up as he had been the first to sign—Old Ambroise found himself in possession of $1,188, easily the most money he had ever made in his life without lifting so much as his little finger to earn it.

Old Ambroise's satisfaction was not destined to come unalloyed, however.

July, the king of months, arrived at last, spreading its sovereign splendour over all living things. Never had the hay looked so beautiful, undulating gently in the fields for as far as the eye could see, swaying under the sun's warm caresses, and promising as bountiful a harvest as had ever been known in the halcyon years of long ago. There was jubilation in the parish, now that the forecast in the almanac was common knowledge and universally believed.

One morning, as Old Ambroise was taking his customary morning ride on horseback, he found himself trotting along the road leading down to the lake. There he ran into Jérémie Coquebin, a fish-faced old codger whom he particularly disliked. Jérémie said to him in passing, in a decidedly mocking tone, "Wal, sor, it looks like we'll be gettin' some hay in this year arter all, ain't it."

The postmaster turned his horse and rode off, feeling doubly chagrinned because he had once had a contract with Coquebin.

July continued fine, as the week that everyone had fixed as the start of haying season drew near. Now, whenever Old Ambroise went for his morning ride, he felt like Tantalus under his accursed grapes, seeing all those superb fields of hay rippling in the breeze, each nodding head of alfalfa seeming to say to him: "No, no, no, my good sir, we're not yours any more, are we?" He had made nearly twelve hundred dollars with no more effort than it took to sign his name, it was true, but at two-and-a-half tons per acre, as the yield seemed certain to be, it wasn't hard for him to calculate the difference between the money he had made and the money he would have made if he hadn't been such a stupid cut-arse as to tear up all those blasted contracts.

Finally, one morning Athanaise Lacaillade, whose farm was more favourably situated than those of his neighbours, announced he was going to begin cutting hay the next afternoon. That evening Old Ambroise sat out on his porch a little later than usual, finishing his last pipe of the day. As he sat rocking, he watched the sun lower itself gently behind the roof of the church in a veritable apotheosis of glory—little puffy, white, cherubic clouds bathed in its soft pink glow. After nightfall, the sky was pin-pointed by a myriad of stars that twinkled like so many golden nail-heads holding up the dark fabric of heaven. There was no denying it: Lacaillade was going to have a beautiful day for haying.

About two o'clock in the morning, Old Ambroise slipped out of bed and tiptoed over to the window. He hadn't been more than half-asleep all night. Outside, it was as black as ink, not a single star shone in the sky. Surprised, he opened the window, and a puff of cool air hit him square in the face. When his wife awakened with a start because of the change in temperature, she asked him what in tarnation he thought he was doing.

"The devil take me if that isn't rain I smell in the air," he answered happily.

And he was right. No sooner had he returned to bed than it began to rain cats and dogs. Lightning flashed, thunder growled, and by dawn it was raining harder than it had ever rained before, with no sign of letting up. The old man got out of bed and fixed his breakfast with a lively step, and at the post office that morning he said to everyone who came in, barely managing to instill a tone of commiseration in his voice: "My, my, it looks like there won't be any haying again this year. Tsk, tsk. Of course, it could let up any minute now...."

But the rain did not let up. Far from it, it continued to come down in sheets, in buckets, in veritable Niagaras; it rained as if the sky had split open and the end of the world were at hand. It rained for four straight days and nights, and when finally, on the morning of the fifth day, a pale, watery sun rose ponderously in a leaden sky, the half-submerged hayfields it revealed looked as though they had been trampled by a herd of stampeding elephants. Not a third of the crop was salvageable, even by the most expensive hay-baler in the world.

Zéphirin, who had been feeling like death itself for the past four days, felt even more desolate on the fifth. Seeing his long, worried face, Old Ambroise felt moved to cheer him up a bit.

"I've got some good news to tell you," he said. "Since you've always been such a good clerk, I've decided to raise your salary to six dollars a week instead of five, beginning next Michaelmas. What do you say to that, eh?"

But Zéphirin merely cried, "No! You can't do that! I don't deserve it. I'm not a good clerk—I deceived you, M. Latourelle. Do you remember telling me not to say anything to the others about your contract with Joe MacEnterre?" And he went on to blurt out the whole story, how he had stolen the almanac and run with it over to the Grenons....

When he finished, Old Ambroise's eyes lit up with a sly sparkle. "And what makes you think," he said, lighting his pipe, "that I didn't intend for you to do just that, eh?"

Zéphirin was so staggered by this that he felt as though his feet had been nailed to the floor. His eyes grew as round as cow patties, and his tongue couldn't have stammered out a word if his life depended on it.

After that, Old Ambroise's fame as a forecaster grew even more, since everyone was convinced that the old fox had foreseen in April the storm that would hit them in July, despite what the almanac said, and moreover had had the presence of mind to pull himself out of the chasm into which his speculative fever had threatened to plunge him.

People now come from far and wide to consult with him on the caprices of nature. Gracious and obliging, the old gentleman basks in the reflected glow of the halo that others have placed on his head. And if anyone happens to mention Dr. Wiggins's famous almanac, Old Ambroise replies with the most innocent expression in the world on his face, that anything written in alamanacs, or in any book at all, for that matter, has to be taken with a grain of salt.

Jean-Aubert Loranger
Translated by Sheila Fischman

THE FERRYMAN

Jean-Aubert Loranger, a descendant of Philippe-Aubert de Gaspé, was born in Montreal in 1896. Orphaned at the age of four, he was raised by foster parents and, at the age of 22, became one of the founding members of the literary group that published the avant-garde art and poetry journal *Le Nigog*. In 1924, he began working as an insurance agent for Metropolitan Life, a position he held until his untimely death in 1942.

Loranger was perhaps better known in Quebec as a poet than as a fiction writer, and he is generally considered the first poet in Canada to abandon poetical classicism in favour of free verse. In fact, he published more short stories than poetry: his first book, *Les Atmosphères. Le Passeur. Poèmes et autres choses*, published in Montreal in 1920, contained both poetry and short stories, and his subsequent short-story collections include *À la recherche du régionalisme. Le Village. Contes et nouvelles de terroir* (*In Search of Regionalism. The Village. Tales and Stories of the Homestead*, 1925) and the two-volume edition *Contes*, published in 1978, which runs to 655 pages. "Le Passeur," the title story included here—translated as "The Ferryman" by Sheila Fischman—is the title story from Loranger's first book.

∽

"The Ferryman" is a translation of "Le Passeur" published in *Les Atmosphères. Le Passeur. Poèmes et autres proses* (Montreal: L. Ad. Morissette, 1920).

Prologue: The River

On the left bank, the lower of the two, sits a village. A single street runs through it, connecting it with the life of the world outside. Small houses line the street, facing each other like guests at a table. At the very end of the street, in the place of honour, stands the church that presides over the brotherhood of small houses.

On the right bank, the steeper one, a broad rolling plain covered with crops stretches towards the horizon, which is covered in the distance by a dense forest. Through the forest runs a little road that crosses the plain to the shore and the ferryman's cabin.

The road is flanked by telegraph poles that look like big rakes standing on end.

Finally, there is the ferry, an extension of the road that floats on the water.

The Ferryman

Now, one day the man became curious to know his age, and when he was shown the register of his life, it contained the sum of his days, which numbered eighty years, and at first he was not so apprehensive at the fact that he soon would die as at the unexpected knowledge of his great age.

He did not know that he had come so far. He had travelled through his life without looking ahead of him, like an oarsman who knows his route so well he can concentrate all his attention upon the movement of his arms without turning to look in the direction he is going. But now, feeling throughout his body the shudder of old age and of the imminent end of his life, he was suddenly faced with the fact that his time was indeed running out.

The man had never plied any trade but that of ferryman; for his home, a shack as old as he himself that stood on the opposite shore at the water's edge, facing the village.

It was an orderly life, with a ferry and a rowboat at its centre: the road was his very reason for existing, and he was charged with ensuring that it continued across the river. He was in a sense a boatman of the road. Foot-passengers he took across in a small white rowboat, while for vehicles and heavy loads there was a large red ferry that moved along a guide-wire from shore to shore.

He spoke little, and this had cost him the friendship of his neighbours.

The fellow was slow at his task, but diligent. If he heard a team of horses on the road he would slowly rouse himself from his nap in the doorway of his cabin and go to his post in the bow of the ferry, his back bent, his hands gripping the wire, ready to pull. Once the vehicle was unloaded he would accept his payment, then set out on the return journey without a word. Slowly, as the swirling water beneath the hull made a quiet little sound like crumpled paper, the ferry would go back to the opposite shore. There the man would resume his nap as if nothing had happened.

And so it was that when the man discovered his true age and was compelled to look back over his long life, he found that as well as his concerns about the future, the notion of death had come to be the focus of his thoughts. What he feared was not so much death itself but what would happen to him before it came, what would become of his arms, the only ones he had. The strength to pump life from his work like water from a well was still in them; but more and more the idea of not being able to pump all of it, to pump until the well had run dry, became an obsession.

The man was assailed then by the selfishness of those who live for their work; he was afraid of being unable to work, he was afraid of existing like some old men whose arms lack the strength to work but still have enough to push away death.

And so it was that on the final day of his eightieth year, the ferryman discovered an idea nestled in his head, one that was starting to make him suffer. He was beginning to know himself: in addition to his arms he had a head, and in the course of the hours he spent dozing, he made contact with his head, holding it painfully between his hands.

The Back

It happened that one morning when he awoke the ferryman made another important discovery. He noted that not only did he have shoulders, from which his arms drew energy, he also had a back.

That had come to him as the result of a great weariness he felt upon rising from his bed. An unaccustomed weight seemed to have settled in his back, as if the heavy straw mattress were clinging to it. He felt as though in a single night all the aches and pains he usually left behind in his sleep had come back to plague him.

A man came, one who spoke in a loud voice and who made him strip naked. He left behind two bottles and these words, which the ferryman had to repeat to himself several times before he had grasped their full meaning:

"It's your back, old man, it's worn out."

This was a considerable revelation, and for two days he kept repeating to himself:

"I have a back and it's worn out."

At first he had been reluctant to believe it.

Accustomed as he was, as a man who worked, to seeing the human body as nothing more than an instrument of work, he could not conceive that there existed a part of himself that was useless. With his arms, he pulled all day on oars that weighed heavily in the water, carrying from shore to shore loads that made his ferry sink as much as one foot deeper into the water. With his legs, he walked to meet his fares, or stood and waited for them to come his way. He knew of course that he had a back: after all, he lay on it when he grew tired. But an aching back served no purpose, unless it was to make him suffer when he caught it.

But now the time had come to go out and get to work, and since the pain in his back followed him everywhere, in his rowboat and in his ferry, he finally had to acknowledge that there was something wrong. And since that thing, whatever it was, did not affect his shoulders or his hips, he finally had to conclude that the trouble came from his back and he was dismayed.

In his mind, then, he came to associate his suffering with his back. They formed a painful part of his body; they were a disease that came upon him in the night, from his sleep, for he noticed his suffering was greatest when he awoke.

Since his back was causing his body such pain, he must have come down with a case of back trouble. And if on certain days that seemed heavier than others his oars remained suspended for a moment in the air, like an orator who pauses in his speech, at a loss for words, the ferryman excused himself by saying he was just a poor man who must bear an aching back.

The Wind

That day, the ferryman rowed more than usual. It was the month of July, and groups of women were crossing to go berry picking on the other side.

All morning it was calm, with the river so smooth it looked polished. The rowboat kept going back and forth like a moving link between the two shores, its oars spread wide like arms crucified by toil.

Then, near midday, at an indescribably beautiful hour, an hour too beautiful to last, a sudden change occurred. The air began to stir in the trees, making them shiver and tremble; the air swept over the hillside where the arms of a windmill began slowly turning in the distance; the air brushed against the river, which suddenly stopped reflecting the shores, like a mirror covered with mist. And so a change had occurred: the wind had come up and the day had grown dark.

Now the afternoon was nothing but wind and grey skies.

When the ferryman came back to the shore where the last of the women were waiting to cross, the river was filled with tremors and shocks, and the rowboat leaped about in the churning water. With a great effort he came ashore, then set off with the women aboard.

Now the rowboat was advancing fitfully, the oars sometimes losing their grip on the water and throwing white spray into the air, because of the countless waves that slapped against the rowboat, because of the need to balance the sweep of the oars as they dipped into the water, then re-emerged as if to catch their breath before plunging again, and above all because of the wind and the ferryman's back that made his entire aching body stiffen and slump as he pulled at the oars, with arms now tense and well-nigh powerless.

The exhausted ferryman felt the wind on his brow, the entire force of the wind that pressed against his forehead and thundered in his ears as if the great wings of a nun's headdress were bracketing his head.

The little craft shuddered to shore and the ferryman collapsed, exhausted, his arms falling heavily to his sides.

In tremendous scrolls the wind rolled over the land and the river, bound tight as a bundle: tremendous scrolls, a huge bundle of heavy scrolls.

The Head

When the rowboat finally bumped into the shore and came to a standstill, the ferryman's arms fell to his sides, like the oars he had just released at the sides of his craft. He felt a shudder run through him, as if cold water was trickling into the hollows of his bones. All his limbs ached as if a fissure had opened in his back and released the pain into the rest of his body. He lay on his seat racked by pain.

And then there occurred the extraordinary thing called paralysis. It came slowly, going up his legs and rising through all his limbs, moving up and up until finally it stopped at his head.

Gradually his entire body changed, as if he had slipped on the shore and fallen into the water until all that could be seen was his head emerging from the water.

The ferryman, who had been a man with arms, legs, shoulders, and a back, now was merely a head that thought of arms, legs, shoulders, and a back.

The next day the man who had come before returned, and this time left without saying a word. Another man moved into the house and the ferryman recognized him as his replacement, another ferryman; and silently he let the man take over.

The Old Oars

From this time on the ferryman's arms hung useless at his sides, like old oars that no longer have purchase in the water, that can no longer tolerate the pressure exerted on them to reach the other shore, the shore that is life, that is his livelihood. The ferryman selected the most comfortable chair in which to rest his tired body, the one consolation of old age.

From the shade of his own roof he gazed out at the shore where the road suddenly widened, as if it were tired from travelling such a distance; he gazed at the river flowing endlessly by; he gazed at the movements of the new ferryman who rowed smoothly and regularly across the water, becoming smaller and smaller until he was nearly imperceptible, then reversed his direction and returned, now growing larger and larger, and stepped onto the shore, with new coins jingling in his pocket.

The ferryman became the aching back that refused to transmit its strength to the arms; he became the fissure in his back; he became the expectation of death in the face of all that is life, the excessive fatigue that always leads to the chair in the shade, at the edge of the sunlight, when there are two arms that will no longer work, two arms that no longer do anything.

The pain in the back prevented his arms from moving freely in their sockets; the old oarlocks were rusty now.

The Old Oars (Second Version)

When the man stopped being the ferryman he became something else. He became the second life, the life lived by old people who have retired from their work and are now waiting for death that will soon arrive because they are no longer doing anything. What he had become was the new chapter that comes into view at the end of a story, when a man thinks that he has turned the final page.

Becoming aware of it, he grew sad.

But then he discovered real life, the other life that he no longer was.

From his doorway in the shade, he recognized that life in everything that had nothing to do with him, in the sun, in the water that flowed by and made ripples in the sand at the edge of the shore; he recognized it in the way the ferryman hauled at the guide-wire of the ferryboat, in the cry that came from the opposite shore, from two hands that formed a trumpet around the mouth of the man who was signaling over there, who appeared very small. Finally, he saw the activity, the great stir in the village across the river which appeared on the shore like a table that had been set, with its little houses of every shape that in the distance reminded you of dishes, and with a factory chimney that rose up like the neck of a flask.

Afterwards

The new ferryman looked after the old one, for he was incapable of doing anything that would allow him to provide for himself. He lived that way during the entire rainy season without complaining, absorbed as he was in the mystery of his joints that now were useless.

Winter came, and with its arrival the river turned to ice, and the man shut himself inside.

In the spring when the sun warmed the earth around his cabin, the ferryman resumed the daily promenades from his bed to a chair placed in his doorway.

He no longer needed someone to support him; the long winter rest seemed to have affected his rigidity. Gradually life returned to his numb limbs, and so long as the day was not too damp he felt almost as strong as he had in the past.

He would have gone back to work had the doctor not forbidden it. But in addition to the fact that he was not very authoritarian, there was another important reason for him not to work: there was the new ferryman who was unwilling to give up the place for which he felt he was suitably qualified.

And so the man to whom life had been restored did not recognize the life that was his in the past. He recognized a diminished appetite for work, and strength enough in his arms to push away death.

Boredom

Since his inactive arms had shown the ferryman how pointless was his very existence, inevitably boredom occurred and with it, little by little, he grew numb.

He was already acquainted with boredom, the thing that is unavoidable when a period of rest goes on too long, he was familiar with it for he had experienced it every winter, once the river had turned to ice and there was nothing for him to do. And so when he felt the first effects, the ferryman was deeply certain that never again would he free himself from it, given the inactivity to which he had been condemned forever, and he felt irresistibly drawn to the notion of death.

It would be the end. And in the face of the boredom that was gaining on him, that was taking him over, all the strength within him melted, just as the colours in a bedroom lit by lamplight begin to fade in the presence of the more brilliant light of day.

Along with boredom came the memory of winters, and the atmosphere of its latest transformation gradually lost its colouring; inside the man's head everything was white, a soft white that came from all sides.

He grew lazy and uncommunicative. His life had been painful and hard, but now he stopped thinking of it, and it seemed as if he was going to do without it.

Of all his life that had been, nothing existed now but time, the different times needed for daytime to pass into night, and nighttime into the waking of another day.

Now there was only the amount of time required when the hour has arrived for sleep: a violet time with slices of red, and the sun setting slowly against the dome of the church like a big gold coin in a collection box; the hour for waking in the great pale slats of light that came from the closed shutters onto his bed; the hour of noon on the river that dazzled with leaping constellations.

Reversal

One morning when the ferryman was on the other shore, for the first time in a year he sat in his rowboat. He was pensive.

The morning was beautiful and the river reflected the blue sky. Small, round, white clouds, like handfuls of soapsuds, stood in a line on the horizon. In the distance, the bell of the village church was ringing.

All at once the ferryboat's guide-wire vibrated. The ferryman was coming back.

Then the ferryman saw the oars, which made him want to rest his hands on them, so he pressed on the oars with both hands. When he felt them on his palms, he squeezed. The muscles in his arms hardened his shoulders and then, as if he had not wanted it, as if he were not even thinking of it, he braced his back.

The rowboat left the shore and when it had reached the channel it began slowly descending between the two shores.

The thrusting oars formed arabesques on the water, and on the river behind him there was a great V.

A few moments later there were no more arabesques, and the two lines of the great V clung to the shores.

Once again, the man felt the shudder of cold water trickling into his hollow bones.

High on the shore in the distance, the arms of a windmill beat the air, and though he concentrated his attention on their turning, he felt an urge to vomit.

The rowboat lay across the channel. The sun was tossing onto the water long shards of light that glowed with tiny dots.

Slowly the rowboat tilted to one side, then it abruptly straightened up. With a muffled sound, a small white spray rose from the water and broad rings spread across the river.

And the current took the rowboat, which was descending by itself, its two oars dangling like two arms that no longer work, like two arms that no longer do anything.

Harry Bernard
Translated by Matt Cohen

THE ITALIAN TEACHER

Harry Bernard was born in London, England, in 1898, but moved to Canada in early childhood. He studied at the Séminaire de Saint-Hyacinthe and at the Université de Montréal, where he received his Ph.D. in literature in 1948. By then he had already published eight of his ten books, most of which were novels. The first, *L'Homme tombé* (*Fallen Man*), appeared in 1924, the year after he left his job as editor and parliamentary correspondent for *Le Droit* and took up a new position as publisher of the *Courrier de Saint-Hyacinthe*. His other novels include *La Maison vide* (*The Empty House*) and *La Terre vivante* (*The Living Earth*), both published in 1925; *La Ferme des pins* (*Pine Farm*), 1930; *Juana, mon aimée* (*Juana My Love*), 1931; *Dolorès*, 1932; and, perhaps his best-known work, *Les Jours sont longs* (*Long Are the Days*), which appeared in 1951. He received a Rockefeller Foundation grant in 1943, and was awarded the Prix David three times: in 1924, 1925, and 1931.

Like his contemporary, Jean-Aubert Loranger, Bernard was very interested in regionalism as a defining influence on culture and character. He wrote a study of the subject, *Le Roman régionaliste aux États-Unis. 1913-1940* (*The American Regionalist Novel, 1913-1940*), published in 1949, in which he maintained that a strong attachment to region was the basis of all good writing. "Catholic and French in their essence, our literature will be Canadian in its achievements," he wrote in *Essais critiques* in 1929. "This means that our books, written by Canadians, will strive to show the souls of our people, to paint and interpret the place in which they live and the landscape that surrounds them."

"Le professeur d'italien," translated as "The Italian Teacher" by Matt Cohen, first appeared in Bernard's only collection of short stories, *La Dame blanche* (*The White*

Lady), published in 1927. It is interesting to read this story in light of Bernard's theories of the importance of regionalism in culture, and in the context of his view that "the French language of the rest of the world . . . is not the language of French Canadians."

Bernard died in Montreal in 1979.

∽

"The Italian Teacher" is a translation of "Le professeur d'italien" published in *La Dame blanche* (Montreal: Bibliothèque de l'Action française, 1927).

Mademoiselle Jeanne-Aimée Bruneau was in a state. She had fallen in love with Luigi Paschetti, her Italian teacher, a soft-spoken man with a gentleman's fine manners. Afraid of her parents, who would never forgive her for loving a man who was both poor and an immigrant, she had told no one about her feelings.

It was the year 1843. Her father was Gilles Bruneau, a shipowner and grain-dealer whose business was located on rue Notre-Dame. He belonged to one of Montreal's richest and most distinguished families and had three daughters of whom the eldest, Jeanne-Aimée, would soon be nineteen. The family lived in a stone house shaded with poplars on rue Saint-Denis, in the Saint-Louis district. They socialized with only the best people: Joseph Bourret, the mayor of Montreal; Jacques Viget, his predecessor; the merchant and philanthropist Antoine-Olivier Berthelet, who was also a former member of Parliament for Montreal East; William Molson, the son of John Molson.

It is to be understood that Gilles Bruneau, who tolerated Paschetti as a teacher, would not have wanted him as a son-in-law. He had never even considered such an unlikely thing. He would have preferred to see his daughters behind the iron gates of the Ursuline convent in Montreal. Knowing her father, Jeanne-Aimée had kept the secrets of her heart to herself.

Luigi Paschetti had only recently moved to Montreal. A handsome man with a serious face and well-kept hands, he said he came from the United States. He started out by giving lessons to the children of the lawyer Zéphir Cherrier, then to the young women and ladies of the city who suddenly developed a passion for learning languages. Received in Montreal's wealthiest homes, he was treated with deference.

Like their friends, Jeanne-Aimée and her sister, Thérèse, wanted the handsome foreigner at their house. Thérèse, who was only seventeen and no longer went to school at the convent, was happy for the distraction. Thus the young ladies conjugated the sonorous verbs of Italy and were initiated into the subtleties of diminutive and augmentative endings. When three or four of them met, it was a pleasure to hear them greet each other with a joyous *Parla italiano?* or the eternally interesting questions: *Che cosa se dice in citta? Che tempo fa oggi?*

Jeanne-Aimée quickly grew to like this game. She even started liking the teacher as much as his lessons. That was more than she had planned for, and she found herself confronted by a serious problem. She could not confess her love but, on the other hand, she wasn't strong enough to give it up. She would cry in her room, but continued her feverish application to the study of Italian verbs. Every week she looked forward to Luigi's arrival, and made herself beautiful to receive him.

A small incident, on a certain April day, would clarify the situation.

Madame Bruneau, who always seemed to remain calm, was intrigued by the way Paschetti sometimes behaved. To her, this man seemed melancholy. As soon as he thought he was alone, his eyes would close and his face harden; he seemed lost in a dream. Surprised one day by Madame Bruneau, he excused himself, saying he had a headache. Her curiosity now aroused, Madame Bruneau noticed that he was often distracted and that sometimes he sighed. Moreover, everything about him was mysterious: from his coming to Montreal to his clothes and his manners, his cold expression, even his strange habit of taking a daily stroll along Rue Saint-Jacques, sumptuously draped in the folds of an expensive coat.

Obviously this was a man who was hiding something.

There things stood when one fine day Monsieur Bruneau arrived home at lunchtime bearing a strange missive, a large letter with a wax seal. It had come from Spain and had been sent in care of Gilles Bruneau, Montreal merchant, but it was addressed to Senor Enrique Olivarez de la Mendoza, the Count of Castile and Marquis de Las Carolinas.

"I have no idea what this is supposed to be," the businessman said, throwing the letter on a table.

"Who knows?" his wife suddenly said. "Could it be for him?"

"Him?"

"But of course . . . Monsieur Paschetti . . ."

"I don't understand."

She then related every detail of her observations—the mannerisms of the Italian, his confusion when she surprised him daydreaming.

"If you want," she said, "I'll take care of this . . . He'll be here tomorrow for the lessons. I'll show him the letter and then I'll know . . . because he'll tell me."

She was right.

At first the teacher was flustered, appeared not to understand, then, encouraged by Madame Bruneau, he confessed to his titles and his true identity. He belonged to an old Spanish family with connections to many of the courts of Europe. But a revolution in his country had stripped him of his fortune. He had come to America and, knowing several languages, he had presented himself as an Italian who taught his language. Since then he had been getting good news from Spain and now he hoped that within a few months he would be able to return and retrieve his fortune. Meanwhile he still had to make a living and he asked Madame Bruneau not to tell anyone his story.

That was easy to promise. But Madame Bruneau told his story so well and so often that soon the whole city, from Rue Saint-Paul to Sherbrooke, from Rue Berri to Guy, knew about the adventures of the Spanish nobleman. From that moment on, he was never left in peace. As a teacher he had been respected, as a marquis he was pursued. He was at every social gathering and in all the salons, a necessary guest at every dinner party.

Things got even worse when, a few weeks later, the Spanish government sent an amply signed and initialled letter advising the marquis that his entire fortune would be restored. This process would require several months, given that certain formalities were to be satisfied, taking into account, of course, the proverbial slowness of government bureaucracies. Now the most exclusive homes opened to the marquis, a multi-millionaire. He accepted these tributes as the due of a powerful lord, accustomed since childhood to every variety of fawning and servility.

Meanwhile our man developed a lifestyle consistent with his birth, his education, his tastes. He left the boarding house of Madame Giroux for a luxurious apartment at the Donegana, Montreal's most expensive hotel, which stood at the corner of Notre-Dame and Bonsecours. He borrowed money and redid his entire wardrobe, his credit being as good at the Robertson establishment as at Joseph-Charles Boulanger's, a working-class clothes store of that era. He now always wore a vest and trousers in white, a necktie mounted high on his impeccable false collar, made from expensive cloth and liberally starched, rising to the height of his ears.

Señor Enrique cut a fine figure, and it wasn't long before all the proper young ladies of Montreal were, it has to be said, duly excited.

Amongst them, as can be imagined, the least upset was not Jeanne-Aimée, the fair daughter of Gilles Bruneau.

Pretty and cheerful, Jeanne-Aimée was much sought after. Her lively, blue-grey eyes sparked with energy. She had fine features and a delicately shaped mouth with small white teeth, and in the sun her hair was the colour of pale gold. In addition, the young lady had studied at the Notre-Dame convent, knew how to keep house and mend linen, was an excellent cook, had a rich father, and came from a good family. To attract suitors and admirers, no more could be asked.

Jeanne-Aimée confessed the secret that had been weighing on her to her mother.

"Why didn't you tell me before?" Madame Bruneau cut in. "These things can be dealt with. My daughter, for something this serious, you should have had more faith in your mother. Woman to woman, we can understand..."

"But the teacher had nothing in common with the Spanish aristocrat . . . Father wouldn't have tolerated him in his house . . ."

Her mother didn't reply. Then she said, "It's not too late. I'll organize a ball in his honour, you will be charming . . . As you know, your father and I have no greater ambition than the happiness of our children!"

Then Madame Bruneau got to work.

The evening of the ball, the marquis arrived in an English carriage drawn by two horses. Curious guests rushed to stare at the spectacle. Las Carolinas slowly descended from the carriage, sure of his effect. He was dressed in an impeccably tailored suit and wore a fashionable stuffed hat, very wide at the top, made of long silky fur.

Jeanne-Aimée was quick to monopolize his attention. In a white dress that emphasized her slender waist, she was radiant with happiness. The one she loved was with her, talking to her. She was in the midst of a marvellous dream, one that was bound to disappear before morning. Meanwhile she danced in the arms of the marquis and laughed when he laughed, with her bright laugh of a schoolgirl on holiday. Italian words came to her lips, they both laughed about those farcical lessons they'd had together.

When the marquis took his leave, he had already promised to return.

From then on, the two were often seen together. They were rumoured to be engaged, and Jeanne-Aimée's friends envied her good fortune.

Sunday afternoons, the Marquis de Las Carolinas would take a walk with the young Bruneau ladies, Jeanne-Aimée and Thérèse, who had the delicate mission of being her sister's chaperon. They took Rue Sainte-Catherine, or Rue Saint-Denis, sometimes going to the small chapel at Notre-Dame de Bonsecours, where Jeanne-Aimée, who was a devout Catholic, liked to stop. On June 29th, with the notables of the city, they were present for the consecration of the bells of Notre-Dame.

And when the French opera company came to Montreal six weeks later, they listened to *Diamonds of the Crown* at the Doric-columned Royal Theatre on Rue Saint-Paul. Together they applauded the two Parisian prima donnas, Madame Lecourt and Mademoiselle Calvé.

During this time Monsieur Bruneau was far from happy about the way the marquis was courting his daughter. Although his bourgeois vanity was flattered, he remained suspicious. For example he found it curious that the Spaniard, despite the sumptuous missives from his country, never actually received any of his promised millions. He didn't like the marquis's casual way of borrowing money here and there, and told himself that a man whose wealth lay mainly in his hopes should be more prudent. In his sly way, he also told himself that a marquis, even a Spanish one, would not be upset to have a businessman like Gilles Bruneau for a father-in-law. He kept worrying over these ideas and did not press the question of his daughter's marriage.

There were also disturbing rumours making the rounds. In business circles, some men would just shrug when the name of the marquis came up. Among the ladies who had daughters to marry off, and whose plans had been ruined by Jeanne-Aimée's success, the enthusiasm for the marquis began to wane.

The Marquis de Las Carolinas, aware of this turn, now invited his friends to a princely dinner.

"I've had excellent news from home," he confided to someone. "This morning I got a letter from Madrid. In response to my last instructions . . . I'll soon be receiving, through the Banque du Peuple, the first installment of my money . . . In fact, I'm on my way to rue Saint-François-Xavier to see the manager. I am relieved, I can tell you . . . I've had to count on my friends here for too long . . . Finally I'll be able to pay back the money that people have so kindly loaned me."

He added, as the other extended his hand:

"I'm counting on you to be there! Sunday evening, at the Donegana..."

The Donegana, on the north-west corner of Notre-Dame and Bonsecours, was the busiest and most luxurious hotel in Canada. Like the Royal Theatre, it was fronted by a Doric colonnade. The building, a former governor-general's residence, was topped by an imposing dome. The hotel was lit by gas, a rare luxury at the time, and the main dining room, which gave out on the Champ de Mars, was no less than a hundred and forty feet long. Around 1840, a reception at the Donegana was the ultimate in elegance, and the invitations from the marquis were well received.

All week no one talked of anything but Paschetti's dinner. The ladies were in a fever of preparation: milliners and tailors were besieged, all the guests wanted to outdo their rivals. Some of the women, normally calm bourgeois ladies, were ready to sacrifice six months' worth of savings. Madame Bruneau, who did her own sewing, didn't know where to start. The houses of Montreal were in a tizzy. Once again the marquis was popular and sought after.

For his part, Paschetti was as busy as his guests. He surveyed the preparations, discussed the hundred details of the menu with Madame Saint-Julien, who had replaced Jean-Marie Donegana as owner of the hotel. They had to agree on the dishes and how they would be served, the wines, the flowers for the tables. The staff was anxious. The manager, a Monsieur Daley, who prided himself on his reputation as an organizer, slept less than five hours a night.

In time everything arrives, even good weather.

The day of the Paschetti dinner was magnificent. About a hundred of the city's richest and most refined residents had been invited. The big dining room was filled with the joyous sound of violin chords, the rustle of dresses, silver tinkling, voices crying out, full and empty glasses clinking together. The waiters, erect as lead soldiers, slid between the tables with platters of food extended. The ladies laughed to show their teeth. Like a volley of gunfire the champagne corks leapt towards the ceiling, while the champagne sparkled and foamed in the glasses.

At the table of honour sat the Marquis de Las Carolinas with Mademoiselle Bruneau at his right side. His head high, his moustache overshadowing his thin upper lip, he was the centre of attention. The cultivated Madame Rodier compared him to a Greek god. His speech was flowing and confident, and he had a way of tilting back his head and looking, without seeming to, at those around him. He knew he was being admired. He drank slowly, nonchalantly, a sensuous man of taste who knew the price of things. Turning towards Jeanne-Aimée, who was a little confused because everyone was staring at them, he spoke gently and treated her as the most important person at the table. The young girl blushed, but she was happy. Her eyes shone with the joy of seeming and being loved.

"You seem happy," she said at a certain moment, as he smiled and looked at the reflections of the gaslight in his glass.

"I am, in fact, as you say. And what about you? Aren't you happy? Because it is for you, you most of all, that I brought everyone together here. So they can see you, honour you, admire you..."

"Flatterer! And when you laugh, looking off in the distance, what are you thinking about?"

"I'm thinking about you, Mademoiselle Aimée, only you... Why are you asking?"

"*Chi lo sa?*" she replied in Italian. "Who knows?"

At this moment the hotel manager came up to the marquis.

"There's someone asking for you," he said in a low voice... "He's over there, in the small reception room."

"Who is it? Look, tell him I'll be here tomorrow morning, that I can't see anyone at this time of night."

But after a few minutes Monsieur Daley returned.

"It's a man I don't know, a tall man in his thirties, he absolutely insists on speaking to you... He says he has an urgent message for you. He says that he will wait for you..."

"All right. Tell him I'm coming."

But his eyes were angry as he spoke to those around him: "Please be kind enough to excuse me. I'll just be a moment, I'll be right back..."

He went out, then returned almost right away.

"A small problem," he announced, as heads swung towards him, "but nothing that should concern anyone. I have to leave for fifteen or at the most twenty minutes... Please forgive this, but it was entirely unforeseeable... Ladies and gentlemen, please proceed as though nothing had happened. I'll be back..."

He left again, everyone's eyes upon him.

People began to talk again. Laughter broke out here and there. More champagne was drunk.

Someone said, "He must have been delayed longer than he expected..."

But after an hour, when he still hadn't returned, people began to worry. Had some misfortune occurred? Perhaps the man who had asked for Las Carolinas, a person unknown to the hotel manager, had done something to him. Monsieur Daley, accompanied by some of the guests, went to check the Spaniard's apartment.

There, they found nothing unusual. The marquis had not even taken his coat, which he had thrown over the back of an armchair.

In the dining room the guests looked at each other, embarrassed. The laughter had stopped. At the slightest sound, everyone turned towards the door, thinking they would see the marquis. Jeanne-Aimée Bruneau, worried and humiliated, bit her lips to keep from crying.

But the malaise kept growing. A few of the men left. Their example inspired others. Gradually the room emptied. Jeanne-Aimée left with her parents. The police were called and they began to search for Las Carolinas.

He never reappeared.

He had left the city and shortly afterwards it was learned he had fled to New York, then taken a boat for Europe.

When his dupes began to grow suspicious, he had made his decision. He would disappear quietly, leaving no traces. But he didn't want to go without, one last time, making fun of his victims. That was why he had organized the sumptuous dinner at the Donegana. Talking with friends, a few days before, he had confided that on the night of the banquet he would give everyone a big surprise.

He had not let them down.

At the hotel they examined his baggage. Everything of any value was gone. In the trunks Monsieur Daley found only worn boots, wrapped in old newspapers, big rocks and scrap iron.

Fifteen days later, the guests at the famous dinner received the bill from the Donegana.

They paid.

Louis Dantin
Translated by Sheila Fischman

THE MASS OF FLORENT LÉTOURNEAU

Eugène Sears (who wrote under the pseudonyme Louis Dantin) was born in the village of Beauharnois in 1865. He attended the Collège de Montréal and later the Séminaire de Montréal, and studied to become a priest at the Congrégation des Pères du Très-Saint-Sacrement in 1883. In 1884, he began work on a Ph.D. in philosophy in Rome, and took his vows in Brussels in 1887. From there he moved to Paris, where he was ordained in 1888, but he soon suffered a crisis of faith and returned to Montreal in 1894.

In Montreal he discovered and became a friend of the poet Émile Nelligan. He also began writing poetry of his own, and in 1900—the year after Nelligan became insane—published *Franges d'autel* in collaboration with Nelligan and a number of other poets, including Lucien Rainier, Arthur de Bussières, and Amédée Gélinas. He lived from hand to mouth for the next three years, editing his order's religious newsletter, *Petit messager du Très-Saint-Sacrement*, and attending sessions of the École littéraire de Montréal. In 1903 he edited Nelligan's first book of poems—declaring in the preface that art and poetry were far removed from ordinary morality, that art could and indeed must exist without religion. That same year Dantin left the priesthood; in fact, he left Canada and moved to Boston, where he worked for many years at Harvard University Press.

Dantin has been cited as Quebec's first literary critic (for his discovery and defence of Nelligan as well as for such books as *Poètes de l'Amérique français*, 1928 and *Gloses critiques*, 1931). He published a book of poems, *Le Coffret de Crusoé*, in 1932; one novel, *Les Enfances de Fanny* (1951); and a book of short stories, *La Vie en rêve*, in 1930.

The literary historian Samuel Baillargeon has noted that Dantin's life was "a lamentable tragedy," but added that "it would be unhealthy curiosity to go into details." The story included here, "La messe de Florent Létourneau," translated by Sheila Fischman, is a fine example of Dantin's classical mind. It first appeared in the periodical *L'Avenir du Nord* on December 14, 1926, and was included in *La Vie en rêve*. "Beauty," he wrote in one of his critical essays, "often strikes you in guises that go against the rules."

Dantin died in exile in the United States in 1945.

༽

"The Mass of Florent Létourneau" is a translation of "La messe de Florent Létourneau" published in *La Vie en rêve, contes* (Montreal: Librairie d'action canadienne-française ltée, 1930); first appeared in *L'Avenir du Nord*, December 24, 1926.

My grandfather shook his pipe and said again: "They're lucky, those folks in Saint-Jovite.

"Fine land, good roads, mail delivery every day, carts, why they've even got automobiles to take themselves into town. In my day all that was woods. Before you got to the new lands you had thirty-five miles of dense woods; and some ways away, by gum, you could go all the way to the North Pole and not see a single clearing. In the winter it wasn't uncommon that you'd open the door and standing there would be a bear seven foot tall rooting around on the gallery; those animals, they'd use their snouts to unlock the barns and they'd make off with whole quarters of beef. And we logged, we stumped, we drove logs down the river, and we sweated, let me tell you. There was misery, and I don't know what would have become of us without the good Lord and Curé Labelle.

"Now I wouldn't claim we were saints; there was a mix of us like there is in any other place. We were mostly good people, but there were some in the bunch who weren't worth much: folks who'd come from far away, some of them, for wicked reasons. In my case, my neighbours were David Latour and Philémon Sécette; we always worked things out, aside from that one time I took David to court on account of a ditch he'd dug across my line. At the other end of the concession road, though, there was a fellow from Quebec City by the name of Florent Létourneau and he had a heck of a reputation. He was a dark-skinned young fellow, well built, around thirty years old or so, not married. He lived all by himself in a sort of rundown shack no bigger, I'm not lying, than a hayrack. Nobody knew just why he'd gone up North, but it certainly wasn't to clear more land. He'd cleared himself a quarter acre, that was all, where he'd planted a handful of potatoes. He hunted from morning till night, that was how he eked out a living for himself. And then he had a good mare and he'd go on trips for this one and that. Never darkened the door of the church. The curé'd got on to him about religion, but he might just as well have taken a pick to some pebbles; not even our holy father the Pope could have softened him up. Sunday, he'd say for his own reasons, was the best day for hunting hare and partridge. Though he didn't have much to do with his neighbours, he'd gone sweet on young Alma Latour, and her house was the only one where he'd drop in. The finest morsels from his hunting were for Alma, and if he earned a dollar it was sure she'd get some frills or fripperies. The little fool was sweet on him, too, but she didn't say so: she was wary about having him as a husband. If he happened to plague her, she knew she could say to him: "When you behave like a Christian, Florent, it'll be time to be thinking about that." And even though he'd have carved himself into four pieces for her, he didn't give in, seeing he was so bull-headed.

Now that individual, the second year he was on the concession road there was something rare happened to him, enough to make every hair on your body stand up; it was something they talked about back then as far away as Saint-Jérôme and Terrebonne.

It was Christmas Eve and as usual everybody was getting ready for midnight Mass. There was a fair amount of snow and the wind was howling, but it was a fine moonlit night with just a few clouds in the west. We visited a while and then when it was getting on for eleven o'clock we hitched up our sleighs, the women prettied themselves, and we set off one after another. We had to drive right past Florent's shack. When old man Morrissette, who was with his daughter-in-law, was across the road from Florent's place, he spied my man standing on his doorstep with a torch and his rifle on his back. He stops his horse. "Evening, Florent," he says with a chuckle, "bringing your rifle to Mass now, are you? Hop in, my friend, you won't get a better offer."

"Thanks all the same," Létourneau tells him, "but I'm just going to check on my traps."

Two or three minutes after that, he sees the Latour family drive past; they see Létourneau there in the middle of the road. Alma shouts to him, "Florent, what are you doing there? Come along to church with me." He stops, looks like he's turning it over in his mind, seeing as how he's fond of the girl, but then he finally turns her down.

"Not this time, *ma belle*, I've work to do tonight."

More than thirty sleighs drive by; the first ones see our man stride across the snowy fields, the others see his torch swinging further and further away in the distance and heading for the woods. Now I ask you, what was in the mind of that man, going to lift his traps at night—and on Christmas Eve! He must have been thinking: "They'll be joking that I went off through the spruce trees while the rest of them were singing their carols." He was an odd sort of individual and he never did anything like the rest of us.

It went on that way for a while and then all of a sudden clouds are beginning to hide the moon, the wind blows up and snow starts to fall. Little by little, things get worse; after twenty minutes we've got a first-class storm on our hands, a fierce blizzard with snow that stings like a needle, a nor'easter that could freeze your bones, and over the entire countryside it was as dark as the inside of an oven.

But we weren't worried: we'd all reached the church and were out on the front steps, gabbing. But Létourneau, meanwhile, he's making his way deeper into the woods. He was relying on some marks he'd carved in the trees, and on the Grand' Coulée that he figured wasn't far away. He'd walked a good ways, struggling at every step, when all of a sudden he trips over a stump that's covered with snow and he lands flat on his stomach with his lantern four feet away. When he goes to pick it up not only has it gone out, all the oil in it has spilled. So there he is in the middle of the spruce grove with nothing to see by. First he swears, then he realizes he has to turn around. He tries to retrace his steps, but his footsteps are all erased, the falling snow is blinding him, and every minute he's banging into a tree trunk. He's lost his way, monsieur, as if he'd travelled fifty leagues; north, south—he couldn't recognize a thing. But you've got to hand it to him, he was a brave man, Létourneau. "Very well," he says, "I'll get there regardless." He reckons where the property line lies, more or less, then he starts walking as fast as he can, though he can't see beyond the toes of his boots, and he's sinking into the snow with every step. He walks for half an hour, stops, then he starts walking again. And now he finds that he's lost in a mass of brushwood, under thousands of birch trees that are practically touching. It's a brush he's never seen before, he has no idea where he is, and he doesn't know what direction to go.

But he still doesn't take fright. "There's just one thing to do," he tells himself, "and that's find a big rock, take shelter behind it, and wait till morning." He looks around to left and right, then finally he spies a rock that looks to be as tall as a house. He starts walking around it; and then he notices something that's darker than the rest and it turns out to be a big hole in the rock. He thinks to himself, "I'll spend the night here. This is a lucky break." He takes a step into the hole and then another; he holds out his arms in front of him but he doesn't touch a wall. "Just as well," he congratulates himself, "I can't feel a breath of wind; I just wish I could see clearly." He looks for his matches: nothing. When he tripped on that stump the box had jumped out of his pocket. He felt his way another couple of steps; he seemed to be in some kind of cave, since he still hadn't bumped up against anything. All of a sudden it seems to him there's a reddish light ahead of him. He asks himself: "What's that? Is there somebody in here? Wouldn't that be something." He's apprehensive but he decides to keep going regardless and he heads straight for the light. He hasn't gone eighteen steps when there's a big opening on his left that leads to a vault, and the whole vault is filled with that same light and it looks like the fire in a smithy. But he can't see a fire or a forge, only a steady glow, not strong, just bright enough for him to make it out. He finds himself in a square cave about twenty feet long and twenty feet wide, and the walls are all covered with frost that's glowing like little stars. He starts looking down at the ground and then, monsieur, what do you think he sees?

In the middle of that grotto, lit by that red glow, there's a little baby lying on a forkful of straw!

He stands there glued to the spot, as you might imagine. "Well now," he asks himself, "is this cold making me see things?" He rubs his eyes, he shakes himself: no doubt about it, there's a child. Not a doll made out of wax or plaster either, it's a real live baby and it's squirming around.

Now, that makes him think about the baby Jesus lying in his crèche in the church; but when he looks at this one he sees it doesn't look like any holy picture. There's short fuzzy hair all over this baby's head; his scrawny little face is the colour of bricks; his eyes have a peculiar glow in them, his body keeps turning this way and that, and he's all bundled up in black.

Florent stands there, dazed. "There's a child that doesn't look too lovable; I wouldn't expect he's been baptized." He wants to come closer, but just then he looks up and here's something else that surprises him. Along the back of the rock, sitting up on their hind paws, he sees two huge bears with their heads lolling from side to side and their tongues hanging out, and a half-bald wildcat with his chops open to show his white teeth. All three animals seem to be giving him a shifty look. Moving fast now, he clamps his hand on his rifle and then he tells himself: "If they don't make a move I won't either; but whatever happens, I'm not taking another step." Now he catches sight of something moving in the corner that turns out to be some smaller animals: it's skunks, monsieur, maybe a dozen skunks prowling back and forth without a sound.

"What's the meaning of this?" he wonders. "It doesn't look natural. What's going on in here anyway." At the same time, brave though he is, he gets a little worried. Just then the baby gives a cry; and as if that was a signal, a mass of broken voices, rocky and rasping, voices that seemed to be coming from all sides at once though there wasn't a soul in sight, they start singing loud enough to deafen a man. It was a well-known song they were massacring and do you know what words Létourneau untangled through all their hullabaloo?

Oh, unto us
A demon is born;

> Unto us
> The devil's son is given!

Some horrible growls from the bears provided the bass accompaniment for this lovely hymn.

Ah! I guarantee you for a minute there Florent felt a whole colony of ants running up his bones. He sees he's landed in the middle of a devils' sabbath, where they're mocking Christmas Eve. And now he's scared; he wants to run away, but it's like his feet have been nailed to an anvil. He stands there, monsieur, he can't move an inch and there's sweat pouring down his whole body. And it's not over yet.

The next thing he sees is a man and a female coming out of who knows where, making their entrance together.

The man, the slimy devil I should say, he's a giant without a hair on him, thin as a salt herring and he's got deep-set eyes, a crooked nose, a face like a crow and a wicked, surly look to him. He's carrying a heavy whip, a solid, ugly thing with lead weights at the end. And the woman, at first sight she seems to be a fine fat creature with good colour, a good shape and all the rest—it has to be like that, you see, so those she-devils can tempt a man—but no need to look any closer, you can see she's cross-eyed, her hair's store-bought, and she's wearing a pound of paint on her cheeks. Most likely she was as black as coal underneath.

The bears were still growling; the man with the whip turned their way: "Shut your yaps you filthy beasts," he yells at them, "or I'll strip your hide for bootstraps." Then he tells the she-devil: "Get moving, you ugly hag, put on your show."

"You needn't push me around, you lily-livered monster," she tells him back, "I know what to do." She comes up to the little baby demon, she bows to him, and then just as she's set to get down on her knees, she spies Létourneau at the entrance to the cave, white as a sheet and with every tooth in his mouth clattering. Right away that Jezebel's eyes gleam like live coals, then she starts laughing and putting on airs. "That's a fine-looking man!" she says. "Come over here, darling sweetheart, let me give you a kiss. You have no idea how handsome you are! Why if it's not Florent Létourneau from over by the Saint-Jovite Hill. Well, well! I know you: and you've seen me more than once though you didn't know it. How kind of you to come and visit me! Alma Latour's very fond of you but I love you ten thousand times more, and I want you to be my dear husband! Won't you come to me, heart of my heart? All right then, I'll go over and kiss you myself."

And without further ado she steps right over that baby and she's heading straight for Florent when her partner stops her short with a stroke of his whip across the legs. "None of that, you hussy," he roars, "you didn't come here to make love. Get on with you, that's enough childishness, come and adore the child of Lucifer."

She says to him, furious: "I'll adore him if I want to. Ha! ha! First of all it isn't his: and that's not the first trick I've played on him. That's good, that's good, hold on to your whip and watch me."

Then she drops to her knees and with her arms outstretched she mutters: "Son of Satan or another, I curse you, I curse my curses, I scratch you, I scratch your scratches; may you be roasted and boiled *in soecula soeculorum!*" And with these words, suddenly enraged, she pinches the baby as hard as she can and gives him a clout in the face. The little Satan makes just one leap; he gives a mewing sound that makes you shiver, grabs hold of his mother's arm and digs his nails into her skin. So then the man, the woman, the little babe, the bears, the wildcat, even the skunks all start howling like the damned that they were, every last one of them.

And to think, monsieur, that all this time the rest of us were gathered inside a fine warm church, well-lit and smelling of incense; that we were all singing hymns, with a single soul and a single heart, in the company of the Blessed Virgin and the Baby Jesus!

When it turned quiet again Létourneau could just barely stand on his two feet, and he kept expecting he'd be swallowed up at any minute and dropped straight down to hell. But no: the snow creaks behind him and he hears heavy footsteps coming closer. He has just enough time to step aside and there are three camels; they walk past him and charge into the cave, shaking their heads and their humps.

The three camels were carrying three Negroes, all decked out in pointed caps and carrying a heap of big sacks. The Negroes get down and make a face at the little devil; then one of them unties one of those sacks, grabs a handful of old pennies from it and sends them rolling across the ground. "Your Majesty," he declares, "this is a present we've brought you from all the countries in your kingdom. It may not look like much but it's worth more than you'd think: every one of these pennies was stolen from the collection box in a church or snatched from some widows and orphans." And with that the young Beelzebub stands up and gives them a little smile, or rather he pulls a face that would make a dog sick.

Now the second darky approaches: "I've got something better than that," he says, pulling a bunch of gold vases from his bag. They were chalices, monsieur, and holy ciboria that those abominable creatures had plundered, from the States perhaps, or from France; and he had a hundred of them! And when he saw them, the infernal heir squirmed on his straw and waved his nasty paws in the air.

Then along comes the third soot-face: "My Sire and King, I bring you incense." He unties his bag and then he makes a run for it, because out of that bag comes a smell that would kill a tanner: a mixture of rotten eggs, castor oil, burnt grease, and cat's filth; it filled the cave and, on top of everything else, the skunks started squealing and scampering about and then they all went into action at once!

And that was it for Létourneau: the minute their perfume hit his nose and his throat he fell to the ground, unconscious.

When we got home from Mass the wind had dropped; there was just a little haze of snow. As he walked by Florent's place, old man Latour said to his wife: "That pagan wasn't at Mass; but never mind, I'll invite him in for a drink and a slice of tourtière." He gets out and knocks at the door. After he's knocked five or six times, he sees the fellow isn't back from the woods yet. "That's odd," he says, "he's been there a good two hours; hope he didn't lose his way in the storm. I'll come back tomorrow morning and see if everything's as it should be."

Early next morning he goes to the little shack: not a soul. All he sees is the mare and she's pawing the ground in the stable. So then he wakes up the neighbours and a dozen men set off on snowshoes and start combing the woods. They finally found him three miles north of the settlement, in a forest of birch trees that's on Roberts' property now, frozen half to death in the hollow of a rock almost as big as his shack. They carried him to Latour's house where they gave him something hot to drink and put him to bed. As soon as he was awake his face was as red as a flame; he'd come down with such a fever it took two men to hold him. For three weeks, monsieur, he grappled with that fever; they had to call for the doctor and without little Alma who took good care of him night and day, he'd have never recovered. That was how we found out bit by bit everything that had happened to him, because at night, you see, he would talk to himself.

As you might expect, he married Alma Latour; but I want you to know, after that she didn't have to pester him to do his duty. He'd never been an agreeable man, you see, nor was he too eager to pay his bills; but as far as religion was concerned, he'd got it. Especially on Christmas Eve, when two teams of horses couldn't have kept him at home. Once, when our curé was sick, he and his wife set out at five o'clock and went to Sainte-Adèle for midnight Mass. But I won't say anything more about poor Florent; there's those around here who knew him.

Marie le Franc
Translated by Matt Cohen

FOREIGN SOULS

Born in Sarzeau, Brittany, in 1879, Marie le Franc studied to become a teacher in Vannes, France, and taught in le Morbihan before moving to Montreal in 1906. She taught French language and literature, first at Westmount College and then at McGill University, and over the course of her eighty-five years published eleven books. The first, a book of poetry, *Les Voix du cœur et de l'âme (Voices of Heart and Soul)*, appeared in Montreal in 1920; the second, poems closely related to the first, called *Les Voix de misère et d'allégresse (Voices of Misery and Joy)*, was published in Paris in 1923. She was the author of six novels, the first of which, *Grand Louis l'innocent* (1927), was awarded the Prix Fémina, making her the first writer living in Canada ever to receive this prestigious French award. This was followed by *Le Poste sur la dune* in 1928. She returned to France in 1929, and her next three novels were all published in 1930: *Grand Louis le revenant*, *Pêcheurs de Gaspésie*, and *Hélier, fils des bois*. Her last novel, *La Rivière solitaire*, appeared in 1957.

From 1930 until her death in 1964, Marie le Franc also contributed stories and essays to many international journals, including *Mercure de France*, *Liaison*, and *Carnets victoriens*. Most of her stories were collected in a single volume, *Visages de Montréal (Faces of Montreal)*, in 1934, and it is from this collection that "Âmes étrangères," translated by Matt Cohen as "Foreign Souls," has been taken.

∽

"Foreign Souls" is a translation of "Âmes étrangères" published in *Visages de Montréal* (Montreal: Éditions du Zodiac, 1934).

I hesitate to talk about you. Your Anglo-Saxon modesty, sentimental paralysis I should say, is starting to affect me. I ought to be afraid of passing judgment on you, based like all human judgment on what we know about ourselves and what we don't know about others.

When you are far from me, I feel a curiously detached tenderness for you. When you are here, in the same city as me, I am consumed by the desire to hear your voice on the telephone, because our relations, friendly though they might be, are of this nature. When I know you're back, every ring of the telephone seems more imperative than usual. I rush towards it, towards you, that is: then I try to cast myself into the coldness I want to display towards you, while thinking about what I call, perhaps wrongly, your indifference. Most often what happens is a complete reversal. A few seconds ago, when it came to you, I was absolutely closed and detached. But the vibration of the ringing telephone broke through the barbed wire. Then I am nothing but joy itself, the mirror of your own, and beneath that I don't know what bitter detachment which may even have its magnanimous side.

Your superiority over me is that you never premeditate your attitudes. The moment comes when you experience the irresistible desire to hear my voice and make my ear resound with a clear and joyous "Hello!" unveiled by any contrary feeling. You follow your impulse and everything is said. Why should I hold it against you that this desire doesn't come over you the morning you arrive in the city and are totally possessed by the need to get to your hotel, to secure for yourself the room to which you are accustomed, then, skin glowing and linen immaculate, to go down to the dining room, to quickly see if there is someone you know, to exchange greetings with the headwaiter who has recognized you, who respectfully punctuates the news he is telling you with "sir" and doesn't insult you by asking, "Tea or coffee, sir?"

This first day is entirely determined in advance. In the evening, sitting at your small table for one, thinking of the innumerable appointments to which you were faithful, of the innumerable transactions you will have undertaken or concluded, the future trips you will have initiated on this first day, the already-organized bridge game at which you will soon meet again your former partners, your face will glow with satisfaction in the lamplight. By the time dessert arrives, your whole long body, so erect, will express repose and contentment. It seems there could be no greater happiness than smoking a cigarette while listening to the orchestra play one of your favourite pieces, as though it knew you were there. The hotel is yours. With a discreet wave you can make your desires known to the conductor, the manager, the bellboy, the cigarette girl who glides so delicately among the diners. She has the air of a refined young lady offering flowers at a charity sale. You'll have something to say to her that is both playful and serious, familiar and distant, protective and friendly. She'll smile at you over her tray, but will greet you with a grave "Good evening, sir!"

What is the secret of your dominion over the workers, usually so casual, at the palace-hotel? Not money. In the dining room there are fortunes compared to which your own is but a grain of sand in a desert. Like so many others of your race, you never stop travelling; like them you are on the board of directors of a certain number of companies. Some people take you for a stockbroker, some for a merchant, others for an engineer; you have opened a mine and managed a ranch, and I've heard you talk about the time you took on the construction of a railroad and, at the head of a team of adventurers, crossed an unexplored region carrying a case of dynamite on your back. You have slept in a log cabin where, on nights when people drank, you had to use your boots to re-establish order; you lived on pork and beans, wore plaid shirts of rough wool and a logger's outfit, and the following winter you played the gentleman in one of the most famous resorts on the Riviera. In business, only the grand adventures interest you. Once the initial deal is concluded, you lose interest, no matter how profitable. You need the poetry and the romance of new undertakings, the pleasure of creation and the art of construction. You have a need to test your power over men, to communicate to them your faith in success and your love of risk. I suppose that is what gives you such an air of authority when you raise a finger or signal with your eyes, and it also explains why the headwaiter whispers so unctuously in your ear while presenting you the menu, naming the dish he recommends, and why the young cigarette girl whom you call M'rie, but whose blue eyes, long lashes, teeth, cheekbones, colouring, smile, and accent could not be more Irish, remembers you smoke only cigarettes of Virginia tobacco.

It also explains why the voice in which I answer you on the telephone, when you find the leisure to call me, is as smooth and superficial as a stone skipping across water. It tries never to grow heavy or dull, it does everything possible to stay light. In the end it sinks, but you only see it bouncing across the surface. Your own tone is like the one you use to make little Marie smile. Perhaps its good cheer is forced. Perhaps you wonder if I am smiling.

You have a lot to say in this first conversation. And what you say is as orderly as a column of figures. I learn the name of the boat that brought you, how many meetings you have had since you arrived (but not their purpose), the exact length of time you'll be in the city, the date of your departure for New Zealand or California, the time at which the taxi will be at my door, because it seems that this evening we will be eating together. Over the little table for two you have reserved at the Windsor, in your favourite corner, we'll make conversation as best we can with the noise of the orchestra in one ear and the gushing of the fountain in the other.

You'll tell me about the meeting you have had, down in the city, with the princes of finance or business, the joke with which they greeted you, your visits to the money changers, the amount you made on the stock market today, which is exactly equal to the amount you lost yesterday, so that you have re-established yourself in your own eyes. It is not the amount of money that counts but the revenge it gives you, the assurance that you've lost none of your flair or your fortune, and that you still rank yourself among those who count, those in the battle, who take risks, men of action, with luck on their side; the certainty that you have not been put on the shelf, that you haven't become what you fear most in the world, *an old man*.

I listen to you, absorbed, as though you were offering me intimate secrets. These figures honour me. I am almost certain to be the only one to whom you would confide them. I share your victory. I say, softly, "Good for you." I am proud of you. I am hearing not your stories but the story of you. Whatever your new dreams and fantasies, I always end up with the same interpretation, which is you. You have a thirst for gigantic achievements. You suffer from a kind of homesickness, which is a longing to go beyond. Your brain is a construction site on which you are always building and rebuilding something bigger than before. I welcome your grand projects like small children off on an adventure. I say, "Yes, that must be them. Yes, that must be him!"

For my part, I tell you a thousand nothings which you welcome with interest; we leave them to the moment of your departure—my long-standing inner debates, the various bogeymen of my existence; we settle the tangled affairs of my friends to their advantage; I bring you up to date on the latest feats of the members of the French colony you have met. We add a few strokes to the portrait of the commercial agent or importer. We finish painting the "major," the doctor, the artist, who come in with every season. I see you silent, courteous, and smiling at these meetings where you are deafened by a rapid and unknown language. You were busy surveying your cigarette and looked as though you were listening to these people who had nothing in common with you and of whom you knew little. I am amazed by your judgment: nothing could be more certain, more concise, more justified, more moderate in appearance and beneath that more severe. You don't bother with details: you take the whole. In your capable hands you weigh a character, a friendship. You look right into the hearts of women, you who boast to yourself about your detachment and pretend to be "a man's man."

We haven't spoken about ourselves, we have not needed to lower our voices; we are content to draw our faces a little closer above the meagre flowers of the small table, to be able to hear each other when the amazing orchestra trades Russian music for loud jazz. You have just murmured how good it is for you that we are together again, you and I . . . When suddenly you are on your feet: the dance card has announced a two-step. You dance like a mature man, a bit heavy-footed but with an astonishing sense of rhythm. We don't say anything more to each other: perhaps each of us continues the conversation internally, and I wonder if what we have to say agrees as much as it did when we were speaking aloud.

Our association is a strange one. I am, I suppose, one of the features of the city to which you sometimes return as to a home base. You would be as uncomfortable at not finding me here as at discovering, when you arrived, that your hotel had been demolished. You, who have accommodated yourself so well to your life of perpetual travel through an always-changing décor of countries and faces, sometimes reveal extraordinary fidelities. I have seen you go far out of your way to buy the newspapers from your usual seller, who is neither blind nor lame nor a returned soldier, but a young Jew, his face puffy and unshaven, his papers offered at the end of a limp, persistent arm. I have also seen you going up a narrow lane of Chinese drycleaners to see if your old Charlie in his grey cotton pyjamas, his braid wound around his head, is still there, bent over his ironing table, his cheeks swollen with the water he has just sucked up from a terrine beside him and which he is going to blow on the linen with the hiss of an angry cat . . . And that suitcase, bruised beneath all its stickers, and the fragile teacup I gave you for Christmas, and which you have been dragging about for years without ever using, yet are always delighted when it emerges from your baggage unbroken . . . And that minuscule edition of the poems of Omar Khayyam—which I didn't give you—that you always carry in the inside pocket of your jacket, along with the address book from which you are never separated. You often leaf through it in my presence. You never talk about the other book; nevertheless the gold-lettered suede cover seems to have been much handled. It is permitted to tease you about the suitcase, but about Omar Khayyam no jokes or questions are allowed.

In all, there are few questions between us. Sometimes, in the moments of silence, our looks traverse long avenues of perplexity. Only our eyes. Then we continue our conversation that, if overheard, would surprise only by its banality. Those who know us would never realize I am listening carefully to dates, figures, statistics with such impassioned attention, nor that you would follow—seeming so amused and absorbed—the feminine verbiage in the language I borrow from you, too vague or too precise, hesitant or reckless, that stumbles just as it gets going and which doubtless is endowed with something of the complex feelings you inspire in me. I appear to you in the inseparable garment of this foreign language that must give me a face as phony as the one you take on when you apply yourself to repeating, in a voice I don't recognize, the few French phrases you use to make yourself understood by the customs officers at Le Havre or the shopkeepers on the Rue de Rivoli. The Parisian tobacconist who hears you saying, in your flute-like voice, "Allumettes, s'il vous plait monsieur?" while holding on to your hat with your hand, has no idea of the formidable man he is dealing with.

Do we suspect, you and I, with whom we are dealing? Or are you spared, when it comes to me, this perpetual questioning I have regarding you? When you are here, these questions are tiresome. Once you are elsewhere they have a role to play. They fill the void. They change the nature of the conversations to which we have become accustomed to limiting ourselves. I like the fact that I have never finished taking your measure, that I still have to examine you from a certain angle, then another, to seek out what you try to hide, the silver lining, to attribute to you that which you suppress, to let your dammed-up personality spill out in me. Absent, I miss you less. We follow our parallel roads without trying to make them meet. Sometimes I see you in my imagination, stretching out your long legs for a moment in front of my fire, and this absurd vision makes me laugh. Your lips might suddenly tremble, an embarrassing quiver that throws you into a panic if it happens while you are talking about one of your romantic businessman escapades and you can't resort to an energetic two-step to regain your balance, or suddenly whip out your address book to find the telephone number of a captain of industry you have an appointment with in the hotel lobby.

At the moment, I am convinced our association will last. You will travel all over the world, but always return to me. You mark the deep divisions in my life, you divide it into its main epochs. Your appearances have the inevitability, the unexpectedness, and also the rarity of the most important events, I was going to say cataclysms. Without the cataclysms, the turning of the world would be monotonous. In the intervals I can catch my breath, amazed that I have survived. Cautiously I advance into this reconquered world of freedom and calm. I think about fortifying myself for the next disturbance. I am not unhappy about being tied to something so strong, so large, so fateful. You emerge victorious in the comparison I sometimes make between the feeling that you represent and the feeling that, according to the code of youth, ought to exist as an absolute for both of us; in appearance it is so exquisite, in reality so meagre. I might have been left with only half a soul; thanks to you, a whole one remains. It is in bumping against yours that I discover a shape of my own. I feed my light to penetrate your shade. Not that you appear to me a shadowy figure: you are shadowy only in the enigma you are for me. In reality you must present few twists, few hidden recesses, few mazes. You are like a huge house with only one room. It's when someone tries to turn you into a modern apartment carved into small rooms that you disappear. It's when someone tries to transform you according to her tastes, wants to make some improvements in order to move in, that she finds herself face to face with you, the easily offended, shadowy owner. The house must be accepted as it is. In you I recognize your homeland, I see in you its methods, its tranquillity, and the innocent way it has of imposing itself.

Any permanent feeling would make you as ill at ease as a door locked, by surprise, behind you, or a room in which it is difficult to breathe. In your emotional life you require the knowledge that you have always retained, in the depths of your soul, your ticket for an unknown destination, the power to close up your heart like an apartment, or to terminate a spiritual understanding as though it were a lease. How simple it is! What intoxication beneath your cold exterior, what over-excitement beneath the calm, you draw from such adventures. The train or the boat won't wait. Your suitcase is packed. You bring with you only what is indispensable. You keep your business papers and burn your personal letters. You leave no old debts behind you. No misunderstanding is possible: it is clear that you are leaving, that nothing could hold you back, that it would be inappropriate and above all useless to protest or be angry. You excel at facing people with the inevitable, the fait accompli. It is entirely obvious that your interest, your peace of mind—one might almost say your everyday desires to eat and drink— are on the other side of the ocean. Each minute of time that remains to you has its purpose. This time is shrinking, this time is growing weak: you consult your watch as though you were taking a pulse. It is useless to decide to ask you for explanations at the same time the concierge has come to get the keys. You hurry the preparations for departure like a man who knows the price of time, but not like one who is making his first crossing, who loses his head, who packs before he needs to, who loses his passport. You do everything elegantly and masterfully, even your farewells. In our taxi you are busy counting your luggage, and it would seem inopportune to you if a disagreeably nervous hand was pressed into yours. You feel your pocket to make sure everything is there: your chequebook, your letters of introduction, Omar Khayyam. You don't need to verify the state of your heart. It's fine, your heart, it is beating, it is awake and it is the colour of the face you are wearing today; it is

English, it has put its affairs in order, it is going on a trip. It is going wherever: a goldmine, the north or south pole, the jungle. It is going off to make conquests, possibly imaginary, or to earn you trophies from the hunt. You are eager to get the best seat on the train, with the *New York Herald* on your knees, or to go down to your cabin to look over whatever companion chance has provided and to hang your hat on an advantageous hook. When they call "All aboard," I won't see you on the bridge, waving your handkerchief. Handkerchiefs are fine for Paris train stations. But perhaps, when I'm nothing but an indistinct shadow at the end of a deserted windswept pier, I will discern, detached from the other passengers and looking in my direction, your immobile silhouette, you in your raincoat, your hands stuffed in your pockets.

Others know why they are upset. You don't want to. You accept it like a chronic condition. From time to time you refer to it, with pride and a touch of regret. You say: "I was born that way!" the way someone else would say: "I'm naturally good at arithmetic." Most of all you were born on an island. The waves beat against your imagination. Every aggravating barrier must be surmounted. Any situation that prolongs itself becomes serfdom for you. Groaning with impatience and looking into the distance, you make the rounds of a familiar personality as though it were a fenced-in bit of ground. For you, it is only in the distance that you can seek yourself, pursue yourself, become yourself. You take your habits with you. They accompany you like friends. A set of dumbbells in the bottom of your suitcase guarantees you can do the same exercises every time you wake up. The moment you arrive in a hotel room you have your same travelling bag, no matter what the latitude. In the evening, when you slide your feet into your sleeping-car slippers, you can be sure they have always been yours, and after so much travelling such a pleasure is not lost on you. It is always possible to find made-in-England ties and collars, whether in Melbourne or Bombay. Because the same impatient exclamation escapes you every time you nick yourself shaving, you are convinced you haven't changed, seeing a countryside fly by through a train window, the sea beating against the porthole, the city rising you don't know how many storeys out the window. Yes, you were born that way. You always go outside the frame. In you there is some mobile element I can't name that might even ensure that no trace of you will be left after you die. I look at you as though you had a mysterious disease. You belong to the country you have never seen, to the emotion you have never experienced. Your dreaming carries you towards the unknown. What empire do you glimpse in the slow smoke rings of the cigarette you are smoking, and why do you suddenly toss it away as though it were burning your fingers?

One evening, in that ballroom they call Venetian, of which the walls, by I don't know what artifice, seem under their frescoes to be bathed in the water of the Grand Canal and from which the music seems to come from the gondolas painted on it, I see you are utterly fascinated by a pair of dancers. The woman in a green dress was a priestess of Bacchus whose pink back flowed magnificently to her waist. She was dancing with her arm curved above her head, and instead of standing in one spot and stamping, the fashion at the time, she went through the crowd with a motion that was at once daring and harmonious, drawing her silver-templed partner in her wake. There was a moment when the projectionist amused himself by following her through the half-darkness of the immense hall. I recognized the heroic dancer. I knew that at women's meetings she displayed only a sullen heaviness. Pleasure had transformed her. You weren't the only one fixed on the curve of her arm, the undulation of her dress, and the passion for freedom and movement that her body was revealing. With nostalgia in your voice you said, "Oh, to dance like that!" What attracted you was less the celebrant than the boldness of her dance. You yourself had the same desire for movement without limit. In her step, you recognized your own.

Despite my efforts, you have managed to remain concealed. I have not been able to uncover your real self. And I think I have remained equally inscrutable to you. A strange fate that refuses to allow us to understand each other yet will not let us remain indifferent.

So it is that now, though you are indeed alive, you are reduced to the status of a memory. I do not dare to try to deduce how you think about me, if indeed I still come to you, from time to time, in a way of walking, some facial expression, a voice that seems to be mine. What is yours is the image you have of me, that characterization of my personality, the interpretation, doubtless false but convincing, that you have made of me. It is also possible that I am the cause of some secret bitterness—I keep myself from saying remorse. You are not one of those people weighed down by remorse.

You must be as impenetrable and solid as rock for me to have never been able to break you down, to shake or diminish you. No matter how my mind assaults you, you remain intact. Not the slightest fissure has been created. I rejoice to see you so. It gives me a secret security. No matter what else fails, you will be there. I will always be able to lean on you, with the impersonality of one who leans, seeks your shade if not your substance, which can be neither given nor penetrated.

I also feel proud . . . To have, no more than you, given in. I continue to come and go around you. I pursue the enquiry with the same persistence. Nothing wears out the wave. It retains its silent patience, its power protected by its depth, a rhythm that belongs to it alone. There is no reason to despair: it will be back just when you think it has gone for good.

These relations satisfy us. In love we would have been uneasy. Our separations and our meetings occur as though they depended on destiny, and our chemistry pushes us apart with a force equal to our attraction. There is no weakening of our feelings. Each day hardens the memory to steel. Each day we test ourselves against each other. I welcome you with the curiosity with which I would open my door to a stranger. I have no idea what you are going to say. Your words are always fresh. The news you bring me comes from the unknown world which is you. We remain intact for one another: whatever we can give each other is only for an hour. Then we each return to our solitude.

I don't miss you very much. Although present in my mind, having put you in place behind—I don't know—that doubtless formidable self of yours, defending you and arguing with you, in reality you are far away, and that distancing soothes. We only become irritated at each other when we are breathing the same air. Because then we feel we are compromising our secret ambition, which is to fortify ourselves in our indifference.

This state, which is not love, is just as durable as love. If in the back of your mind there is a preoccupation from which you can't quite free yourself, I am sure it must be me. Your memory of me keeps mixing itself up with your figures and your balances. You find it lurking in the place you least expect to meet it. A light step crossing the corridor, at your door, catches your ear; a French voice saying *bonjour* or *monsieur* or *oui* or *non* in the street makes you turn around. And the first snow falling on the tree outside your window reminds you of how we once watched it together. Because we never know how memories manage to insinuate themselves: you put them out the door and they come back in through the window. There is something comical in the contrast between the fortress that you are and the cracks through which you allow the past to creep in.

What is so exceptional about you that you have survived? Are you not made out of what I attribute to you? Are you not simply myself? Why is your memory the only one I mourn?

We could have fallen into friendship. But friendship would still have been a weakness, a condescension. Friends look at each other at terribly close range. The closer they get, the smaller they become. All intimacy implies a dangerous proximity. We hear the echoes of the soul, the breathing in sleep, the dream babbles, the moans from nightmares through the wall. We witness the quarrels each has with himself every morning, just when we need to be re-energized, when our minds must start to function. You wouldn't know how to be the friend of a woman. The idea implies something abnormal to you, almost immodest. You, who are a remarkable swimmer and for whom swimming in the sea is a sport of choice, detest being undressed together on the beach. As you would detest the free movement of an intimacy unjustified by love.

Few words have passed between us. Those we have exchanged endure. Each one is imprinted. Each is attached to the day, the hour, the moment, the circumstance when it was pronounced with the clarity of an inscription. We can secretly come back to them as often as we want without fear of finding them changed. Your words have your intonation, your long lines and muscles that make me think, every time I look at you, of an anatomical illustration. They are as well dressed as you. As soon as they come into my apartment they look for the ashtray. They refuse the armchair, they need that high-backed straight chair for their long limbs. Sometimes they tease me, they take me by the shoulders, they try a sudden or awkward caress, they hide blushing in my neck. They have your breath.

Sometimes they are spoken in public, that brilliant and cosmopolitan public that you love, the only one you know, the one that is of another breed than me, but to which I seemed to belong that evening you took me with you. I came down from my tower. I found myself in a current of which the waters were set in motion by powerful dynamos called money, vanity, deception, though the surface bubbled with worldly politeness. I have to admit you were at home there. I saw you relaxing. Your face opened up in a way it never did at my place, sitting on the high-backed, straight chair of your choice, listening to your watch tick. In these places you were no longer constrained. Your expression with me was one of happy intimacy. Nothing was tightening in your throat. You were reassured by the voices around you. Your confidences made their way among the words of strangers. You needed a crowd to balance your own massive weight. Not that you would become vulgar. I don't know what protects you and keeps you apart. To your running about the world you bring a relentlessness that is a disease, and in the midst of the swarming masses I see you as a point of light, immobile. You melt away only at the edges: the inner self remains intact. Only your corolla is aging. There is something about you on which nothing has taken hold. I could say your smooth, hard skin covers your soul as well as your face. From every point of view you are a man in magnificent health. You swim easily in every kind of water, and I think you use the weight-lifting exercises you perform every morning in front of a window, open to the winter weather, to strengthen yourself mentally as well as physically. You manipulate your dumbbells with such deliberation, such perseverance, sometimes in such a fury, to the right, to the left, above your head, around your waist. What marvellous displaced dirty jokes, what sneaky flattened paws, what wonderful Punch and Judy puppets! Bravo!

Isn't it time to go home, to break the restraints around our limbs and shoulders, around our faces that have become weak with smiling; the smoke, the lascivious vapours of eyes and mouths, the stench of contented hearts, the sour smell of unsatisfied desires? Should we not flee, hand in hand, through some deserted alley, or walk side by side along some avenue drenched in the hour's tranquil light? But you are afraid of the alley or the avenue where we are followed only by our two shadows. You fear the echo of our steps, light as they are, the resonance of our voices, however careful we might be to preserve our banality. You refuse to see my true face. You cover it with its social mask. You close your heart against emotion the way you button your coat against the cold. Because emotion is a physical pain to be battled against. Sensitivity could upset the well-organized and well-defended creature you are. It is something for those who are weak. You would be as ashamed to discover that you are sensitive as you would be to have been born with a harelip. If I said to you, laughing, that I thought you sentimental, you would blush with mortification. Even if this undesirable sensitivity were content with causing a tiny little stir inside you which was completely invisible from the outside! But the very fact that it makes you contract your lips, the way children do when they are about to cry, is odious to you. There is no salvation except in flight. You boast about preparing for your trip in a few minutes, bundling up your things and stuffing them in your bag, as though you were crushing any little bits of sentiment. You are also sure to supply yourself with an armful of newspapers on which you can crush your eyes, as soon as you reach your reserved seat in the parlour car.

What a puppet I make of you! Parlour cars, sleeping cars, steamships, and hotels stinking of luxury, where the human beast seeks refuge, pursued by its own weariness; stockmarket offices, clubs, elegant banquets, the great public edifices raised by this century's pharaohs, built on the desert of man, there is the frame in which I place you. The frame that you overfill with your powerful shoulders, that you burst with your noble and luminous face, your eyes that are always looking straight ahead. You are here only as in a foreign land. At our small table we are an island. Only I am amazed at our surroundings. I am the only one submerged by it. I see you isolated by the smoke from your cigarette, the amusement in your smile. Your voice, instead of being lost, comes straight to the unique interlocutor I represent. The circle we make constitutes your home. The shade of our lamp makes an oasis of sterile light.

That is enough. You pull happiness over you like a blanket. You have no need to drag it around like something you have caught. Nothing stays on your hands, those hands which are so tough, so delicate, so hardy, which I never see gloved. When the best furred mitts are touched with frost, you bury your hands in your pockets with an air of disdain for the superfluous, of finding enough heat in yourself. By this gesture you bluntly reject social caste. You soak your hands in the cold like the labourers you pass on the highway in the morning, who break the frozen earth with their iron picks. Your hands want neither to give nor to accept. They draw from their own source. Yours are hands which give away no secrets.

Let me stop deluding myself and reducing you to the role of pillar of the house of pleasures in which I disdain to set foot. If it pleases you to go there, it is because you have no fear of leaving any part of you behind. You are made with a lacquered shell beneath which you stay perfectly unscathed . . . Your taste for worldly things is not really what separates us. You have known how to create for yourself a solitude that equals my own. The roads that lead to you are as roundabout, long, and wild as those which I frequent, and I have often had the impression of insurmountable fences raised around your person. And especially an impression of sudden cold. When you feel yourself in danger you radiate cold, the way certain animals, in order to defend themselves, release an unpleasant stench. I am thoughtlessly caught up in your gaiety, in your warmth, I believe in your sunny skies. And then, at a turn in the road, I begin to shiver. It feels as though I have gotten lost.

Incomprehension, that is what joins us, that is the grand common ground on which we meet, the one which never grows smaller, into which each of us ventures equally, with the sensation of being stripped naked, exposed, and visible from afar. Across the ground of this place blows an austere wind, sad and drying. To state our differences is a way for us to meet. We represent two nations of souls.

Albert Laberge
Translated by David Homel

MRS. FILLY

Albert Laberge was born on February 18, 1871, in Beauharnois, the son of a farming family. He was educated in Beauharnois and, later, at the Jesuit Collège du Gesu (Sainte-Marie) in Montreal. In 1891, he suffered a crisis of faith, however, and the following year was expelled for "improper reading" of books on the Index. He subsequently worked in a law office for several years, and in 1896 began writing for *La Presse*, first as a sports writer and then as an art critic.

Laberge's most famous literary work was the novel *La Scouine*, a *roman naturaliste*, the first instalment of which appeared in a Montreal journal in 1903. A second appeared in 1908 and was immediately attacked by the clergy— Monseigneur Bruchési condemned it as "low pornography." Perhaps as a consequence, the complete novel was not published until 1918, and then in a private edition of only sixty copies, so it remained largely unread, or at least unacknowledged, for many years. *La Scouine*, translated as *Bitter Bread* (1977) by Conrad Dion, has enjoyed a kind of subterranean success, however: André Major was strongly influenced by its harsh realism, and the novel now stands as one of Quebec's most significant works of realist fiction.

Although Laberge never wrote another novel, he published five books of short stories: *Images de la vie et de la mort* (1936); *La Fin du voyage* (1942); *Le Destin des hommes* (1950); *Fin de roman* (1951); and *Le Dernier souper* (1953). "Madame Pouliche," here translated by David Homel as "Mrs. Filly," first appeared in *La Fin du voyage*, and in 1962 it was included in Gérard Bessette's *Anthologie Albert Laberge* as one of Laberge's twelve best stories. It is no less starkly realistic than *La Scouine*, but as Bessette has remarked, "the blackness or degradation that perhaps constitutes a defect in

La Scouine may actually be seen as a quality in Laberge's short stories."

Laberge died on April 4, 1960, in Chateauguay.

∽

"Mrs. Filly" is a translation of "Madame Pouliche" published in *Anthologie d'Albert Laberge* (Montreal: Cercle du livre de France, 1972).

She'd surely emptied her share of spittoons in her life, Mrs. Filly had!

And swallowed down her share of paregoric, too! You've got to seek consolation somewhere, right, and forget your troubles. Some people do a lot worse than that, for sure.

Every day, for almost forty years, she had cleaned the offices of a large insurance company that occupied an entire floor of a vast building. Some sixty men and women worked there. There were a dozen private offices and a large meeting room. At the end of every afternoon, once the employees had left, Mrs. Filly and her assistant would go to work and do most of the cleaning. The next morning, before the clerks arrived, the two women would return to finish their tasks. Sweeping, washing, wiping, dusting, emptying wastepaper baskets and spittoons, cleaning out the washroom—that was the daily ritual. Mrs. Filly had been practising her trade since the age of twenty-four.

She was a long plank of a woman, grey and thin. Her hair was grey, her eyes were grey and round and stuck out of her skull, her skin was dry and grey, as grey as the rags she used to wipe the desks. It was impossible to imagine that once her skin had been young and smooth; she looked as if she'd always been grey. To go with that, she had a flat pug nose and a voice like a locust. No, she was neither beautiful nor attractive nor made to excite a man's desires. When she plodded by with her bucket and broom, she seemed to have been born to the job.

In a strange way, her mannerisms were astonishingly like those of a chicken. In the morning, before stepping into the manager's office where there was a rug, she wiped her feet on the floor, sliding them back and forth like a chicken scratching with first one foot, then the other, to uncover a kernel of corn, a worm, or an insect in the dusty ground.

For nearly forty years, her life had been consumed in sweeping floors, emptying spittoons, and cleaning toilets. Of course, it's more pleasant to be a saleslady in a store, or a waitress in a restaurant, or a stenographer, but you can't always choose the way you earn your keep. Most often, you take what you can get. When she was in her twenties, she worked in a shoe factory, but the job made her sick. In the rooming house where she was staying at the time, there lived a charwoman from the insurance company; aging, losing her strength, she needed help. And so Mrs. Filly was hired. The older woman died a few months later. Her assistant took over and assumed the title and responsibilities of charwoman, the way another woman might take on the title of queen by ascending to a throne.

That was years ago, but nothing had changed in the meantime, for all her years were the same, all unfolded in the same way: emptying spittoons, cleaning out toilets, and drugging herself with elixir of paregoric. Actually, she had gotten married once, which is how she'd acquired the name Filly. But the marriage had never amounted to much, and the poor woman preferred not to think about it, for the union had brought her more bother than enjoyment. When she was about thirty, she made the acquaintance of Mr. Filly, a short, reed-like man in his fifties. He scraped by on the money he made renting a hall once weekly or monthly to societies, clubs, and organizations that held their meetings there. He had founded his own musical club and named himself director. Mrs. Filly had met him several times when he was wearing his conductor's uniform, which consisted of a short coat with metal buttons and a gold-braided cap. To tell the truth, Mr. Filly was no Don Juan, nor any other brand of seducer. In fact, he looked rather insignificant and silly, but his cap and coat with the gold trim impressed the thirty-year-old charwoman. One evening, she watched him conducting his musicians at a soirée where he'd been hired to play. He liked those simple tunes, tra la la and fol de rol.

His baton set the measure, lightly, lightly, lightly, light . . .

It wasn't easy to take Mr. Filly seriously with his rigadoon rigadoondah music, but as he was, he didn't displease the charwoman, and one day when he asked her to marry him, she accepted and became Mrs. Filly. With the few hundred dollars' savings she had, they set up house. It would be an exaggeration to say that Mr. Filly had appetites. Mrs. Filly had expected something better. She was disappointed; she hadn't gotten her money's worth, since after all she paid for everything, all the household expenses. Meanwhile, her wages disappeared, down to the last penny. And there were no rewards in return. Mr. Filly let himself be kept. Their union was six months old when a sensational event occurred. Tipped off by someone, the police raided Mr. Filly's hall during a musical rehearsal. What the police discovered when they burst in was never revealed, for the trial was held in camera, but Mr. Filly was sentenced to three years in penitentiary for "public acts of indecency," according to the verdict. With tastes like that, no wonder he didn't have any appetites, Mrs. Filly said to herself. She was widowed the very next year. The name Filly was all her husband left her. She kept the little apartment that she had furnished, and rented out a room to her assistant; the costs would be lower that way.

Every day brought the same tasks, the same routine: sweeping, washing the windows, emptying the spittoons, cleaning out the washrooms. Naturally, life was no picnic for her, so in search of comfort, she turned to elixir of paregoric. But she didn't discover this precious balm until much later.

You'd have to have known the business, you'd have to have practised the trade, you'd have to have been there to realize how dirty men are. Worse than swine. One of them caught cold once and developed a cough. Instead of using his spittoon, out of pure meanness, to humiliate her, to make her job more repugnant, he peppered the floor with fat, viscous wads of spit that she had to clean up. But that was only the beginning. You should have seen the mess they made in the toilet. Some of them, deliberately, just to make her life harder, threw the paper they used onto the floor. They threw so much of it there that they made a kind of litter, which they liberally watered down. Just for the sheer pleasure of it, out of spite, to make her life more unpleasant, to make her job harder and dirtier. When you opened the door, it was like stepping into a manure-pile in a stable.

Regular animals, those people. Stinking beasts, those men were. After leaving their droppings, they amused themselves by writing inscriptions on the wall which displayed their gutter minds. The gutter—that's where their minds resided. Oh, they were educated, they dressed like gentlemen, but underneath, their minds were cesspools. One day, in one of the stalls, she discovered her own portrait, a nude one at that, sketched out in a few strokes, but very accurate and even amusing. The author of this farce had drawn her with broom in hand, and the way she clung to the stick was absolutely side-splitting.

Every evening and every morning, Mrs. Filly returned home in a cloud of disgust. One time, as she came in the door, she said to her assistant, "I can't eat supper tonight, I'm too heart-sick."

Her assistant—it was Mélanie at the time—told her, "Let me give you something that'll do you a world of good."

She went to her room and returned with a little vial. Then she poured a teaspoon of the potion into a little sugar-water.

"Take it," she said, holding out the spoon.

Mrs. Filly brought it to her lips. The potion tasted a little like licorice. Not unpleasant. She swallowed down the liqueur. True, it did help out. It stimulated her. She began to forget all about the spittoons and the stinking filth in the washroom.

"What is that stuff?" she asked a minute later.

"Elixir of paregoric. It's not dangerous, it's not expensive, and it does you a world of good."

The two women sat down at the table for a cup of tea and something to eat. She had the mannerisms of a chicken, Mrs. Filly did. Instead of taking a healthy mouthful with her fork, she fenced with the food on her plate, like a chicken pecking with its beak, first to one side, then the other. She picked at her food, snagging a fleck of meat, a leaf of salad, a string of spaghetti at the end of her utensil—never a real mouthful.

After her dose of paregoric took effect, Mrs. Filly felt a great sense of peace come over her, she felt her nerves relax, and sitting on her chair, she surrendered to the drowsiness that weighed upon her. That evening, she went to bed early and had a good night's sleep. The next morning, on her way back from work, she stopped at the pharmacist's and bought a bottle of paregoric. And so, she got into the habit of taking it three times a day. Not a large dose, of course, just a teaspoon in a little sugar-water. How good it made her feel! A miracle, a true panacea. The alcohol stimulated her, then brought her sleep.

When you earn your living emptying spittoons and cleaning out toilets, a liqueur like that is a great relief. Mélanie had certainly done her a big favour by introducing her to the elixir.

During the year, there are ordinary days and extraordinary days—the holidays, for example. In the course of Mrs. Filly's existence, every winter brought with it one exceptional day: the Day of the Big Mess, the morning after the staff party. It was a tradition. Once a year, bosses and employees got together to celebrate with an office party. They danced, they played music, they amused themselves, they ate and drank (because there was always a luxurious spread), and they vomited, too. The morning Mrs. Filly came in to do the cleaning up after the first of those parties, she was stupefied and disgusted by what she saw. Lord Jesus! Never in her life had she seen such filth. They had eaten and drunk like pigs, and thrown up everything they couldn't keep down. The toilet was in a repulsive state. Not only had they vomited in the toilet bowl, but on the seat, too. Even the walls were spattered. The smell was strong and acrid and made her stomach turn. In some of the private offices, the spittoons were filled with puke, others with urine. It seemed as though they had done their utmost to make the biggest mess possible. Now it was up to her to clean it all up. So, with mops and pails and brushes, she and her assistant worked through the afternoon, spending hours cleaning up the human filth.

Every year brought the same thing. It seemed every year was worse, as if they'd tried to outdo themselves in the production of human filth, to give her ever more obscene trash to clean up. It was a celebration for some; for her, it was a repulsive chore. But she had to earn her pay, her pittance, so she washed down and cleaned up those pools of vomit. She emptied some fine spittoons the morning after those nights of drunken revelry! After a spectacle, a job like that one, disgust followed her for the rest of the day. At noon, she wouldn't risk a meal, so strong was the odour of vomited food. To try to forget and stiffen her courage, she took a dose of paregoric. And not just a teaspoon, either; a big soupspoon, sometimes more. She needed to purge her mind of all that filth. Soon, she lapsed into drowsiness, then slept, but often her dreams were painful.

With time, she began wanting more of her panacea, and took stronger doses of it. It brought her the strength she needed to do her repulsive task. She stopped measuring by the spoonful; now, she tipped the bottle and swallowed.

Every morning, she would rise, dress hurriedly, and take the streetcar downtown to empty her spittoons and clean out her stalls. That was the routine: every day, week in and week out, one month to the next, one year leading to the other. And that would be the routine for the rest of her days.

Her life was no bleak desert, arid and monotonous; in the desert the vistas are large, there is a wild kind of grandeur, there are mirages and great gusts of wind, and at times a cool and verdant oasis. No, her life was more like a long, poor, sordid street, without trees or flowers, bordered by ugly houses, all the same, filled with hostile faces with mocking, ironic expressions.

But she had her elixir of paregoric.

Paregoric was her friend, her support, her consolation. It was her walking stick, her comfort, her viaticum.

The poverty of her pitiful life melted away, the ugliness of her poor pariah existence faded when she took the precious balm, when she swallowed the blessed potion.

Without that comforting cordial, how would she have faced the evils and calamities that every day brought?

The only pleasures Mrs. Filly had, she owed to paregoric.

She felt as though she'd been put on earth to wash floors, empty spittoons, and clean toilets filled with foul, stinking filth.

The older she got, they greyer she became. Her hair turned grey, as did her skin, her eyes lost all their light. She wasn't so much getting thin as she was drying out, like a skeleton hung with skin.

Emptying the spittoons, cleaning out the toilets, that's how Mrs. Filly earned her daily bread. The same routine every day; nothing would ever change. She'd never receive a surprise inheritance or any of those happy windfalls that let you untie your apron and toss it in the garbage, and send your job to the devil, and take it easy the rest of your life. Luck wasn't going to smile on her. For thirteen and a half months, she bought a ticket in the weekly lottery that one of the commissioners organized—and never won. In the end, tired of paying out and never receiving anything in return, she quit the game.

"No, that's enough. I've given enough of my money to you," she told the man the next time he offered her a ticket.

"You're making a mistake," he teased her. "You would have won this week."

Then he turned to Mrs. Filly's assistant, a new girl who was working her first week.

"Here, buy the ticket. I bet you'll win the jackpot."

The woman took the coupon, paid her twenty-five cents, and won the lottery. Her very first ticket, and she walked away with fourteen dollars.

"That's the limit! I put down twenty-five cents for more than thirteen months and I never won a penny," Mrs. Filly said bitterly as she watched her happy assistant count her winnings.

Plain bad luck.

One day, in the streetcar, she had her wages stolen. She was going home on a Saturday morning with her envelope in her bag. At a stop, two riders got into the car: an elegantly dressed gentleman who sat on her right, and an average-looking woman who took the seat on her left. The man was holding an illustrated magazine and began paging through it casually once he'd sat down. The pictures were quite daring, even obscene. The rider considered them with nonchalant eyes. Off-handedly, he turned one page, then the next. A bit curious, Mrs. Filly stretched out her neck and gawked at the sporting pictures ever so dicreetly. Meanwhile, the woman on her left had gotten off without Mrs. Filly realizing it, and at the next stop, the gentleman also got off, taking his time, his magazine in one hand. Mrs. Filly watched him go. When the streetcar started up again, she put both hands on her knees and suddenly discovered that her purse, which she'd been holding in her left hand, was gone. So that's what had happened: she'd gone and gaped at salacious engravings, and lost all her wages. For six days, she'd emptied spittoons and cleaned out the restrooms, only to have her envelope snatched.

One day, as she was cleaning the manager's office, Mrs. Filly found a five-dollar bill that someone had obviously dropped. Fundamentally honest, she got to work earlier the next morning.

"I found this on the floor," she said to the person in question, holding out the banknote.

"I wondered where I'd lost it," he said, taking the money. Then he rummaged through his pocket, came up with a twenty-five-cent piece, and handed it to her.

"It's not much, but it comes from the heart," he assured her.

"Thank you, but it's not mine and I couldn't keep it," Mrs. Filly declared.

A few months later, she decided to ask for a raise.

"I'll have to submit your request to the administrators," the manager informed her. And when they met, he told them of Mrs. Filly's wishes.

"What do you think?" one of the directors asked the manager.

"I think it would be extravagant, it would be like throwing our money out the window. She doesn't need it. A little while back, she found a five-dollar bill and gave it back to its owner!"

Her simplicity moved them all to laughter.

"Fine, then, tell her that at the present time the company can't afford any raises," said the director, settling the issue once and for all.

Some men can say, "I sold a hundred automobiles this year, a hundred and fifty radios, I repaired a hundred and fifty pairs of shoes." Or, "I delivered two hundred loaves of bread every day, and a hundred and fifty pints of milk." Some men say to themselves, "I drank my share of beer in my life." Others mentally add up the number of women they had. Those are the kind of thoughts that buoy a man up. But all Mrs. Filly could say was that she'd emptied more spittoons than any other woman in town.

Her assistants were luckier than she was. They'd found a way for themselves, you might say. Rose, the first one, a tall, pretty blonde, former seamstress whose eyes started playing nasty tricks on her, took on the job because she had to work for a living, but she got married six months later. Mélanie, the second, a dark-haired girl who came to work every morning with her face made up, found an old guy to take care of her. Emilienne, who'd followed in her footsteps, held the position for thirteen years, then died, a victim of pneumonia. Her troubles were over. Mrs. Drapeau was abandoned by her husband, and worked the job for ten years. Then one day, her son, who was a grown man by then, told her, "It's my turn to work now, so you don't have to." Since that day, she'd put her feet up. Then came La Bourrette, the fat widow who was her current assistant. She was shacked up with an unemployed fellow who was separated from his wife. La Bourrette was nothing more than a mass of jelly, and Mrs. Filly had sworn to fire her more than once; she was slow, negligent, she wouldn't move unless you pushed her. No, they couldn't go on like that. She'd have to be replaced.

But all those women lived, whereas she. . . .

With the years, she became greyer, thinner, and uglier with her protruberant grey eyes, empty of all expression.

Then one day she realized she'd been a charwoman for this big insurance company for thirty years. She knew the personnel. Some had been young when she'd started working; today, they were grandparents. They went on trips, some of them had even gone to Europe, they owned automobiles, they were well dressed, they lived good lives . . . You, old hag, empty that spittoon!

In search of consolation and forgetfulness, to do her daily duty without being overwhelmed by disgust, she poured herself ever stiffer doses of paregoric. Afterwards, she would slip into drowsiness, only to awaken later, her head heavy, her thoughts in a jumble, her body anesthetized.

She had no more appetite; she never ate. Paregoric was all she had a taste for. She was so skinny she scared people in the street. At night, she had frightful, painful, pursuing nightmares. A day full of misery wasn't enough—it had to go on into the night.

She kept her nose to the grindstone, but some days it was harder. Her strength was deserting her. Her heart seemed to be off-kilter, like an old machine that wouldn't pump any more. Sometimes, she felt as though she were about to collapse and fall to the floor. But despite it all, day in, day out, sick or not, she emptied the spittoons and cleaned out the toilets.

And when the job was done, for the time being at least, she swallowed down a generous dose of paregoric.

One morning, she got up late for work. She missed her streetcar by seconds and had to wait five minutes for the next one. That's the way it always worked. At the building, as it often happened, the elevator man hadn't shown up yet. "His wife was sleeping on his shirt-tail and he couldn't get up," Mrs. Filly said out loud, furious at this particular setback. She started up the stairway, but found herself gasping for breath, her heart pounding, and she was completely winded by the time she reached her floor. Naturally, La Bourrette was late, too, that lazy dog. Never on time. Still shacked up with her lay-about. She'd have to show her the door and find herself another girl. Things were going from bad to worse. Couldn't anybody get up in the morning? Damn it to hell! Mrs. Filly was in a devil of a mood! Hurriedly, she went to her closet, took off her old grey overcoat that was threadbare and wrinkled, with the sewer-rat fur collar, then her washed-out, misshapen, banged-up hat. She hung both up and put on her apron, took her brush, her wiping rags for the desks, and her bucket for the spittoons. Her key ring swinging and jingling at her belt, she bustled off towards the assistant-manager's office, since he always was the first to show up. Feverishly, she opened the door and took a few steps inside, then, struck down by heart failure, she crashed to the floor, hitting the standing receptacle of filth and knocking it over. Its contents spewed out on the linoleum. She lay dead there, Mrs. Filly, she'd died on the job, her old grey head and grey face steeped in the dirty water, in the spittoon juice, a cigar-butt lying next to her mouth . . .

Yves Thériault
Translated by Wayne Grady

MOTHER SOUBERT'S PIG

Born in Quebec City on November 28, 1915, of Montagnais descent, Yves Thériault studied at the École Notre-Dame-de-Grâce in Montreal, but at the age of seventeen decided to travel throughout the entire province of Quebec rather than pursue his studies. Subsequently, he worked as a trapper, a cheese merchant, a truck driver, a night-club impresario, a tractor salesman, and a Radio-Canada announcer before turning to writing. He became a scriptwriter for the National Film Board in Ottawa in 1943; the following year his first book of short stories, *Contes pour un homme seul*, was published in Montreal.

From then on, Thériault was one of the most prolific writers of his generation. Among his twenty-five novels, *Aaron* (1954) won the Prix de la province de Québec; *Agaguk* was awarded the Prix France-Canada; and *Ashini* won the Governor-General's Award for literature. Thériault was awarded the Molson Prize for lifetime achievement in 1971. He also served for many years as cultural consultant for the federal Department of Indian and Northern Affairs.

Thériault was a prodigious writer of short stories: his eight collections include *Le Vendeur d'étoiles* (1961); *Si la bombe m'était contée* (1963); *L'Île introuvable* (1968); *Œuvre de chair* (1975); and *La Femme Anna et autres contes* (1981). Although Thériault's novels have been well received in English translation, his short fiction has not fared so well: *Contes pour un homme seul*, curiously enough, has never been translated into English in its entirety. A study of primitivism, violence, and eroticism, in which characters struggle, often in vain, against basic and sometimes brutal human passions, it is a startling and disturbing work by a writer whose vision of society differs greatly from that of his contemporaries. Nevertheless, as "Le cochon de la mère Soubert," translated

by Wayne Grady as "Mother Soubert's Pig," shows,
Thériault was among the first Canadian writers to explore
some of the fundamental themes of modern literature.

Yves Thériault died on October 20, 1983.

∽

"Mother Soubert's Pig" is a translation of "Le cochon de la mère
Soubert" published in *Contes pour un homme seul* (Montreal: Éditions
de l'Arbre, 1944).

When Maugrand's wife heard the noise coming from old Soubert's cabin, she said to herself: "Sounds serious, all that whining. I'd better go take a look."

Which she did, and found Mother Soubert almost ready to give up the ghost, the pain in her stomach was so bad.

"What!" said the old woman, between groans. "I'm not a young woman anymore, and yesterday I ate like a woman about to have her first baby. So today"—she barked painfully between each word—"I'm paying for it. Go away!"

But the woman Maugrand was a midwife, and she knew about sickness, having taken care of enough women in the village; and even though it was true Mother Soubert was no spring chicken, she might be sicker than she thought. So Maugrand made her a tisane and said a few prayers for her, the kind that are supposed to rid a person of gastric complaints.

As the day passed and Mother Soubert didn't seem to get any better, and maybe even got a bit worse, Maugrand's wife had to think about her own family, which needed looking after too. The older ones would be eyeing the table, the youngest one would be crying for the nipple.

Just as she was getting up to go, having decided to leave the old woman's bedside for a while, Mother Soubert gave a loud groan, clutched at her vitals as though she would tear her stomach out, and gave up the ghost. Which annoyed Maugrand's wife no end, because she was there by herself and would now have to describe the old woman's death to the whole village, because everyone would want to know every last detail.

But since that was the way of it, she pulled off the old woman's stockings and stripped her body, which did not make for a pleasant spectacle seeing that it was hard as a crust, and yellow, and anyway she ended up pulling a sheet over it.

"I'll come back later to wash it and get it ready for the burial," she said to herself.

And, blowing out the lamp on the table, she left the old woman's tumbledown cabin and went home.

When she got there, she nursed her youngest, who was howling loudest, then served dinner to the others. The two boys, the Maugrand girl who had been the first to come along, and Maugrand-the-Strong, who was tall enough to knock his head against the ceiling joists and strong enough to pick up a bull and throw it across the barnyard.

She didn't say much to them about the death that had taken place that day. Just that the old woman had died and someone would have to bury her. Which moved Maugrand to reply: "I wouldn't mind getting my hands on that pig of hers. It's a fine pig, fat and full of grease. You might have spoken to her about it."

His wife shrugged her shoulders. But the daughter spoke up:

"Do you think it's proper to talk about the pig so soon after she's dead? Can't it wait?"

"Sure, it can wait until someone else makes off with the pig," said Maugrand. "But I want it myself."

Maugrand's wife stopped halfway between the fireplace and the table, and fixed her husband with a long, cold stare. She knew what the words, "I want" meant in the mouth of her husband. That's what he'd said before the last one was born, against all reason, long after the others were grown—almost ten years after.

"I want" was what he had said then, and what he had got.

But she didn't say anything. There's no reasoning with a mule.

For his part, Maugrand fell into a calculating silence, in which the fat pig of the late Mother Soubert figured prominently.

When dinner was over, Maugrand's wife went out to gather up the other women in the village: Lorgneau's wife, Mother Druseau, Coudois the blacksmith's wife, and anyone else she could find who would respond to the obligation implicit in her appeal and the curiosity brimming from their eyes.

There were many commentaries on the death which, though it surprised no one in its coming, took everyone unawares by its rapidity.

Especially when Maugrand's wife removed the sheet from the body, and everyone saw the old woman's scraggly body.

"Sad, isn't it," said Lorgneau's wife. "She didn't eat much, to judge by the way her skin stuck to her bones like that."

To which Judith, the one with the huge thighs and the ample bosom, added: "Look at the way her breasts hang down over her sides, I hope mine never get like that."

And more than one woman present felt a moment of envy for Judith's generous flesh, which jiggled with life every time she took a step.

But it was Mother Druseau who had the last word.

"Madame Maugrand," she said, "you should have closed this woman's eyes and pinned her lips together. It's not right we should be looking into her eyes wide open as they are, or staring down her gaping mouth. It's not Christian that these things should be, and it gives the person who forgot to do her duty a bad name."

Maugrand's wife hung her head in shame. She was humiliated, and for a long time said not a word. She remained silent during the entire washing of the body. And she was still quiet as they looked through the old woman's cupboard for a decent dress, one that was good enough to bury her in.

Coudois came. He was the one in the village who made caskets.

All the time the funeral preparations were going on, Maugrand was thinking.

Alone in his kitchen, he was thinking about the pig. He could hear it squealing in the yard behind the old woman's house.

He thought about the pig so much that he began to feel it was his pig, and when he couldn't stand it any longer, he went out to take a better look at this pig of his, to see how fat it was. He looked at it a long time.

"A lot of meat on that pig," he said to himself out loud. "A lot of good, juicy meat. It'd fetch a good price. Three more summers and off to the market, it'd get twice what it'd get today, if I took real good care of it, fattened it up nice and good."

The pig looked up at the man who was talking to himself, squealed back in response, then lay down and rolled around in the mud.

Maugrand looked at the huge sun setting over the sea amid shocks of red and blue, and at the dark green foliage of the trees as the harsh light of the sun receded, and he dreamed of the following day when the pig would belong to him. The dream seemed so real that it became an obsession, and he promised himself that...

"Tomorrow the pig will be mine. There," he said, "so be it."

And he went inside to join the women who had already begun praying for the dead woman, and who were preparing to hold their wake throughout the long night.

They had left Mother Soubert in her bed, with her eyes open and her mouth hanging down.

It made a macabre sight, the room in a shambles, the sow-bellied bed with its none-too-clean sheets, and the small, thin body of the old woman lying on it. A rosary was threaded through her fingers, and her simple black dress was buttoned up to her throat, above which her mouth sagged open as though she were catching flies.

It was just too bad. Not a woman in the room could look at Mother Soubert without thinking how horrible it would be to die looking so ugly.

Maugrand approached the bed and knelt beside it, still thinking about the pig. He remained on his knees long enough to say a prayer, but he didn't say one—praying wasn't something that appealed to Maugrand—then he got up and went into the kitchen.

Just about the whole village was there.

Men, a lot of women, and most of the children.

Some of the people were saying their beads, others were telling stories.

Daumier was even telling stories that would make a saint blush, but he was telling them quietly, in a corner, and just to a few men.

Maugrand wandered back and forth as if he had lost his bearings, looking for somewhere to park himself, still possessed by the idea of the pig, which was squealing in the yard and could be heard quite clearly in the kitchen.

He ended up joining Daumier's group.

He stood for a long time without speaking, listening to Daumier's ribald stories, laughing when the others did, but not as hard. Then he came to a decision.

"Listen, Daumier, I don't mean to put a damper on things, but there's something on my mind and I want to say it. It's about that pig of old Soubert's. That's a fine pig."

Daumier nodded, and Lorgneau, who was one of the group, said:

"It's a damn fine pig. It'll come in a good weight."

Maugrand said slyly: "I'm just wondering who's going to inherit it."

"The old woman had no family."

It was Lorgneau who said that, and Maugrand thought he could hear the greed in Lorgneau's voice.

"That we know of," he said. "She could well have family somewhere we don't know about."

"That's possible . . ."

Maugrand fell silent, and Daumier began another one of his stories, but the men seemed distracted and hardly laughed. Daumier knew that each of them was thinking about the pig the way a hawk thinks about a rabbit. Maugrand, too, realized that they were all thinking about the pig—it was written all over their faces—and he was sorry he'd ever mentioned the animal.

"If I'd kept my trap shut," he told himself, "they'd never have thought of the pig, and I could have just taken it."

And when Judith passed the wine around the table, he took three huge gulps of it.

The wake continued, but it was quieter. After a while some of the women left, and some of the men went with them. Maugrand stayed, and Lorgneau. Maugrand knew that the question of the pig would now be settled between himself and Lorgneau, and that Lorgneau was no mean adversary.

Maugrand's wife saw what was bothering her husband, and went over to him.

"Listen, Maugrand," she said, "that's not your pig."

"Not mine? What do you mean, not mine? Why not? The old woman had no family, so the pig goes to me."

"It does not go to you. I found a paper in her cupboard."

"What paper?"

"A paper written by the old woman."

Maugrand became suspicious: "And what was written on this piece of paper?"

"Words . . . words saying that the pig does not belong to you."

"Not to me? Who to, then?"

"To Troublé. The old woman wanted the pig to go to Troublé."

"Let me see that paper."

But Maugrand's wife was not Maugrand's wife for nothing, and when he tried to snatch the paper from her hands she stood up quickly and addressed everyone in the room, in a loud voice:

"The old woman has left a will," she said. "I found it in her cupboard. In her will she wrote that she wanted the pig to go to Troublé."

To which Judith replied: "It's almost like, when you get real old, you sort of sense death coming on, like you almost know you're going to die . . ."

In the corner, Lorgneau was biting his lips.

As for Maugrand, he had stomped out of the room when his wife began to speak.

Outside, in the darkness, there was a fine rain.

He walked, unaware of where he was going, until he realized he was heading for the bend in the Sablière, heading in fact for Troublé's cabin.

He hesitated for an instant when he realized where his instincts were taking him, but then he shook himself and continued walking, thinking how stupid it was to give a pig like that to someone like Troublé. To an idiot!

Troublé was in his cabin, sitting on a chair drawn up close to the table.

He didn't get up when Maugrand came in. He only said, in a small voice: "I knew you would come to get me."

And he looked over at the sack hanging on the wall, the sack that had Annette's legs in it, which he had cut up earlier that day.

Maugrand said nothing.

"You've come to get me, haven't you, Maugrand? Because of what I did? I'll go away, I won't say anything, I'll go away."

Maugrand still didn't speak.

Troublé began to think that maybe Maugrand hadn't come to get him after all.

And he didn't understand what Maugrand meant when, all of a sudden, he heard Maugrand yelling at him:

"You'll not have that pig! That's my pig, it's coming to me, not to you!"

And when Maugrand pulled out his knife and plunged it into Troublé's throat, killing him with a single twist of the blade, Troublé was still trying to figure out what it was that Maugrand was talking about. But he never had time to get out of the way, or even to raise an arm in his own defence.

Alain Grandbois
Translated by Matt Cohen

FLEUR-DE-MAI

Alain Grandbois was born in Saint-Casimir de Portneuf on May 25, 1900, and was educated at the Collège de Montréal and the Séminaire de Québec, and later at Saint Dunstan University in Charlottetown. He took a law degree at Université Laval in 1921. An inheritance allowed him to travel and, using Paris as a base—he lived in Montparnasse at the same time as Ernest Hemingway, F. Scott Fitzgerald, Morley Callaghan, and other celebrated exiles—he travelled in Italy, Spain (where he fought in the Republican Army), Austria, and Germany, as well as China, Japan, southeast Asia, the former Soviet Union, and Africa, returning to Canada just before the Second World War, in 1939.

His first book, *Né à Québec* (*Born in Quebec*), a work of creative nonfiction about the life of the explorer Louis Jolliet, was published in Paris in 1933; it was followed in 1934 by *Poèmes*, the first edition of which was printed in China and lost in its entirety in a shipwreck. His next book, *Les Voyages de Marco Polo*, in part inspired by Grandbois's own peripatetic existence, was awarded the Prix David in 1941. Grandbois won the Prix David in 1947 and in 1970, the year his *Poèmes choisis* was published in Montreal. One of the founding members of the Académie canadienne-française, Grandbois has also received the Prix Duvernay (1950), the Lorne Pierce Prize for poetry (1954), the Prix France-Canada (for *Poèmes*, published in 1963), and the prestigious Médaille d'or de l'Académie canadienne-française for his life's work.

Long considered one of Quebec's most important poets—a special issue of the literary magazine *Liberté* was devoted to his work in 1960—Grandbois also distinguished himself as a writer of short stories. *Avant le chaos*, published in 1945, is widely regarded as one of the first hints of

Quebec's emergence into the harsh, realistic light of the modern. "Fleur-de-Mai," translated here by Matt Cohen, has been taken from that collection, and was also included in Adrien Thério's influential anthology *Conteurs canadiens-français* (1965). A work of great poetic intensity and psychological insight, it is one Grandbois's most original and exotic works.

Grandbois died in March 1975. A book of his unpublished works, *Délivrance du jour et autres inédits*, illustrated with drawings by the author, was published posthumously in 1980.

༷

"Fleur-de-Mai" is a translation of "Fleur-de-Mai" published in *Avant le chaos suivi de quatre nouvelles inédites* (Montreal: Éditions H.M.H., 1964).

The boy's gong was truly and excessively loud. When he came into the small salon for the first-class passengers, where for the tenth time I was trying to light a cigarette limp with humidity, he redoubled his infernal clanging. I was alone. The room might have been twelve feet square. Perhaps fifteen. The boy stayed in the doorway, his torso naked, legs bare, beating his metallic disc as though he wanted to smash it in. I signalled him to stop but that only made him bang louder. Then I shouted at him—a few offensive and energetic insults—no success. Finally I got up, grabbed him by the shoulders, turned him around and quickly gave him a few kicks somewhere, but gently, gently, because I am not an uncivilized brute. He ran out to the gangway and said to me:

"Me love gong. Me love gong."

Then, with a laugh, he disappeared—meanwhile continuing to make his awful racket.

The captain's table was decorated with giant, fleshy orchids. The captain was laughing. Everyone laughed in East Asia. Except old men and children. The captain said to me:

"It seems you don't particularly care for the sound of the gong."

"On the contrary, I like it a lot," I replied. "But this gong boy seems to be trying to compete with the trumpets of Jericho."

"You're in a bad mood."

"Perhaps. I also have a bit of a fever."

"So that's it . . ."

We each drank a whisky, strong and with ice. It's not the best medicine for malaria but it's an excellent way to take care of the symptoms. For a while.

The captain and I were old friends. We had just spent a few days together isolated like rats on the island of Shameen, in the very heart of Canton. All around the island, Canton seethed with riots, spitting out hatred and death. Every bridge was protected by barbed wire flanked with machine guns manned by barefoot soldiers in ragged uniforms, screaming, gesticulating, itching to shoot. At night, from the roof of the hotel, we could see the monstrous purple flowers of fires rising from every part of the city. On the evening of the fifth day, following some mysterious negotiations, we had been allowed back on the boat. The Ngao-men was an old hulk of six hundred tonnes that went back and forth between Canton and Macao. There were three first-class cabins, the small salon, the officers' wardroom. As for the rest, the steerage was in the hold.

The captain said to me, "We won't be arriving in Macao until tomorrow evening. I've had to modify my course towards the southwest. The waters are infested by pirates. As soon as there's a problem they spring up like mushrooms after a warm rain."

"It's all part of the job," I replied, just to say something.

"Yes . . . It's the job . . . But I have been navigating these coasts for twenty years. I know every nook and cranny. I . . . I'm getting bored. I feel that I'm not a sailor anymore but a bureaucrat. The kind of incident you've just experienced is becoming more and more frequent, with the exactness of a clock or the seasons. The most amazing thing would be if, one fine day, a lasting calm began. That would be a change from methodical and organized disorder."

Again the boy filled our glasses. I asked the captain, "Why don't you request a change of command?"

"Because . . . because it's too late. I'm sixty years old. I'm married. My wife and I have a small villa in Macao. There are flowers all around. In fact, I'm counting on you to come visit us . . . In all likelihood that's where I'll die . . . I was born in Noordwijk, on the North Sea. I will die in Macao, in the South Seas. That's how life is."

We heard the gong again. The captain, laughing, said to me, "You can see that my gong boy takes his job seriously. That is how he makes himself feel important. When he strikes his instrument he believes he is the Master of the World. There are two cabin passengers, but he plays for two hundred. Sometimes we have no passengers at all. But he bangs away just the same . . ."

That was when Fleur-de-Mai appeared. She was short, very thin, and her face was strikingly beautiful. She was dressed in a dark blue silk tunic embroidered in gold. Her arms were crossed, her hands sunk into her wide sleeves. Like a mother superior addressing her novices. She bowed slightly to the captain. The captain introduced us. He had suddenly become very ceremonious.

We sat down at the table. The boys were busy. The captain spoke only to direct the serving of the meal. Sometimes, between courses, she raised her eyes to the captain or myself. She had an extraordinarily serious expression. Her movements while eating were so graceful, so delicate, that she could be imagined picking lilies at the edge of a perfumed fountain. When the dinner was finished she bowed and left us, preceded by the headwaiter. They served the cognac.

"She is sixteen years old," the captain told me.

We were stretched out on the poop deck, the captain and I. The night air was exceptionally mild. A reddish moon, with halos from the northern lights, swung back and forth through the rigging. Sometimes a big junk would cross our path, its sail like the underside of the wing of a monstrous bat, and we could see naked men crouched around a fire on the deck, gleaming and immobile like bronze statues. The humidity of the South drowned the line of the horizon. We were adrift on a sea without beginning or end. A sea of eternal space. Nothing existed. Neither Canton, nor Macao, nor Noordwijk, nor Paris, nor Quebec. Nothing, no one. A sort of slow march across ghostly limbos.

Suddenly we heard light footsteps, and Fleur-de-Mai was with us. The captain invited her to sit down. Two, three hours passed. Without any of us saying a word. The darkness of the night began to lift. Fleur-de-Mai got up and spoke a few words in Chinese to the captain. He said to me, "Miss Cheng wants to know if you would like to hear a short poem by Siu Tche-mo . . ."

Fleur-de-Mai looked at the sea and began to her recital. She had a strange and veiled voice, a sweet contralto.

> Go away, World of Mankind, go away!
> Alone, I stand at the summit of a high mountain;
> Go away, World of Mankind, go away!
> Here I stay face-to-face with the immense dome of the stars.
>
> Go away, birthplace of my dream, go away!
> I throw the jade cup of illusion and it breaks;
> Go away, birthplace of my dream, go away!
> Smiling, I accept the compliments of the wind
> Of the mountain and the ocean waves.
>
> Go away, everything, go away!
> In front of me mountain peaks pierce the sky;
> Go away, Everyone, go away!
> In front of me flows the vastness of the vast.

Then Fleur-de-Mai disappeared. The next day she didn't come to the captain's table. She was ill. The sun was setting when we arrived at Macao. Already the city of all sins was turning red in the light of its fires. I went to say goodbye to the captain, who repeated his invitation to me.

"I'm on compulsory leave," he told me. "I have to wait until Canton becomes peaceful again before recommencing my job. I'm going to trim my rosebushes."

On the flowered terrace of the villa, after lunch, the captain's wife, who was half Chinese and half Portuguese, served us perfumed tea. We were talking casually when the captain asked me, "What do you think of my goddaughter?"

"Your goddaughter?"

"Yes, Miss Cheng, Fleur-de-Mai."

"I would never have thought that . . ."

"I know, I know . . . In any case it's a secret I am asking you to be sure to keep, at least for the remainder of your stay in Macao, because if old Cheng found out, there would be trouble."

"Old Cheng?"

The captain lit his pipe.

"Old Cheng is Fleur-de-Mai's father. He is the richest and most respected man on the peninsula. He is more than generous to every charitable cause, regularly distributes rice, tea, and clothes to all the needy on the coast, and even makes sure that the dead are properly buried. In addition, he is a special adviser to the governor of the colony. An extremely important man. In books, is this kind of success not termed the crowning of a long life marked by noble deeds and high virtue?"

"Indeed," I replied politely.

But the captain insisted on continuing. "Indeed! No doubt. But sometimes, my dear young friend, sometimes even books make mistakes. And they mislead us, as well. Because old Cheng is the most disgusting piece of scum you can imagine. The worst pirate of the South Seas. Fifty years ago he was a coolie in Canton. He was a pickpocket, a pimp, a pirate. He became head of a gang. Soon he had a whole network of businesses that sold women and drugs. During the revolution of Dr. Sun, he got himself made a general. He bought, sold, repurchased, then sold again several armies. He went to the North where he joined up with several other warlords. In 1917 he supplied weapons and ammunition to the Germans; in 1920 to the White Russians; in 1923 to the Bolsheviks; in 1925, two sets of clients: the Northern armies and the Southern armies. Currently he is active in three scenes: Chiang Kai-shek, the communist army, and Japan. With him, the embassies and the consulates never know on which foot they're supposed to be dancing. I don't know whether he himself knows, but he is always in the right place. Here in Macao he controls the gaming houses, the theatres, the bordellos, the racetracks, drugs, alcohol, the private banks, and, it goes without saying, all of the region's politics, which are, I can assure you, complex in a way only Asia can be. He lives in Macao, under close guard, because if he shows up publicly here or in Hong Kong, his life would be worthless. Sometimes they find bombs in his palace gardens. But the boys are the ones who get blown up. So that's old Cheng. He is very respected and he is scrupulously observant of the rituals..."

"And the goddaughter?"

"The goddaughter, well, the old bandit, for reasons I don't know, several years ago entrusted her education to the nuns of X convent, in Hong Kong. Cheng trusts me. To the extent he can trust anyone, naturally. So that is why he has me look after her when she travels . . . But two months ago, unknown to her family, Fleur-de-Mai was baptized, and I was the godfather . . . That's the whole story. So, what do you think of her?"

"I . . . I think your goddaughter is an extremely serious young person. She has a way of looking at you . . . She almost intimidates me . . ."

The captain started laughing. Then he continued. "If I'm talking to you about her, it's because she has told me she wants to see you again. She will be inviting you . . . She asked me questions about you. She knows you are a Catholic and that you write."

"She knows many things," I replied to the captain. "However, my stay in Macao is too brief for me to be able to waste time paying visits to young society girls. I'd rather meet old Cheng."

"No doubt. But old Cheng has expressed no desire to see you."

"What's that supposed to mean?" I asked the captain.

"I haven't the slightest idea."

"And what would you do in my place?"

"You are free and over twenty-one. I never give advice. It's a waste of words."

"All right. I will tell the young lady that my many preoccupations unfortunately prohibit, that I am extremely sorry, etc. . . ."

"You are a sensible man," the captain said to me.

But the captain's wife was smiling.

Someone knocked at the door. I called for whoever it was to come in. A boy handed me a letter. I opened it. Miss Fleur was informing me that tomorrow, at eleven o'clock, a car would arrive to take me to the residence. The boy didn't budge.

"Answer?" I asked him.

"Ya ya, mastah sah, answah."

I wrote to Fleur-de-Mai thanking her, that I regretted, that I was very sorry, etc., I put the sheet of paper in the envelope. Then I tore up the envelope and wrote that I accepted her gracious invitation with great pleasure.

The next day at eleven o'clock I got into a carriage pulled by two small, white horses. An old Chinese woman was huddled in the back. This was Fleur-de-Mai's governess. The "amah." She looked sullen and very unhappy. We crossed the Praia Grande at a trot and came to a wide boulevard shaded by royal palms and carob trees with brilliant green leaves. There were villas along the side, faded pink, pale ochre, faded blue, buried under heavy vegetation. Then the road began to rise and twist, sinuous as a snake. Suddenly the amah began to talk, her tone plaintive.

"The Master has a terrible temper, truly terrible, he mustn't find out . . . I would be finished. I tried to persuade Miss Fleur. I begged her, cried . . . I'm just a miserable old woman . . . but what could I do against the wrath of the Master? Tell me the truth, what would I be able to do?"

And she started to emit small muffled sobs. "Ah, I am a miserable old woman, a guilty criminal . . . I didn't know how to stand up to Miss Fleur . . . I couldn't stand up to her . . ."

She fell silent. We continued to climb the hill. After a while I saw the walled enclosure of the residence. The amah, who had stopped crying, said to me, "The Master has gone down to the city to visit the governor. A servant is watching for his departure from the palace. Others are along the road. We will be signalled in advance. You will return along the road we came on. The Master has a powerful car and will take the main road."

She spoke like a general giving his officers a lesson in strategy. We went along the wall and the carriage stopped in front of a heavy door made of dark wood. We got out. The amah shook the bronze ring and the door opened. Like sesame. We were in a long, covered walkway. On either side were marble-paved courtyards, gardens of flowers, fountains surrounded by willow trees, ponds filled with pink lotus, pavilions in the shape of pagodas. The amah led me to one of these pavilions. It was shaded by a giant banyan tree. I went into a tiled room, very high, its ceiling of crossed beams among which lounged brightly coloured painted dragons. Scrolls hung from the walls, covered with brushed characters. There were purple-bordered black lacquer tables, chairs, a divan, knickknacks in jade and ivory, and an enormous Buddha, smooth and gleaming.

Then Fleur-de-Mai appeared. She was perfectly beautiful. She bowed, motioned me to sit down. A boy brought a tray with tea. She officiated with the precise and elegant movements I had admired at the captain's table. We drank the tea. The boy took away the tray.

She was sitting opposite me.

In her sweet contralto voice she said, "The captain has undoubtedly told you, I authorized him to do so, that I am a Catholic..."

"He did," I replied.

"I must return to my convent in eight days. I will be there for three more months. Then I will have to come back here, to my father's house."

I must have betrayed my surprise by some movement because she immediately added, "You are undoubtedly wondering why I am telling you these things. Here is the answer. I must return in three months but... but I cannot come back."

"—"

"I can't come back because I am to be married. My husband has been chosen. I have never met him. According to the custom, I will not see him until after the marriage. I know nothing about him except that he is from Yunan and that his father is rich... I cannot come back because I cannot marry him. And I don't want to. I am a Christian."

Her mouth quivered. Like that of a child about to cry.

"I am a Christian. I will have to go and live with his family. He will forbid me the free worship of my God. He will live like my brothers..."

"—"

"I have three brothers. All three are married. They live here, in the residence. Their wives are my friends. They are delicate and gracious. My brothers spend their nights going out to theatres and gaming houses. They have taken concubines who also are lodged here, in the most beautiful pavilions... Their wives cry in secret. What can I say to console them? I don't want their fate. I don't want to cry in secret..."

Her face was that of a wounded angel. Her eyes were lowered. She got up, opened a jewellery box, came back to me holding out a large envelope. I was bitterly regretting that I had come, that I had given in to my stupid curiosity.

"The Captain told me you will be spending time in Shanghai. Take this picture. Look at it sometimes. I've been told that... that I am beautiful... I feel very ashamed talking to you this way. But I have to. And if, three months from now, you..."

The amah burst into the room, very agitated. "The signal, the signal has been given. The Master just left the governor's palace."

Fleur-de-Mai continued, very quickly. "If, three months from now, you send this photograph to the captain with your address on the other side, he won't understand what it means but I will know... And I will set out for Shanghai."

She turned her head away and added in a low voice: "I would be a faithful and obedient wife for you..."

Then she raised her eyes to me. She was crying. She tried to smile. I left. The amah led me back to sesame and I went back along the road to Macao. Later, in Shanghai, I wrote to the captain. But I kept the picture of Fleur-de-Mai.

Ringuet
Translated by Wayne Grady

Happiness

Philippe Panneton, who wrote under the pseudonym Ringuet, was born in Trois-Rivières on April 30, 1895, to a family that had first settled in the region in 1640. At the age of eighteen, he went to Montreal to work as a reporter, then one year later enrolled at the Université de Montréal to study medicine. In 1920 he went to Paris to specialize in ear-nose-and-throat disorders, later returning to Quebec to set up eye clinics in Montreal and Joliette. Under his real name, publishing in several leading periodicals, newspapers, and medical journals, he quickly became famous in Quebec as an iconoclastic thinker and physician. Also under his own name he published in 1925, in collaboration with Louis Francoeur, *Littératures . . . à la manière de*, a satirical spoof on many of the period's leading literary lights, including Henri Bourassa, Lionel Groulx, and Camille Roy.

His first novel, *Trente arpents* (*Thirty Acres*), published in 1938 in Paris under the nom-de-plume Ringuet, was a brilliant but controversial twist on the traditional Quebec novel of *terroir*, or the homestead, whose assumptions, perpetrated for the most part by the clergy, were that adamantine faithfulness to the land, the family, and religion was rural Quebec's only defence against encroachment from outside the province. Ringuet, who refused to idealize or romanticize life on the land, suggested that traditional attitudes merely guaranteed that Quebec would be left behind in a future of rapid change and growing internationalism.

Ringuet's later novels, *Fausse monnaie* (1947), *Le Poids du jour* (1949) and *L'Amiral et le Facteur* (1954), are less known and, according to Gérard Bessette, "far from possessing the vision of his first book."

"Le bonheur," translated here as "Happiness" by Wayne Grady, is a tale of urban despair, taken from

Ringuet's only book of short stories, *L'Héritage* (1946). The story suggests that the only route to happiness in working-class Montreal was through madness and delusion. In some ways, it justifies several of Ringuet's severest critics, who accused him of a bitter and fruitless pessimism. But "Happiness" also reveals the author's gift for exact observation, meticulous writing, and his delight in a subtle, black humour.

Panneton died in Montreal in December 1960, on the eve of a literary and social revolution he would greatly have enjoyed.

∽

"Happiness" is a translation of "Le bonheur" published in *L'héritage et autres contes* (Montreal: les Éditions Variétés, 1946).

First there was marriage, then fifteen years of hardship with his wife, a tall, thin, bony woman with a sharp tongue and a pallid face, as though she'd been blanched by a lifetime in the kitchen over tubs full of hot water. They'd had eleven children, five of whom survived, miraculously. That year they were all living in four rooms on the second floor of a tenement on Labrecque; he often wondered what kept the building from collapsing into its own cluttered yard, not that he cared. They were moving in May anyway, throwing together their few belongings, their three-legged chairs, their sunken mattresses, looking for a new place to stay as they did every year. It was more than an annual habit: it was a necessity. They hadn't paid the rent on this hovel. His wife had quarrelled with everyone within earshot. His children had broken three windows in two weeks. Every February the search began again. His wife didn't seem to mind. It gave her an excuse to stick her nose into some other family's dirty linen, under the pretext of inspecting their apartment. For a while he kept track of their years together by recalling their addresses; lately, he was beginning to forget some of them.

His whole life revolved around the textile plant, where for ten hours a day he took his part in the thunderous ballet of bobbins and spools. Every night he walked home with his ears still throbbing with the machine's deafening drone. He ate his dinner, read his newspaper, heard the doors slam as his daughters went out on their nightly prowls. Then he went to bed and slept like a dead man until morning, when he got up and left for work.

And yet he wouldn't say he was unhappy. Nothing in the world existed for him except his vertiginous machine and the safe harbour of his kitchen, where he sat at night amid relative quiet. He enjoyed his lunch breaks, sitting with his co-workers, his lunch-box perched on his lap, telling stories and cracking jokes with men who knew the parry and thrust of a good conversation. And he loved getting his pay on Fridays, walking home with the envelope in his pocket, imagining he could buy anything he wanted, even if the feeling didn't last long; he wouldn't be home ten minutes before the few dollars had disappeared, snatched up in his wife's cold fingers and dropped into the grocer's till.

Every night he left the factory at the same time as the owner, and each time he passed through the gates he saw the owner's limousine waiting by the curb, the silent, disdainful chauffeur sitting in the driver's seat. He'd slow down as he passed that car, take a long look inside, his empty lunchpail dangling in his hand. The car symbolized for him the whole idea of being rich, it was what he thought of when he heard the word "happiness." He'd drink in the smoky windows, the fenders polished like mirrors, the narrow hood like the muzzle of a greyhound, the brilliant chrome. It was perhaps the only time he ever gave a thought to his lot in life, to the difference between himself and other people. It made him think, passing that car. It made him think, and it made him feel cheap and ashamed.

Cars were his secret passion, a strange and private love that was forever unrequited. Saturday nights he would snatch up the newspaper supplement and look for the car ads; he would search through them with the haste of one who felt pain coming on and couldn't wait to get it over with. He would caress the new models with his eyes, only at the most luxurious ones, those that cost three, four thousand dollars; five years' salary! What he liked about them was the way they fed his bitterness. He would feel almost overcome with delight when an ad for a new, even more expensive car came along to haunt his Sunday.

But he never spoke about this to anyone.

One night something snapped in him; it was as though the thread of his thought had slipped off one of the bobbins at work, spinning along in their regular fashion, each one identical to the one next to it, each year undifferentiated from the year before, undefinable, and he went from there to the break in the thread that no spinner could mend. The thing was vague in his mind at first, and out of habit he reached out to return the errant thread to its proper place on the spool.

But then what had started out as an indefinite idea, a thing without shape, began to firm up, to come to a certainty whose roots reached deep down into the depths of his troubled being.

It was that he suddenly knew, knew with absolute clarity, that before long he would own his car; a luxury car with chrome that shone like the Milky Way, with a silhouette as sleek as that of any greyhound.

He felt as though he had been hit between the eyes by a bright light, with such sudden intensity that he stopped eating, sat there stupefied as he watched the idea take shape in his brain, an idea that was almost painful in its precision, its brutality.

He thought about it all that night with an eagerness that returned to him again and again as he lay in his bed.

He thought about it all the next day at work, and when he left the factory that night, he was still thinking about it so hard that he stopped right beside the owner's limousine and stared at it with an almost possessive eye. Even the chauffeur looked at him in surprise—which made him hurry along, not wanting anyone to guess his secret. He wanted to keep the pleasure of it, the surprise of it, all to himself, until . . . imagine what his wife would say, what the neighbours would think, when he drove up to the door in a car a hundred times more beautiful than . . . and driven by a chauffeur, why not, a chauffeur wearing a golden uniform, like the car. A longing as for revenge floated up from deep within him, though it remained very obscure.

That night at dinner he started laughing; it was a private sort of laugh that made his thin shoulders shake under his frayed, woollen vest of which he was no longer aware. His children looked at him with a bold curiosity. His wife pointed her astonished chin in his direction.

Three weeks later he was taken to Saint-Jean-de-Dieu Hospital in a taxi. As he stepped out of the car, he turned to the driver and told him to stop in at the Bank of Montreal on his way back and pick up a hundred thousand dollars, for a tip.

They had caught it early, they said, and there was some hope for recovery. The chief psychiatrist himself was interested in the case; he'd been experimenting with a new drug that seemed to be justifying the most extravagant claims made for it.

The patient was in a pitiable state. He spent his days in the common room, surrounded by inoffensive idiots, adding up his fortune on stray bits of paper that came his way, or counting on his fingers. Millions and millions of dollars. When one of his companions came up to him, as happened from time to time, he would tear off a slip of paper and sign with an authoritative flourish, as though it were nothing, a cheque for a thousand, two thousand dollars, which the recipient would take and stare at for some time before popping it into his mouth and swallowing it with murmurs of pleasure.

He was enjoying his stay at this luxurious establishment. He strolled about with a glorious and condescending mien. He took an enormous, not to say morbid, delight in his surroundings. Nothing in his view retained its ordinary human dimensions. Every meal was a feast; every intern's visit a state occasion, a kind of audience.

Twice a week he was escorted with great ceremony to the clinic for his treatment. In the car he was friendly with his attendants. At the clinic he held out his arm magnanimously for the injection, which was administered by an aide whose duty and pleasure it was to serve him. Doctors, nurses, and other menials maintained a respectful distance. There were servants everywhere; one took him by the arm, to steady him, another offered him a cotton swab. When the ritual was accomplished, he said thank you and smiled to everyone, to show that despite his wealth he could still be affable to ordinary people. Then he was driven back to the hospital and seen to his room, at the entrance to which he would turn and dismiss his flunkeys and hangers-on with an amiable but categorical wave of his hand, exactly as he had so often seen the factory owner dismiss the chauffeur.

A passion for generosity overcame him which, once satisfied, was enflamed again by each new act of generosity, as each mouthful of food to a starving man opens vast new gulfs of hunger. In his entire life he had never received a single thing he hadn't earned a hundred times over, and even then he had never had a single thing he could afford to give away. Now he gave in to a veritable orgy of largesse.

It started, of course, with cars. He gave them away wholesale: Packards, Lincoln Zephyrs, Mercedes Benzes, Isotta-Fraschinis. One each to each of his former fellow employees, two to each of their children. He gave his wife a platinum-plated Pullman Car; and so that she would continue to respect and honour him, he gave her a weekly allowance of one million dollars. When he thought about all the happiness he was spreading, he remembered an epitaph he had read somewhere and which he now thought applied to him; some day, he hoped, they would say of him: "He died doing good deeds!"

While waiting for the cruise-ship *Normandy* to be redecorated in preparation for his trip around the world, he had consented to spend a few days in this, well, this sort of retreat, among these poor unfortunates whose lot might be improved by his munificence.

At first, the nun inspired in him only a feeling of mistrust: so much gentle patience seemed to him to be a cover. Surely, he thought, she only wanted to get her hands on some part of his fortune—maybe the diamond mines he could see from his window, protected from thieves by stout iron bars. Then he realized that the theft of a few million would hardly put a dent in his immeasurable resources; and without saying a word, casting upon her what he thought was a forgiving eye, he let her make off with what she could. Thus did the madman and the nun regard one another with mutual generosity and pity.

From time to time, an unsummoned memory of the thundering factory would come back to him, and of the threading machine in whose thrall he had spent so much of his life. When the roaring started, he would sit down on the asylum floor and go through the old motions. But before long his imagination would carry him off again in an immense confusion of wings, and he would find himself calculating tenfold increases, his already incalculable fortune. The factory! He'd bought that ages ago, paid for it in cash and given it away to Louis, the janitor, who was a little soft in the head!

And he would start to laugh, a deep, delirious, maniacal laughter that rose up from his chest and lifted the eyebrows of those working beside him making paper hats out of old wallpaper samples, or trying to listen to the words of the Archangel Gabriel, who had taken up residence in their lower intestine.

His treatment went on for eleven weeks without discernable results, and the chief psychiatrist was beginning to have his doubts when a gradual improvement in his condition began to manifest itself. The first sign was that the patient began to appear calmer, more taciturn. Then he began to exhibit brief spells of rationality, as faint glimmers of light begin to appear at the end of a long, dark night. Bit by bit, one could say that the patient was beginning to become aware of himself as a sentient entity; that he was becoming capable of touching, albeit with a hesitant and perhaps incredulous finger, at least the surface reality of his day-to-day dealings. And as his mind slowly re-established its grasp of everyday logic, he began to be ashamed of his own madness. Instead of the defiant, skeptical smirk that hid a triumphant laughter, there began to appear a frown of concentration.

After five more months of injections, the doors to the asylum were finally opened onto the real world. The chief psychiatrist added another name to his already impressive list of patients who had been successfully treated by his new method. A great advance in the treatment of insanity had been made, a new era in psychotherapy was born.

They took him back at the factory; they didn't even ask where he'd been. The machines hadn't slowed down a fraction of an instant while he was away; they still churned out their fifteen hundred spindles a week, and it soon seemed even to him that he had never ceased to be a part of their interminable piercing rhythm.

The months he had spent in the asylum left no more residue in him than a night of troubled sleep, than a dream peopled with strange fantasmagoric creatures. A few fragments stuck in his brain, as upon wakening the scattered and confused images from a dream might wade through one's consciousness: the glint of sunlight on the polished ironwork of a bench; a row of glass bottles on a counter; and most often, since he had been declared well, the brisk, smiling face of the chief psychiatrist as he signed the papers that had released him from that house of horrors.

Every morning and every evening he walked from his home to the factory and from the factory back to his home on Labrecque. On the first pay-day his wife was waiting for him at the door, eager to grab the money that was needed to settle their accounts with the baker and the grocer.

And every night as he left the factory he brushed against the owner's limousine, with the arrogant chauffeur sitting in the driver's seat as immobile as a mannequin in a shop window. Every night the car was there, as if it had never moved at all, hadn't budged an inch all the time he'd been away; as if it had sat there waiting, cold and patient, for his return.

Slowly, slyly, it all began to come back to him. The dinner waiting for him every night at the same end of the same though somewhat dingier tablecloth; the newspaper minutely scrutinized before going to bed to escape, for a few hours at least, the constant railing of his wife against the injustice of her embittered life. And all the while his daughters fighting over a pair of nylons that cost forty-nine cents, and his oldest son coming in swearing and smelling of drink.

He used to laugh, if rarely; but now it seemed to him that he had laughed himself out during his captivity, that all the laughter in his life had been used up in that place. Those miraculous injections, they seemed to have cured him of laughter as well as of madness.

Sometimes, when no one was watching, he would look at the car ads in the newspaper. But his eyes, gliding down the columns, sliding over the sleek machines, would see nothing but his aging wife, the sleeves of her soiled housecoat trailing in the water as she did the supper dishes; the beds piled with soiled linen and stained sheets; the grimy windows of the sheds whose grey boards blocked out the horizon. When he was with other people he would wince if anyone mentioned his absence; but deep within himself he felt a growing remorse for the illusions he had bitten into and lost, for the sweet deliriums he had tasted.

His awakened memory gave him a better idea of what had happened to him. One day, when his wife was complaining about the treatment she had received at the hands of the local butcher, to whom they owed money, he found himself recalling the day he had bought the Mount Royal Hotel because he needed a place to keep his things. When he realized with a start that the memory was nothing but a perverse dream, he blushed with shame; but privately, although he was perfectly conscious of the falseness of it, and although he forbade himself to slip back into its tantalizing warmth, he still felt profoundly sad at having to give it up.

Soon he began to re-create his mirages in a deliberate attempt to escape into their unreal, magical world. Before going to sleep at night, he would close his eyes and force his brain to run down their forbidden corridors, and when with feverish efforts he succeeded in conjuring up a chimera, he would draw it in so deeply that he became intoxicated with it. But these nocturnal chases gave him only a moment's satisfaction; he no longer believed in their reality. They came and went without sustenance, leaving nothing but a bitter taste in his mouth.

In the end he became even more aware than ever of the miserableness of his life. His precious dreams existed in his own past, and so could no longer shield him from the reality of his present misfortune. From that moment on he was banished from illusion, and bound to live in regret. The corners of his mouth drooped sadly.

One morning as he arrived at work, the chief psychiatrist from the asylum passed the factory in his car. The two men recognized each other and waved. At first he was filled with respect for this influential doctor who held in his careful hands the happiness, the health, the very life of so many people. But then the doctor's face reminded him too strongly of the wonderful vacation he had taken at the oasis of his illusions. Here was the man who had sent him back out into the desert!

The doctor had published a paper on the treatment of certain mental disorders with injections of iridium chloride. Out of forty-five cases treated, twenty-eight patients left the asylum completely cured; half of the rest showed marked improvement and were able to resume a relatively normal life, even to the point of going back to work. The success of the treatment had made the doctor famous. His photograph was in all the papers and he had been appointed a full professor at the Faculty of Medicine.

In time, the former patient realized that he was one of the twenty-eight who had been completely cured. He also realized that that meant there were twenty-seven others out there who, like him, felt as though their hearts had been torn out of them by wild dogs. According to the newspapers, the doctor's clinic had received a generous grant from the government, so that the miracle cure could be made available to a much wider clientele: so many fortunate people to be dragged from the Jerusalem of their illusions and tossed into the Gehenna of reality!

He felt his duty flood into him like a surging tide. His tongue burned with the acrid joy of the sacrifice he was about to make.

The taxi ride to the doctor's house took only a few minutes. Fortunately, it was the doctor himself who opened the door. The knife deflected off a rib, barely missing the heart, and pierced the left lung.

Anne Hébert
Translated by Sheila Fischman

THE TORRENT

Anne Hébert was born August 1, 1916, in Sainte-Catherine-de-Fossambault, the daughter of literary critic Maurice Hébert and the first cousin of the great Québécois poet Hector Saint-Denys-Garneau. A childhood illness prevented her from attending school, and she was educated at home by her parents. With her cousin, she began writing poetry and stories at an early age; in 1939 she began publishing in several literary journals, including *Le Canada français* and *Amérique française*. She attended Collège Notre-Dame-de-Bellevue and Mérici, and in 1942—the year before Saint-Denys-Garneau's death—she published her first book of poems, *Les Songes en équilibre*, which won the Prix David.

She began working as a scriptwriter for Radio-Canada and the National Film Board in 1950. Four years later she made her first trip to Paris; she stayed three years, then began dividing her time between France and Montreal, until finally moving permanently to Paris in 1967.

Hébert has written many important novels. The first, *Les Chambres de bois* (1958; *The Silent Rooms*, 1974), won the Prix France-Canada. Her subsequent novels include *Kamouraska* (1970), *Les Enfants du sabbat* (1975), *Héloïse* (1981), *Les Fous de bassan* (1982; *In the Shadow of the Wind*, 1983), *Le Premier jardin* (1988; *The First Garden*, 1990) and *L'Enfant chargé de songes* (1992; *Burden of Dreams*, 1993), the last four translated by Sheila Fischman, who has a beautiful affinity for Hébert's delicate but incisive prose style.

The short story "Au bord du torrent" was published in October 1947 in *Amérique française*, and appeared in book form in 1950, when *Le Torrent* won the Belgian Royal Academy's prize for the best book in French by a non-Belgian. Its theme is the death of the old régime, personified by the dark and dominating mother of the hero, François Perrault. Often called Quebec's first modern short story, it occupies the same niche in Quebec as do the early stories of Alice Munro in English Canada. The critic Ben-Zion Shek has noted that "Le Torrent" is written in the form of "a powerful allegory . . . in starkly tragic and violent images, pessimistically announcing that the breakdown of the old would not necessarily usher in a new, freer social climate," and it is true that Perrault does not seem to be significantly better off following his mother's death. But after the publication of "Le Torrent," there was little doubt that the old order was gone, and that a new kind of literature was being written.

"Le Torrent," first translated by Gwendolyn Moore in 1973, is presented here in a new translation by Sheila Fischman.

∽

"The Torrent" is a translation of "Le Torrent" published in *Le Torrent* (Montreal: Éditions Beauchemin, 1950); first appeared as "Au bord du torrent" in *Amérique française*, October 1947.

I

I was a child bereft of the world. A will that took precedence over my own decreed that I was to renounce any possession during this life. I touched the world in fragments, only those that were immediately indispensable to me and that were taken away as soon as their usefulness had ended: the notebook I was to open, but not the table on which it lay; the corner of the stable to be cleaned, not the hen that perched on the windowsill; and never, never the countryside that was offered through the window. I would see my mother's big hand when she brought it up to strike me, but I did not see my mother in her entirety, from head to foot. I only had a sense of her terrible grandeur and it chilled me.

I did not have a childhood. I have no memory of any leisure before the singular experience of my deafness. My mother worked without respite and I accompanied my mother, like a tool in her hands. After she rose with the sun, the hours of her day fitted together so precisely there was no room left for any recreation.

Aside from the lessons she gave me until I entered boarding school, my mother did not speak to me. There was no room for speech in her order. If she was to depart from that order, I had first to commit some infraction or other. Which is to say that my mother spoke to me only to reprimand me, before she punished me.

On the matter of study, there too everything was counted, calculated, with never a free day and no vacation. Once the hour for lessons had ended, utter silence would creep over my mother's face again. Her mouth would close, strictly, hermetically, as if held that way by a bolt drawn from inside.

As for me, I would lower my gaze, relieved that I no longer had to follow the operation of the powerful jaws and thin lips that uttered, with each syllable enunciated clearly, words like "punishment," "God's justice," "damnation," "Hell," "discipline," "original sin," and above all this precise statement that kept coming back like a leitmotif:

"One must master oneself through and through. No one has any idea of the evil force within us! Do you hear me, François? And let me tell you, I shall master you..."

And then I would start to shiver and tears would fill my eyes, for I knew very well what my mother was about to add:

"François, look me in the eye..."

That torture could go on for a long time. My mother would stare at me mercilessly while I would be unable to meet her gaze. And then as she got to her feet she would add:

"Very well, François, the hour is up... But the time will come when I shall remember your bad grace..."

In fact, my mother recorded in meticulous detail every one of my lapses so that one fine day, when I least expected it, she could draw up a tally. And then, just as I thought I was going to get away, she would swoop down on me, implacably, having forgotten nothing, detailing day by day, hour by hour, the very things I had thought were the best hidden.

I did not understand why my mother did not punish me then and there. Especially because I vaguely felt that it was difficult for her to control herself. From what came afterwards I realized she was acting that way out of self-discipline, in order to "master herself," and also, I am certain, to make a stronger impression on me by establishing as firmly as possible the hold that she has over me.

There was another reason too that I did not learn about until much later.

I have said that my mother kept herself constantly busy, in the house or the stable or the fields. To thrash me she would wait for a respite.

The other day I found in the shed, on a beam behind an old lantern, a little notebook that had once belonged to my mother. In it was carefully written the schedule of her days. One Monday she had been intending to spread the sheets on the grass to bleach them; but then as I remember, it suddenly started to rain. On that same Monday, I saw in her notebook, that peculiar strange woman had crossed out: "Bleach sheets" and added in the margin, "Beat François."

We were always alone. I was about to turn twelve and had not yet gazed upon a human face aside from the moving reflection of my own features when, in summer, I bent down to drink from a stream. As for my mother, I knew only the lower part of her face. My gaze dared not travel any higher, up to the wrath-filled eyes and the broad forehead I would later see hideously ravaged.

Her autocratic chin, her tormented mouth, despite the attitude of calm she tried to impose through her silence, her black blouse like a breastplate, with no soft place where a child's head could snuggle: such was the maternal universe in which I learned, so early, harshness and rejection.

We lived too far from the village even to go to Mass. That did not prevent me from sometimes spending the better part of Sunday kneeling on the floor, in punishment for some offense. That was, I believe, my mother's way of sanctifying the Lord's day—at my expense.

I never saw my mother pray. But I suspected her of doing so sometimes, locked inside her bedroom. At that time I was so dependent upon my mother that her slightest inner movement had repercussions on me. Needless to say I understood nothing about the woman's own drama, but I could sense, in the way that one can sense a coming storm, even the most deeply hidden of the sudden changes in her mood. On nights when I thought my mother was praying, I dared not move on my pallet. The silence was deathly still. I was anticipating I know not what torment that would sweep aside everything else, dragging me along with my mother, linking me forever to her dire fate.

The desire I felt grew from day to day and it weighed on me like nostalgia: to see at close range and in detail a human face. I tried to examine my mother surreptitiously, but nearly always she would turn towards me sharply and my courage would fail.

I resolved to go in search of the face of a man, not daring to hope for a child, and vowing I would run away if it were a woman. To do so, I decided to position myself at the side of the main road. Surely someone would pass by.

Our house stood well away from any thoroughfare, in the middle of a property covered with woods, with fields, and with water in all its forms, from calm streams to the agitated torrent.

I walked through the sugar bush and across the rocky fields that my mother persisted in ploughing, gritting her teeth as she clutched the handles which the shock sometimes forced her to drop. The work had killed our old horse, Éloi.

I had not thought the road was so far away. I was afraid of getting lost. What would my mother say when she came in from the milking and realized I was not there? Anticipating them, I shrank beneath her blows, but I continued walking. My yearning was too urgent, too desperate.

After crossing the burnt-out clearing where I came with my mother every summer to pick blueberries, I found myself facing the road. Out of breath I stopped short, as if a hand had touched my brow. I wanted to cry. The road stretched out before me sad and pitiful in the sunlight, soulless and dead. Where were the processions I had imagined I would see there? There must be footsteps on this ground that were neither mine nor my mother's. What had become of them? In what direction had they gone? I saw not a single print. The road must certainly be dead.

Not daring to walk on it, I followed the ditch. Suddenly I stumbled over a body lying there and landed in the mud. I got up, filled with consternation at the thought of the dirt on my clothes, and then I saw the hideous man beside me. He must have been sleeping and now he was slowly sitting up. Rooted to the spot I did not move, expecting to be killed at the very least. I could not even find the strength to shield my face with my arm.

The man was filthy. On his skin and clothes there were streaks of dried and fresh mud. His long hair merged with his beard, his moustache, and his enormous eyebrows, which fell over his eyes. Good Lord, what a face it was, made up of bristly hairs and spattered mud! I saw the mouth appear inside it, sticky, with yellow teeth. I tried to break away. The man held me by the arm. He grabbed hold of me as he struggled to his feet and made me fall head over heels.

The man laughed. His laughter was in keeping with the rest of him. As revolting as he was. Again I tried to get away. He forced me to sit on the edge of the ditch, beside him. I could smell his musky odour mingled with the stench of the swamp. Very softly, I made my act of contrition and I thought about God's judgment that would come after the terror and disgust this man inspired in me. His heavy, grimy hand was on my shoulder.

"How old are you, young fellow?"

Without waiting for my reply he added:

"Know any stories? You don't, eh . . . I do, though . . ."

He wrapped his arm around my shoulders. I tried to free myself. Laughing, he gripped me even more tightly. His laugh was very close to my cheek. And then I spied my mother standing before us. She was holding the big stick she used for driving home the cows. For the first time I saw her in her entirety. Tall, strong, clean, more powerful than I had ever imagined.

"Let go of that child!"

Surprised, the man lumbered to his feet. He seemed as fascinated by my mother as I was. She turned to me and in the tone of voice you use with a dog, shouted:

"Home, François!"

Slowly, feeling my legs give way beneath me, I got back on the path through the burnt clearing. The man was talking to my mother. It seemed that he knew her. In his drawling voice he said:

"If it isn't the lovely Claudine! Fancy seeing you here . . . Left the village because of the boy, did you? Fine young lad he is . . . yes, indeed . . . Seeing you here . . . Everyone thought you were dead . . ."

"Go away!" roared my mother.

"Good old Claudine, used to be so sociable . . . Don't get mad now . . ."

"Don't you dare speak to me like that, you pig!"

Then I heard the snapping sound of a blow, followed by a thud that marked a fall. I turned around. My mother was standing, immense, at the edge of the woods, the cudgel shuddering in her hand, the man stretched out at her feet.

She must have used the big end of the stick to bash him on the head.

Big Claudine (that was how I started mentally thinking of my mother) assured herself the man was alive, then she picked up her skirts, jumped across the ditch, and set off again along the road to the house. I broke into a run. The echo of my startled footsteps rang out in my ears along with the sound of my mother's robust stride behind me.

She caught up with me near the house. Dragging me by one arm, she marched into the kitchen. She had thrown away her stick. I was so frightened, so exhausted, yet I could not help feeling an inexplicable curiosity and attraction. I believed obscurely that what was going to follow would be equal to what had just taken place. My senses, numbed by a constrained and monotonous life, were now awakening. I was living through a magnificent and terrifying adventure.

My mother said sharply:

"A human being is a fine thing, isn't it François? You must be glad you've finally seen a face up close. A tempting sight, isn't it?"

Dismayed to realize that my mother had been able to guess at a desire I'd never confided to her, I looked up at her, like someone who has lost all self-control. And it was with my distraught gaze held by her own that the whole conversation unfolded. I was paralyzed, mesmerized by big Claudine.

"The world isn't beautiful, François. You mustn't touch it. Renounce it, here and now, magnanimously. Don't wait. Do as you're told, without looking around. You are my son. You are the continuation of me. You will battle evil instincts until you achieve perfection."

Her eyes were shooting flames. Her entire upright being, standing in the centre of the room, was expressing a violence that could no longer contain itself, that rooted me there with both fear and admiration. She said again, her voice not so hard now, as if she were speaking to herself: "Self-possession . . . mastery over oneself . . . above all, never give in to oneself . . ."

Then she stopped. My mother's long hands were already calm and through them calmness filled her entire being. She went on, her expression now remote. Only the brilliance of her eyes remained, like leftovers from a feast in a deserted house.

"François, I shall go back to the village with my head held high. They will all bow before me. I shall be triumphant. Triumphant! No drunken pig is going to slobber over me and touch my son. You are my son. You will fight your evil instincts until you achieve perfection. You will be a priest! You will be respected! What a victory that will be over all of them!"

A priest! The idea was overwhelming, especially on this day when I had been so wounded in my poor search for a pleasant face. My mother often explained to me: "Mass is a sacrifice. The priest, like Christ, is at once the sacrificer and the victim. He must immolate himself upon the altar mercilessly, along with the Host." I was so young and I had never been happy. I burst out sobbing. My mother nearly threw herself on me, then she turned on her heels, saying curtly:

"Crybaby! Weakling! I've received the principal's answer; you will start at the boarding school next Thursday, September fourth. Now bring me an armful of kindling so I can light the stove for supper. Go on, get moving!"

My schoolbooks had been my mother's when she was a child. That evening, under the pretext of preparing my baggage for boarding school, I picked up the books one by one and eagerly looked at the name written on the first page of each one: "Claudine Perrault." Claudine, lovely Claudine, big Claudine ...

The letters of her Christian name danced before my eyes, writhing like flames, taking on fantastic shapes. It had not struck me before that my mother's name was Claudine. And now it seemed to me strange, and painful. I no longer knew if I was reading the name or hearing it uttered by a hoarse voice, a demon's voice, so close that it touched my cheek.

My mother approached me. She did not lighten the atmosphere. She did not rescue me from my feeling of suffocation. On the contrary, her presence gave weight to the supernatural nature of this scene. The kitchen was dark, with the one pool of brightness cast by the lamp falling onto the book I held open. In that circle of light my mother's hands went into action. She grabbed the book. For a moment the name "Claudine" written there in big, deliberate letters held all the light until it disappeared; in its place I saw, inscribed in the same haughty calligraphy: "François." A freshly inked "François" beside "Perrault" written in old ink. And so inside this narrow beam, within the space of a few minutes, the long hands played and sealed my fate. All my books were given the same treatment. That sentence of my mother's hammered at my head: "You are my son. The continuation of me."

Once that extraordinary day had ended I struggled to follow my mother's orders and erase it from my memory. Long since accustomed to her iron rule, it was fairly easy for me to stop thinking consciously about what had occurred and to perform mechanically the tasks she had imposed. Deep within myself, however, I sensed at times an unfamiliar, formidable richness whose languid presence stunned me and disturbed me.

The practical result, so to speak, of my first meeting with another, had been to put me on my guard and to suppress any spontaneous gesture of human feeling. My mother had scored a victory.

It was in that frame of mind that I entered boarding school. Unsociable and uncommunicative, I observed my classmates. I rejected their advances, whether timid or mocking. Soon there was a void around the new student. I told myself it was better that way, since I must not form any attachments in this world. Then I imposed penance on myself for that pain I was suffering in my isolation.

My mother wrote to me: "I am not there to tame you. You must impose your own mortifications. Above all do not give in to softness, your greatest flaw. Do not let yourself be moved by the mirage of some special friendship. Everyone, teacher or student, is there only for the length of time needed for your education and your training. Take advantage of what they must give you, but hold back. Do not at any cost abandon yourself, or you will be lost. Remember, I am informed of everything that goes on at the boarding school. You will give me a precise accounting during your vacation, and to God on Judgment Day. Do not waste your time. As for recreation periods, I have made an arrangement with the principal. You will help the farmer, in the stable and in the fields."

Farm work was something I knew and I preferred to keep myself busy with that than to be with my classmates during recreation periods. I did not know how to play or laugh and I felt I was in the way. As for the teachers, rightly or wrongly I considered them to be my mother's allies. And I was particularly on my guard with them.

Throughout my years at boarding school, I studied. That is, my memory recorded dates, names, rules, axioms, formulas. Faithful to my mother's teaching I wanted to retain only the outward signs of the material I studied. I was wary of true knowledge, which is an experience and a possession. And so on the subject of God I clung with all my strength of will to the countless prayers I recited every day, using them to build a rampart against any possible shadow on the naked face of God.

My grades were always excellent and I generally met my mother's insistence that I stand first.

I considered the structure of a classical tragedy or a piece of verse to be a mechanism of principles and formulas joined together by the author's will alone. Once or twice, however, I was brushed by grace when I perceived that the tragedy or the poem might well depend only upon its own inner inevitability, a condition for any work of art.

These revelations affected me painfully. In a second I could measure the emptiness of my existence. I had a foreboding of despair. But then I hardened myself and absorbed whole pages of chemical formulas.

When our grades were read out, and particularly when prizes were distributed, I experienced the same deep aversion that I could not overcome despite all my efforts.

During my year of rhetoric I stood first and won a great many prizes. Arms laden with books, ears buzzing with the polite applause of classmates for whom I was still a stranger, I went from my seat to the platform and felt such keen anxiety, such despondency, that I could barely take a step.

Once the ceremony was over, I lay on my bed in the dormitory that was bustling with the comings and goings of students preparing to leave on their holidays.

Suddenly I had a glimpse of what my life could have been. A sense of regret that was brutal, almost physical, had me in its grasp. I felt oppressed, a tightening in my chest. I saw my classmates going away, one by one or in groups. I heard them laughing and singing. But I felt no joy. I was unable to feel it. It was more than a prohibition. What had been first a refusal had become a sense of impotence, of sterility. My heart was bitter, harrowed. I was seventeen years old!

There was only one boy in the dormitory now. He seemed to be having trouble closing his trunk. I was going to offer to help him, but just as I was getting up from my bed he asked:

"Can you give me a hand with my trunk?"

Surprised and annoyed that he had spoken first, I played for time:

"What did you say?"

My question rang out in the deserted room and had the effect of putting me on edge. My curt, hoarse way of speaking always sounded unpleasant and irritating to me.

I lay down again, tight-lipped, squeezing my pillow in both fists. My classmate repeated his question. I acted as if I did not understand, hoping he would repeat it a third time. I counted the seconds, convinced he would not call on me again. And I did not move, as I experienced the voluptuous pleasure of doing something irreparable.

"Thanks for all your help and have a good holiday, jerk!"

And then this classmate whom I had secretly liked more than the others disappeared, sagging under the weight of his trunk.

My mother never came to meet me at the station, nor did she watch for me at the window. She waited for me in her own way, that is wearing a housedress and in the midst of doing some task or other. When I arrived she would interrupt her work to ask me the few questions she considered necessary. Then she would go back to work, after assigning me the chores to be done before the next meal.

Despite the heat that day I found her on her knees, weeding a row of beets. She sat up on her heels, briskly pushed the straw hat to the back of her head, wiped her hands on her apron and asked:

"Well, how many prizes?"

"Six books, Mother, and I won the scholarship."

"Let me see!"

I held out the books, which looked like all prize books, with their red bindings and gilt edges. They struck me as ridiculous, pathetic. I was ashamed of them, I despised them. Red, gilt, false. The colour of false glory. Marks of my false knowledge. Of my servitude.

My mother rose and went inside the house. She picked up her bunch of keys, a great knot of iron where all the keys in the world seemed massed together.

"Give me the money!"

I thrust my hand in my pocket and took out the purse. She almost grabbed it from me.

"Come here! Do you think I've got time to dawdle? Change your clothes and help me finish the weeding before supper!"

I looked at my mother without flinching and had the growing certainty that I hated her.

She locked the money in the little desk.

"I'll write the principal tomorrow to register you. It's a good thing you won that scholarship . . ."

"I'm not going back to boarding school next year," I said, so clearly I thought I was hearing someone else's voice. The voice of a man.

I saw the blood rise to my mother's face, flooding her sunburned forehead and neck. For the first time I saw her hesitate. It gave me great pleasure. I said again:

"I'm not going back to boarding school. And I'll never go to the seminary! You'd better not count on me to restore your reputation..."

My mother sprang like a tigress. Very lucidly, I watched what happened next. While I moved back towards the door I could not help noticing that tall woman's supple strength. Her face was ravaged, almost hideous. I thought to myself that was probably how hatred and death would disfigure me one day. I heard the clinking of her bunch of keys. Raising it, she brandished it at me. I caught a glimpse of its metallic dazzle as if a bolt of lightning were crashing down on me. Several times my mother struck my head. I lost consciousness.

When I opened my eyes again I was alone, stretched out on the floor. There was a violent pain in my head. I had become deaf.

Beginning on that day, a crack appeared in my oppressed life. The weighty silence of my deafness swept through me, along with a tendency to dream that appeared as a sort of accompaniment. No voice, no external sound could reach me now. Neither the roar of the waterfall nor the chirp of a cricket. Of that, I was quite certain. And yet I could hear the torrent's existence within me and our house and the entire farm. I did not possess the world but I found it had changed: a part of the world now possessed me. The expanse of water and mountains and secret hiding-places had just settled upon me its sovereign touch.

I thought I had been set free of my mother and I discovered a new kinship with the earth.

My eyes would fasten on our house—long and low—and facing it, the farm buildings in the same style and identified with the austere earth, with the mean clearings of the cultivated fields, and the woods unfurling to the halting rhythm of the wild mountains all around. And above it all, the water's presence. It was in the freshness of the air, the species of plants, the song of the frogs. Streams, the smooth river, ponds clear and still, and close to the house, seething through the rocky gorge, the torrent.

The torrent suddenly took on the importance it should always have had in my existence. Or rather, I became aware of its hold on me. I struggled against its domination. It seemed to me that a mist that rose incessantly from the falls drifted in and gave to my clothes, my books, the furniture, the walls, indeed to my daily life, an indefinable taste of water that wrung my heart. Of all the sounds on earth, my poor deaf head had retained only the intermittent turmoil of the cataract that pounded my temples. My blood flowed in cadence with the hurried rhythm of the turbulent water. When I became more or less calm, it was not too painful, it was reduced to a distant murmur. But on those terrible days when I recalled my act of rebellion, I could feel the torrent so powerfully inside my skull, against my brain, that my mother's striking me with her keys had not hurt me any more.

The woman had not said a word to me since the spectacular occasion when I had opposed her will for the first time. I felt that she was avoiding me. The summer chores were following their course. I arranged to be alone. And neglecting hay, mower, vegetables, fruits, my soul allowed itself to be overcome by the spirit of the place. I would spend hours gazing at an insect, or watching a shadow make its way across the leaves. And for days at a time I would recall those occasions, even the most remote, when my mother had mistreated me. Every detail was still present. Nothing disappeared, not one of her words or her blows.

It was at about this time that Perceval came to us. This horse, nearly wild, would not allow big Claudine to break him, though she had tamed many others. He resisted her with a boldness, a perseverance, a cunning that enchanted me. All black, with nostrils always steaming and his body covered with foam, the shuddering animal resembled the creature of spirit and passion I would have liked to embody myself. I envied him. I would have liked to consult him.

Living so close to that intrepid fury seemed to me an honour, an enrichment.

In the evening after my mother was asleep, I would get up and perch in the hayloft above Perceval. I was delighted, astonished, to see that he never relaxed the force of his rage. Was it out of pride that he waited for my departure before he went to sleep? Or did my still and hidden presence irritate him? He did not cease breathing noisily or kicking his hooves against his stall. From my hiding place I could see his splendid black coat shimmering with blue highlights. Electric currents ran along his spine. Never before had I imagined such a feast. I was savouring the true, physical presence of passion.

I left the stable, my head and ears throbbing with a din that nearly drove me crazy. Always that sound like the surf in a storm. I would take my head in both hands, and the shocks would rush at such a speed, I was afraid I would die. I promised myself not to stay so long the next time, but the spectacle of Perceval's anger attracted me so powerfully, I could not bring myself to leave until the roar of the torrent within me took hold and kept me from paying attention to anything else.

Then I would go down to the edge of the waterfall. I was not free to stay away. I would go towards the movement of the water, I would bring its own song to the water, as if I had become its only guardian. In exchange the water would show me its swirling eddies, its foam, like necessary counterparts to the blows pounding against my forehead. There was not one great cadence that rushed along the entire mass of water, but the spectacle of many exasperated struggles, of many currents and inner eddies ferociously joined in combat.

The water had hollowed the rock. I knew the spot where I now stood jutted out over the water like a terrace. I pictured the creek underneath it, dark, opaque, fringed with foam. False peace, black depths. Stock of dread.

Here and there springs seeped through. The rock was muddy. I could have slipped. What a leap of several hundred feet! What fodder for the gulf that would decapitate and dismember its prey! Shred them to pieces ...

I went back down the road to my pallet on the floor without having really parted from the torrent. As I fell asleep I added to its roar that was already part of me, the image of its raging fever. Elements of a dream or of some work to be done? I sensed that before long the face of one or the other, already formed and monstrous, would emerge from my turmoil.

The first day of school was approaching. My mother had steeled herself and now was only waiting for the moment to make an about-face, all her vigour concentrated and heightened by that long and conspicuous resignation, which in reality was nothing more than a victory over her own quickness to act. Not one of my moments of idleness when there was work to be done nor a single moment of the time I wasted at the edge of the falls or elsewhere was unknown to her.

I knew she was in full possession of her power. Curiously the continual setbacks she encountered in breaking Perceval did not seem to affect her. She rose above everything, sure of her ultimate triumph. It dwarfed me. And I knew that soon it would be pointless to try to avoid a confrontation with the gigantic Claudine Perrault.

I turned to Perceval.

That night the animal was unleashed. When I walked into the stable I almost turned around. The horse was struggling so hard I was afraid he would smash everything in his way. Once I was safely in the hayloft, I gazed down at that astonishing rage. There was blood mixed with the sweat on his coat. And though he had been cruelly hobbled, it did not prevent him from struggling.

I think my first feeling was one of pity at the sight of such a superb creature wounded and tortured. I was unaware that what I found most unbearable was to see his hatred, so ripe and so ready, tied down and held back, while my own hatred felt inferior and cowardly.

That captive demon in full power dazzled me. I owed it to him, as a tribute and in justice too, to enable him to be himself in the world. What evil force did I want to set free? Was it inside me?

Suddenly the torrent roared with such force inside my skull that I was gripped by horror. I wanted to scream. I could no longer draw back. I remember being stunned by the mass of sound that struck against my head.

There was a gap in my recollections that I have been badgering myself to shed light on since that time. And when I sense the possible approach of the horrible light in my memory, I struggle and cling desperately to the darkness, troubled and threatening though it may be. Inhuman circle, circle of my unending thoughts, material of my eternal life.

The torrent subjugated me, shook me from head to foot, it broke me in an eddy that nearly tore me limb from limb.

Impression of an abyss, an abyss in space and time where I was rolled into a void that came after the storm. The limit of that dead space had been crossed. I open my eyes on a luminous morning. I am face to face with the morning. I see only the sky that is blinding me. I cannot move. What struggle has left me so exhausted? A struggle against the water? Impossible. And anyway my clothes are dry. In what depths have I drowned? I turn my head with difficulty. I am lying on the rock, at the very edge of the torrent. I see its foam gushing in yellow sprays. Is it possible that I am coming back from the torrent? What atrocious fight has covered me with bruises! Have I done battle hand to hand with the Angel? I do not want to know. I push away consciousness with harrowing hands.

The animal has been set free. He has taken his horrifying gallop through the world. Woe to anyone who finds himself in his way. Now I see my mother lying there. I look at her. I measure her great size, now laid low. She is immense, marked with blood and with hoofprints.

II

I have no point of reference. No clock marks my hours. No calendar counts my years. I am dissolved in time. Regulations, discipline, shackles—all have been thrown to the ground. The name of God is dry and crumbling. No

God has ever inhabited that name for me. I have known only empty signs. I have worn my chains for too long. They have had time to put down their own roots. They have broken me from within. I shall never be free. I tried too late to emancipate myself.

I walk upon the wreckage. A dead man amid the debris. Anguish alone sets me apart from dead signs.

Nothing around me is alive except the landscape. Not that my contemplation is affectionate or aesthetic. No, it is something deeper, more closely bound; I am identified with the landscape. Delivered over to nature. I feel myself becoming a tree or a clump of earth. All that separates me from that tree or from that clump of earth is anguish. I am porous beneath the anguish as the earth is to the rain.

The rain, the wind, the clover, the leaves have become elements in my life. True limbs of my body. I am part of them far more than of myself. Terror, though, is on the surface of my skin. I pretend not to believe in it. At times, though, it lets me distinguish my arms from the grass that it flattens. If my arm trembles it is because fear has suddenly made it tremble. While the grass does not depend on fear, only on the wind. Though I abandon myself to the wind, fear alone sways me and perturbs me.

I am not yet ripe for the final escape, the ultimate abdication to cosmic forces. I do not yet have the permanent right to say to the tree: "My brother" or to the falls, "Here I am!"

What is the present? On my hands I feel the fresh, lingering warmth of the March sun. I believe in the present. Then I look up and spy the open door of the stable. I know that there is blood, that a woman is lying on the ground, marked with the stigmata of death and rage. It is as present to my gaze as the March sun. As real as my first vision some fifteen or twenty years ago. That dense image putrefies the sunlight on my hands. The limpid touch of the light has been spoiled for me forever.

I go home. Dread alone sets apart my muddy footsteps from the muddy path leading to the house.

In the old pine tree, the oldest and the tallest, a crow must be singing his return from the south. I can only make out his contortions. I have lost the sound and the song. Speech no longer exists. It has become a mute grimace.

The torrent is silent now. With the heavy silence that precedes the rising water levels of spring. My head is silence. I analyze scraps of it. I repeat my ordeal. Complete it. Shed light on it. I take it up again where I had left it. My investigation is lucid and methodical. Little by little, it corroborates what my imagination or my instinct let me suppose.

I admire my detachment, which astonishes me. And then all at once I realize I am deceiving myself. I think that I am without pity, and I disguise the truth, I stray from the path in order to escape from reality. I lie! What is the good of seeking? Innate truth presses upon me with all its weight. It corrupts even the simplest of my acts. I am in possession of the truth, and through it I recognize that none of my acts is pure.

How long since I have experienced such calm . . . It worries me. What greater fury will reinforce the next inner tumult? What is the meaning of this absence in my night? Does it bring some sweetness? I do not believe in sweetness.

Desire for a woman has come to me in the desert. No, it is not sweet. It is pitiless, like everything that touches me. To possess and destroy the body and soul of a woman. And to see that woman play her role in my own destruction. To look for her is to give her that right.

I have gone out to find her. Taken again my childhood route, along the main road. The route from the days of my innocence when I sought a fraternal being and was denied it.

After so many years, I am once again rising to the surface of my solitude. Emerging from the depths of an opaque pond. I lie in wait for the lure. I know now that it is a trap. But I too shall break it and I shall have tasted fresh meat.

There are peddlers' odds and ends on my land, by the side of the road. And two formless individuals, draped and hooded, stand there like grey trees. Their coloured hands, raised towards a small fire made of branches. Their motionless hands in the air above the fire as if to bless the fire, endlessly.

I can feel my hard muscles and the robust breath in my chest. At last I will be able to measure my strength by chasing away these intruders. In one glance I observe that they have cut some kindling. They are camping on my property! They see me approach and do not move, are like impassive standing stones! O my anger, gather your sure strength!

I call out to them. No reaction whatsoever from these people. For so long I have spoken to no one at all, what if I have forgotten how to speak? I shout, I scream. I do not know what words are escaping from my throat. Do they correspond with my thoughts? I do not know. In any case, I have arrived at the stones. There is a stirring beneath the cloaks. Hands leave the fire. One of the two shadows approaches me. It is an elderly man, grey-haired, his expression sly. His bizarre and mock-solemn getup makes him look quite ridiculous.

I raise my fists. The man bows profusely. He talks incessantly. But his babble is lost to me. I lay him on the ground with one blow. He rebounds from the end of my arm like a bullet. I laugh. My laughter must have a sound. I do not know what it is.

The man gets up, his cape streaked with mud and melting snow. He proffers more bows and more apologies. He appears to be offering me his merchandise as reparation. From his small cart he takes an armful of necklaces, rosaries, almanacs, knives and so forth. He drops the lot in my arms, accompanying his action with a look of distress, more for his bleeding cheek than from regret for his actions. The whole production is equivalent for me to a clear remark, something like: "Go ahead, choose! Take whatever you want, but for pity's sake don't hit me again! I'll leave your property as fast as I can . . . Just let me gather up my things . . ."

I drop all his trinkets on the ground, keeping only a glass bead necklace because I like its naive vulgarity. I look at the man. He gestures to me that I should keep the necklace. Happy to get off so easily, he would smile if his cheek were not forcing him to pinch his lips. I offer him money but he refuses it, gloomily shaking his head.

I am still advancing. I am right beside the second shadow crouching by the fire, the hood over its eyes. I tug the shadow towards me, pulling it firmly by the shoulders. It is a woman. She laughs. Her face is raised towards mine. I lose some of my self-confidence. I move away a little. She laughs. The man too tries to smile. They seem to be laughing at me. By way of reply I come closer to the woman, so close I can feel her breath on my neck. I tear off her cloak. I want to tear off all the rags that cover her, the way I tear the bark off a birch tree. She makes no attempt to move away . . . She is still breathing onto my neck. Laughing onto my neck. Her dazzling teeth scoff at me. I feel her heart beat, she is barely winded by the laughter I cannot hear. She holds her upraised arms above her head, hands on the nape of her neck, apparently hiding something.

Have I really spoken or have I merely thought these things to myself? I wish I knew what she was hiding. Without moving away from me she takes off the scarf her hands were tying around her heavy hair. The hair now falls loose to her shoulders. I step back. Her hair is black and very long. A mass of blue-black hair. I step back again. She is walking towards me. Her eyes are greenish-blue. Her black eyebrows, set high, emphasize the perfect setting of her eyes.

I turn and shout at the fellow who has been following the scene with a bored expression:

"Is this your daughter?"

He shrugs.

Using gestures and words I explain that in his whole bazaar only the girl tempts me and that if he does not let me have her, I'll smash his face. She laughs more softly now, close to me. I can feel the warmth of her breath against my chest. She has lowered her head a little. I breathe in her smell.

The man seems dismayed. I throw him handfuls of money. (I don't understand how I have all that money in my pockets.) The man picks up the bills and coins that have fallen all around, hopping excitedly. He rolls his eyes in ecstasy. He thanks me, bowing to the ground.

Then I put an end to the vagabond's show, gesturing to him to douse the fire, take his belongings, and clear out. He gets busy. Now that everything has been piled into the hand cart, the man hesitates. The woman goes and speaks to her associate. He listens, shaking his head. Then she comes back to me. From her demeanour I understand that I have won my prize.

The role of solitude has been reversed. Now it weighs upon the peddler's shoulders. With my companion, I am part of a couple. The solitary man clears off. And that man isn't me.

The woman has donned the burnoose-like cloak again, after taking a small bundle of clothes from the cart. Her face is expressionless. I notice her mouth at rest; blooming and fleshy, it replaces the taste of her laughter without erasing it inside me.

And now I give her a name. I, the wild man, feel a woman's name rise to my lips, like a gift to be offered. I who have never received anything, taste the miracle of that first gift. I call her Amica. She probably has another name, but I will never hear her say it and this one, I have just heard for the first time. I heard it gathering within me, then bursting out of me for her to take. And she took it, for she is mine now and I have been given the right to name her.

I waited a long time after the man disappeared, struggling along the road, pushing his cart. After that I took Amica through a series of detours along the mountain in order to scramble forever in her memory the road to my property.

I imagine her asking all kinds of questions: "Where are you taking me?" "Is it much farther?" "Will you keep me very long?" "Do you like me that much?" "Is the necklace for me?"

Nothing. She does not open her mouth, which has taken on a disdainful pout.

She is walking beside me, buried again beneath her hood. Her eyes are watchful. At times she gives me a piercing look that breaks her passive expression and startles me. Too late. I am already bound. I am not waking from an illusion; on the contrary, as soon as I saw this woman, what attracted me more than anything else in her was precisely that hint of slyness and evil in her eyes.

I am still advancing, never retracing my steps. I shall go all the way to the end, all the way to the plenitude of the evil that now is mine alone, though I knew nothing of it this morning. And then I shall feast my eyes upon her face when we are in sight of the house and the torrent. When she realizes there are miles and miles between us and any neighbour, I shall tell her about the torrent. I shall introduce her to the eyes of my solitude. She will see that of the two, I am the more to be feared and she will shiver . . . I shall feel her shiver against me. My hands on her throat. Her supplicating eyes . . .

I observe her, I spy upon her expression. For the second time I have pulled back her hood and she does not protest or emerge from her apparent apathy. We enter the house. I have shut the door behind us. Not a muscle moves in her face. Yet the house is sinister. Dirty, dark, it still contains the shape and smell of the dead woman and of the terrible living man that is me. There is no retreat, no concern; impassive, Amica appears inside my home, enters my drama.

Amica is the devil. I have invited the devil to my house.

With much laughter she twines her arms around my neck. Her fine firm arms seem to me unwholesome, destined to play I know not what role in my downfall. I resist their enchantment. (What cold snakes have embraced me?) Roughly, I pull her obstinate arms from my neck. Their resistance pleases me. I twist them. It feels good but it does not reassure me. The use of my physical might shows all too well the defection of my spiritual force. Brutality is the recourse of those who have run out of inner strength.

I go outside. A gust of moist air on my forehead. Already I have only one desire. To go inside again, back to the snare of Amica's arms. The evening air is nothing. I know another freshness now, another agitation.

When I open the door I see her standing at the back of the room, slicing bread. I drop my armful of wood; and motionless, without stepping through the doorway, I cry out to her:

"Good day, my wife!"

We eat our meal facing one another. The flame is brighter in the lamp because she has washed the globe. Her shawl on a chair, her cloak hanging from a nail. What is this peaceful household I catch sight of all around me? For nothing seems to penetrate inside me now. I see a stranger who is eating opposite an unknown woman. Each one is as secret as the other. No, I have inhabited neither this place nor this man.

And now I welcome into my bed the woman and the man who is with her.

For how long now have I been using my mother's big bed? I have not yet had the strength to occupy all of her bedroom; but one night I took the bed into my attic to replace my childhood pallet. Was I afraid of seeing the horror of my nights become insipid? I am playing with a sore, tending it. I am the sore and it is me. And then, what good does it do to hold forth about the reason for my acts and impulses. I am not free.

I introduce Amica to the remnants of my nights. Ah, you do not know, you of the long blue-black hair, nor you, phosphorescent irises, nor you, flesh of cool arms, what bed it is that is welcoming you, you and your deaf companion. What old waking nights stand watch around you, proffering countless fevers and terrors! Nor is sleep any better. It is only a descent into the deepest gulf of the unconscious, where I can neither play nor defend myself, not even as feebly as I do when I am awake.

I observe the strange couple on their wedding night. I am the guest at the nuptials. Amica displays a facility, a skill at caresses that plunges me into a dreamy bewilderment. She sleeps. The familiar demons are matched with the bed's black carvings. Ah! No longer shall I alone be tormented! No, they are sparing her calm sleep. They spread all about her in the distance. She forms an island of calm on my cursed bed.

Day is breaking. I sense the distant murmur of the torrent moving towards me, inside me. Am I dreaming? Why are these little slippers at the foot of the bed? These flimsy fabrics on the chair? And why is this sleeping head against my chest?

I take it in both my hands like a ball. It makes me uneasy. It bores me. Irritates me. What am I going to do with it? Throw it away? I feel such dryness. Neither desire nor voluptuous delight. Only dryness. Utter drought. And so from the beginning of time an arbitrary will has deprived me of any principle of emotion or sensual pleasure. Ah! My mother, I had not imagined the extent of your destruction within me!

I get up and lean out the window, wanting to escape from the vision of the strange wedding celebrated in my home. I move discreetly, trying not to let the sleeping couple be aware of my frustrated presence in their nuptial chamber.

Days have passed. A routine has been established. Amica takes care of the meals and the housework. I, the stable. It is not yet time for the fields and the garden. I do not want to leave her alone in the house for a moment. I follow her constantly. My nerves are at the breaking point. I do not vouch for anything.

Why did I not take her back after the first night? Already she was a burden. If I did not do so it was from fear of the main road, of the peddler who may still be there and has perhaps assembled some idlers to come here and gawk at me, to question me, perhaps intending to follow me here. The thought was unbearable. I thought I was safe here in my hiding-place. My bridges with the inhabited universe have been cut. I have cut them beneath Amica's footsteps, too. She wanted to be a witness to my life. And she will not leave it that easily. Witness: the word wounds me, obsesses me! Amica is a witness . . . to what? A witness to me, to my presence, to my house. That is all it takes to frighten me to death, as if I could see a huge mirror where ineradicable images hold my deeds and my gaze. At no cost must I set my witness free into the world.

Sometimes at night when I wake, I see her sitting at the foot of the bed, combing her hair. I am invariably surprised at the extreme attention in her eyes as she stares at me. She observes me tensely, ready to flee at the slightest warning. To tell the truth I can feel her gaze even under my closed eyelids. It presses upon my sleep with all its strange weight. It is what wakens me, through the force of concentration. It is almost like hypnotism. What is she trying to do? Does she hope to possess me altogether? I would kill her first.

Once, unable to tolerate her exasperating insistence any longer, I started to strike Amica. With one leap she jumped to the floor. That elastic stride was such a revelation that I stopped thinking about running after her. The poignant malaise that was given me by her eyes that were open too wide on me was completed by the impression of her supple fall. It reminded me of a certain cat.

My mother had never wanted a cat. Probably because she knew that no cat would accept servitude. She accepted only those creatures she could control and make crawl, trembling, to her feet. (Ah Perceval, then who were you?) I have never seen a cat here except during the final days of my mother's life. At the time there was a cat prowling in the vicinity. He only showed himself, surprisingly, when I was alone. I remember being troubled, irritated by the sensation that the animal was watching me intently with his dilated eyes. He seemed to be following the development of something latent in me that escaped me, whose inevitable outcome he alone could penetrate.

The last time I spied the cat I was measuring my ravaged mother. The creature, conscious and out of reach, was still fixing me with his eternal gaze. Had someone surprised me then? Had someone gazed at me uninterrupted, day or night? Had someone known me at the very moment when I no longer had any knowledge of myself?

Amica's eyes are like the cat's. Two great discs, apparently motionless but quivering like flames. She peers at me while I sleep. She looks at me when I no longer see myself. She can discover in my waking dreams those deeds that are buried in the darkest regions of my being, those that sleep turns over at will, leaving the bitter stench until morning, just enough to nourish the torment of the day.

After that I never saw the cat again. I often had a curious impression of him. It seemed to me that the evil animal had disappeared inside me. It knew everything and it existed within me, bearing down with the full weight of its certainty.

And today, finding that woman with eyes so astonishingly similar riveted on me, I think I see my witness looming suddenly into the light of day. My hidden witness emerging into my consciousness, facing me, quite plainly. Torturing me! Wanting me to confess! What is that witch doing here? I do not want her looking at me! I do not want her questioning me! I know perfectly well that I shall never rid myself of her. A creature came to know me at the very moment of Perceval's flight. That witness now is questioning me, directly, from outside me, separated from me, without complicity, like a judge. That witness pursues me into my most secret refuge, into what was his own dwelling. He violates something deeper than my consciousness. I know nothing! Nothing! If the cat knows, he does not belong to me. No! No! Do not smile, Amica. He is not mine. As for me, I know nothing.

Her skirts and shawls drape her and seem to be held in place only by the moving fasteners of her hands that clutch them more or less tightly according to the whims of her movements, brisk or nonchalant. A network of pleats slipping from her hands is later reborn in eager waves. Interplay of pleats and hands. A knot of pleats on the bosom held in a single hand. A gleam of silk too tight across the shoulders. The balance broken, recreated elsewhere. Gliding of silk, the shoulder bared, the arms unveiled. Fingers so brown against the red skirt. The skirt is lifted in handfuls, nimbly, to climb the stairs. The ankles are slender, the legs perfect. A knee stands out. Everything has disappeared. The skirt sweeps the floor, the hands are free and the bodice no longer holds.

That morning Amica had lined up on the table the few spoons, forks, and knives that I possess. She seemed to be thinking as she gazed at them. When she spied me she talked to me with animation as she pointed to the mean utensils. I understood absolutely nothing of whatever she might have been trying to say. And then for the first time she scribbled something on a bit of paper: "Is it silver?"

I couldn't help chuckling, and I wrote on the paper below it: "Of course not, you idiot!"

Amica bit her lips, looking very annoyed and furious.

Still, it is peculiar. Why should she be so anxious to know if my cutlery is silver?

Amica has an odd way of doing the housework. She can scrub, or rather ferret, for hours in the same cupboard, the same corner, while there are other tasks she never tackles. Blacking the stove, for example, or scouring the pots and pans. As I watch her I think: she is looking for something. Why has she come here? What if our meeting was no accident? If on the contrary she had been waiting for me deliberately so she could come and investigate the dead woman and the living man who dwell here? Why then did I bring her here? I see no way of getting rid of her now. What if I were to measure her capacity for suffering against my own? No, I must handle her carefully. I am too afraid that she will leave here and take my secret while I sleep. I must stop sleeping. I must keep watch. Keep watch over myself. It is that, finally, which is implacable. All I do now is keep watch over myself, live inside myself. The only voices I can hear come from within. No mouth translates them, no intermediary gives shape to them. They strike me, sharp as arrows. I have plunged to the centre of myself, relentlessly. After a childhood turned to torture by the strict prohibition of intimate, profound knowledge, all at once I was facing the innermost human abyss. I foundered there. While still alive I am tasting the last judgment: that true confrontation with oneself. It is too much for human strength. I am burning. No, I am not always lucid. My sick mind distorts voices. But it is enough for me to know that they speak and accuse me. Indeed, I accuse myself. At times a thought occurs to me that could be an alleviation, a grace, if only I could believe in appeasement, if only grace had not been refused me. Every man carries within himself an unknown crime which seeps out, for which he atones.

When I was small, I would fall asleep stunned by hard work and by fear. And sometimes I would feel, just for a moment, a presence that was a kind of consolation, superior to everything I had suffered. I dared not abandon myself to the sweetness that my mother called the temptation of softness. I would harden myself, knowing I was perhaps killing an angel by accepting this responsibility. To justify myself, I would tell myself that it could only be an evil angel, for the good ones are God's police and they punish little children who are too tender.

I was forbidden the experience of God, yet they wanted to make a priest of me! I was turned away very early from the possible savour of God.

If grace exists, I have lost it. I have pushed it away. Dismissed it. No, it is deeper than that: someone before me, of whom I am the continuation, turned down grace on my behalf. O my mother, how I hate you! And I have not yet explored the entire range of your devastation within me. One phrase haunts my nights: "You are my son, you are my continuation." I am bound to a woman who is damned. I took part in her damnation, as she did in mine ... No! No, I am responsible for nothing! I am not free! I tell you again, I am not free! I have never been free! Ah! Who is striking me with such ferocity? The torrent surges inside my head! And I am not alone! That girl I picked up from the roadside is before me, observing me and spying on me: she must not see me in this state. I am drawn to the falls. I must peer at my inner image. I lean over the seething gulf. I am leaning over myself.

How many hours have passed? What instinct makes me climb back up the steep shore? The instinct of a terrier who retrieves wounded animals? If I have gone back it is because the torrent is not yet my ultimate dwelling. The house of my childhood is still acting upon me, and perhaps Amica is as well . . .

I am not fully prepared for the ultimate integration with the fury of the falls, nor for the deeper abyss within myself. I am still running away from myself. The outcome, the final flight into myself, into my despair, remains in suspense. For how many hours? Or days? Consenting to my destiny does not depend on my will. The next crisis will sweep it away.

The rock springs flow, swollen by the recent rains. I am walking in the water. I am so weak that I must stop at every step.

I drink from the pump. I dash water on my head. Amica is not here. I climb into bed fully clothed, my head pounding. I am not yet concerned (I think so slowly) that she has not come in. Usually I do not let her out of my sight. In any case, she never goes away. What can she be doing now? And yet night has fallen. I have already told her about the wolves on the mountain.

Amica has come back. I am too weary to question her. She is more sensual, more affectionate than usual. She appears rich with unfamiliar caresses. She has attained her full powers. I wish I could banish that sated girl. Why am I being so difficult? What companion do I require in my humiliation?

She lays her hands on my forehead. I cannot prevent myself from enjoying her soft hands against my burning. All at once I am seized with panic at a certain revelation. I did not think I had opened my mouth, only desired mentally to have some water. Amica nods and holds up my head, helping me to drink like a child. I roll stupefied eyes at her. She laughs.

And then I am certain I have no control at all over my voice. I do not know if I am speaking out loud or continuing my inner monologue. Amica can read my thoughts. My brain is stripped bare before her. I had not imagined that peak of my horror! I am delivered up to this worthless woman! I bite my lips to stop one more word from getting out. She laughs.

I do not possess the strength to get up. My vain efforts exhaust me. My head is bursting. I want only to drive Amica away. Since she came here she has probably surprised me like this many times. What exactly does she know? She gives me something to drink. I smell a strange odour on her skin. A foreign smell that offends me. Then I think I recognize a particular aroma, one I have smelled before, made up of the hide of a human no longer young, of tobacco, paper, and ink . . . It makes me think of the chief of police, of his interrogation after my mother's death! I let out a cry that I am aware of only from a contraction in my chest, and by the way Amica jumps up until she is standing quite erect. She is pale. Her shawl tumbles to the ground, uncovering her shoulders and arms. I wish I could tear with my teeth and nails her proffered flesh.

I have no inner shelter now. The sacrilege is complete. The invasion of my most secret being has been accomplished. I am naked, outside, before that girl who is plundering me for the police. She will know far more than is needed for a police report. She will penetrate my agony.

The fever is on me. If I say anything in my delirium I do not hear it. While Amica replaces my lost sense of hearing. She usurps my own role as the first to hear. I communicate with her instead of with myself. My soul has been violated. I once was told that God alone had that power and that right. The final judgment will be pronounced by a slut. Just now I wish I could believe in God, in his terrible righteousness, his perfect grandeur. Let him hear my confession and absorb me into my truth. Not that girl! Not that wretched nonentity! How powerful the devil is! And I am his accomplice.

I can smell the damp springtime that comes in through the window. The springtime holds the odour of the falls. I have a dog's sense of smell. Since my deafness that sense has developed, has been enhanced in a singular fashion. My sense of smell, that of a tracked animal, made me fear the scent of the police on Amica. But what if I was mistaken? There is no scent of ink or paper . . . No, I think it is rather the peddler's rancid taste!

Amica tucks me in like an infant in its cradle. I struggle. She laughs. What I would give to hear the sound of her laughter! I know that ever more savage grimace.

Amica is leaving me. She is downstairs. She must be turning everything upside down. The way is clear. She has everything she needs. She wants material proof of the crime. I myself have been searching for perhaps twenty years: will she be better served? There are of course some nooks and crannies in the house I have forbidden her. In the stable a certain stall, a certain place in the dusty hay, now twenty years old. A certain weightiness in my dead memory where seals have been affixed . . . For Amica, nothing is forbidden; she will go everywhere, to the deepest part of a badly sealed horror . . .

I have the coroner's verdict before my eyes: "Accidental death." What business does that girl have snooping around here? There is nothing to be learned. The peddler won't know anything. He won't be able to tell the police anything whatever. Nor will Amica.

The fever chills me and consumes me. What is Amica doing? What will she find out? Can it be that she will find something? I have no strength to get up, but when she comes up the stairs I shall strangle her. Or rather, I shall wait for my strength to be fully restored and then I shall throw the spy into the water. Briefly, my arms will swing her over the precipice. She will struggle. I shall not savour her cries, only the convulsions of her terror. And then Amica will be decapitated and dismembered. Her remains will be shattered on the rocks. No! No! I do not want her severed head on my chest! Nothing of hers! Nothing! And her long blue-black hair around my neck. It smothers me.

I must have slept. It is morning. Amica has not come back. She has fled. I am certain she must have fled. Does that mean she has found what she was looking for? What sign did she uncover? In what drawer? What chest? Oh! the rough floor of the stable that is absorbing the black blood!

The mountain must be surrounded. The police and their wolfhounds are lying in wait for me. Amica has sold me out. She will pay me back in kind for the goods that I paid the peddler for in cash. Now it is my turn to be sold. By her and by myself. Did I know what the price would be? The price of my poor ravaged bones? What added pain? I perceive no stabilization. Soon I shall be merely a rag.

How did I manage to get up? I drag myself downstairs. Everything is in disorder, the cupboards open, their contents turned inside out. The door to my mother's bedroom has been smashed! I stop, gripped by the presence that even the poorest objects scattered every which way reveal so powerfully. Everything my mother ever touched has retained her form and is rising against me.

The lock of the little desk has been forced. The last and only time I dared to open it was on the day I acquired Amica. That was where I took the sum of money she cost me. In my impatience to be on the road then I paid no attention to a certain sealed envelope that I tore open after I had felt it. One detail, however, is still clear in my memory. After I had filled my pockets I am sure I replaced the envelope, still half-full, inside my mother's big ledger from which I had taken it.

The ledger is open. I leaf through it. No trace of the envelope. I cannot explain the curiosity that leads me to search these pages. I do it with a concern, a meticulousness, a kind of avidity that is distressing. I note that all her attempts at bookkeeping, which were sometimes amazing, seem intended to wipe out a debt. On the last page I read this final sentence, traced there in her lofty hand: "The evil debt is closed."

I bend down and take the empty, torn envelope from the floor. I piece together the same words I saw in the notebook: "Money of evil"; and in smaller letters: "To be burned tonight." There follows the exact date of my mother's death.

And this is what Amica has done. She has run away with the money of evil! She will go out into the world, telling everyone that she found it here, that I am the son of evil, the son of big Claudine. The whole world will know that evil chose me at the moment of the first breath of my existence.

What more must I renounce? Must I renounce myself, my own drama? I have never thought of perusing oneself as the condition of the pure being. Besides, I cannot be pure. I shall never be pure. I surrender myself to my own end. I absorb myself and I am nothingness. I cannot imagine my end outside myself. Perhaps that is my error. Who will teach me the way out? I am alone, alone within myself.

I am walking. I can take a step back, a step forward. Who said that I am not free? I am weak but I am walking. I can see the torrent but I barely hear it. Ah! I would not have believed in such lucidity! Waking, I play with the elements of a fever that is subsiding. The water is black and filled with eddies, and the foam is spitting yellow. I see Amica's head above the waves. That head I no longer know what to do with! Why does it stay inside me? Everything is alive within me. I refuse absolutely to emerge from myself. Her hair is caught in the wind like a veil of darkness. It mingles with the water in a long scroll, filled with roaring black and blue and hemmed in white. Her hair flows to me in swirls. It smells of the sweet water of the falls and of the unique perfume of Amica. Her severed head, no, I don't want that! It spins like a ball. Ah! Who will buy it? I have already paid too much for it!

I am tired of watching the water and of taking from it fantastic images. I lean over it as far as I can. I am inside the torrent's spray. My lips taste the insipid water.

The house, the long harsh house, born of the soil, is dissolving inside me as well. I see it distorted in the eddy. My mother's bedroom has been ransacked. All the objects of her life are spread through the water. Such mean things! Ah!

I see a silver mirror someone gave her! Her face in it gazing up at me: "François, look me in the eyes."

I bend over as far as I can. I want to look into the gulf, from as close to it as possible. I want to lose myself in my adventure, my sole and appalling wealth.

～

Gérard Bessette
Translated by Wayne Grady

LAST RITES

Gérard Bessette was born on February 25, 1920, in Sainte-Anne-de-Sabrevois, Quebec. He attended the Université de Montréal, receiving his master's degree in 1946 on the poems of Émile Nelligan, and a doctorate in 1950 on poetic imagery in Québécois poetry. From 1946 to 1948 he taught at the University of Saskatchewan, and from 1951 to 1958 at Duquesne University in Pittsburgh, Ohio. He accepted a post at the Royal Military College in Kingston, Ontario, in 1958, and from 1960 until his retirement in 1980 he taught in the French department at Queen's University. He was made a Fellow of the Royal Society of Canada in 1966, won the Prix David in 1980, and has twice received the Governor-General's Award for literature.

Bessette's first publication was a slim volume of poetry called *Poèmes temporels* (1954), but since then he has published only fiction and criticism. His first novel, *La Bagarre* (1958), is about a man who turns his back on the common people. *Le Libraire* (1960; *Not for Every Eye*, 1962) is also about the dangers of too narrow a world view. In 1960 he also published *Les Images en poésie canadienne-français*, a book of literary criticism. *Les Pédagogues* (1961) was his last stylistically "traditional" novel; with the publication of *L'Incubation* in 1965, Bessette adopted the form of the French "nouveau roman." *L'Incubation*, which earned Bessette his first Governor-General's Award, was followed by *Le Cycle* (1971), which won a second Governor-General's Award. His other novels include *La Commensale* (1975, but written before *L'Incubation*); *Les Anthropoïdes* (1977), and *Le Semestre* (1979).

Bessette's only book of short stories, *La Garden-Party de Christophine*, was published in 1980 and has never been completely translated. It contains stories from many periods in Bessette's development as a writer. "L'extrême-onction" first appeared as "The Conversion" in *Queen's Quarterly* in 1960, translated by Glen Shortliffe; included here in a new translation by Wayne Grady as "Last Rites," it is a fine example of Bessette's early blending of traditional style and avant-garde ideas. Bessette's work hovers between the writers of the 1950s and the literature of the Quiet Revolution, which, in his second book of criticism, published in 1968, Bessette called *"une littérature en ébullition,"* a literature in ferment.

⌒

"Last Rites" is a translation of "L'extrême-onction" published in *La Garden-Party de Christophine: Nouvelles* (Montreal: Québec-Amérique, 1980); first appeared in *Liberté*, 5, no. 3 (mai-juin 1963).

Last Monday at about eleven o'clock at night, just as I was getting ready for bed, I received a telephone call: my old friend Étienne Beaulieu had been struck down by a sudden attack of paralysis. I quickly got dressed again and, without even taking the time to put on my hat, hastened over to his house, which was only a few blocks from mine.

I had known Étienne for a long time. We'd been to college together, and then to university, and after graduating with our law degrees we had set up a joint practice in an office down on St. James Street. And two years ago almost to the day of his attack, we had both retired. But we still got together regularly, two or three times a week, either to play bridge or chess, or sometimes just to talk.

Émilie, Étienne's daughter, and her husband Julien— with whom Étienne had been living—met me at the door. They seemed frightened. The doctor had arrived a few minutes before me, and was already in with the patient in his room. He came out just as I entered the living room.

"How is he?" I asked him.

The doctor, who was also an old friend, shook his head sadly: "There's nothing we can do, I'm afraid," he said. "He only has a few hours left."

The news brought a painful lump to my throat, and Émilie buried her face in her husband's arm, sobbing uncontrollably. But she soon rallied, and said with an air of decision: "We must call the priest."

The doctor and I exchanged embarrassed looks. Although I had expected something of the sort, I could think of nothing to say. In fact, there didn't seem to be anything one could say. Émilie and her husband were devout Catholics; they were very active in their parish, and had raised their children in the strictest orthodox manner. Étienne's atheism had long been a matter of considerable pain to them. They had always hoped he would recant before his death, but they had no doubt preferred not to give it much thought. But now that Étienne was on his deathbed, they obviously felt it was time to act.

Étienne was not one of those indecisive and frivolous free-thinkers, always ready to change their beliefs at the drop of a hat, and refusing to talk seriously about religious matters. Neither had he been one to beat his chest and shout insults at priests and fate, trying to hide their doubts beneath the violence of their attacks.

He had, rather, been a cold, systematic materialist, absolute in his sincerity and unwavering in his conviction. And he had been since our days in college.

Even though he rarely brought up the subject of religion himself, he seemed to enjoy discussions with anyone who challenged his beliefs. But he always spoke with reasoned calm, without the slightest hostility, and with a sincere desire to convince his interlocutor that he or she was missing out on so many real pleasures by holding on to their religious "chimeras," as he called them. He never pressed his case or tried to convert others to his own view, and always withdrew from the discussion the moment it seemed about to escalate into an argument.

If he occasionally chided his daughter for her faith, it was always without malice, more like teasing, in exactly the same tone he would use to question her taste in clothes, or the shape of her hat. He had a number of friends who were priests—former schoolmates, for the most part—with whom he would pass long hours talking religion, smoking his pipe, and drinking whiskey.

It was one of those friends who had said to him one day that, like everyone else, when faced with imminent death Étienne would renounce his atheism and embrace God. "It's possible," Étienne had replied. "It's quite possible. But at such a time I won't really be my normal self, will I? I won't be calm and lucid, as I am now."

"You'll do it just the same," said the priest. "Just you wait and see!"

"Perhaps," said Étienne. "But it won't mean a damned thing. Where's the glory for the Church in triumphing over a sick man whose suffering has clouded his judgment?"

These memories were flooding through my mind when I heard Émilie asking me in a plaintive voice: "You are his closest friend, M. Dorval—you must try to convince him, to prepare him for the priest's visit..."

I had to refuse, although I did so politely, explaining that religion was a personal matter and that, in any case, until then all my efforts in that direction had been futile. I then excused myself and went into the sick man's room.

As I approached his bedside, I saw how much the partial paralysis had altered Étienne's appearance. The whole left side of his face was pale and shone like taut silk; it seemed pulled back as if by a heavy weight, presenting a painful contrast to the right side, which seemed entirely healthy, as creased and florid as ever.

He must have heard me enter, because as soon as I was close enough he opened his right eye, lifted his left eyelid with his finger, and looked up at me. I saw that he had recognized me, and that he seemed to be perfectly lucid.

"How are you, old friend?" I asked him, and felt instantly shamed by my own banality.

"How do I look?" he replied. "As you can see, I'm not long for this world."

Having no heart for the traditional words of encouragement we usually dredge up when talking to the terminally ill, I simply asked: "Do you need anything?"

"No," he said, "nothing, thank you. Only to be left alone for a while, if you don't mind. I'll call you later... When you came in just now I was... working on my balance sheet, trying to think things out as clearly as I could. It's very important, to think clearly. It's amazing how knowing that you have only a certain amount of time left... focuses the mind."

He fell silent, and I was about to leave the room when Émilie and her husband briskly opened the door and came in with a determined look on their faces. The violence of her effort to control herself showed in the contraction of her features.

"You are very ill, Papa," she said to Étienne. "Would you like us to call a priest?"

Étienne, who had closed his eyes, opened them again as he had before. His daughter's request obviously came as no surprise to him. He seemed only to be somewhat annoyed that his last few moments were being stolen from him, that he was being prevented from devoting his final energies to clear thought and meditation.

"No," he said, simply.

"But Papa, you might be dying. Aren't you afraid?"

"Wouldn't you like to make a confession?" Julien added. "You'll feel so much better afterwards. The priest will be here in a few minutes—we called him earlier . . ."

Étienne had closed his eyes again, and seemed to have drifted off. He lay perfectly still, a small, asymmetrical figure whose left side seemed stretched like the skin of a tambourine.

"Papa, Papa!" cried Émilie. "Papa, don't you understand what we're saying?"

"No," said Étienne, in exactly the same tone as before, as though he were not replying to her last question, but still responding to her initial request.

At that point the doctor came into the room.

"You're going to tire him out," he said quietly. "Leave me alone with him for a bit. You can come back in fifteen minutes."

I heard Étienne give a deep sigh, and then I left with Émilie and Julien. We had barely sat down in the living room when Étienne's two other children, Gustave, the eldest, and Lucille, the youngest, came rushing in with their respective spouses in tow.

"Have you called the priest yet?" Gustave said to Émilie.

"Yes, of course," she replied. "But it's no use. He won't see him."

"Are you sure?"

"Of course I'm sure," she said testily. "I've asked him twice and he's refused both times."

Gustave appeared to be stupefied by the news. He was a large, barrel-chested, red-faced man who expressed himself with violent gestures and a thunderous voice. He was vice-president of the Order of St. Basil, a patriotic and religious society, and entertained political ambitions that he felt were being compromised by his father's atheism.

"Oh hell, what difference does it make?" asked Lionel, Lucille's husband. He had always said he only went to church "to keep peace in the family."

"What difference does it make!" demanded Émilie.

"Yes, what difference. As long as he remains true to himself, he'll be 'saved,' won't he?" Lionel prounouced the word 'saved' in single quotes, as though to say he was only using it in its 'technical' sense, so that the others would understand what he was talking about.

"But he's been baptized!" cried Émilie. "He's a Catholic!"

"And Catholics are not free to believe whatever they want . . . But it is just as impossible for the Unbeliever to—"

"And what about me!" Gustave broke in. "What do you think it'll do to me, eh? Do you have any idea how much harm this pig-headedness of his could do me? Do you think I can stand up at the next elections and—"

"No, you're right," interrupted Émilie. "We must try again—"

Just at that moment the doorbell rang. It was the priest, a pale young man with a thin, ascetic face. Émilie had chosen him over Étienne's friends because she thought that they would not have been sufficiently insistent with the old man. She brought him up to date on the latest development, and for a moment he seemed to hesitate. But in the end he said:

"I'll go in anyway. It's my duty."

"Might you refuse to give him a Christian burial, Father?" asked Gustave.

"If he doesn't confess, if he shows no repentance, then yes," said the young priest. "I'll have no choice."

"But you could always say he gave in at the last minute, couldn't you? I mean, once he's dead, who's to know?"

"Out of the question. The Church—"

The priest's response was cut short by the doctor, who came into the room.

"No change, I'm afraid," he said, in response to our questioning looks. "I would imagine he still has a few hours."

"We'll go in and tell him you're here, Father," Gustave said as he headed toward Étienne's room, accompanied by Lucille and Émilie. "We'll try to convince him, but . . ." I hesitated for a brief moment, then followed them, out of an obscure desire to be there in case Étienne needed someone on his side. I left the living room just as the priest was lowering himself into an armchair.

Étienne had not changed position. He was lying on his back with his eyes shut, one side of his face destroyed by paralysis.

"How are you feeling, Papa?" Gustave asked.

Étienne opened his right eye. "Not bad," he said. "Not much pain."

There followed a long silence, broken only by the sound of Étienne's breathing.

"The priest is here, Papa," said Émilie, tentatively. "Would you like to see him?"

"No."

Gustave, Lucille and Émilie all started talking at once:

"Have you thought about it, seriously?"

"You can't just die like this, like some heathen!"

"The priest says they may not even let you in the Church!"

"You're jeopardizing my whole career!"

To all these arguments Étienne remained impassive, lying with his eyes closed as if he were deaf. Not a muscle in his face moved.

"So, you agree, then?" said Gustave. "We bring the priest in?"

"No." It was a firm, final "No" that contained not even the shadow of a hesitation.

The three looked helplessly at one another, then lowered their heads and left the bedroom. Once again I could hear Étienne heave a sigh, and I went up to his bedside and spoke to him:

"You're sure you don't need anything?" I asked.

"No, nothing, thanks. Just a bit of peace! Why is it that that's the one thing no one seems to want me to have?"

"You shall have it now, old friend," I said. "They won't dare come back again. I'll see you later."

And I left. Back in the living room, the young priest was saying: "It doesn't matter, I'll go in by myself."

"Father," I interrupted him. "Étienne is very tired. He wants to rest . . ."

"The repose of his soul is much more important than that of his body, M. Dorval," he said. "Perhaps God will inspire me with the right words to change his mind . . ."

"But he doesn't want his mind changed," I insisted. "He wants to be left alone! He wants to die in peace!"

"God's mercy *is* peace," said the priest. "He may change his mind yet."

"He's right," said Émilie. "We can't overlook anything. We would feel terrible afterwards."

I sat down, not daring to raise more objections. After all, it was a family affair. The priest went slowly towards Étienne's room while the rest of us remained silent. Only Gustave moved, pacing back and forth like a beast in a cage. The others sat still, looking down at their feet. Our vigil didn't last very long.

Suddenly the priest burst back into the room, his eyes wide and his voice shrill:

"I think the patient has lost consciousness," he said. "He can't hear me . . ."

Émilie ran into her father's room. "Papa, Papa, are you awake? Can you hear me?" she cried. "Did you understand what the priest was saying to you?"

"NO!"

This time there was no mistaking the exasperation in Étienne's voice. Émilie returned quietly to the living room.

"You see?" she said to the young priest. "It's no use."

We all resumed our places and our silence, while the priest began reciting the Prayers for the Dying. The others lowered themselves to their knees, all except Lionel, who seemed absorbed in the contemplation of a painting that hung above the fireplace. The priest's voice rose and fell in monotonous rhythms as he intoned the Latin words.

Suddenly, Lucille sprang to her feet and cried:

"Émilie, why don't we send Monique in to see Papa? You know how he dotes on her...."

Monique was Émilie's ten-year-old daughter, and the apple of Étienne's eye. The old man had never been able to refuse her anything. At Lucille's suggestion, the faces of the others lit up with renewed hope—all except that of the priest, who remained kneeling, his prayer book pressed between his hands, looking about the room with a doubtful expression.

"That's not a bad idea," exclaimed Gustave.

Émilie and her sister practically ran upstairs to wake up Monique.

"You never know," Gustave shrugged. "It might work."

The young priest had had time to gather his thoughts. "The idea is an inspiration from Heaven," he said. "I am certain that God has heard our prayers, and has taken pity on his lost lamb..."

The two women reappeared, with the little girl in her pajamas and wrapped in a house coat. Her hair was mussed, and she was still rubbing the sleep from her eyes.

"Now, you know what you have to do, Monique?" said Emilie.

"Yes, Mother."

"Tell him that you are very worried about him... Ask him—no, beg him.... Tell him everyone wants him to—"

"Yes, Aunt Lucille."

"And don't forget to give him a big kiss, like you do when you want a new doll or something."

"Yes, Uncle Gustave."

"Please allow me to bless the child," the priest said solemnly, "before she undertakes this supreme effort."

The child knelt down with a grave and even meditative air, no doubt flattered and perhaps a bit frightened by the importance of her mission.

"Remember everything I've told you," said Émilie.

"Yes, Mother."

And they directed her gently toward the door to her grandfather's bedroom.

She was in there a long time, perhaps half an hour. The rest of us didn't utter a word the whole time. Gustave resumed his nervous pacing, and from time to time Émilie would get up, tip-toe nervously to Étienne's door and place her ear against it, then return to her seat without saying anything. Lucille toyed with her bracelet. Lionel seemed to have returned to his deep contemplation of the painting above the fireplace.

Suddenly the bedroom door opened and Monique ran into the living room shouting: "He said yes, Mama, he said yes!"

Without saying a word, Émilie sprang to her feet and hurried toward Étienne's door, followed by the rest of us:

"Is it true, Papa?" she said. "You've agreed?"

"Yes," said Étienne, in the same tone of voice with which he had said "No" half an hour before.

"You wish to make your confession?"

"Yes."

The priest ran to get his stole, and we left him alone with Étienne.

This time, the conversation in the living room was animated.

"That was a brilliant idea you had, Lucille," said Gustave. "Absolutely brilliant."

"You see, M. Dorval," Émilie said to me, "one must never give up hope. If we had listened to you, he would still be a lost soul."

"I hope this will make you see things differently," Lucille said to her husband, who merely nodded.

Before long the priest came back into the room, his face beaming with joy.

"My friends, let us give thanks to God and be without fear: M. Beaulieu has made an exemplary confession. I have never heard such an edifying confession in my entire life."

"Oh, thank You, dear God, thank You," sobbed Émilie.

"That's excellent, Father," said Gustave heartily. "You have done a fine job here."

The young priest turned to me and said: "The penitent has expressed his wish to speak to you, sir."

When I entered his room, I could tell immediately that Étienne's breathing had become more difficult. There were beads of sweat on his forehead, and the paralyzed side of his face seemed to have become tighter and redder.

"You wanted to see me?" I asked quietly.

"Yes," he said. "Come closer. Closer. I have a . . . confession to make to you."

"A confession?"

"Yes. Those others, they don't matter. Let them think what they want. But you, I want you to know the truth. I have been . . . I have been weak."

"Weak, Étienne?"

"Yes. I haven't changed my beliefs, you understand . . . I am still as disbelieving as ever . . ."

"But you're afr—"

"Afraid? No, certainly not. Not a bit. Afraid of what? No, I just didn't have the strength to resist. That poor child, she was so worried. She cried so pitiably I couldn't. . . . And you know, it meant nothing to me, really, to confess to that—"

"Of course not," I said. "Don't give it another thought."

"No," he said. "I'm not worried about that. I suppose the dying are allowed their occasional lapses in faith." A thin smile played over the right side of his mouth, but I couldn't tell whether it was due to his last words or at the thought of the trick he had played on the others, on the "gulls," as he used to call them.

As I left the room, the priest, followed by his assistants, entered to administer Étienne his last rites.

Adrien Thério
Translated by David Homel

A CASE OF SORCERY

Born in Saint-Modeste, near Rivière-du-Loup on the lower St. Lawrence, on August 15, 1925, Adrien Thério was five when his family moved thirty miles inland, to the Chemin-Taché that appears in many of his short stories (including "A Case of Sorcery"). He began his studies at the Séminaire de Rimouski in 1947, later spent four years in a sanitorium recovering from a respiratory illness, then attended the University of Ottawa and Université Laval, where he received his doctorate in literature. He began his teaching career at Bellarmin College, in Kentucky, and subsequently taught at the University of Notre-Dame in Indiana; the University of Toronto; the Royal Military College, in Kingston (where he met Gérard Bessette, and founded the magazine *Livres et auteurs québécois* and the publishing house Les Éditions Jumonville); and the University of Ottawa, from 1969 to the present. He helped found the influential literary magazine *Lettres québécoises*, and is an outspoken proponent of Quebec culture and literature.

A prolific writer, Thério has published more than fifteen books since his first novel, *Les brèves années*, appeared in 1953. Among the rest are three works on Jules Fournier, a journalist and thinker of the nineteenth century, and his first book of stories, *Contes des belles saisons* (1958). A second novel, *La Soif et le mirage*, appeared in 1960, and *Mes beaux meurtres*, a second book of stories, was published in 1961. His anthology *Conteurs canadiens-français*, published in 1965, was the first anthology of modern Québécois short stories: in his introduction, he wrote that "a new country has been brought to light in these contemporary stories, a country that breathes to the rhythm of the modern world."

Thério began writing what has been referred to as the chronicles of Chemin-Taché with *Les brèves années*, and continued them in such later novels as *Le Printemps qui pleure* (1962), *La Colère du père* (1974); *C'est ici que le monde a commencé* (1978); and *Marie-Eve, Marie-Eve* (1983). "L'Enchantement," translated here as "A Case of Sorcery" by David Homel, is from *Ceux du Chemin-Taché* (1963). "It took me many years to realize just how much that barren piece of land had left its mark on me," Thério told Donald Smith in an interview published in *L'Écrivain devant son œuvre* (1983; *Voices of Deliverance*, 1986). Though its origins are in early folktales of magic fiddles, "A Case of Sorcery" is also about how a country can be transformed by art.

༄

"A Case of Sorcery" is a translation of "L'Enchantement" published in *Ceux du Chemin-Taché* (Montreal: Éditions de l'Homme, 1963).

If you'd visited the Chemin-Taché fifty years ago, and were to pass by it again today, you wouldn't recognize a thing.

Everything has changed!

I might as well tell you that the land I come from is anything but fertile. Sitting on a mountain, a mountain that turns into a plateau once you get there, a wide plateau with an evil glare that first shows you its notches and crags, its tortuous hills and its lowlands where your feet bog down in the bad earth, it seems to defy the horizons and all the human beings who ever ventured there.

I never knew that time and it's difficult to imagine such a thing. But the old folks from where I come from still talk about those days with a misty kind of horror in their eyes, a kind of regret that's hard to describe, part satisfaction and part pride. Because they're the ones who brought the big change! Or rather, they were the witnesses of the event that changed the whole country. If you saw their eyes, one evening when they were in the throes of nostalgia, you might be able to imagine what the Chemin-Taché once was.

A hard land, difficult to get to, it was opened to settlement late. For a long time, a bad road ran through it, and only the bravest would cross over to the neighbouring villages, and never would they stray from the path.

One day, surveyors arrived, divided the plateau into lots and, shortly after, offered these new parcels to whomever showed up. They even promised help for the building of houses and barns. But everybody had been warned and settlers were few and far between. Just three the first year! They struggled to clear a few acres of land. But discouragement got the better of them and they disappeared, leaving a half-built house, or part of a stable with its doors wide open, like a giant maw that might have spat out the wave of misfortune that covered the countryside. The land they had worked produced only rocks, and what was underneath promised more of the same harvest.

"By the Cross," they would swear, "we'll never manage to grow any grain in this bedevilled land! Rocks, rocks, and more rocks!"

The next year, newcomers arrived to take the place of those who had left. At least they had a shelter for themselves and a stable for the few animals they owned. Following their example, attracted by the grants given those who could clear a parcel of land, more people showed up to take possession of the neighbouring lots. After a few years, along the narrow road that crossed the landscape, you could see a string of some thirty defeated-looking little houses.

But the inhabitants of the Chemin-Taché never got used to living on barren land. Every year, seven or eight more families would disappear, happy to be pulling out and quitting such ungenerous land whose only recompense for the effort spent was rocks that seemed designed to break the shares of their ploughs.

Even the climate conspired against them. In winter, the storms were so frequent and the wind blew with such rage that several houses lost their roofs. In summer, the sun seemed to hold back some of its warmth, as if the very sight of the countryside covered it with a cloud.

The people would turn surly, cursing the temperature, the rain, the wind, the snow; cursing the naked rock crags, the rocks that never stopped turning up under their ploughshares; cursing the lowlands that had no business being there and never seemed to want to dry out; cursing destiny with flinty, pitiless eyes. At times, surrounded by stumps and slashes, they would call curses down upon the misfortune that dogged their steps.

Yes, the people of the Chemin-Taché would go that far!

When they had choked back their curses against destiny long enough, they would pick up and leave. Without regret. They wouldn't even turn back for a final look at the slashes that were still smoking.

No one ever saw them again. Others took their place and little by little learned to complain about the misfortune that had taken up residence on this mountain. After a few years, when they'd decided that their dog's life had lasted long enough and that it was time to feel the sunshine on their hardened faces again, they, too, departed, damning the land with curses of their own devising.

Then, suddenly, everything changed!

The people's spirits is where the transformation first took place. Then, the farmers began remarking that there were fewer rocks, and that the climate was more amenable, and that the plateau itself had taken on a new face.

This change was the work of a man who had only just come to the Chemin-Taché. The man's name was Laurentin—for a long time, all anyone knew about him was his first name—and he had set himself up on a farm abandoned the year before, at the edge of the village, on a crossroad that led to Raudot Township.

Laurentin didn't stand out from the others. When he went off to work, people would say the same about him as they would have said about Pierre or Charles: "There goes Laurentin."

And that was that. Laurentin would go into the store, come out again, go down the road and head for his place. He would do the same as his neighbours did: cut down trees, heap up the branches, pull out the stumps, pick the stones, and seed the new earth. He worked hard all day. In the evening, after supper, he would sit on his steps and from there gaze wordlessly upon the village, happy with the day that had been completed, proud to hear the children's voices as they played in front of the house.

When night fell, he would go inside and, a few seconds later, come out and sit in the same spot again, but this time with a fiddle in his hand.

Then came the sharp report of plucked strings, and a brief lament whose tune was off-key. Then the tune became a song, a song everyone recognized, one that had been born generations ago and was still remembered by everyone.

Through the long spring evenings, Laurentin would make his fiddle sing. He played every song the people knew. The villagers listened to him, sometimes their hearts would grow heavy with feeling, they would sing the words that accompanied the tune and, when the music faded, go off to bed, their minds at peace.

Those common tunes helped the people forget their troubles, but they didn't keep them from deserting the Chemin-Taché. One morning, discouragement would worm its way into them like a snake among the rocky crags and stumpy lands. Then the news would come that two or three more families had left. That was the price to be paid for a relentless fate that scoured the belly of the great plateau that had given birth to this sorry little village.

But Laurentin had an idea.

He worked on it ceaselessly that first winter after his arrival on the Chemin-Taché. While his children did their homework and his wife spun the wool, he would sit with his eyes closed and try out new tunes on his fiddle.

"You forgot how to play!" his wife would tell him.

"How could I forget?"

"Since you stopped playing for the village, we never hear the old tunes."

"I'm composing a song! That takes time, you know!"

His wife stared at him, not knowing whether to laugh at him or with him, out of happiness. Her Laurentin, a composer? Who had ever heard such a thing? She never imagined that someone had actually composed the tunes she knew. Now, a single word from her husband conjured up a long line of fiddlers, all bowing their bows in different ways. The sound of it confused her ears so badly she couldn't recognize any of the tunes she knew by heart; now, she began to understand what Laurentin meant.

"You can't do it, you've never been to school!"

"You don't need to go to school to play the fiddle."

"To play—no. But composing's different!"

"We'll see."

Laurentin continued to experiment with his bow, trying a note, starting over, sliding up and down the scale, moving into a crescendo. Then he would put down his fiddle, close his eyes, and try to grab at a bit of melody or the lilt of a waltz. Suddenly, he would take up his instrument again and the strings would sing as a flash of joy lit up his damp eyes.

By winter's end, the melody was born! In the spring, when he could finally sit outside, he began playing the old tunes again. His melody would wait, for the day had to be perfect.

One warm July evening, as the village rested in the calm air, as a kind of porous veil, soft as velvet, stretched over the ripe hay and a new perfume covered the mountain, Laurentin decided that the time was right.

He stepped onto the porch, fiddle in one hand, bow in the other. He stood and waited. Then suddenly, with his trembling fingers, he ran the bow over the waiting strings.

First came a gentle, soft song, a haunting waltz whose tempo seemed to rise from the earth itself. Then a quick-paced refrain set in, bursting with happy notes that slipped through the open windows and brought enthusiasm to every ear. Next, a trembling crescendo ended in an explosion of sad joy, a great outpouring that engulfed the Chemin-Taché, becoming one with it, telling its sad tales, taking possession of it, caressing it.

The people understood that something extraordinary was happening, and that the melody enveloping the village in a loving embrace had a particular meaning.

Everyone listened as the strings sang anew. A long shiver ran through the village, past the ripe hay, through the clearings, under the roofs of the houses, to the very heart of the dwelling-places, it penetrated the secret corners of the soul and transformed the way people had thought for years.

The need for joy filled the plateau. Endless joy like a hammock woven from fruitful labour where thousands of memories were gathered, recalling the harshness of the countryside, its discouragement, pain and the misery endured together, all dissolving into the gentleness of this warm night.

The people understood that the long years of unease and yesterday's obstacles would finally bear fruit. The country, once so barren, would become prosperous; no more would they damn its rocky crags and desert it with a hateful backwards glance.

In the distance, the fiddle still played. As darkness gathered, the spirits of the people seemed to be undergoing a complete change. The rhythm of the music was so new, so appropriate to the land, the inhabitants had to wonder whether they hadn't all lapsed into a dream that would soon come to an end.

In the distance, the fiddle stopped. And no sooner had it done so than a man's voice, strong and tuneful, full and round like the trees of the land, issued forth in a song whose words flowed from the melody that had only just faded from the strings of the fiddle. Laurentin was explaining the meaning of the music with words. His words were the great plateau of the Chemin-Taché, they stood for its back-breaking road, its simple houses, its pasture-land reddening in the sun, its naked, arrogant rocks, its burned stumps and smoking slashes; they stood for the hard eyes of the men who built that country and the graceless voices of the women who had lost the habit of gentleness and the caress of the female voice. The soul of the country sang in those words; a kind of sorcery, an inexplicable wave of happiness swelled every breast.

When night covered the earth, the song fell silent. And when it came time for the villagers to sleep, their dreams were alive with the incantations of Laurentin's fiddle unfurling like a flag.

The next evening, and the evening after, Laurentin took up his fiddle. When he started to play the old tunes, people asked him for the song of the land again. All summer long, Laurentin played it. But one autumn evening, the wood of the instrument splintered in his hands, and Laurentin stood there, alone, for what seemed like forever, stroking the divine strings and the sacred wood from which that unforgettable melody had sprung.

That was the end of Laurentin and his fiddle, but the people knew the song, and they never forgot it. From that moment on, the Chemin-Taché had become a different place.

Rare are the days when the sun does not show its face. And rare are the people whose faces do not glow with pleasure when you meet them on the new road that has replaced the old, back-breaking track.

To ward off misfortune, all they have to do is whistle the tune that everyone along the Chemin-Taché knows, the tune composed by Laurentin long ago.

Now, you won't be surprised if I tell you that the Chemin-Taché has become a prosperous bit of country, a wide plateau with long, straight fields, all in harmony, glowing green in the springtime, yellow in the summer, reddened by the autumn—and that the rock crags are scarcely visible now, scattered here and there.

Once you've been to that land, you'll always return. When you've been away too long, your heart will issue a call from within, and that call will become a song as great as a river, and stir the feelings inside you.

Several generations have gone by since that famous evening. A new family has replaced Laurentin's on his farm, but the spot is still known as Laurentin's Place; it's the people's way of remembering.

If one day you should go there, linger a while beneath the trees at the road's edge, across from Laurentin's Place. I'm sure you'll hear the fiddle's lilting tune and the song of the country's soul.

Jacques Ferron

Translated by Wayne Grady

THE CHRONICLES OF L'ANSE SAINT-ROCH

Jacques Ferron was born in Louiseville, near Trois-Rivières, on January 20, 1921, and attended first the Séminaire de Trois-Rivières and then Université Laval, from which he graduated with a degree in medicine in 1945. After a year with the Royal Army Medical Corps, he opened a practice in the Gaspé, in the village of Rivière-la-Madeleine, and then in Ville Jacques-Cartier, near Montreal, where he lived until his death on April 22, 1985. Doctor, writer, dramatist, journalist, iconoclast, and political maverick, Ferron was president of the Canadian Peace Congress in 1954, founder of the serio-satirical Rhinoceros Party in 1963, and the only person both Pierre Trudeau and Paul Rose would trust to negotiate the surrender of the FLQ in December 1970.

Ferron was a prolific writer of fiction, drama, criticism, and essays. His first play, *Le Dodu*, was published in 1956, the same year his first novel, *La Barbe de François Hertel*, appeared. His other novels include *Cotnoir* (1962; *Dr. Cotnoir*, 1973), *La Charrette* (1968; *The Cart*, 1981), and *L'Amelanchier* (1970; *The Juneberry Tree*, 1975). His short stories began appearing in French in 1962 with the publication of *Contes du pays incertain*, followed by *Contes anglais et autres* in 1964. These were translated in a single volume, entitled *Tales from the Uncertain Country*, by Betty Bednarski in 1972.

In 1968, a complete edition of Ferron's stories appeared. Called simply *Contes*, it included the stories from the two earlier collections as well as four previously unpublished stories, one of which was "Les Chroniques de l'anse Saint-Roch," translated here by Wayne Grady as "The Chronicles of l'Anse Saint-Roch." Ferron, writes Donald Smith in *Voices of Deliverance*, "attaches a great deal of importance to Quebec's history"; Ferron wrote a series of what he called "historiettes," or historical tales, in which he writes "the true history without any window-dressing or prettifying." While the protagonist of this story, Reverend William Andicotte, is not a strictly historical figure, the story is "true" in every other important sense, and a fine example of Ferron's juxtaposition of fact and fiction.

∽

"Chronicles of l'Anse Saint-Roch" is a translation of "Chronique de l'anse Saint-Roch" published in *Contes* (Montreal: Éditions H.M.H. Ltd., 1985).

I

Between the lighthouse of Madeleine and the Mont-Louis bridge, the line that separates land from sea, when seen from the top of the cliffs, is unmistakeable. The shore itself, however, can only be reached by four valleys, three of which are clearly visible and one that is almost impossible to detect. The first are called, from east to west, Manche d'Épée, Gros-Morne, and L'Anse-Pleureuse; they cut deeply into the cliff-face, but the bays they feed are small and exposed to all weather. "From Madeleine to Saint-Louis," the old sailors used to say, "you can't believe what you see; just pass right on by without a second look." The fourth valley, situated between Gros-Morne and L'Anse-Pleureuse, is not readily visible because it is narrow and twisted; it empties obliquely into a deep and sharply defined bay. It was christened the Valley of Mercy because, as the old-timers said, "You can't depend on it; when you look for it you won't find it, and you'll only come across it when you're least expecting it." This dubious reputation meant that its harbour was hardly ever used; at best the sailing ships of a larger tonnage could enter it only at high tide. It was forgotten, and if today you hear them talking about a Valley of Mercy, they would not be able to tell you where it is; it has become a legend.

Sailors, who experience coasts only from a distance, think of them in terms of valleys and mountains, while fishermen who skirt the shoreline from much closer in ignore its backdrop and concentrate on the coast itself. The names they use to describe the coast differ accordingly: Mont-Louis and Gros-Morne bear the mark of the sailor; Manche-d'Épée and L'Anse-Pleureuse of the fisherman. When the Valley of Mercy was rediscovered the area was called L'Anse Saint-Roch, because the fishermen who spent their summers there came from Saint-Roch-des-Aulnaies.

In November 1840, an epidemic of typhus, brought over on an emigrant ship called the *Merino*, swept through the parishes of the lower St Lawrence. Abbé Toupin, the young and scrupulous vicar of L'Islet, wasn't surprised in the least. He had long been fearing some kind of vengeance from Heaven. As the epidemic raged into February the young abbé spent all his energy explaining it. His preaching became so popular that people came from neighbouring parishes to hear him. The sermons grew gloomier and fiercer from one Sunday to the next, until one day he rose in his pulpit, a strange expression on his face, and cried: "My friends, the end of the world is at hand!" And he fell down dead. The epidemic died out soon afterwards, but the abbé's words lived on in the hearts of his parishioners. Next spring, most of the fishing boats of L'Islet remained drawn up on the beach, the spirit of adventure seemingly content to work itself out by staying at home. From all of Saint-Roch only Thomette Gingras and Sules Campion went out into the Gulf.

II

After breakfast, the Reverend William Andicotte asked his wife what she thought about Canada. Intrigued, she looked down at the table, but there was nothing on it to explain the question.

"William, have you had enough to eat?"

The pastor pushed aside his plate; he was serious, he awaited her answer. Canada, Canada . . . really, she hadn't the vaguest idea.

"God be praised"' he cried. "Then you have nothing against my project?"

"Your project, William?"

"Well, properly speaking, my mission. I believe, my dear, that we are needed in Canada."

Reverend Andicotte was the minister of the cathedral in Liverpool. He had a red mane and a mournful mien, although he knew when to leave his mournfulness and laugh when occasion demanded. He was thin but had enough appetite for a whole fraternity of fat monks; preached asceticism but hardly practised it; was nonetheless a good minister and a well-informed theologian. The archbishop of the diocese had him earmarked as his successor.

His wife loved him; he returned her love and added to it; she loved him back all the more, and by these augmenting endearments Time had brought them closer and closer together. Since they were hardly ever apart, they grew ever more strongly united. This didn't prevent them from having their own private worlds: he had his church and she had her house. They had three daughters: the eldest resembled her father without quite succeeding in being ugly; the others took after their mother. All three were accomplished young ladies.

"What about the episcopate, William?"

The Reverend had been awaiting his episcopate for ten years. The archbishop had promised it to him; when the old fellow died it would go to him. Except that for ten years it had not been the archbishop's pleasure to die; in fact, he looked better and better each year, and seemed well on his way to celebrating his centenary.

"Fie," he said, "on the episcopate."

"No, let's wait a little longer."

"The old boy will live to bury us, my dear. No, believe me, our future is in Canada."

She did believe him, having always done so. Moreover she was still at an age when missionary fervour seemed preferable to a sedentary episcopate. With a deep flutter of the heart, praiseworthy and healthy—though not perhaps in the eyes of the Church of England—she gave her assent. Marriage, about which she knew as little as she did about Canada, no longer deceived her.

"Shall I do the dishes?" she asked.

"No, my dear, break them. Break them."

But she couldn't do it; twenty years of frugal living had made such waste painful. In the end she washed them. It was not a good omen.

III

One month later the pastor, his wife, and their three daughters boarded the *Merino*. The previous evening the archbishop, learning of their departure, had died of an apoplectic fit; they were still laughing about it. Gulls swooped above the girls' heads with shrill cries. The Reverend was content: an ancient herring gull was escorting them with the greatest dignity, its neck drawn in, its wings held stiffly out, from time to time emitting a hoarse croak just to remind itself that it still could. The mother followed, slightly dazed by all these birds.

The captain was shaving. He heard the noise: "What's up?" he called out, and was told that it had something to do with a pastor. He hurried out of his cabin just as the laughing party arrived on the bridge. The captain thrust himself in front of them, one cheek pink, the other black, and his straight-razor held aloft like a scimitar. The gulls fell quiet. The old gull, when the laughter died, thought he had suddenly gone deaf: trying to keep in his head the sounds he could no longer hear, he floated above the silence.

"Who are you?" asked the Reverend of their unexpected guest.

"Who are *you*?"

"I am the Reverend Andicotte."

"And I am the captain of this ship."

The two men looked each other up and down. Then, turning abruptly, the captain stomped back into his cabin. Followed closely by his flock of females, the pastor continued on to their own.

"What do you think, William?"

"My dear," he replied, "we will doubtless encounter many such men in Canada."

The *Merino*'s captain was not a church-going man. He disliked pastors, firmly believing that they never laughed. Well, it seems they do laugh. This piqued his curiosity. When he finished shaving, he presented himself at the Reverend's cabin. He put on a better face, they listened to him, he explained himself, and everyone was happy.

"But what were you laughing about?" he asked.

"The archbishop died," explained Mary, the youngest.

The captain slapped his thighs. From now on, he'd be an Anglican.

IV

The *Merino* was a former slave ship. No sooner were the emigrants on board than the anchor was weighed. The emigrants forgot their miseries and looked forward to the promised land. They left behind them a trail of human wreckage, of broken bellies and petrified children, of demented souls and severed hands. They set their sails; the sails were clean and white. The vessel that left Liverpool was a great, black edifice propelled by hope.

"They don't care a damn about me," the captain grumbled.

Her Majesty's regulations prevented him, at least while in England, from taking on more than two hundred passengers—Her Majesty was gracious, but her regulations were stupid: hadn't he already made a crossing with two thousand blacks?

"Might as well go with no cargo at all," he said. "Just to amuse the crew."

They steered for Hamburg, where they took on another three hundred emigrants. The captain's mood improved: with fewer than five hundred passengers on a ship built to carry a hundred, he would have felt lonely.

"I like having souls in my charge, lots of souls," he confessed to the pastor.

The latter praised the captain's zeal, although the promiscuity occasioned by such overcrowding seemed somewhat un-Anglican. But the Reverend didn't want to complain: one mustn't press a convert too hard.

"Besides," he told himself, "we're going to see plenty more like him in Canada."

V

Sules Campion and Thomette Gingras left Saint-Roch at the beginning of May. Two weeks later they were off Mont-Louis. The following morning, the sun rose over a sea of infinite calm. It was no good unfurling the sail; it takes more than a bit of cloth at the end of a mast to get a boat under way. The two fishermen waited for high tide to get them out of the bay, then, when they were in open water, they shipped their oars and let the sea carry them west. Below L'Anse-Pleureuse they hugged the shore and watched as huge chunks of ice disengaged themselves from the cliff-face, a sure sign that they were too early to fish for cod. They were in no hurry to get anywhere. They got there anyway. Just off a cape, like its shadow, a clear, dark stream wove its way out to sea; here and there the troubled water warned them of submerged boulders. They got in among some reefs; the hull scraped over a round rock covered with moss. Campion, standing at the bow, pushed with an oar. Suddenly the sea-bed slipped out of sight and they found themselves in a harbour, and there was the valley. A single detail held their attention: from a cabin above the cove a thin whiff of smoke rose up, pale and violet, and disappeared without a trace into the still air.

"Christ!" exclaimed Thomette Gingras. 'They're burning our store of hardwood!"

VI

The thrill of departure lasted only as long as the departure. As soon as they lost sight of land they began to get sick.

"Bah!" said the captain. "Nobody dies of seasickness."

On the fifteenth day of the crossing four of the passengers died. They were Poles. The captain shrugged his shoulders: they'd paid their berths in advance. "They're not slaves," he said. "They're free men; they can die whenever they like."

Besides, they probably died from some Polish disease that wouldn't bother British subjects.

VII

In her pretty cabin on the upper deck, Mrs. Andicotte has caught a disease that seems to have come up from the hold. She goes out, but the vertiginous nothingness beneath her rises up with raucous and discordant cries, and she soon goes back inside to lie down. Elizabeth and Mary stay with her. Their youth makes her break into tears. Jane, the eldest, accompanies her father; she puts the word of God before everything and hardly worries about what is proper for her sex.

VIII

Typhus is better than the plague; it tends one toward resignation. A violent shivering grips the patient, he is flushed with small red macules, his tongue becomes paralyzed, he can no longer articulate his suffering. He can only sing it, softly, sadly, without struggling against it. He can be thrown overboard before he is actually dead.

IX

One day Jane learned that Tom, the captain's slave, was dying in his hammock in the hold. She went down to talk to him about God, and fell into the hands of sailors who left her, covered with bruises, tears, and dust, alone with the black man. Tom pulled himself toward her and, with a trembling hand, wiped her face. Observing his charity, Jane was touched. That was how the captain found them.

X

The spotted fever took hold of the pastor's wife. The *Merino* tacked back and forth in the Gulf for a week. She died off Gros-Morne. Her body was brought out onto the bridge.

Above her hung Tom, the slave, from the yardarm. The captain placed one of the ship's boats at the bereaved family's disposal, and the *Merino* sailed on to Quebec without them.

XI

At the sight of the smoke a violent indignation seized Thomette Gingras. He threw himself below, rummaged about in his gear, reappeared on deck with a loaded rifle, and shouted to his mate:

"Sules! Bring 'er in to shore!"

Sules worked at the oars, and the boat went running up on the sand. Gingras jumped onto the beach. Campion got up to follow suit; a girl came out of the cabin, blushing, young, well built, but very scantily dressed. Campion froze in the bow like a wooden figurine. The girl, as taken aback as he was, opened her mouth and forgot to close the front of her dress. This oversight did not improve the situation. Campion joined his companion.

"Don't shoot," he said, "I think she's tame."

"What'll we do?" asked Gingras, whose gun was making him excited.

"Go up and get a closer look," proposed Campion.

They made as if to approach: just then two more girls came rushing out of the cabin, completely hamstringing the two fishermen.

Gingras, powerfully moved, raised his rifle: "Christ, I'm gonna shoot, I'm gonna shoot!" he yelled instead of shooting. Campion held him back.

"Take it easy, Thomette, take it easy!"

At that moment the girls, who were still grouped before the door, parted to let a huge man, dressed all in black, with flaming red hair and a Bible in his hand, emerge from the cabin and advance on the two men. "Holy Christ, what in hell is that?" The figure kept moving down the path . . . Gingras fired. The figure opened his mouth as if to swallow the bullet, then pitched forward and fell to the ground, his nose buried in his big book.

XII

At Saint-Roch-des-Aulnaies, autumn came and went, and the villagers waited in vain for the two fishermen. They believed them drowned. Two years later a fishing boat from Cap Saint-Ignace brought news that the men were alive and sound of body if not of soul, living under the spell of three she-devils. The next spring the number of fishermen from the lower St Lawrence attracted by the Gaspé cod was greatly increased. When they returned, they confirmed the news: Gingras and Campion had settled in L'Anse Saint-Roch with a woman apiece and the children they'd had from them by the left hand, happy, and even disposed, if the opportunity should ever arise, to get married properly. Meanwhile, their souls were intact, their women were both magnificient creatures, white as milk, hot as fire, and quite distinguished; they spoke English, just like society ladies. As for witchcraft, that came from the eldest sister, a strange, thin, red-faced woman who read from a big, black book and carried in her arms a little black child she had had by Satan before the two fishermen got there.

XIII

> A sea-filled day a single gull
> That I see ever from afar
> Floating turning like a sail
> Tell me seagull what you are
>
> Are you a beacon shining clear
> A sea-rose flower without stem
> Whose petals scatter in the air
> Like love to make my senses swim
>
> A whirling winding sail divine
> Prepares a fated tenderness
> Its flight deflects from its design
> You lift your face to the caress

Born in turbulence you feel
Engulfed by wings of wind and sea
The ocean marks you with its seal
And now I fear what you must be

The bird will float and turn again
In air a god stirs from above
My heart your body take their plan
And you a goddess now of Love

XIV

Man is a vagabond, woman holds him back. A country without women, a land fit only for passing through, a barren desert that lacks even a stake to tie animals to: for a long time that was the north coast of the Gaspésie. Fishermen from Montmagny, from Cap Saint-Ignace, from L'Islet, went down to it every spring and returned from it every fall; no one ever wintered there. The adventures of Gingras and Campion changed all that. The Canadienne who triumphed over the Indian woman, her rival in whose arms her men would discover a whole new continent, was not a woman who would give up without a fight. She let them go only when she was sure they would come back. If she couldn't be sure, she'd go with them. That's what the women of the lower St Lawrence did: because they could never be sure of the Gaspésie, they said goodbye to the old parishes, to their well-tended land, so serene, so Catholic. They came down with their men, not just for a summer, not to give life to some dream of late afternoons by the sea, but dressed to the neck, prepared for all four seasons, to give life to a country. Before long, every cove from Méchins to Rivière-aux-Renards was inhabited.

XV

Tucked under a cliff, facing the sea, your house is not very grand. Your man is brave, but he doesn't master you. Giants hover over you during the night. At dawn the wind drops from a great height and all in one piece. It passes just above your roof like a thousand shrieking birds. You shiver even in warm weather, when you have nothing to be afraid of. If you're carrying a child in your belly, its little life strangles you. Why didn't you stay in the old country, where men dominated the land, where the houses were large and the countryside was small? What made you come to this wild bay to follow the call of a fisherman?

XVI

Jane halted on the beach. She made a gesture of uncertainty that took in the jarring cries of the gulls and the natural disorder of space, but recovered herself when she saw her son, who was playing with some seashells and was beset by a flock of friendly, hungry crows. She had been bewitched, she knew, but then a child had been born. In the anger of his crying he had reconfirmed her world.

When the little black child noticed his mother, he left his shells and the crows. She took him up in her arms and cradled him. She was tired. She would have liked him to go to sleep, but his laughing eyes never left her. A while later, his uncles' fishing boat entered the harbour. They threw their catch up onto the shore and stepped out of the barque, happy as children. Sules picked up a pebble from the beach and threw it: to his complete surprise it hit a crow. The bird stayed where it was, its wing stretched out, its neck drawn in, its beak half open.

Jane cried out and tried to stop Sules, but she was too late: the stone struck. She took up the bird in her hands. It stared fixedly at her. She told it she was sorry, but she knew that no one would ever forgive her. She put the bird down, and it hobbled off a few steps, dragging its broken wing.

Sules and Thomette laughed at her dismay. Two days later her son stepped on a shell and cut his foot. The wound festered, his woolly head glistened with sweat. All one night he was delirious; in the morning the shrill wind that cut down from the cliff like a thousand shrieking birds carried off his soul.

Several weeks went by and Jane did not recover from this final blow. One morning, as the sun came up, she was sitting on a stump holding in her lap the huge Bible she no longer read, when she saw the wounded crow. She got up; the bird ran toward the path that led to L'Anse-Pleureuse. She followed it. From time to time she lost sight of it, but when she stopped it reappeared. The path was steep; it turned up the mountain in order to twist around the peaks along the cliff. Jane was soon out of breath, her knees began to give out; she went off the path into a burn-out that cut across it. When she looked around her she saw all the crow-people who had come together to judge her.

XVII

The abbé Ferland, a professor at the college in Sainte-Anne-de-la-Pocatière, a giant with a heart of gold, spent that summer ranging up and down the northern coast of the Gaspé peninsula, baptizing, hearing confessions, marrying, bringing with him the peace of God. At Madeleine, with a single stroke of an axe, he silenced the mighty Braillard who had been terrorizing the village. After his stay at L'Anse Saint-Roch, Sules Campion and Thomette Gingras had each taken his Englishwoman, white as milk, hot as fire, by the right hand; they were the happiest men in the world and they lived to have many more children. As for Jane Andicotte, the abbé found her half dead on the footpath near L'Anse-Pleureuse, and he took her with him to Quebec. She found her final rest in the Convent of the Urselines.

This chronicle records facts that may not be to our liking, but life itself is not always to our liking. The main thing to keep in mind is that everything finds its proper order, and that around the untamed bay, little by little, the customs of the old country triumph over native fear, softening the harsh bird-cries of the wind passing over the houses as it sweeps down from the cliffs.

Hubert Aquin
Translated by Alan Brown

BACK ON APRIL ELEVENTH

Hubert Aquin was born in Montreal on October 24, 1929. He attended the Université de Montréal, where he studied philosophy, and then the Institut d'Études politiques in Paris, from 1948 to 1951, before returning to Montreal to work for Radio-Canada and the National Film Board. In the 1960s he helped found the political and literary journals *Liberté* and *Parti pris*, the latter a left-wing publication set up in opposition to the federalist journal *Cité libre*, to which Pierre Elliott Trudeau was a principle contributor. Aquin was arrested in 1964 for carrying a gun—he was vice-president of the Rassemblement pour l'Indépendance Nationale at the time. While detained in a psychiatric hospital, he wrote his first novel, *Prochain épisode* (1965), about a man detained in a psychiatric hospital. His other novels include *Trou de mémoire* (1968; *Blackout*, 1974), for which he was awarded—and refused to accept—the Governor-General's Award; *L'Antiphonaire* (1969; *The Antiphonary*, 1973), and *Neige noire* (1974; *Hamlet's Twin*, 1979), for which he was awarded the Grand Prix de la ville de Montréal. He became literary editor of Les Éditions la Presse in 1975, but resigned the following year. On March 15, 1977, he shot himself on the grounds of the Villa-Maria convent, in Montreal.

"De retour le 11 avril," translated by Alan Brown as "Back on April Eleventh," first appeared in *Liberté* in the March-April 1969 issue, and was later reprinted in *Point de fuite* (1971) and in a posthumous collection of Aquin's writing, *Blocs erratiques* (1977). In this story, Aquin depicts the self-destructive element he saw in many of Quebec's intellectuals. "A dialogue of the deaf is taking place," he wrote in an essay entitled "La Fatigue culturelle du Canada français," "between thinkers who, by reducing their listeners to conditioned products, disabuse them at the same time of any illusions concerning their own intellectual strength." "Back on April Eleventh" depicts this intellectual frustration pushed to a feverish extreme. It not only foretells Aquin's own death, but also warns against the death of independent thinking in modern Quebec.

∽

"Back on April Eleventh" is a translation of "De retour le 11 avril" published in *Point de fuite* (Montreal: Cercle du livre de France, 1971); first appeared in *Liberté*, 11, no. 2 (mars-avril 1969).

When your letter came I was reading a Mickey Spillane. I'd already been interrupted twice, and was having trouble with the plot. There was this man Gardner, who for some reason always carted around the photo of a certain corpse. It's true I was reading to kill time. Now I'm not so interested in killing time.

It seems you have no idea of what's been going on this winter. Perhaps you're afflicted with a strange, intermittent amnesia that wipes out me, my work, our apartment, the brown record-player . . . I assure you I can't so easily forget this season I've passed without you, these long, snowy months with you so far away. When you left, the first snow had just fallen on Montreal. It blocked the sidewalks, obscured the houses, and laid down great pale counterpanes in the heart of the city.

The evening you left—on my way back from Dorval— I drove aimlessly through the slippery empty streets. Each time the car went into a skid I had the feeling of going on an endless voyage. The Mustang was transformed into a rudderless ship. I drove for a long time without the slightest accident, not even a bump. It was dangerous driving. I know. Punishable by law. But that night even the law had become a mere ghost of itself, as had the city and this damned mountain that we've tramped so often. So much whiteness made a strong impression on me. I remember feeling a kind of anguish.

You, my love, probably think I'm exaggerating as usual and that I get some kind of satisfaction out of establishing these connections between your leaving and my states of mind. You may think I'm putting things together in retrospect in such a way as to explain what happened after that first fall of cerusian white.

But you're wrong: I'm doing nothing of the kind. That night, I tell you, the night you left, I skidded and slipped on that livid snow, fit to break your heart. It was myself I lost control of each time the Mustang slid softly into the abyss of memory. Winter since then has armed our city with many coats of melting mail, and here I am already on the verge of a burnt-ivory spring.

Someone really has to tell you, my love, that I tried twice to take my life in the course of this dark winter.

Yes, it's the truth. I'm telling you this without passion, with no bitterness or depths of melancholy. I'm a little disappointed at having bungled it; I feel like a failure, that's all. But now I'm bored. I've fizzled out under the ice. I'm finished.

Have you, my love, changed since last November? Do you still wear your hair long? Have you aged since I saw you last? How do you feel about all this snow that's fallen on me, drifting me in? I suppose a young woman of twenty-five has other souvenirs of her travels besides these discoloured postcards I've pinned to the walls of our apartment?

You've met women ... or men; you've met perhaps one man and ... he seemed more charming, more handsome, more "liberating" than I could ever be. Of course, as I say that, I know that to liberate oneself from another person one has only to be unfaithful. In this case you were right to fly off to Amsterdam to escape my black moods; you were right to turn our liaison into a more relative thing, the kind that people have, any old love affair, any shabby business of that kind ...

But that's all nonsense. I'm not really exaggerating, I'm just letting myself go, my love, letting myself drift. A little like the way I drove the Mustang that night last November. I'm in distress, swamped by dark thoughts. And it's no use telling myself that my imagination's gone wild, that I'm crazy to tell you these things, for I feel that this wave of sadness is submerging both of us and condemning me to total desolation. I can still see the snowy streets and me driving through them with no rhyme or reason, as if that aimless motion could magically make up for losing you. But you know, I already had a sedimentary confused desire to die, that very evening.

While I was working out the discords of my loneliness at the steering wheel of the Mustang, you were already miles high in a DC-8 above the North Atlantic. And a few hours later your plane would land gently on the icy runway of Schipol—after a few leisurely manoeuvres over the still plains of the Zuider Zee. By then I would be back in our apartment, reading a Simenon—*The Nahour Affair*—set partly in a Paris blanketed in snow (a rare occurrence), but also in that very city of Amsterdam where you had just arrived. I went to sleep in the small hours of the morning, clutching that bit of reality that somehow reconnected me to you.

The next day was the beginning of my irreversible winter. I tried to act as if nothing had changed and went to my office at the Agency (Place Ville Marie) at about eleven. I got through the day's work one way or another. When I was supposed to be at lunch I went instead to the ground-floor pharmacy. I asked for phenobarbital. The druggist told me, with a big stupid grin, that it called for a prescription. I left the building in a huff, realizing, however, that this needed a little thought.

I had to have a prescription, by whatever means, and information about brand-names and doses. And I needed at least some knowledge of the various barbiturate compounds.

With this drug very much on my mind, I went next day or the day after to McGill medical bookstore. Here were the shelves dealing with pharmacology. I was looking for a trickle and found myself confronted by the sea. I was overcome, submerged, astonished. I made a choice and left the store with two books under my arm: the *Shorter Therapeutics and Pharmacology*, and the *International Vade Mecum* (a complete listing of products now on the market).

That night, alone with my ghosts, I got at the books. To hell with Mickey Spillane, I had better things to read: for example, this superbook (the *Vade Mecum*) which has the most delicious recipes going! Your appetite, your tensions, your depressions—they are all at the command of a few grams of drugs sagely administered. And according to this book of magic potions, life itself can be suppressed if only one knows how to go about it. I was passionately engrossed by this flood of pertinent information, but I still had my problem of how to get a prescription. Or rather, how to forge one that wouldn't turn into a passport to prison. A major problem.

His name was in the phone book: Olivier, J.R., internist. I dialled his number. His secretary asked what would be the best time of day for an appointment and specified that it would be about a month as the doctor was very busy. I answered her with a daring that still surprises me.

"It's urgent."

"What is it you have?" asked the secretary.

"A duodenal ulcer."

"How do you know?"

"Well, I've consulted several doctors and they strongly advised me to see Doctor O."

"Tomorrow at eleven," she suggested, struck by my argument. "Will that be convenient?"

"Of course," I replied.

I spent forty-five minutes in the waiting room with the secretary I'd phoned the day before. I flipped through the magazines on the table searching for subjects of conversation to use on this doctor friend I hadn't seen for so long.

He appeared in the doorway and his secretary murmured my name. I raised my gloomy gaze to greet this smiling friend. He ushered me into his overstuffed office.

After the usual halting exchange of memories from college and university days, I took a deep breath and, talking directly to Olivier, J.R., I told him straight out that I was having trouble sleeping. He burst into laughter, while I crouched deeper in the armchair he kept for patients.

"You're living it up too much, old boy," he said, smiling.

Just then his intercom blinked. Olivier lifted the phone.

"What is it?" he asked his secretary.

(I had been hoping for something like this.)

"Just a second. I have something to sign. You know how it is. They're making bureaucrats out of us."

He got up and went out to the reception room, carefully closing the door. At once I spied on his hand-rest the prescription pad with his letterhead. I quickly tore off a number of sheets and stuck them in the left inside pocket of my jacket. I was trembling, dripping with sweat.

"Well, bring me up to date," said Olivier, coming back. "Is she running around on you?"

He obviously found his own humour as irresistible as I found it offensive, and our chat didn't get much farther. We fell silent and Olivier took his pen. Before starting to write on his prescription pad he looked up at me.

"What was it, now? You wanted some barbiturates to get you to sleep?"

"Yes," I said.

"Okay, here's some stuff that'll knock out a horse." He tore off the sheet and held it out to me.

"Thanks, thank you very much." I suppose I was a bit emotional.

"I've put *non repetatur* at the bottom, for these pills have a tendency to be habit-forming. If you really need more after a couple of weeks come and see me again."

I folded the prescription without even searching out the *non repetatur*, an expression I had learned only a couple of days before. The intercom blinked again. Olivier, annoyed, picked up his phone but I paid no attention. I was already far away. Afterwards Olivier started telling me how his wife complained—or so he said—that she never got to see him any more.

"I'm working too hard," he said, hand on brow. "I probably need a holiday, but there it is. My wife's the one who's off to Europe. And it's only a month or so since she did the Greek Islands."

In my mind I saw you in the streets of Breda and The Hague. I imagined your walks in Scheveningen, your visits to the Maurithuis. I wasn't sure any more just where in Europe you were: at the Hook of Holland, the flying isle of Vlieland, or the seaside suburb of Leiden at Kalwijk aan Zee . . .

I was out again on the chilly street. The sky was dark and lowering. Black clouds scudded by a rooftop level, presaging another snowstorm. Let the snow come to beautify this death-landscape, where I drove in a Mustang while you moved in the clear celestial spaces of the painters of the Dutch school . . .

Back in our apartment, I analyzed the prescription I had obtained by trickery. Twelve capsules of sodium amobarbital. I had no intention of remaining the possessor of a non-repeatable number of pills and began practising Olivier's handwriting. On ordinary paper. I had stolen ten sheets of his letterhead but that precious paper must not be wasted. In two or three hours I'd managed four good prescriptions. I fell asleep on the strength of my success.

It took me some days to accumulate a *quoad vitam* dose with the help of my forged scribbles. But I wasn't satisfied with the *quoad vitam* dose indicated in the *Vade Mecum*. I went on accumulating the little sky-blue capsules, each with its three-letter stamp—SK&K. There were nights when I slept not at all rather than dip into my stock of precious sodic torpedoes.

Quite a few days passed this way. Strange days. Knowing that I had my stock of death in hand I felt sure of myself and almost in harmony with life. I knew that I was going to die and at that moment it would have been upsetting to receive a letter from you, my love, for I had come too close to the end of living.

When your letter came on November sixteenth, it in no way disturbed this harmony, as I had feared it might. After reading it I still wanted to end my life by using, some evening, my surprising accumulation of sodium amobarbital. You'd written in haste (I could tell by your hand) from the Amstel Hotel, but the postmark said Utrecht. So you'd mailed it from there! What were you doing in Utrecht? How had you gone from Amsterdam to that little town where the treaty was signed ratifying the conquest of French Canada? Symbol of the death of a nation, Utrecht became a premonitory symbol of my own death. Had you gone with someone? A European colleague, as you usually describe the men you meet on your travels? Are there many interior decorators in Utrecht? Or perhaps I should ask if they are friendly and charming. I imagined you sitting in the car of a decorator colleague, lunching on the way and perhaps spending the night in Utrecht. I grew weary of calling back so many memories of you, your charm, your beauty, your hot body in my arms. I tore up your letter to put an end to my despair.

By the twenty-eighth of November I'd heard nothing more from you. My days grew shorter and emptier, my nights longer and more sleepless. They finally seemed barely to be interrupted by my days, and I was exhausted. Recurrent insomnia had broken my resistance. I was destroyed, hopeless, without the slightest will to organize what was left of my life.

For me, an endless night was about to begin, the unique, final, ultimate night. I'd at last decided to put an arbitrary end to my long hesitation, a period to our disordered history; decided, also, no longer to depend on your intermittent grace, which had been cruel only in that I had suffered from it.

That day I made a few phone calls to say I was not available and spent my time tidying the apartment. When it was evening I took a very hot bath, copiously perfumed from the bottle of Seaqua. I soaked for a long time in that beneficent water. Then I put on my burnt-orange bathing trunks and piled a few records on our play-back: Ray Charles, Feliciano, Nana Mouskouri. I sprawled on our scarlet sofa, a glass of Chivas Regal in my hand, almost naked, fascinated by the total void that was waiting for me. I put Nana Mouskouri on several times. Then I finally made up my mind and swallowed my little sky-blue capsules four at a time, washing them down with great gulps of Chivas Regal. At the end I took more scotch to help me absorb the lot. I put the nearly empty bottle on the rug just beside the couch. Still quite lucid, I turned on the radio (without getting up) so that the neighbours would not be alerted by the heavy breathing which, according to my medical sources, would begin as soon as I dropped into my coma.

To tell you the truth I wasn't sad but rather impressed, like someone about to start a long, a very long voyage. I thought of you, but faintly, oh, so faintly. You were moving around in the distance, in a funeral fog. I could still see the rich colours of your dresses and bathrobes. I saw you enter the apartment like a ghost and leave it in slow motion, but eternally in mirror perspective leading to infinity. The deeper I slipped into my comatose feast the less you looked my way, or rather the less I was conscious of you. Melancholy had no grip on me, nor fear. In fact, I was blanketed in the solemnity of my solitude. Then, afterwards, obliteration became less complex and I became mortuary but not yet dead, left rocking in a total void.

And now, you ask, how are you managing to write this letter from beyond the tomb?

Well, here's the answer. I failed! The only damage I received in this suicide attempt resulted from the coma that lasted several hours. I was not in the best condition. My failure—even if I had no other devastating clues—would be proof enough of my perfect weakness, that diffuse infirmity that cannot be classified by science but which allows me to ruin everything I touch, always, without exception.

I woke up alive, as it were, in a white ward of the Royal Victoria, surrounded by a network of intravenous tubes that pinned me to the bed and ringed by a contingent of nurses. My lips felt frozen and dried and I remember that one of the nurses sponged them from time to time with an antiherpetic solution.

Outside it was snowing, just as it had been on the day you left. The great white flakes fell slowly, and I became aware that the very fact of seeing them silently falling was irrefutable proof that I was still, and horridly, alive. My return to a more articulated consciousness was painful, and took (to my relief) an infinity. As soon as I reached that threshold of consciousness I began to imagine you in the Netherlands or somewhere in Europe. Was there snow in Holland? And did you need your high suede boots that we shopped for together a few days before you left?

Suddenly, I feel a great fatigue: these thoughts, returning in all their disorder, are taking me back to my stagnant point again. . . .

It was really quite ironic that your telegram from Bruges should have become the means of your tardy (and involuntary) intervention on behalf of my poisoned body. I suppose the message was phoned first. But I didn't hear the ring and Western Union simply delivered the typed message to my address. The caretaker, who has no key to the letter boxes in our building, felt the call of duty and decided to bring me the envelope himself. There is something urgent about telegrams, you can't just leave them lying around. People can't imagine a harmless telegram that might read: HAPPY BIRTHDAY. WEATHER MARVELLOUS. KISSES. And yet that's exactly what was written in that telegram from Bruges.

I suppose the caretaker rapped a few times on our door. He probably couldn't see how I could be out when the radio was blasting away. Finally, his curiosity must have got the better of him. He opened the door with his pass-key and stepped in to leave the envelope on the Louis XV table under the hall mirror. It's easy to imagine the rest: from the door he saw that I was there, he noted my corpse-like face, etc. Then, in a panic, he phoned the Montreal Police who transported me—no doubt at breakneck speed—to the emergency ward of the Royal Victoria. I spent several days under an oxygen tent. I even underwent a tracheotomy. That, in case the term means nothing to you, involves an incision in the trachea, followed by the insertion of a tracheal drain.

I must tell you everything, my love. I'm alive, therefore I am cured. The only traces are an immense scar on my neck and a general debility. While I was surviving one way or another in Montreal, you were continuing your tour of Europe. You saw other cities, Brussels, Charleroi, Amiens, Lille, Roubaix, Paris . . . Bruges had been just a stopover where you perhaps had dinner with a stranger, but no one hangs around in Bruges when the continent is waiting. Though God knows Bruges is a privileged place, an amorous sanctuary, a fortress that has given up a little terra firma to the insistent North Sea. I feel a soft spot for that half-dead city, which you left with no special feeling. I stayed on in Bruges after you left, immured beneath its old and crumbling quays, for that was where you wished me (by telegram) a happy birthday.

There is no end to this winter. I don't know how many blizzards I watched from my hospital window. Around the fifteenth of December some doctor decided I should go home, that I was—so to speak—cured. Easy to say! Can one be cured of having wanted to die? When the ambulance attendants took me up to the apartment I saw myself in a mirror. I thought I would collapse. As a precaution, I lay down on the couch where I had almost ended my days in November. Nothing had changed since then, but there was a thin film of dust on our furniture and the photos of you. The sky, lowering and dark, looked like more snow. I felt like a ghost. My clothes hung loose on me and my skin had the colour of a corpse. The sleepless nights again took up their death march, but I no longer had my reserve of suicide-blue amobarbital pills. And I'd used up all my blank prescription forms. I couldn't sleep. I stared at the ceiling or at the white snowflakes piling up on our balcony. I imagined you in Rome or Civitavecchia or in the outskirts of Verona, completely surrendered to the intense experience of Europe.

From my calendar I knew that you were coming back to Montreal on April eleventh, on board the *Maasdam*. If I went to meet you that day at the docks of the Holland-American Line I would be in an emotional state. Too emotional, unable to tell you about what I did in November or about my disintegration since. Of course you'd give me a great hug and tell me all about those marvels, the fascinating ruins in Bruges, the baths of Caracalla, the Roman arches of triumph: the Arch of Tiberius, of Constantine, of Trajan, and so on. And all through your euphoric monologue I'd feel the knot at my throat.

It's for that reason—and all sorts of others, all somehow related to cowardice—that I'm writing you this letter, my love. I'll soon finish it and address it to Amsterdam, from which the *Maasdam* sails, so that you can read it during the crossing. That way you'll know that I bungled my first suicide attempt in November.

You'll understand that if I say "first" it means there'll be a second.

Don't you see that my hand is trembling? That my writing is beginning to scrawl? I'm already shaky. The spaces between each word, my love, are merely the symbols of the void that is beginning to accept me. I have ten more lucid minutes, but I've already changed: my mind is slipping, my hand wanders, the apartment, with every light turned on, grows dark where I look. I can barely see the falling snow, but what I do see is like blots of ink. My love, I'm shivering with cold. The snow is falling somehow within me, my last snowfall. In a few seconds, I'll no longer exist, I will move no more. And so I'm sorry but I won't be at the dock on April eleventh. After these last words I shall crawl to the bath, which has been standing full for nearly an hour. There, I hope, they will find me, drowned. Before the eleventh of April next.

Roch Carrier
Translated by Sheila Fischman

THE GOLDFISH

Roch Carrier was born in Sainte-Justine-de-Dorchester on
May 13, 1937, and studied at the Collège Saint-Louis in
Edmunston, New Brunswick, a city where he also worked as
a journalist from 1958 to 1960. He attended the universities
of Montreal, Paris, and the Sorbonne, where he received his
Ph.D. in literature for a dissertation on Blaise Cendrars, and
in 1965 began teaching at the Royal Military College in
Saint-Jean, south of Montreal. He has since served as president of the annual Salon du Livre in Montreal and as resident dramatist at Montreal's Théâtre du Nouveau Monde;
he is currently director of the Canada Council in Ottawa.

Carrier's first two books were of poetry, *Les Jeux incompris* (1956) and *Cherche tes mots, cherche tes pas* (1958), but since then he has published fiction, mostly novels but also plays and several collections of short stories. His best-known novels in English are the trilogy *La Guerre, Yes sir!* (1968), *Floralie, où es-tu?* (1969; *Floralie, Where Are You?*, 1970), and *Il est par là, le soleil* (1970; *There's the Sun, Philibert*, 1971), all translated by Sheila Fischman. His other novels include *Le Jardin des délices* (1975; *Garden of Delights*, 1978); *La Dame qui avait des chaînes aux chevilles* (1981; *Lady with Chains*, 1984); *De l'amour dans la ferraille* (1984; *Heartbreaks along the Road*, 1987); and *Fin* (1994; *The End*, 1994).

Carrier's short fiction has achieved a wide audience in both French and English Canada. His first collection, *Jolis deuils*, appeared in 1964 and won the Prix littéraire de la province de Québec. His other collections include *Les Enfants du bonhomme dans la lune* (1978; *The Hockey Sweater and Other Stories*, 1979), and *Prières d'un enfant très très sage* (1988; *Prayers of a Very Wise Child*, 1991).

"Le poisson rouge" ("The Goldfish," as Sheila Fischman has translated the title), first appeared in the anthology *Nouvelles du Québec*, edited by Katherine Brearley and Rose-Blanche McBride in 1970. A magical story, it shows Carrier's early fascination with the child-like naiveté and wonder through which profound truths are often discovered. It is interesting to trace in Carrier's work the development of this theme—the adult world seen clearly from a child's point of view—from this early story to such similar works as *Prayers of a Very Wise Child*.

∽

"The Goldfish" is a translation of "Le poisson rouge" published in *Nouvelles du Québec* (Scarborough: Prentice-Hall of Canada, 1970).

Tonight my father and I are entertaining my mother and her husband at our house.

My girlfriends at school didn't think it was funny when I told them my father and I were entertaining my mother and her new husband.

I think it's a good idea.

In the past, my father and I would meet my mother in a restaurant. They would have me served a Château Champlain sundae: ice cream of every flavour and colour, butterscotch, chocolate, marshmallow, with grenadine syrup, fresh strawberries, cherries, walnuts, sliced banana and pineapple, green grapes and raisins—and a chocolate milkshake to drink. My father and mother would exchange trite remarks of no interest either to me or to them. While I ate my sundae. When they ran out of things to tell each other they would speak to me:

"Be careful, sweetheart. You're going to make an ugly stain on your dress."

And I would reply:

"I am so glad to be here with both of you."

They believed me.

"She's delightful," my mother declared.

"My daughter would feel at home at an ambassador's table."

"Our daughter," my mother corrected him.

"How are you getting along?" he asked, concerned.

"I'm gradually getting back on my feet. It's been hard, you know."

My father felt sorry for his poor wife who had left us.

"Life isn't easy, alas!"

Having listed all their principles and their sorrows, they had nothing left to say to one another. My father twirled his cup in his saucer. That nervous habit used to annoy my mother when she was living with us; now she seems to put up with it more easily. My father concentrated on his game; my mother smoked cigarettes. Then all at once my father resurfaced:

"Don't be greedy, angel."

"A pretty girl like you has a duty to be refined," my mother added.

"What good is it to know the name of the Indian chief Bessabez if you don't know how to eat a sundae?"

My father called the waitress:

"May I have a sundae like my daughter's..."

"Like our daughter's," my mother insisted.

"... but not ten storeys high. Hers makes me dizzy."

He laughed, the waitress smiled, and my mother declared:

"Georges, your problem is, you're just a child."

While he was tucking into his ice cream, my father talked about what he had been reading in the newspapers or in his engineering magazines, while my mother described what she had seen in store windows. And that was what went on at our happy monthly meetings.

I was beginning to hate ice cream. My parents must be aware of it because tonight my mother and her husband are coming to visit me at my father's house. They'll make me weep with emotion, those three!

My father is an ordinary man. My friend Denise's father is an airplane pilot, but my father gets dizzy just climbing into his slippers! Hélène's father is a hunter: he's even been to Africa. My father sometimes hunts mosquitoes, if he's been bitten really badly! But he's so funny! All my friends know that their fathers have mistresses; I can guarantee that my father doesn't have even one! My father does the job of a mother! That's why I defend his honour to my friends. They know that my father once danced with Elizabeth Taylor in Los Angeles. I proved that exploit to them with a newspaper clipping. The photo showed my father from the back . . . But they believed me. I talked about a racing-car accident to explain my father's gangly way of walking. Why should I tell them that he always hogs the road and that people yell at him:

"Move it, Gramps, you'll be late for the old folks' home!"

I like to protect my father's reputation among my friends. No one but me knows how funny he is. I want him to be funny because if nobody thinks you're funny, it must make you sad.

I know perfectly well that my father's not Napoleon or Julius Caesar or John Kennedy; I know that he cares more about whether I've taken my bath than about following the stock market, but I also know that when he claims to dislike hunting for humanitarian and aesthetic reasons, the truth is that he forces himself to stay home with his little girl—me. In a few years from now, when I'm a young lady, my father won't be my prisoner any more, and then he'll be very different. Perhaps he'll be able to catch up on the time he's lost and be funny for everyone. While I, well, perhaps I'll be worried.

Does my father observe me the way I study him? In any case he doesn't have an easy life and it's all on account of me. If I weren't there . . . (which is ridiculous, because I am there . . .). I do my best to see that he's not unhappy. When all's said and done I'm glad he asked my mother and her husband for dinner. It will be a change from Château Champlain sundaes, and I'll have the honour and the very very (that's a superlative) great pleasure of meeting my mother's husband, a very distinguished man, as my father warned me, a professor of ancient Greek and a polyglot. In our school we have a Greek teacher: a lady who looks like a goldfish. One Greek teacher must resemble another. In spite of all her faults, my mother deserves more than a goldfish!

My father is better than a goldfish. My mother should have stayed with him. Perhaps he's glad she left. The dinner table will be like an arena, but polite: on one side, the phony Greek who looks like a goldfish and across from him, my father. The trophy to be won: me. The Greek goldfish won't get any sympathy from me. My father is the winner in advance. I suppose that from my mother's point of view he'll be the loser . . .

The doorbell rings.

"I'll get it," says my father. "Are you wearing your bracelet? I hope you haven't forgotten your perfume."

He unties his apron as he speaks. He slips on his jacket, hurries. Here is my mother, extending her hand to him. My father kisses it. He is carrying on like a man of the world. Accompanying my mother is a tall blond man with his hair cut like Julius Caesar's (before he went bald). I allow my mother to kiss me. Is the man with her going to kiss me too? I don't like my mother's perfume. What a weird get-up the man has on! A pink suit. Pink? No, pale mauve; in any case, it's violet. It's hideous, with big checks. Hideous. What terrible taste! He's a pederast! He is holding my father's hand. What a meal we're going to have. The pink-clad pederast comes up to me, holding out his hand.

"So you're the big girl your mother talks about so often. I'm happy to finally meet you. We're going to be good friends."

He looks me in the eyes, then his eyes slide down to where my little breasts are growing. The pig, he wants to seduce me! To tell you the truth, he's quite good-looking.

"Sweetheart, this is Franz."

"Yes, you must call me Franz, since we're nearly friends."

"Franz—is that a German name?"

"Yes."

He is more handsome than my father.

"I don't like Nazis."

A battery of voices protests, outraged: the German, my mother of course, even my father. Too much is too much.

"Bachau!" I shout, "Bachau! Bachau!"

My mother is indignant, my father is white, Franz is smiling.

"Does the young lady mean Dachau?"

My mother's face is bright red; I can tell that my father wishes he were a moth and could disappear into the carpet. All alone, the German stands there stonily, just like a Nazi.

"My parents were Brazilian," the Nazi goes on, "I was born in Germany, in a maternity clinic."

The Nazi hasn't stopped looking me in the eyes. He is very handsome.

"Franz is a very gentle man," pleads my mother.

"I don't care."

They burst out laughing; I laugh too, to keep from sobbing with rage.

"What a wonderful daughter you have, Mr. Martin!"

"How I'd like to have such a daughter," says my adorable mother quite spontaneously.

My father, turning pale, heads for the kitchen. The Nazi turns around and walks towards the library. Hoping to be forgiven, she takes it into her head to say:

"I miss you so much, my little girl."

When a mother talks so affectionately, you absolutely have to kiss her.

"Dear friends, let's have a drink!" declares my father.

That's how all their dramas end.

When my father fixes drinks he seems to be building an H-bomb.

They drink their aperitifs. I drink my grenadine. They talk. I say nothing. I'd like to go and hide in my room. What is more boring than an adult? Another adult. They know that they're boring. They all get bored together. They get together to be boring. They get bored as they forget that they're boring. Their greatest ambition is not to let it show that they are bored. Why can't I have a scotch? I feel sorry for them. I slip away. To the bathroom. When the door is locked I can finally live. I look at myself in the mirror. I'm not at all ugly. I like myself. I'm in the mood to read. To read and think about something else. There ought to be a bookcase in the bathroom. I leave and go into my bedroom. The books in my personal library are childish. The ones I like are from my father's library. It's been a long time since I've taken a book from my shelves. Nothing here interests me. I read the titles. How about this one? I'd forgotten it, needless to say: *Wonderful Tales for Children Taken and Adapted from Homer's Odyssey*. I'll find something in there. To tell the truth I prefer *The Erotic in 18th Century Painting*. Let's have a look. Let's see. At random. I read. The tone here is rather youthful. Naive. At least I can get some peace and quiet in here. "The rosy-fingered dawn," isn't that laying it on a little thick? If I wrote like that I'd get eighty percent! Isn't that ridiculous? Elephenor? Do you know who Elephenor is? What a name! I read. Elephenor. I read.

There is a knock at my door. I hide the book under my pillow. I open the door. It's the Nazi, sweet as sugar, athletic.

"Sorry to disturb you. Your father and mother would appreciate your presence. I hold out no hopes for myself, since you've already passed sentence on me. I wish you could have got to know me better. As long as I have just one enemy I cannot live. And I'm twice as unhappy if the enemy is a lady."

That Nazi talks the way a spider spins its web. Now it's my turn to set a trap.

"You're a Greek teacher, aren't you?"

"My students think so."

"Then you must know who Elephenor is . . ."

The Nazi is so gullible, he's surprised at my knowledge. He searches. Gotcha!

"You know, young lady, the civilization of Greece, her history and her literature, are vast fields. It would take more than one lifetime to cover them all."

I'm happy, I congratulate myself, I rejoice inwardly: the spider is going to die.

"Elephenor," he continues, "was a companion of Ulysses, who died on the island of Circe. He reappears on earth when Ulysses calls him."

The Nazi can't know all the details.

"He was killed in a war," I insinuate, "wasn't he?"

"No, not at all, it was wine that killed him. Alcohol, you know, has killed more men than wars have!"

I'm going to lose my temper if he keeps provoking me.

"Shall we make peace, you and I?"

"For the time being."

He holds out his hand. It feels soft. Holding me by the waist he takes me back to the living-room. It's nice to have a man hold you by the waist, even if he's a Nazi. When they notice us, my father and mother break off their conversation.

"I was sure they'd become good friends," says my mother. "Franz is irresistible."

"You mustn't minimize my daughter's charms."

Everyone agrees. He's a funny man, my father.

For dinner my father made a coulibiac, he announces while he is serving us a first course of shrimps, mussels, and other monsters.

While they struggle to devour their horrible animals, my mother and her Nazi wonder just what a coulibiac can be. They are unable to make us tell them that it's a traditional Russian peasant dish.

"You've become quite a cook, haven't you?" asked my mother.

"I had to learn," says my father, resigned.

I outdo him:

"Papa is a master, especially when it comes to difficult dishes. Last week when we entertained the Steins Papa cooked a toutitatou. Mr. and Mrs. Stein swore it was the most delicious toutitatou they'd ever eaten."

"You're exaggerating, darling," my father chides me.

Now, there's obviously not a word of truth in what I said. But who will stand up for my father unless I do?

"What exactly is a toutitatou?" the Nazi inquires.

"It's a very well-known dish from Greece," I say.

The Greek professor is humiliated.

"Darling," my father insinuates, "don't you think . . ."

"Didn't Mr. and Mrs. Stein like your toutitatou?"

My father no longer has the courage to contradict me. He refills the glasses, adding some water to my wine.

"These shrimp are delicious," Franz assures him. "In the past I used to say, 'It's criminal to eat shrimp anywhere but in Madrid at the Puerta del Sol, at five p.m. while waiting for the sun to set, and to wash them down with sangria.' Now I shall declare that the best shrimps are to be found at Mr. Martin's."

"Franz," coos my mother, "show our darling daughter the scar you have from when the bull attacked you in Seville.

Unbutton your shirt, darling. Show her."

When my mother still lived in our house she used to slap my fingers if I dropped any crumbs. And now she's urging her Nazi to do a strip-tease at the table. Luckily I know how to lie.

"My father likes danger too. His new sport is motorcycle racing."

"Georges on a motorcycle!" laughs my mother. "That's impossible."

"My father's not a champion yet. He came third in the race last Sunday. But there were two people dead and five injured."

Franz is not smiling now. He looks me coldly in the eyes.

"That sport is pointlessly dangerous. You must convince your father to give up motorcycles. It's too dangerous."

"That will be hard."

Could I have touched the heart of that murderer of Jews? I go on lying.

"Yes, I promise I'll convince him to give up those reckless sports."

Now my father is proudly carrying in the coulibiac and setting it in the middle of the table.

"I'm not the culinary genius my daughter claims but I hope you'll enjoy this. If you like salmon . . ."

Why does my father always have to apologize whenever he does something? Since my mother's new husband is with us he seems ready to apologize for being my father.

The glasses are filled. We nibble at the golden crust, scented with herbs.

"Georges, darling, will you let me have your recipe?"
"Gladly."

Why didn't he say no? My father is too nice.

The Nazi lays down his knife and fork.

"Mr. Martin," he says, "my wife" (he hesitated, I noticed, before saying *my*) "my wife has often told me about you. You are such a considerate man. We can become good friends if you want to."

"The first condition for our friendship is that you like my coulibiac."

"But I do, I do like it!"

"I adore it, Georges."

"Then let's drink to our friendship!"

The glasses clink. I didn't raise mine.

"Won't you join us, darling," pleads my mother.

My father is too humble, I defend what should be his honour.

"I don't feel like drinking: there's too much water in my wine."

"You're a voracious reader, young lady, do you know where you can read about the biggest salmon?"

I don't, but I won't admit it.

"In a Greek book!"

Franz laughs.

"Isn't she the sly one! She hates me, but I'm already fond of her."

My father's eyes are bright and he is beaming.

"If I'd been able to pick any daughter, she's the one I would have chosen!"

I blush. Sentimental declarations like that embarrass me.

It bothers my father that I am here, but he assures me that he likes being bothered by me. Dear Daddy!

"The biggest salmon," continues Franz who holds on to his idea like a real Nazi, "is found in the works of Rabelais. Gargantua, who is a giant, has dumb-bells made from two lead salmons, each one weighing 8700 hundredweight. Isn't that amusing?"

I laugh very rudely.

"No!"

My father's eyes reproach me for being impolite. He tries to correct my gaffe.

"Oh!" he says, "I haven't checked to see if the salmon I served you was made of flesh or lead!"

Franz laughs, my father fills the glasses, scattering some red spots on the tablecloth.

"Oh, Georges, you're so funny!"
"You didn't know me very well, Marie!"
"I don't even know myself," says Franz.

Simultaneously they bring their glasses to their lips. Together they burst out in a throaty laugh that stops them from drinking.

"A lead salmon!"
"Ha! Ha!"
"Roasted lead! Ha! Ha! Ha!"

Choking with laughter, they rock back and forth on their chairs, slapping the table and gasping for breath. They're disgusting! Why doesn't my father kick them out? He'd have to go with them, he's so much like them now. What am I going to do with these people?

I push my chair back and run to my room. I lock my door.

"Sweetheart," pleads my father, "please come back."
"No."
"Sweetheart."
"Young lady" (it's Franz, the Nazi) "how can I get along without you, when I'm so fond of pretty girls!"
"Darling, don't upset your dear Mama who loves you so much."

The viper who is talking to me is my mother. Poor Daddy . . . Poor Nazi . . . I'll resist just a little while longer.

"No! No! Never!"
"Open the door, darling, we want to apologize."
"Please sweetheart, be polite to our guests."
"I don't want to see anybody."

I hear my mother:

"What a naughty little girl she is. She must have psychological problems."

I think: "With a mother like you . . ."

I announce:

"I don't want to see anybody, I want to die" (that last word makes me shiver) "I'm going to jump out the window."

I walk to the window, stamping my feet. I push up the screen-window.

"Darling!" pleads my mother.
"One..."
"My treasure!"
I count very slowly:
"Two..."
"My child!"
"Three..."
"My little girl!"
"Farewell..."

I listen. There's no one fainting on the other side of the door. My mother is absolutely insensitive.

My father and Franz wait for me to fall, under the window. I leave my room. My mother isn't there now, she went out with the others. I sit down, I fill my glass with real wine, with no water, I finish eating my coulibiac: it's a little cold. I go back to my bedroom window. They're still waiting for me to fall. The fruit's not ripe yet! They're such gullible fools! I lean out the window and shout:

"Is it time for us to go swimming?"

Not wanting to contradict me they reply:

"Yes!"

Aren't they wonderful, they think they've saved me from suicide! Happy that I'm not angry any more, they all pile into Franz's car. I'll be spiteful and make them wait. I change into sports clothes and to kill a little time, I open my *Wonderful Tales for Children Taken and Adapted from Homer's Odyssey*. I read: "The Sirens charmed all those who came near them." I read. They wait for me. I read. They blow the horn to call me. I read. They grow impatient. Finally I call out the window:

"I'm ready."

My father would look funny driving a sports car like Franz's. Those cars aren't suitable for big families. That's what we are: one child, one father, one mother, and her husband. We drive across Montreal. It looks like a cake that didn't rise. Basically, my father is a perfect man. But I can't see him driving this car. My father is perfect the way a turtle is perfect.

You don't picture a turtle at the wheel of a sports car. With Franz the Nazi, though, you could say that sports cars were made for him. No one says anything. I may be the only one who is thinking.

"Young lady?"

Franz has opened his mouth.

"I'd like to tell you a little story . . ."

"Without thinking I reply:

" I'm very interested in stories from ancient Greece: murders, princes . . ."

"My little story isn't Greek. It's about a hermit crab. Do you know about that strange little animal? He moves into an empty shell when he's very young and never comes out. At the slightest alarm he pulls in his little claws and disappears."

"Explanation: the hermit crab is me."

Franz the Nazi is watching me in his rear-view mirror. My mother turns around with a sickly sweet smile. My father squeezes my hand and says:

"Franz, if you want to talk about my daughter, you'll have to tell a story about a tigress."

They all chortle. He's funny, my father.

"The hermit crab," Franz goes on, "is a timid animal, a quick-tempered little creature like all self-centred little creatures."

I chortle, alone and very loud.

My mother is stung to the quick.

"You're going too far, sweetheart."

"She's adorable!" says Franz.

"Didn't I warn you," simpers my father's former wife.

"And yet my daughter is mediocre today," says my father, squeezing my hand in a sign of complicity.

"She's adorable," Franz repeats. "I'd be very happy with a daughter like her. Are you not happy, Mr. Martin?"

In the rear-view mirror I can see his eyes looking deep into mine. Franz is handsome.

We drive along the highway for a long time, at ninety miles an hour. We slow down only at the toll booths. Now the journey is just an ordinary car trip. Franz has attractive, nicely formed ears. He isn't nearly as old as my mother and father. In the sunlight everything I see is precious. I think: this is where I would like to live. I no longer think about far-off lands.

At the lake I'm the first one to jump into the water. It's a little cold. Gradually my skin gets used to the chilly silk against it, and soon the water is like the most wonderful dress. I am swimming. That's freedom. To advance by myself, through just my own strength, in the water that is holding me up because I want it to, that's living. I swim. I could swim right across the lake without getting tired. My mother has spread a blanket on the beach. Here are my father and Franz.

"Yoo hoo! Come here!"

And I dive and I swim. My arms make broad movements and my face cuts through the water that bubbles against my ears and cheeks. I can go even faster. My legs make energetic scissor kicks that push me along. The water caresses my belly. What is a caress? No man has ever caressed me. I swim. Whew! I've swallowed some water. Spit it out. I'm choking. I'm coughing. My feet are paddling now. The water is black here. It is here in this black water that you find seaweeds that lick your thighs with their rough tongues. I cough. I cough. At last I can breathe freely. I'm a little tired. Back to shore now. But I'm so far out! I start swimming again. My arms turn in the water, my hands with their tightly clenched fingers paddle in the water. I can't go any further, my legs are so heavy they're throwing me off balance. I call out.

"Franz!"

"Daddy! Franz!"

I wave both arms but that just sends my body deeper into the water. I start swimming again but I won't be able to keep going for very long. If I slow down I'll sink, if I speed up I'll swallow water. Now I'm choking. This water is thick molasses. Franz has seen me. He's signalling to me. He darts towards me. Daddy can't follow him. Franz is executing a perfect crawl. He is going to save me. My eyes are stinging. I am swallowing water through my nose. Franz is coming closer. When he's all wet he's not handsome. His eyes are puffy.

"Come here, siren," he says.

He hooks his arm under my chin and tips me onto my back. He drags me like that. I feel the tense muscles of his arm. His legs are beating the water powerfully. With every move he makes his chest is pressed against my back. It's so hard and I can feel his breath inside. I feel as though I could swim by myself now. I tell him so, I tell Franz. He lets me go. The muscles in my limbs are too limp. They won't obey me. I'm going to sink. Franz takes hold of me again, my chin in his folded arm.

"Oh, Franz!"

I can't help crying.

On the beach my father is waiting for me. How funny he looks in his swimming trunks! He wishes he could have saved me, I can tell. He kisses me.

"Poor darling," says my mother, wiping away a tear, "you'll have to learn to be careful."

She goes back and lies down again on the sand.

I am condemned to be happy!

André Langevin
Translated by Basil Kingstone

A BLUE ROSE PERFUME

Born in Montreal in 1927, André Langevin worked as literary editor of *Le Devoir* before becoming a broadcaster for Radio-Canada, and has written numerous radio and filmscripts as well as novels and short stories. His first novel, *Évadé de la nuit*, appeared in 1951 and won the Prix du Cercle du livre de France, as did his second, more famous novel, *Poussière sur la ville* (1953; *Dust Over the City*, 1955). The novel is set in a mining town called Macklin—a thinly disguised Thetford Mines, where Quebec's most bitter labour dispute had taken place in 1949 between workers and the owners of the asbestos mines. Concerned not only with workers' health issues (the central character is the town doctor), the novel also deals with such issues as marital infidelity and existential angst. In the words of critic Gilles Marcotte, it gave readers "more to think about than most of the other books that have come out of French Canada in many years." It may have given them too much to think about, because Langevin's later novels, *Le Temps des hommes* (1956), *L'Élan d'Amérique* (1972) and *Une chaîne dans le parc* (1974), translated by Alan Brown in 1976 as *Orphan Street*, never achieved the critical or popular success of *Dust Over the City*.

"Un parfum bleu-rose," translated here as "A Blue Rose Perfume" by Basil Kingstone, first appeared in 1974 in the Montreal magazine *Liberté*. It is a simple story—a man whose wife has committed suicide tries to trace her last movements—but it explores many of the themes that have occupied Langevin since his first novel: marital infidelity, existential doubt, and the lack of a truly committed social conscience.

∽

"A Blue Rose Perfume" is reproduced from "A Decade of Quebec Fiction," a special issue of *Canadian Fiction Magazine*, no. 47 (1983) and was originally published under the title "Un parfum bleu-rose" in *Liberté*, no. 62 (March–April, 1969).

"She saw the city from this window?" the man asks. Motionless, his hands flat on the spread-out newspaper, he is looking at the livid emptiness, suddenly dotted with a thousand clusters of light. The tall buildings mired in the dying January daylight are lit up, straighten up with a jerk, just as they are about to keel over and disappear.

"She tried to see the river and the mountains—then she got dizzy, I suppose," he adds, in a faint voice which hardly carries in the deepening gloom, but which I can hear clearly above the loud digestion of a snowblower on the street, twelve floors below, and a shrill music trickling out of the radio like water from a dripping tap. The presence of this tall figure with its back to me, silhouetted against the picture window of the apartment, hems me in, almost physically.

"Anyway, she came here? It *is* her? You recognized her!"

"I can't see now. Let me put a light on."

"No. Later."

As he turns back towards me he raises his voice, but not in anger. His overcoat gives him unnaturally broad shoulders. With both hands he brandishes the newspaper, now rolled up.

"As you wish."

"This time of day is like her."

His voice becomes even fainter. Behind him now, the countless lights draw a picture of an almost warm city in the night. I turn the radio off and sit down in an armchair a few steps from him. The snowblower has suddenly fallen silent, and between us there is an interminable wave of silence.

"I'm sorry. How can you be expected to understand? I'm looking for . . . something like a perfume, or a breath . . . I've often come across her in the dark . . . away from home . . . Jeanne liked to get lost."

"Jeanne, you said?"

"She came here, didn't she? Why did they find nothing in her purse but a ticket which she had written your address on?"

"Her name was Anne."

"Anne or Jeanne, it makes no difference. You recognized her? It's her picture?"

"Yes and no. Anne had a different expression, a different smile, a passion—"

"It's her!"

"If you wish."

"It's not a question of what I wish!"

"I'm sorry. Yes, it's Anne."

"Jeanne! What was she doing in your place?"

I see his silhouette storm up to me. He leans over, grabs me by the shoulders and shakes me furiously. Without anger. A sort of stunned pleading. A question held in too long.

"What was she after? What did she tell you?"

Suddenly he lets go of me.

"What's the use? When I came across her alone in the dark, she hated me."

I say nothing. This perfume he's looking for, I can smell in profusion. The whole apartment is saturated with it. Anne's little cool hands on my back, the blonde storm of her hair on my shoulders, and her gaze where the waves of a terrible anguish broke. Anne's breathing suddenly cracking my ribs, her warm lips closing over her thirst. And the renunciation which, during all those hours, I never figured out. So distant when she opened her arms to me. Her perfume chills me. I would like to run away.

"Give me a drink, please."

He walks up and down for a while, then bumps into a coffee table and drops into an armchair across from me. I turn on a lamp. The light makes the room dangerously smaller.

"Before I rang the bell, I still hoped it was a woman's address. But it doesn't matter, does it?"

I pick up a bottle at random and pour him a drink, unable to take my eyes off him, fascinated by the strong hands slowly crumpling the page of the paper. Thirty maybe, milky blue gaze, athletic and youthful. He swallows his drink in one gulp, then very carefully sets the glass down on an end table beside him. His blue eyes rest for a moment on the picture in the paper.

"Of course it isn't her. A photo can't run away. Jeanne did nothing but run away. A little note scribbled on a scrap of paper: 'I have to get away, for a week or two, or longer. I'm stifling. You're breathing my air.' You, meaning the kids and me. I ask you."

"Anne had children?"

He looks at me in silence, surprised or annoyed, there's no telling which, his blue eyes are so expressionless.

"Why do you insist on calling her that? We're talking about Jeanne, my wife. Two children—three, rather. You wouldn't understand."

With a broad sweep of his hand he wipes out everything I can't understand, an image he alone sees and which is painful to him.

"What do you want from me? I knew her for twelve hours at most. And her name was Anne. She didn't tell me about you or the children or even herself. Listening to you, I'm finding out I don't know anything about her."

"Didn't she tell you she was married?" he asks, his voice choked, but with no emotion in his imperturbable gaze.

"Yes, but not a word more. She wasn't wearing a ring."

"She couldn't, it got in her way when she played the piano."

"She was a pianist?"

"Didn't you know that either? She could have been a professional. Musicians have told me so. She only played when she was alone. I can't understand that."

"Shall I refill your glass?"

"No, thanks. Twelve hours. Two people can talk for twelve hours, and part without having gotten to know each other . . . What I'm looking for here . . . I don't know. Maybe a sentence, which may have no meaning for you but would mean a lot to me."

The snowblower is still chewing up the city, in wider and wider circles. The building is coming to life. Doors slam. A smell of boiled cabbage suddenly wafts into the fresh silence between us. The bedroom door is ajar and I can see the foot of the bed. The man stares at it as if stupefied.

I feel his presence as a painful and at the same time inevitable intrusion. I am shocked by his desire to find something of a moment he didn't experience, or an explanation, but I feel I can't get out of it. This blind man is groping around in my life because unhappiness gives him rights. I offer him a cigarette.

"No, thanks, I don't smoke."

After a while he adds, almost with wonder in his voice, "She left lighted cigarettes everywhere! She burned everything—"

"Anne told me she didn't smoke!"

I raise my voice in triumph. Hoping against hope, I persuade myself that this stranger has the wrong address. Everything he says about her seems so absurd that it's obvious he's made a mistake. Why can't he see that?

"That's no more important than her name. No doubt she was playing a part."

He smiles faintly, his blue eyes overflowing with indulgence. He adds, obstinately, "What did she tell you all that time? You must remember certain things she said. Was she happy?"

His understanding, almost fatherly tone of voice makes me indignant.

"And who are you, sir, to—"

He interrupts me at once, quietly and firmly.

"We have settled that, I think. I will add that I am a lawyer in Quebec City. I'm not judging, I just want to understand what happened."

"What if it all happened in your household, before that?"

"Oh certainly, in the course of more than seven years . . . I will tell you anything I think useful."

His blue gaze has darkened a little, hiding painful secrets I don't know. The man is quite shamelessly proposing a trade, with himself as sole judge of the value of the goods exchanged. I'm speechless.

The brief encounter he's asking me to recall is a precious and fragile moment of grace which is now among my most personal memories, and not something to be shared, the missing piece to be added to somebody else's happiness or unhappiness.

For those few hours Anne had no past and no future; whether she was Jeanne or Anne, linked to this man or another one, she was an appeal addressed to me alone, an unforgettable, unknown woman.

"When did you meet her?"

Every time he talks about her, he points with his right hand at the paper in his left. This habit is annoying me.

"A few days before Christmas."

"More than three weeks ago, then . . ."

He notes this fact in a sad and defeated voice, as if my answer demolished a whole theory.

"Where did she go then?"

"I don't know. I left her here. I was going on a week's trip."

"Didn't she tell you where she lived?"

No. She said something about a waiting room in a railway station, but she was joking."

"How do you know? Did she have the car?"

"No."

"A suitcase, anything?"

He has grown vehement and his questions are coming faster. I have the strange impression that despite everything, somewhere deep inside himself this man is triumphant as if he's playing a sinister game.

"Is all this really necessary? I don't see—"

"I need to know," the sharp voice interrupts. "Did she have a suitcase?"

"No. But she had several packages."

He sits forward on the edge of his armchair, suddenly very interested.

"Packages? What became of them?"

"She left them here. I'll give them to you. I didn't know where to send them."

This new factor plunges him into deep thought. I say, almost despite myself, as if Anne were speaking again, through me:

A BLUE ROSE PERFUME

"It's awful what they're doing in Vietnam!"

He stares at me in disbelief.

"It—it was Jeanne who said that to you, wasn't it? That's something Jeanne said, I'm sure of it."

He's delighted. She is among us again. He wasn't wrong.

"It's awful what they're doing in Vietnam! She had an armful of Christmas gifts for Vietnamese children. She was ready to mail it all, with just the address 'Children, Vietnam.' She was obsessed by pictures of children burned alive by napalm. She talked about it a lot."

"Children—napalm." His voice is choking and his eyes are brimming with tears.

"Shall I fill your glass?"

"No. Go on. What else did she say?"

"The eyes of the Vietnamese children. You'd think they were two thousand years old. Nothing is more serious than a Vietnamese child's smile."

"Like Mozart's adagio."

"She never said that!"

My sharp reaction surprises me. As if I've been hit by something I don't recognize. He's managed to create a sort of conspiracy between us that's sucking me down.

"Maybe not. Go on."

I work myself up, so as to break free of him once and for all.

"There's nothing else to tell. Disjointed remarks, lost amid long silences, which cannot mean anything to you. She was cold. She was always cold. And sometimes she was so completely somewhere else. The wandering expression of a child who refuses to go to sleep."

"'I never sleep,'" he says in a voice not his own.

"Yes, she said that too."

"Go on."

"There's nothing else. Minor details. 'In Palma de Majorca, by the sea, there were huge blue roses that were absolutely indecent.'"

"Blue roses? She was never in Palma."

"'I killed a bear once. Those huge animals die like little children, they don't resist. I've given up hunting.'"

"A grasshopper on the lawn terrified her."

"'I didn't feel anything when my parents died. They were so calm . . .'"

"They're still alive, but she hasn't talked to them in years."

"'I learned Spanish because I was cold.'"

"It was Italian she tried to learn. It lasted two hours at most. She'd bought fifteen records."

"'I was raped in a church once, by a choirboy. I like the smell of incense. I never drink milk because I don't like white. I'd like to only have yellow children.' And so on. You can see there's nothing there."

He's sitting bolt upright on the edge of his armchair, in amazement. Not till I hear the paper crumpling do I notice his hands are shaking.

A child is crying somewhere in a neighbouring apartment, the barely audible, feeble voice of somebody walled up. The smell of boiled cabbage is making me ill. The silence is growing deeper between us and oppressing me. I stand up to put an end to the interview.

"So there you are. I don't think there's anything else to say."

He pays no attention to my outstretched hand. A single tear gleams in his right eye and annoys me. I turn away and walk over to the picture window to let it fall. Everything I've said is meaningless. Anne did say those words, in her almost inaudible voice that hardly emerged from the silence—scraps of her train of thought that escaped her almost without her knowing it—but without that voice, without her wandering gaze in the dark, without her presence, so slight and yet so serious, those words cannot reveal anything. Thus when she came into the apartment she said at once, "Close the curtains. I can see the cold." And she had a way of huddling in her coat, with her two fists under her chin, which instantly made the cold visible.

Not only are the words meaningless now, but saying them has wiped out Anne's image. Now I can only see her fixed, as if in the photo in the paper. Anybody. Somebody's wife.

I hear him helping himself to drink. By the time I turn around, he's already emptied the glass. He flashes me a brief, automatic smile.

"She liked to play games a lot," he said, as if to reassure me. "But maybe somebody suffers in any game. Thank you."

Once again I hold out my hand, but he pretends not to see it. He leans over and rummages in the briefcase he set down on the coffee table when he came in.

"Do you have a record-player?"

Seeing my bewilderment he adds, as if giving an order, "I'd like to ask you one last favour. Let me listen to this record here, in this apartment where I've lost her trail for good."

I recognize the record. Mozart's clarinet concerto in A. I feel a great tumult rise in me and I lose grip. I stammer, "Why—a record?"

"I'll tell you afterwards."

Never till now have I been afraid of him. But now I am. As if he'd played a card that makes it clear he's in control, that he knows my whole hand.

He finds the phonograph himself, turns it on, sets the record on the turntable. And the long phrases of the adagio suddenly fill the room, a light and poignant song that sets me aquiver and tears me apart. The clarinet's piercing tendrils unfold all through my body. I want to cry out but I have no voice. The treachery of it leaves me paralyzed. What does this man want of me? An hour ago I didn't even know he existed.

He's sitting with his eyes closed, his fists so tightly clenched around the paper that his nails are digging into his flesh. A strange grin is twisting his mouth. His expression is one of intense suffering or intense happiness, there's no telling which. I cannot stand to even look at him. I go back to the window.

On the highest note the clarinet freezes for a few interminable, agonizing seconds. Then the long breathing resumes, a child's breath, powerful and fragile at the same time, born again on the edge of life.

Her feet went clean out from under her and she landed on her back in the slush melting on top of the ice. The packages in their Christmas wrapping were hurled in all directions. She smiled pitifully when I offered her my arm to help her up. Her fur coat and her stockings were too muddy to be cleaned off. The passers-by were stepping around the packages.

She leapt to her feet so lightly, the lift I had given her was far greater than necessary.

"That was a pretty good fall," she said, taking off a glove that was full of dirty water.

I went fishing for the packages, having to hold them at arm's length as though they were absolutely disgusting.

"Please don't bother. I'm soaking wet already, so it doesn't matter."

She leaned down and picked up some of them, tucking them firmly under her arm, ignoring what they did to her coat.

"What are you going to do now?"

"I don't know. Dry out in the sun on a park bench, I suppose."

Her teeth were chattering pathetically in the dirty, slushy dusk.

"I live close by. The building superintendent will let us clean you up a bit."

She kept trying to brush the dirt off with her glove, or to keep from shivering.

"No thanks, I'm all right. When it freezes it'll be pretty, like terra cotta."

In her dark gaze, beneath the fake amusement, there was a gleam of panic. Seizing the packages, I said in a gentlemanly but firm tone, "Come on, it's just around the corner."

She gave way with a smile full of distress.

"All right, just to please your building superintendent."

Thus began a very slow, very gentle night, constantly threatened by an undefined breakoff, because the whole thing was a game. Neither of us tried to find out anything about the other. We put on a show for each other which was the truth of the moment, and nothing else counted. But she was gravely and distantly playing an inner melody of which I heard only very occasional disconnected notes. Like a sick child who stops playing a game, and comes back to it, as the illness dictates. I don't think she was ill, but a hidden fire was consuming her. She was in the grip of a sort of icy fever. As though she had spent the night by the fire with her back to an ice-cold space.

She was still shivering in the superintendent's apartment. Under her coat she had on a tight-fitting navy blue dress, very plain, cut just a little low at the neck, which made her look both young and austere. When I invited her to dinner she murmured, as she touched up her lipstick, "Oh, I see."

We left the packages with the superintendent and she followed me, unsmiling, in silence. In the restaurant she didn't open her mouth until after the soup, to say, as if at the end of a long train of thought, talking to herself:

"It's awful what they're doing in Vietnam!"

Her voice was so strange, so quiet, that I was struck speechless, as if by a confidence painfully extracted from her. She didn't seem to notice my surprise. She added almost at once, very proudly, "I'm a very bad cook!"

"Why would you cook?"

"I don't know. Because I'm married, I suppose."

"And is Vietnam important to you?"

"Oh, nothing. Pictures."

"Pictures?"

"You see them everywhere. Little bald children mutilated by napalm. So skinny their arms are just bones."

"They're awful. Don't think about them anymore."

She raised her glass in front of her face with both hands, and her gaze sank into the red glow of the wine.

"It's a warm country," she said with a long sigh. "I've stored up enough cold for more than one lifetime."

She drank slowly then disappeared elsewhere, staring at the light in the empty glass between her hands. She reappeared at dessert to tell me about the Christmas package and the eyes of the Vietnamese children.

"You haven't eaten anything."

"I don't eat anymore, I don't sleep anymore, and I'm cold."

The distant voice wasn't joking. It was a lifestyle summarized in three points. She added, "It must be scurvy, an illness of the ice-cap."

Thus the evening passed in conversations that broke off as soon as they started, words thrown at random like pretend buoys to two pretend drowning people. Then we had brandy in three different places, each of which we left solely because we had finished our drinks. As soon as we were in the street she felt cold and we had to go into another place. She stopped taking off her coat, which still bore the traces of her accident.

"The gentleman was accompanied by a lovely lady covered in dirt. It's the beginning of a fairy story..."

I was looking at her without trying to hide the fact that I violently wanted her. Sometimes our gazes brushed together dangerously, and for a very brief moment I believed she was willing, but a sort of invisible screen would suddenly appear and allow her to get away. Or she would say something playful:

"I got married because organ music sends shivers down my back."

We picked up her packages from the superintendent, then she followed me into my apartment, perfectly naturally, without being formally invited in. She asked me to close the curtains, then she took her coat off and lay down on the sofa, navy blue and blonde, and shivering. I brought her a blanket and a glass of brandy which she set down on the carpet without drinking.

"Put the TV on. I can't sleep and I'm bored."

I put the TV on, discreetly laid a pair of my pyjamas and a robe on the coffee table and, having shown her where the bathroom was, went to bed—a bit angry, but happy anyway, because I was sure she wasn't cold anymore. I was leaving at six in the morning on a week's trip. What would become of her? I fell asleep hearing a white man on the TV talking about Indians in fractured French.

Her perfume woke me up, a blue rose perfume, very cool, unlikely. And her little cool hands around my neck, and her soft body stretched out beside mine, the tide of her body flowing towards me, and the music, the music of Mozart's adagio, a hymn to joy that swallowed me up, unfolded in long successive waves through the apartment, and rolled us towards each other. She was all thirst and fire. Her heart beat in her chest as though it would burst. We panted as though in a frantic race. Then her breathing became a long moan, and she abruptly pulled away as if falling back into the sea, in a dizzying loneliness. I slipped one arm under her and waited for morning, squeezing her against me. She was cold for a long time.

I left her at dawn. It was still pitch dark. A blizzard was plastering snow over the picture window. Before I left I kissed her and said goodbye, hesitating a long time after "goodbye" because she hadn't told me her name yet. She didn't open her eyes.

"Anne," she said.

"You'll wait here for me, Anne? You'll be here when I get back?"

"Maybe."

She wasn't.

I look at the man in his tense ecstasy, letting himself be indecently penetrated by this music that is harrowing my feelings, till I can't stand it any longer. I turn the record-player off. It takes him forever to react. At last he looks at me and says gently, "You're wrong. It's music to make love by. Jeanne and I loved each other to that music. You wouldn't understand . . . or maybe you do . . ."

I'm afraid I'm going to start despising him. First he tried to pick up the crumbs, and now he's betraying Anne so as to destroy something. The picture in the paper he has in his hand doesn't give him that right; it doesn't justify him breaking into my memories and mixing them up with his.

"Anne never saw the city from this window."

"Why, on a perfectly dry empty highway, in a brand-new car, would she wrap herself at over sixty miles an hour around the only tree in sight?"

"I don't know. Let me give you the packages."

"Perhaps she had just found out she had cancer."

I put the still mud-stained packages beside the briefcase. Cancer or whatever, I don't feel like discussing it with him.

"I don't know."

"I'll give them to him."

"Pardon me?"

"That's right, I'll give them to him, two weeks late. He's used to that. I'm talking about our third child. Two years old. She put him in a foster home as soon as he was born and never saw him again. Look, here's his picture."

It's an Asian child, with dark eyes that swallow his whole face.

"Thank you," he says, and leaves.

The calm smell of boiled cabbage is blotting out the unlikely blue rose perfume.

∽

Gabrielle Roy
Translated by Alan Brown

PART II OF
CHILDREN OF MY HEART

Gabrielle Roy was born on Rue Deschambault, in St. Boniface, Manitoba, on March 22, 1909. Her father was a colonization agent for the federal government, responsible for bringing immigrants from the east and Europe into Saskatchewan (her short story "Ely! Ely! Ely!" describes this period). Upon the death of her father in 1927, she entered the Winnipeg Normal School and taught in St. Boniface until 1937, when she went to England to attend the Guildhall School of Music and Drama. In 1939, with the impending war, she returned to Canada, settling in Montreal and working as a journalist, first for *Le Jour*, then for *La Revue moderne*.

During this time she wrote her first and best-known novel, *Bonheur d'occasion* (1945; *The Tin Flute*, 1947), about the effects of the Second World War on the workers of Quebec. She became known as a clear-sighted realist, a writer who was very aware of the lives of quiet desperation lived by Quebec's urban poor. This reputation was enhanced by her next novel, *Alexandre Chenevert, Caissier* (1954; *The Cashier*, 1955). But with her next book, *Rue Deschambault*, she returned to her semi-rural roots in Manitoba, and in most of her subsequent work she delved ever more deeply into her past as a Manitoban of Quebec descent, and as a teacher. Gérard Bessette has called *Rue Deschambault* a work of "fictionalized memoirs," and the same may be said of *La Montagne secrète* (1961; *The Hidden Mountain*, 1962), and *La Route d'Altamount* (1966; *The Road Past Altamount*, 1966).

Although *Ces enfants de ma vie* (1977), translated by Alan Brown in 1979 as *Children of My Heart*, has also been called both memoir and novel, it transcends genre classification, just as its author transcends regional analysis. Alan Brown's fascination with Roy's work has spanned four decades: his essay "Gabrielle Roy and the Temporary Provincial" appeared in the first issue of the literary magazine *Tamarack Review* in 1956, and he retranslated *The Tin Flute* in 1984. The following story is Part II of *Children of My Heart*, and whether memoir or fiction it is a superbly self-contained story, and arguably Roy's most fully realized work of literature. As Hugo Macpherson has noted, "Gabrielle Roy feels rather than analyses, and a sense of wonder and mystery is always with her."

Gabrielle Roy died in Quebec City in 1983.

∽

"Children of My Heart" is reproduced from *Children of my Heart* (Toronto: McClelland & Stewart, 1979) and was originally published under the title "Ces enfants de ma vie" in *Ces enfants de ma vie* (Montreal: Stanké, 1977). Reprinted by permission of Fonds Gabrielle Roy and McClelland & Stewart Publishers.

The school to which I was appointed that year could, I suppose, be called a part of the village, though it hung back at the very end, separated from the last houses by a good-sized field in which a cow used to graze. Despite this gap, there was no doubt that I belonged to the village—a dreary place with its poor houses, most of them in unpainted wood, already decrepit before the last board was nailed; and its tiny chapel, built out of antagonism to the next village with its rich and fancy church. But it was out of antagonism, too, that the priest from the rich parish had never set foot in the little chapel, which was gradually crumbling from neglect.

From the school windows I could see the bleak railway station, like all those built at the time, with its grain elevators, its water tank, a caboose that had been sitting on the ground for years. Everything was painted in that hateful oxblood colour that had no life or sparkle; but very likely because it was lifeless, it was durable and money-saving. The main street predominated, of course, treeless and too wide, a melancholy dirt road, plaintive and dusty as the main streets of almost all the villages of the Canadian West in the first year of the Great Depression. It was a village of retired farmers, bitter or acrimonious, with barely enough to live on, old folk, homebodies, little businesses just scraping by. There was nothing in the place to give you courage or confidence or hope in any tomorrow. But I had only to turn the other way and everything changed: hope came back in giant waves; I seemed to be looking toward the future, and that future shone with the most alluring light it ever released in my lifetime.

Yet there wasn't anything to see. Not the roof of a house, nor a barn, not even one of those tiny granaries you found all over the prairies when the harvest was too big to sell. Just a stretch of dirt road that rose a little, turned a little, then was lost in infinity. After that, nothing but the sky, a shoulder of rich, black earth against the rich blue of the horizon and, occasionally, clouds rigged like old-fashioned sailing ships. Why, in a country so young, does hope come to us from desert spaces and the marvellous silence!

It's true that more than half my pupils came from that wild side that looked so uninhabited. Until it grew too cold, toward mid-October, they all came on foot, except for a few mornings when there was heavy rain.

From the very first week, sitting at my desk, which looked out toward the plain, I got in the habit of watching them arrive. I came early to prepare my lessons. I had to: I had forty pupils divided into eight grades, from the first to the eighth year. Having so many classes was the great problem of those country schools, but it was also their incredible advantage. With children of all ages they constituted a sort of family, a world in itself. Today they'd call it a commune.

I was very often ready well before school-time, the blackboard covered with examples and problems to be solved. Then I'd sit down and start looking impatiently for my pupils to arrive. My eyes never left the lonely rise in the road where I'd see them appear one by one or in groups that sketched a little border against the sky's edge. I would see their tiny silhouettes pop up in the immensity of the empty prairie, and I felt the vulnerability, the fragility of the children of the world, and how it was, nonetheless, on their frail shoulders that we loaded the weight of our weary hopes and eternal new beginnings.

I remember how overwhelmed I was that from all directions they were converging on me, an outsider to them after all. To this day I'm still astonished and touched to think that people should entrust to a total stranger—fresh from Normal School as I was then—the most delicate, the newest, the easiest thing to break in this whole world.

Soon, even at that distance, I could tell them apart: the Badiou children, who held each other by the hand, not only on the last stretch but, as I later found out, for the whole two miles from their farm, their anxious mother having put the boy of five and a half in the care of his sister who was six and a half, and her in the care of her little brother; and they no doubt felt some protection in holding hands. The Cellinis formed a compact group, the five of them, only Yvan the terrible, Yvan the rebel, dragging behind, with

Adele, the eldest, turning to make signs for him to hurry. Then there were my children from the Auvergne, who kept to themselves, never mixing with the Italians, still less with those from Brittany, easy to recognize by their slogging step; the two little Morissots who, rain or shine, late or early, I saw arriving on the run, like madmen; the Lachapelles, making a ladder on the horizon, the tallest in front, the smallest last, walking at an unchanging pace, keeping equal distances between them; and finally, almost always alone, often last of all and a few minutes late, a little silhouette that hurried, his shoulders bent forward, his schoolbag on his back, seeming over-burdened.

Oh, that boy! There's still a tightening around my heart when I think of him!

His name was André Pasquier. And he wasn't a bad pupil, far from it, nor lacking in any way. But—how can I put it?—while he was hard-working, with the best will in the world, one that I could reproach with nothing in particular, he was always off somewhere. Preoccupied, you would have said. No doubt worried by some cares at home that wouldn't be shaken off. And he seemed tired even as the school day began. How could he make the effort I expected of him?

One day when I saw him struggling over a problem that the others had solved in half the time, I stopped at his desk.

"What's the matter, André? Are you tired?"

"Yes, a bit," he said, and his eyes had the wandering look that one sees in some men who are broken by physical exhaustion.

"Do you help a lot at home?"

"Oh, not that much. I have to do some. I'm the oldest. It's my job to help my father."

"Do you have far to walk?"

"It's two and a half miles."

Dear me! And I'd scolded him just yesterday for being late!

"That's quite a stroll, isn't it?"

"Oh, it's not so bad," he said, managing a smile. "The fresh air is good for you."

I helped him solve his problem—the little one of the moment—and went back to my desk. From then on this child was never far from my mind. I was determined to bring to his life, which I felt was difficult in the extreme, at least the possibility of escape through education. At all costs I wanted him to succeed in class. But how to go about it? Keep him after school to go over his lessons? I'd make his day that much longer. Give him special attention in school hours? He was touchy and proud. If he noticed, he could withdraw even deeper into himself. Yet this was the only way; but I had to use the utmost discretion. After a week I had the joy of seeing him finish his work almost as soon as the others.

I congratulated him and hardly recognized in this child—astonished at himself, dazzled by his own performance—the poor little boy who some days came to school so tired that I'd have thought he had been drinking.

"See, André! When you try!"

And I put out my hand to pat his cheek or his forehead. And now, unlike other times, he didn't recoil, acting the little man, but allowed a fallen lock of hair to be pushed back.

It seemed to me from that day on, if he arrived late, weary, sometimes sad, that little by little in the course of the day his soul, light and tender, would surface above the worries that were too much for his age; and he would be astonished to enjoy a moment without care.

One day I heard him laugh, for the first time, at I don't know what. I was struck by this, and went to look at his notebook. There was no doubt he had made a great deal of progress.

I asked him:

"Are your parents anxious for you to get an education?"

"Oh, yes! My father says he doesn't want me to be like him, with no schooling, no trade, nothing."

I wanted to chase away the seriousness and concern that had come back in his eyes at the mention of home, and I said to the others, half laughing, half seriously:

"You just look out for André. He's a slow starter like the tortoise, but who knows if he won't come in ahead of all of you hares and rabbits!"

André gave me a hesitant look that had something of a man's reproachful glance: Don't push it too far, now . . . But there was also a flash of a child's wild belief in the impossible.

What had got into me, to make me put such intense hope in his head?

Of the two of us, I must have been the bigger child.

By four o'clock, full of vitality though I was in those days, I would be so weary and exhausted that I would sit idle at my desk for a long while, gathering courage to attack the pile of notebooks in front of me.

If I looked up toward the lonely little slope, I could see the morning's film projected in reverse against the horizon. Now André was in the lead, his shoulders hunched forward, hurrying with the pace of a man returning to pressing duties. Then came the Lachapelles, not in single file now, but—what next!—with the bigger ones giving their hands to the smaller ones for the evening walk. Only the Badiou children never changed, morning or evening, week after week, holding hands and gracefully, tirelessly, swinging their two arms joined together. All my little people were making their way up the gentle slope, each at his own pace, in his own manner, each in turn printed for a second on the sky, which was often fiery at those early sundowns. For one instant, I would see them in an aureole of light at the top of the road, then the unknown would snatch them from me.

At those times I found myself wondering about their lives on the distant farms about which I knew nothing. I suspected that an infinite distance separated their lives there from our life at school, but I was still far short of the truth: between those two lives rose a frontier that was almost insurmountable. Yet I dreamed of setting foot in those isolated farmhouses, of perhaps being accepted by those silent, sometimes hostile households. Then, miraculously, the chance was offered me by the little Badiou girl, whose mother had taught her what to say, and who came one day to say it at my desk, word for word, chirping gently like a sparrow:

"My mother, mamzelle, she says for me to say this that it would give her the greatest pleasure if you would do us the honour of having supper at our place one of these evenings at your convenience."

So as to forget no part of this solemn invitation, little Lucienne had rattled it off without a pause. And even with her eyes closed.

I said, very pleased:

"Of course, Lucienne. I'd love to go with you. And why not tonight? It's such a nice day."

In fact, after one or two nights of hoar frost we were being treated to Indian summer. It was as hot as the finest day in the summer; but everyone knows that these radiant days in October are an exceptional gift, to be withdrawn promptly. I felt like taking advantage of it.

The child hesitated, caught between a great satisfaction and a certain disappointment.

"It's just that mama won't have time to houseclean, or at least sweep up the worst, or even bake her cake."

And she underlined each regretful phrase with a gesture of one old gossip to another, letting her hands fall to her sides.

"She wouldn't want to not have her cake ready, at least."

"What's the difference? It's not the cake, it's the company that counts."

At four o'clock quite a few pupils were waiting for me on the front step, out of politeness, because I was going their way. We left together, but with one group within the other, so to speak, as the Badiou children had made it clear that I belonged to them for that evening, and they had come to take my hands, Lucien on my left and Lucienne on my right, swinging them at a great rate as they did between themselves, so that in no time my arms were aching and I had to beg them to set me free. As they did so, they were no doubt surprised to find themselves free of each other, for they were off at a run, Lucien to peer and poke into a gopher hole with a stick, and Lucienne to put two or three mushrooms into her skirt. Then they came back to their places at my side, threatening any who would usurp them. They relaxed their surveillance only when it became clear that I couldn't really escape. My little Auvergnats, however, were stubbornly gaining ground.

Soon we formed a single group, if not a friendly one at least more or less united. Only André kept the lead, yet without dissociating himself from the group, for when he saw that he was getting too far ahead he would slow down, forcing himself to wait; but soon, as if he couldn't help it, he was leaving us behind with the pace of one who has never learned to take his time.

We arrived at the top of the little knoll. We stopped. Looked back. I could see myself at my desk, watching me go up to the top of the road with the children, and I was pleased with the picture that rose in my imagination. From here the school looked bigger than I had thought, and higher, with its second floor formerly occupied by another classroom when there had been more children. Its worn paint, still faintly white at this distance, stood out rather well in the dull landscape. The graceful belfry on its roof even gave it a certain refinement. For the first time I realized that, poor and all as the village was, it had put its money on the school as being an essential possession.

Then I turned and saw the prairie, that endless gulf into which my children plunged every evening. The sight did not lift my heart in joy as when I looked at it from the village. Perhaps deserts, the sea, the vast plain and eternity attract us most when seen from the edges.

I grew silent. The children, finding me different from what I usually was in their eyes, were disconcerted. They looked questioningly at me, pointedly, as if they were wondering:

Is that still her? Is it?

My moment of gravity passed. It may have come from a presentiment of sadness still hidden in the future—a thing that has happened often in my life. I was back with the children now, and as soon as they were aware of it, they came back to me, gay and confident and chattering, real little magpies. In ten minutes they told me more than I had taught them in days.

Toutant's cow had calved. They'd had a lot of trouble with her, for the calf came out wrong-way around. Jos Labossière had taken his sow to the boar. She'd have little pigs in a few months. And Mrs. Toutant had lost her baby when it was just on the way—months too soon.

"And you know how big a baby is, mamzelle, a baby born six months too soon? Not very big."

Lucienne tugged at my sleeve and confided:

"Mama had her baby three months ago at our place, a real one, and he's big and beautiful."

I saw that I had nothing to teach them about birth, human or animal; and both appeared to have the same importance to them.

At last we came to a house. Here the Lachapelles were going to leave us. A woman with a ponderous breast, in a dress of flowered cotton, her thick arms bare, opened the door and shouted to me from the threshold:

"Where are you leaving to go, then?"

"To the Badious."

"That's right. Go and see the French, never your own people."

"But madame!"

"I just said that for something to say. Will you drop in at least on the way back?"

"Of course, madame."

"A'right, then. Come on, kids. Off with the new, on with the old.

At that instant the five Lachapelles, who were quite affectionate toward me at school, became like little strangers who had never heard tell of me. If I hadn't known to what madness embarrassment can push certain children, I would have been stupefied. But I just said to the five wooden faces looking past me toward the picket fence:

"Good-bye, children, see you tomorrow!"

A little farther on, at the junction of the road and a section byway, we lost the Auvergnat children whose farmhouse was a quarter of a mile away, alone in the immensity of its fields.

Before they left us, the little girls began to lament:

"Mama's going to be really happy when she finds out you started your tour with the Badious!"

"In the first place, it isn't a tour. In the second place, if your mother wants me to visit, tell her I'd be delighted to come."

Our group continued, thinned out now. We talked less, walked more slowly, perhaps because we were a little tired; and, for my own part at least, in order to admire the landscape. In the light of the sun, which was about to disappear, it was uniformly bright in colour, drowsy and tranquil in a way that perhaps disquieted the spirit because of its infinite depth. Almost all the harvest was in the barns. What remained to cover the earth was stubble, golden in itself and tinted a fairer blond by this soft light of the day's end. Few and far between, trees reddened by autumn stood flaming in their bursts of colour. All the rest was sweetness and peace, or rather the occasional harmony found in nature as it huddles over its secret.

We crossed a long stretch of prairie without a single building, and heard no cock crow and no dog bark, nor even the wild birds of the place. André was walking with us now, his hurry appeased at least. He didn't join in the conversation, but his head, a little to one side, seemed to spring up to listen after a moment's silence. In this way we would exchange a few words, mostly about the harvest, which had been good in this place, bad in that. Then we would fall back into a vague reverie, perhaps due to the walk in the fresh air or the magic influence of the day's end on the prairie.

As the road climbed out of a slight hollow, a house became visible, still far away, surrounded by fence-posts, each of which had a milk-pail for a hat. The little Morissots began to shout with joy:

"That's our place! That's our place!"

As we approached, their mother came out to the fence to greet me with a rapid-fire monologue that never stopped. It was about me, the children, the harvest, the school, a trip to town she was about to undertake, the hard life, the good weather these days, the winter coming and God knew how we'd get through it . . . Finally she grabbed her two children by the hands and the three went into the house, running.

Only a short way farther, Lucienne, who always pulled at my sleeve when she had something to confide, gave a great tug and said:

"You can never get a word with her. Mama says there's not a woman alive talks more than Madame Morissot."

"Maybe she's bored, alone out here at the end of the world."

Lucienne put on an offended expression because it seemed I did not share her ideas completely, and went on pointedly:

"We're even more alone at our place."

I thought I saw the shadow of a smile pass over André's face, but he said nothing.

There were four of us now. We continued on our way. The Morissots' house was soon hidden by one of the rare patches of trees in the area, and we found ourselves again penetrating what seemed to be the earth's hidden face.

"The sun is dead!" Lucien suddenly cried in a plaintive voice. He had been watching its descent below the horizon and came to press against me, trembling with sadness.

I could not imagine what these tots must feel as they went through the small wood—which to them might seem like a forest—at the moment the sun was setting.

To me, this hour that hesitates between night and day has always seemed enchanted. It has always called to me; it calls me still, like a dream in which our torments will be stilled. It has happened that without realizing it I would walk for two hours in a row under the darkening sky toward the last flush of the horizon, as though it held for me the answer to the question that haunts us from birth. And that evening—so young then and even more than now given to dreaming—I crossed through that hour of sweetness, holding the hands of Lucien and Lucienne to reassure them, with André just a shade ahead. And it seemed to me that we were climbing infallibly, the three children and I, toward happiness, still out of sight but certain to be waiting for us before too long. Emerging from a hollow we were struck by a last arrow of light darting from the horizon. André received it full in his face, and I discovered with astonishment the strange and splendid colour of his eyes; a spring leaf traversed by sunlight.

Silence still enveloped us, not oppressively as when it signifies the absence of life, but swollen with a happy revelation on the point of being made. And then in the golden stubble we heard a burst of bubbling song in the distance. I stopped the children with a gesture and laid my other hand on André's shoulder. "Listen! Wait just a moment, we'll hear the meadowlark!"

Lucien and Lucienne pretented to listen, looking all over to find the bird; but André listened from within, his head tilted, not caring from what point might come such an expression of joy that perhaps no one has sung it better than this bird—yet a queer, solitary figure when we came upon him at last, sitting on a stone in a bare field.

When the song ended, André turned his eyes toward mine, and I saw a delight that was equal to my own.

After that the road was level for a long time. The blue of evening grew darker all around until all shapes were imprecise. The Badious started pointing somewhere in the great emptiness.

"We're home! That's our place!"

Finally I was able to make out a poor, colourless cabin, no porch, just a cube fallen there like dice on a table.

The Badiou children were pulling me along with all their strength, announcing with loud cries that carried far through the infinite silence:

"Mama! Mama! We've brought our mamzelle!"

Much in the same way, it seemed to me, they might have boasted: We've caught her!

Then, out of the little house that stood at the end of a faint trace of laneway, came a small, round woman, agile and agitated, lively as a weasel. When she saw who I was she began to flap her arms at her sides and in the same breath cried that I was so nice to have come . . . and then, abashed: "My house is a mess! And my kitchen's not scrubbed!"

I later understood that it was better manners to give people some time to make special preparations for your visit. But it seemed in this case that the joyous exuberance of this little woman was stronger than her shame at being caught in her "old rags" with the house "all upside-down."

On the point of going inside, I looked back to the road. André was already moving on. Now in the gathering dusk he seemed terribly alone. His shoulders had sunk forward again.

"Hey! André!"

He turned.

"Have you far to go?"

He pointed in the direction of a kind of combe from which emerged a few large, black treetops and, among them, the roof of a house that seemed uninhabited. In that direction everything seemed darker than elsewhere on the plain. You'd have said that was where the night came from.

"How far is it still?"

"Half a mile," he said. "That's why I have to hurry now."

He stood there, unmoving for a moment, not saying a word, as though he regretted not having the right, like other children, to say to me: You'll come to my place one of these days . . .

He simply made a curious, despairing gesture with his arms.

"Well, good night, André. See you tomorrow!"

"Good night, mamzelle!"

As I watched him go, almost at a run, I never dreamed how little I was to see of him in the future.

Less than two weeks after that walk under the Indian summer sky, the icy rains came, and piercing winds; and then—just on the first of November—we woke up to find the poor prairie village surrounded by dunes of snow, like a desert fort amid the sands.

As I kept watch over the little slope that morning, I had the pleasure of seeing, instead of small silhouettes with shoulders hunched, a whole series of cutters. First came Cellini, a man in a hurry, who stopped in for a minute to warm his big hands over the register, telling me that from now on he would bring his children to school and pick them up at four o'clock sharp, and let's be clear about it, he wouldn't wait for anyone who had a detention, let them walk home, it would serve them right. Then came Odilon Lachapelle, in such a rush to leave that the last child barely had one foot out of the cutter and he was on his way home. Then an enormous man with a moustache, with the little troop of Auvergnats cuddled around him under the same buffalo robe. And finally Morissot, who also brought the Badiou children. When I saw that, I wondered why they hadn't all thought of asking him, or one of the parents, to gather all the children from that side of the world and pay him a little for his trouble, rather than have each family underway with the sleds. Everybody would have gained. But apparently our people weren't ready to think that way, at least in those days.

While the children, happy that they didn't have to walk, were hanging up their coats and chattering gaily, a pleasant smell of cold and snow spread through the room, tempered by the waves of heat from the stove.

I rejoiced with them. Now they would start their day rested, good-humoured, and everything would go much better. Then I noticed that André was missing. I asked the Badious, the Morissots:

"You didn't see him on the way?"

"No."

He didn't arrive until about one hour later, walking, his cheeks burning with the cold, and he was still shaking with it after he'd stood over the register a good five minutes. Again he had trouble concentrating on his grammar and geography and arithmetic. And it seemed to me, as I looked at this exhausted child, that those subjects weren't worth making such a fuss about. He came to my desk to show me his notebook, and I took the opportunity to say to him, almost in a whisper:

"Won't your father be driving you to school too, very soon?"

"Not a chance!" he said. "He's already got too much to do in the mornings, all the chores, feeding, milking . . ."

"But couldn't you make some arrangement with the Badious or the Morissots? You could walk to their place and they'd bring you from there."

He put his shoulders back.

"We don't like being obliged. They'd have to wait if I wasn't on time. And they don't always leave at the same time every day. No, we thought about it, but it's too much to ask."

"Well! At least your father's going to pick you up in the afternoon! It gets dark so early now."

In his eyes, which were not so much sad as resigned, those of a man who has seen it all, there passed an expression of annoyance . . . perhaps because I was poking my nose into his life with such persistence.

"It's the same thing at night," he explained, but still politely, as if our roles were reversed and I was the child whose eyes had to be opened to hard realities. "It's the livestock, the chores, the milking. And our horse couldn't do it. He's all we have in winter. And he has to go a mile and a half twice a day for water. It's hard in this weather. You have to break the ice. My father's tired out when he comes back the second time . . . You can't ask too much," he said with pity.

"Of course, André. I didn't know all those things. But at least you could go home at night with the Badious. You'd only have another half-mile to walk. Do you want me to ask for you?"

He seemed hesitant, torn between his secretive nature and the confidence I had been able to inspire in him. Lifting his arms as if to say, what can you do?—he finally murmured:

"It's not worth it, mamzelle."

"What do you mean, it's not worth it?"

His lips trembled.

"Oh, well. I didn't want to tell you just now. Mama said to wait a week or two yet and get what I can out of it. But I know there's no other way. I'm going to quit school, mamzelle."

"Leave school! André! You mustn't think of it!"

He lifted his arms again, like a pair of powerless wings.

"My father can't get on alone. And where does it get him, working like a horse? He's going to a logging shanty up north. He'll earn enough there to keep us going. So I have to keep the house."

"What about your mother?"

"She's been in bed nearly two months now."

"You didn't tell me she was ill."

"She's expecting . . ." he said briefly.

Barely getting out his words, he continued close to my ear:

"If she gets up in those times she'll likely lose her baby, and anyway she's too sick to do anything but give orders from her bed."

"Is there no one else at your place to help out?"

"Just Émile."

"Your little brother? How old is he?"

"Five."

A flash of intense pride, almost of maternal joy, lit the depths of his worried eyes.

"You'd be surprised how he can work, bringing in wood, washing dishes . . . He's a real little helper, Émile is. At night when I have time I give him lessons. He can read already. You'll see, mamzelle, when he comes to school, he's going to be a lot smarter than I was."

His defences down, he was, for that moment, dreaming aloud of a happy furture for his little brother Émile.

"But you're only a child yourself. And far too young to keep house, come now!"

"I'm past ten. I'll be eleven in two months."

That afternoon I managed to get him into Guillaume Morissot's cutter, and to ask the driver in secret if he couldn't wait for André in the mornings and take him back at night.

He answered good-naturedly:

"If those folks weren't so proud, of course we'd do a favour between neighbours. But with them it ain't easy, believe me, mamzelle."

Sitting warm with the others under the robes in the sled that took off with a start, André was the only child who showed no joy. His little face with its big, worried eyes was elsewhere, already busy with the chores that awaited him. He was never to come back to school again.

Weeks and finally months passed by and I realized that not for a single day had I stopped telling myself: It can't be, he's going to come back. Nor had I given up watching the lonely rise in the road, now a high barrier of snow, in the hope of seeing again, as I had the last time, the frail silhouette with the thin, hunched shoulders... And I hadn't even any news. Not a word!

I often asked the Morissots and the Badious. Had they any news?

Lucienne shrugged and flapped her arms. She said:

"Not a thing, mamzelle! They never get in touch, the Pasquiers. So we just wait. No use stickin' your nose in other people's business."

One day I met Mrs. Morissot at the general store.

"That poor woman," she said, meaning Mrs. Pasquier, "it's a downright shame, lying in bed almost all the time she's pregnant. It's her constitution, not the same as other women. We'd go and help out but it's not easy, you know. Those people, when they get that miserable, they won't let you near them."

At Christmas I had sent André by way of the Badious the little present which the school board allowed for every pupil. I added some candies and also sent fruit for Émile. It wasn't until the end of January that I received a note of thanks, and I supposed that the Badious had not been in too great a hurry to deliver my package. The little thank-you note was signed in André's already firm hand, and underneath, in capitals contained between two pencilled lines, Émile had put his name.

Then came February and days of startling beauty. The sun was gaining strength. One afternoon of fine weather was enough to start the surface snow melting, only to crystallize in the cold of the night, and next morning offering to the fire of the rising sun the glinting of a cut stone with a million facets. This hard crust carried well, and one Saturday morning I put on my skis and, ignoring the road, set off across the prairie toward the Pasquiers' farm.

This time, seeing it first from the back, from the top of a knoll, I had no trouble finding the house in its narrow combe surrounded by leafless trees. There it squatted, along with its outbuildings, weathered by time but not ugly in shape, with the high gables stretching to capture a piece of sky above its sombre nest. And no doubt in the years when its paint was new—light yellow, so far as I could judge—it must have looked very spruce in its green background.

I glided down the slope to the back door, which seemed to be the only one in use, as was the case with many farmhouses in winter. A deep path, like a trench in the snow led up to it. As I took off my skis I thought I heard vague sounds coming from inside, which stopped as soon as I knocked on the door. I imagined a lively commotion within, as most likely no one had seen me coming. At last I saw the doorknob turn, very slowly. The door opened a crack, revealing half the face of a child with green-gold eyes like those of André. It expressed the stupefaction of a shipwrecked sailor seeing another turn up on his island.

"So you're Émile!"

Then he opened the door and let me in without saying a single word, staring at me with intense curiosity. I was in a large, bright kitchen where washing hung from cords strung from side to side. From a room that opened off it, a weak voice called:

"Is somebody there? Who is it, Émile?"

Then Émile's voice was raised in triumph, high and shrill:

"It's the lady from the school, Mama."

"Good Lord!" cried the voice, taking on a warmer tone. "Bring her in, Émile, quickly. Put a stick in the stove. Take her coat. As soon as she's warmed up a little bring her in to me."

Then she spoke directly to me, without having seen me, perhaps a little embarrassed:

"You must excuse the mess, mademoiselle. Do come in."

I went through the open bedroom door and saw, lying flat on her back on a wide iron bed, the quilt outlining her swollen belly, a woman with a beautiful face whose immense, sad, but gentle eyes met mine with warm emotion.

"Quick, Émile, clear off a chair for the lady . . . No, put those things on the chest . . . Oh, there's dust on the table! Give it a wipe with the cloth, Émile, my dear."

And to me:

"Sit down, mademoiselle, please sit down."

As soon as I was seated near the bed, she stretched out a thin hand to seize mine and shake it, while tears ran down her cheeks. Standing in the doorway, Émile was trying to hold back his. Seeing this, she sent him away, but tenderly:

"Now then, make yourself useful, you rascal. Get up on the chair. Open the draught a bit in the stovepipe, but don't forget, as soon as the wood starts crackling climb up and turn it shut again. And while you're on the chair you can take down some of the washing. It must be almost dry. Fold it properly, now."

When the child, busied with the stovepipe, was making enough noise to cover our voices, she made her excuses to me:

"What are you going to think, I don't even get up to greet you, mademoiselle! But the doctor has forbidden it completely. And now I've gone such a long way with him I wouldn't want to lose him," she said, stroking her belly gently with her hand. "But we didn't want this one, at the start."

Her eyes grew moist again.

"Émile, yes, we wanted him, even though I was in bed six months before André came and we knew what I was in for. Antoine and I, we thought it was worth it all the same. But then, after Émile, we said, never again! Never again! But you see! I guess nature has its needs..."

Émile was once more in the doorway, his little face craning to catch our conversation. His mother sent him back to mind the fire and sweep the kitchen.

And she took my hand again, smiling almost gaily through her tears.

"André's the one who'll be really pleased. He's doing the chores. We sent quite a few of the livestock to the farmer next door. An Icelander. A fine man he is! Thorgssen. But we still had to keep the milk-cow for ourselves. And the old horse in case Thorgssen was away. There's the chickens to feed, the cow to milk, the stable to clean. It's a lot for a child of eleven... not to mention meals."

I took it on myself to ask her why she didn't accept help from Mrs. Badiou, who seemed quite ready to give it.

"Ah, yes!" she answered. "That's a good woman if there ever was one! But she has six children of her own, and the oldest isn't seven yet. One a year, never a miss. And if her pregnancies are normal, her births are not. They go on forever. She was screaming for three days the last time...."

Suddenly I couldn't stand it, and I wept with her over the lot of women.

"At least your husband will be back when..."

"Oh, if he only could! But his full winter's wages up there, that's our only salvation. Enough to finish our payments on the combine and get us out of debt. If we don't..."

The sound of feet stamping off snow made us stop talking. André came in, sent his cap flying to land on a nail in the wall, took off his jacket and stooped to unlace his high boots. His gestures, his attitude, his facial expression, were those of a man coming tired and a little deadened from his daily job. Émile, folding linen on the other side of the room, whispered to him, Look . . . see who's there . . .

André looked up and saw me sitting beside his mother. His face grew red with emotion. He came in, his hand stretched out, somewhat ceremoniously, but as soon as the greetings were over he leaned with solicitude toward his mother.

"No more pains? Are you all right?"

She stretched out her hand and, as I had so often wanted to do, smoothed back the lock of blond hair that fell over his eyes.

"Just fine," she said. "But we're going to keep your mademoiselle with us. Do you want to try an omelette?"

He agreed with joy and went off to the kitchen to put on a great apron with shoulder straps, and took his turn at issuing commands to little Émile:

"Now, then! Get some bark or kindling to get the fire up. A little speed, eh? No, get up on the chair and open the stovepipe draught and I'll bring some shavings."

Get up on the chair! Surely in all my life I had never heard this order repeated so often and so promptly obeyed. Every time I looked out into the kitchen, there indeed was Émile standing on tiptoe on the chair to reach the Sunday crockery or fetch the best tablecloth from the high cupboard, or close the stovepipe draught which was by now snoring too healthily.

André was busy too. His mother asked me to pull her bed over so that she could better observe the children at work, constantly giving them good advice:

"Beat your eggs till they're light, André."

I offered to help him.

She whispered:

"You mustn't. André likes to do it all by himself. He takes offence easily and anyway he has to get used to it."

At last I was invited to take my place at the table. I took a mouthful of omelette, and began to chew a tasteless substance with the texture of rubber. I succeeded, just the same, in swallowing the oversized serving André had given me. He watched me closely, and when I had downed the last forkful he said roughly to Émile:

"See? My omelette was good!"

Émile, making a face, shoved his plate away.

"I can't eat that. It's tough as an old boot."

I turned to the mother. We exchanged a furtive smile. André had brought her a small tray. She was eating, sitting up slightly in bed, with pillows behind her back.

For dessert they went and stood beside the bed, one on either side, each with a small dish, and fed her by the spoonful with viburnum jelly sent over by Thorgssen. They took turns in the process.

"One spoonful for André!"

"One for Émile!"

She was not hungry, but she gulped it down to please them.

I thought of the queen mother of the bees, fortified by her small servants to the best of their ability in her terrible task as funnel to the species.

When the meal had ended, André set about washing the dishes from the morning and noon meals, helped by Émile who dried and, from his chair, put away the cups and plates.

I suggested that the mother sleep for a while, and I would rest as well, to prepare for an early start homeward, so as to arrive when it was still daylight.

She took my hand again.

"If you wanted to . . . If you'd just be kind enough to help André. I haven't been able to help him with his last arithmetic question. He's discouraged, he doesn't want to open his books these days, and I feel it's such a shame!"

I said that I'd help him, of course. He wiped the oilcloth tablecover with a damp rag, scratched with his nail at a stubborn spot, then went to bring all his school material, books, scribblers, ink bootle, until the big table was covered with it and the room looked like a school. Émile followed all our movements as if they were mysterious preparations for an unknown celebration.

I saw at once the difficulty that had caused André to stumble, and began explaining it to him. His face, grey with fatigue, suddenly grew heavy and lolled sideways, his eyes closing. He slept thus, sitting almost straight in his chair, for five or ten minutes. I didn't dare to move, but contemplated this defenceless face before me with a mixture of discomfiture and relief.

Nothing was left of him now but the fragile child. In his sleep, his head weighed to one side, he made me think of a flower bowing on its too-delicate stem. He woke as suddenly as he had gone to sleep, shook himself, apologized, attributed his "going-to-sleepiness" to the heat of the house, said that he was ready now to follow my explanations. And in fact I had the joy of seeing him understand at last. He was proud and happy.

"It's not so much for me, it's so I can help Émile later on when it's his turn."

"For you, too, my dear," his mother corrected him. "If only there was a way for you to get your year!"

I went over the problem again with André to make sure he had understood. I told him to keep the solution hidden somewhere and try to do the question a few times without looking it up. I also made a work plan for him, other arithmetic problems, a few rules of grammar, some guide marks that would help him work alone. He became tense as he tried to grasp the lesson, just as he had in school, his forehead reddening with effort and a kind of solemn joy. The time passed so quickly that I was surprised to hear the mother's soft voice saying from her room:

"Émile, my dear! I don't know how you can see a thing. Get up on a chair and take down the lamp. Bring it to me with a match. I'll brighten up the room for you."

I looked up from the scribblers and the open books. Above the edge of the combe, the plain was already pale and the sun had dropped below the horizon. A kind of mysterious happiness seemed to fill the darkened house. Émile was the first to yell with joy:

"The lady won't be able to leave now. It's almost dark. She could be eaten by the wolves."

Less bubbling, but just as determined, André agreed:

"It's true, mamzelle, you can't leave at this hour. Night would catch you on the way. We'd be too worried about you."

The mother backed them up:

"It's true, at this time it wouldn't be wise."

After a few seconds of hesitation I gave in to their objections. I was not tempted, in any case, by the notion of venturing across the prairie with its lonely, tragic face at this time of day. The moment I nodded agreement, a heart-felt activity took over the household, but all in an orderly way, with everything directed from the great iron bed.

"André, lift the trapdoor, go up to the big bedroom upstairs and get some linen sheets. The ones we brought from France. You can hang them on some chair-backs, spread out, to warm them in front of the open fire. But right now, before you go upstairs, open the door of the other downstairs bedroom and let some heat in."

They sent packing any fear of a chimney or stovepipe fire, stuffing the stove with softwood which crackled merrily. Émile was asked to climb on a chair and regulate the draught by turning the handle once again. While the sheets, spread out from one chair-back to the next, grew warm they filled the room with a delicious smell.

What we ate for supper I don't remember. Unforgettable was the comforting, tender beauty of this interior, with its two lamps, one in the mother's room and one in the kitchen, their gleam reflected in the windowpanes which were invaded by the dark of night.

After supper the dishes and stable chores were done so quickly that I wondered if André had only half-milked the cow. Then Émile inquired:

"Are we going to have a party? A real party?"

As if relieved of the weight of his day's labour, André agreed indulgently. He went into the parlour, kept closed so that it need not be heated, brought out a phonograph with a horn speaker, which he set up on the table and cranked up. He put on a record. Out came something which remotely resembled an old Chevalier song. Mostly what I heard was a series of whistles, scratches and general caterwauling . . . then everything began to come apart. André hastened to give a few turns to the crank. The squeaks, the meeowing, the bleating, picked up again. The children were in seventh heaven.

Their three records played again and again. Émile came and knelt on the floor at my feet, planted his elbows on my knees, and looked up at me with a supplicating air.

"Are you going to tell us a story?"

Sitting astride his chair like a man, his hands joined behind the chair-back, André nonetheless had an expression that agreed with Émile's request.

I asked them to come closer and then, O Lord, why did I start off, dead with fatigue as I was and wanting nothing better than to go to bed, with the long story of Aladdin and his wonderful lamp?

No doubt because of the miraculous effect brought about in this poor, isolated house by nothing more than the timid light of the lamp. But, as we all know, the story has no end.

I was falling asleep myself as I told it. I watched Émile as his eyes grew heavy and thought: There we go, he's dropping off, I'll be delivered at last. But he'd rub his eyes and hold them open forcibly until the sleepy spell passed and then spur me on without pity:

"Don't stop now! Your story's not finished!"

It came to an end at last. I went with the children to prepare their mother for the night and wish her rest. Then we all went to bed, I in the East Room, as they called it, Émile in a kind of little nook off the kitchen and André on a couch near his mother's room so that he could hear if she called.

In order to heat my room, André had built the fire up so high that I was far too warm even with the covers thrown back, and I spent some time getting to sleep. But two hours later I awoke chilled to the bone.

The mother was calling softly, with the desire, one felt, not to really wake him up:

"André, the fire's out! It's getting cold! André!"

The call came again a little later. André seemed to hear nothing. I got up and went to the couch where he was sleeping. A white, full moon, soft and peaceful, poured its light directly through the kitchen window. It fell on André's face, resting at last, with no cares, no anxiety, no weight of responsibility. His forehead was smooth, the lines of his mouth were pure. Suddenly I saw his half-open lips form the beginning of a smile. What dream-thought had brought him relaxation at last?

In the light of the moon it was easy to find the makings of a fire. As I waited to make sure it had caught properly, I went and sat beside the mother. Her eyes shone in the half-light. She had her rosary in her hands.

I asked her:

"When your time comes . . . what will you do?"

"That's easy," she reassured me. "André will run to Thorgssen, our good neighbour, and let him know. He'll hitch up and go for the doctor."

"And if the weather's bad?"

"Thorgssen will go anyway. He promised my husband. And anyway, you mustn't worry about me like this, mademoiselle. My pregnancies are hard but I give birth easily. You know, you can't have all the bad luck on your side."

I was going to go back to bed, but she took my hand with that touching gesture that I had seen several times already, as if to mark a deep need of her spirit, combined with confidence.

"If my husband comes back, as he's supposed to, about the end of April or the beginning of May, do you think it might be possible, in spite of everything, for André to pass his year? I'd give I don't know what for that."

In my heart I doubted it. I said only:

"I'll do my very best."

A pressure of her hand thanked me. I went back to bed after adjusting the draught of the stove yet again. This time

I slept like a log. When I awoke it was broad daylight. The smell of freshly ground coffee and bread toasted over the flames wafted through the house.

Astonishingly, André succeeded in serving us an excellent breakfast. The butter especially had a very delicate taste, churned at home according to the mother's directions.

I said I had never tasted any with so fine a flavour since I used to visit my grandmother as a child. André blushed with pleasure.

No question of lingering this time. Under the high sun the plain was as it had been on the previous morning, a smooth, soft and shining sea. I would have to hurry to make the most of these luminous hours. I remembered the sudden, almost sinister coming of night that had surprised us yesterday in mid-afternoon. I said goodbye to the mother and the children, who all at once grew serious when they saw me ready to leave.

I hurried away in the belated realization that while, by staying with the Pasquiers, I might have reassured them, I must have thrown my landlady in the village into a panic.

I came to the rim of the combe, passed it, climbed a little higher and reached a small knoll. There I stopped to look back. At the bottom of the funnel, I could still see the little lost farm.

Suddenly the back door opened. A silhouette appeared, the thin shoulders hunched forward. In one motion he sent the contents of a pail flying out on the snow and slipped the handle over his arm; then he picked up a few sticks of firewood and some other object—perhaps a piece of clothing hung out to air—and went in, drawing the door shut behind him with a deft movement of his foot. Shortly after, a strong column of smoke rose out of the combe.

I went on my way, telling myself there was nothing to fear. The house was kept, well-kept.

André Major

Translated by David Lobdell

The Good Old Days

André Major was born in Montreal on April 22, 1942, and left school at the age of eighteen to pursue a career in journalism and literature. He wrote for the weekly *Petit journal*, became a frequent contributor to *Liberté*, and in 1963, with Hubert Aquin and others, he began publishing the magazine *Parti pris*. From 1967 to 1970 he wrote for *Le Devoir*, and from 1972 to 1979 for *La Presse*, and was also active in the founding of the publishing house La Coopérative d'éditions les Quinze. He is currently a reader of manuscripts for Éditions du Jour, and since 1973 has worked as a cultural programmer for Radio-Canada.

Major's first novel, *Le Cabochon*, was published in Paris in 1964, and this was followed the next year by *La Chair de poule*, a book of stories published by *Parti pris*. His study of the influential novelist Félix-Antoine Savard, author of *Menaud, maitre draveur*, was published in 1968. The following year, while living in Toulouse, France, Major began writing a trilogy of novels set in the Laurentians and Montreal: *L'Épouvantail* (1974; *The Scarecrows of St. Emmanuel*, 1977), *L'Épidémie* (1975; *Inspector Therrien*, 1980), and *Les Rescapées* (1976), for which he won the Governor-General's Award for Fiction in 1977.

A second book of short stories, *La Folle d'Elvis* was published in 1982 and translated by David Lobdell as *Hooked on Elvis* in 1983, and it is from this book that "The Good Old Days" has been taken. In reviewing the book, Joyce Marshall noted that it contained "wry stories about possible encounters that fail to take place, or when they do take place are merely tentative or disillusioning." Though perhaps less overtly political than many of Major's other works, "The Good Old Days" is definitely a story about disillusionment—a theme that runs through all of Major's writing.

"The Good Old Days" is reproduced from *Hooked on Elvis* (Montreal: Quadrant Editions, 1983) and was originally published under the title "Le bon vieux temps" in *La Folle d'Elvis: nouvelles* (Montreal: Québec-Amérique, 1982).

I

She'd ended up accepting; she still wondered why. Simply to avoid having a guilty conscience? For months he'd been going on about Bernard, the good old days with his friend Bernard, all the things they'd done together, the sleepless nights spent smoking in front of an open fire. Jean-Louis's eyes glowed whenever he spoke of these things, recalling new details each time that caused him to marvel. It was a Friday evening. The forecast was for a sweltering weekend.

"We could go out there, if you're so set on it."
"To Bernard's, you mean?"
"What do you think I'm talking about?"
"Oh, just you wait! You're in for a treat!"

Exultant, he rushed to the phone to announce their visit, not forgetting to ask Bernard how to get to his place.

"You understand, my friend, it's been such a long time..."

She had stopped listening, preferring instead to soak in the tub.

And now they were moving up the narrow, winding road, whose dirt surface was bleached white by the summer sun. The foliage had lost its lustre beneath the fine coating of dust raised by passing vehicles. The road kept climbing, with sudden abrupt curves; it hadn't been used much lately. Already, she was beginning to regret having suggested this excursion to such an out-of-the-way place. The landscape made her feel lightheaded. It was as if, deprived of all familiar points of reference, she could find nothing to cling to. But that was something Jean-Louis would never have understood, he was so excited by the view of the moutains and all the youthful memories they evoked.

"It should be around here somewhere."
"Keep your eyes on the road," she replied curtly.

She was the navigator, sitting beside him with the list of scribbled directions in her lap. He was so afraid of missing the place. Really, it was absurd! But she said nothing.

For the past few weeks, they'd been at each other's throats almost constantly, and usually over the most trifling matters. The last time was still fresh in her mind. The previous evening, following his conversation with Bernard, he had begun to boast about a twenty-mile hike they had once taken in the pelting rain. "Well, you certainly didn't have that belly in those days!" she had retorted. And he had taken offence. He'd told her to go to hell. At least an hour had passed before peace was restored. What was happening to them? The beginning of the end? Curious that this thought left her so cold. She had once found a certain charm in Jean-Louis' reminiscences, but not anymore. And now she was having second thoughts about suggesting this visit to Bernard.

The bright sunlight was dazzling. The car left a long trail of white dust in its wake. This must be the ranch, she thought. Horses were grazing in a field, but there was not a soul to be seen beneath the clear, blue sky, which seemed almost low enough that you could reach up and touch it.

"Slow down," she said. "You have to turn left in about half a mile."

"Left?"

She didn't feel like repeating herself. What she wanted right now was a cool drink, a beer or a lemonade.

II

The famous mansion of which Jean-Louis had so often spoken was, in fact, nothing but a big, white clapboard house with bay windows. The cool air of the interior struck them like a wall. Bernard didn't seem to be in any great hurry to come and welcome them. They found him weeding his garden, wearing a big straw hat with a frayed brim. The thing that struck her most was that he didn't remove the hat, not even when he invited them into the kitchen for refreshments. The room was sparsely furnished. A pale wooden table with four matching chairs stood near the window, which looked out onto the garden. There was nothing else except a cast-iron stove and a truncated barrel holding a few sticks of wood. The walls were bare, embarrassingly so. Her gaze wandered over the room without finding anything to rest upon. Their host had been content to shake her hand and incline his head, as if he were at a loss as to what to say. It was Jean-Louis who did all the talking, delighted to find things unchanged since his last visit. "How long ago was that?" he asked. Bernard shook his head, showing little interest in the subject. But he did remove his hat once he had served them iced tea in beer mugs. He seemed content just to stand there, a shade taller than Jean-Louis and somewhat more youthful in appearance, looking as though his mind were on other things, nodding his head from time to time. She felt as though they were intruding. He hadn't even bothered to change out of his faded jeans and khaki shirt, which was missing two or three buttons. It was always these details that she noticed first. Then, so as to know who she was dealing with, she would submit a person to a sort of interrogation. But she was given no opportunity to do this now, for Jean-Louis was chattering deliriously away while Bernard stuffed his corn-cob pipe.

"Doesn't it get hot?" she asked him.

"Depends on the tobacco. With a mild blend, there's usually no problem."

He looked like a gentleman-farmer from the Deep South. When she told him this, he didn't even flinch, he merely met her gaze with an intentness that made her stomach twitch. Then he lowered his eyes, as if he was afraid of her, and his face recovered the impassivity she thought must serve as a mask. She didn't hear what he was saying to Jean-Louis, she caught only the word "horses."

"Horses? What horses?"

"Bernard has fitted out some horses for us."

"Well, you'll have to go without me," she declared, panic-stricken. "Can you see me on a horse in this?" The dress she was wearing was split to the thigh and clung to her like a sheath. "If you'd told me, I would have worn something else." She gave Jean-Louis a withering look.

He claimed it had completely slipped his mind. But he knew perfectly well that if he had made the slightest allusion to horses, she would have refused to come.

"Can you see me on a horse in these heels?"

"I can lend you a pair of sandals," said Bernard. "Or if you prefer a pony, that can be arranged. I have one that is as docile as a dog."

She resented the fact that he had seen through her so easily, standing there and looking her over with his condescending male smile. She glared at him until he lowered his eyes and left the kitchen. Meanwhile, Jean-Louis went in search of their things.

You'll pay for this, she thought, just you wait. She had the impression she had been made the dupe of their virile complicity, which allowed them to feel for a moment that they were in charge. Bernard returned with the sandals and some blanket rolls. They've planned everything behind my back, she thought. She removed her shoes and slid her feet into the sandals. Jean-Louis came in with his back-pack.

"You won't want to lug that thing around," said Bernard, "not on horseback."

"What do we take, then?"

"The very minimum. We'll make do with what we find."

"The very minimum," repeated Jean-Louis, opening his pack. "Matches, mess tins, groundsheet, rope, axe. But what'll I put them in?"

Bernard pointed to a game bag hanging from a hook on the wall. "I've already packed the food," he said.

"I didn't forget the most important thing," said Jean-Louis with a wink, brandishing a flask of brandy.

Bernard set his straw hat back on his head and slid his arms into a buckskin jacket that had seen better days. She went in search of the shawl she'd left on the rear seat of the car, hesitating a moment before putting on her hat, a stylish little thing that she knew would be an object of ridicule.

They were waiting for her in front of the jeep, basking in the sweet odours of the natural world distilled by the blinding sunlight.

"Smell!" said Jean-Louis.

"Smell what?"

"It grows all around the house," explained Bernard, relighting his corn-cob pipe.

Squeezed between the two of them in the jeep, she had to hold onto her hat, which threatened at any moment to fly off.

"It'll be cooler in the woods," said Bernard. As if she had complained about the heat.

III

Riding a bay mare devoid of markings, Bernard led them down a forest trail. Jean-Louis had finally fallen silent, clearly delighted by this unexpected reunion with his past. But he couldn't help naming the things he saw from time to time.

"Birches," he said, pointing them out.

"I know what they are," she replied sharply.

"Tell me what those are, then."

"Hardwood trees."

"Yes, but what kind?"

"I'm waiting for you to tell me."

"Elms."

"Beech," corrected Bernard, who had overheard them.

"Are you sure?" asked Jean-Louis, looking disconcerted.

"See the smooth, grey trunks? They can't be anything else."

"Yes, of course," conceded Jean-Louis a little reluctantly.

She was about to smile when her pony suddenly swerved, making her heart skip a beat. The ground they were moving over now was covered with little, shiny, wet stones. The tree trunks were oozing resin.

Holding the shawl around her shoulders, she kept her eyes fixed resolutely on the pony's grey mane. At one point, Jean-Louis dismounted a little awkwardly and slapped his mare on the rump.

"I'll be back in two seconds," he said, disappearing into the woods.

She caught Bernard looking at her leg, which was pressed against the pony's soft flank. Feast your eyes, she thought, returning his stare. He looked away finally and continued on his way without waiting for Jean-Louis.

She wondered what time it was; it might have been two o'clock or four. She was thirsty, though the air was cool in the woods. Holding the reins in one hand, she let herself be carried along by the pony, rocked by its steady gait. The animal seemed to know the way. From time to time a butterfly would dart into a shaft of sunlight, looking like a miniature stained-glass window. A sort of feeling of wellbeing permeated her, leaving her a little numb. When she raised her head, she saw the two men up ahead of her, waving to her. Somewhere nearby, she could hear the gurgling of water. The men were looking for a way across the torrent, which was narrow, but seemed impassable.

"You go on ahead without me," she called to them.

Bernard said something she didn't hear as he moved down the edge of the stream. She and Jean-Louis followed. Suddenly, up ahead, there appeared a little bridge. Just like in a storybook. She was very frightened while crossing it. On the other side, there was a sun-drenched clearing. The horses waded through the high ferns, which crackled under their hooves. The men stopped in the middle of the clearing, shading their eyes from the overhead glare, and she understood that at that instant they were back in the past, reliving some earlier, similar moment in their lives. While Bernard had chosen to go on living here, exactly as he had in his youth, Jean-Louis had moved on to other things, and now he was consumed by nostalgia. It was probably this that put him in awe of his friend and left him a little bitter. Well, why didn't he move back here, then, and settle down in the countryside? She would have made no move to stop him. She might even have been a little relieved. She was tired of feeling guilty all the time, as if it were she who was preventing him from living. The horses were tearing at the lush grass. Bernard raised his hat and, squinting, pointed to a grove of maples.

"We'll move into the shade."

The moment they entered the undergrowth, the cool air washed over them like water. Why are you looking back at me like that? she thought. I'm following you.

IV

They had reached the flat summit of the mountain, from which vantage point their eyes took in the distant constellation of metal roofs scattered amongst the hills. She had had to plead with them to stop to rest, for the feeling had gone out of her legs. Jean-Louis laughed at the sight of her rubbing her thighs. She cursed him under her breath. Bernard began chopping up some dead wood, working slowly but methodically. The horses were grazing peacefully. From time to time, she could hear shrill cries in the undergrowth.

"What's that?"

"Only a squirrel," said Jean-Louis, emptying the game bag.

She had not known a squirrel could make such a sound. Bernard ignited a strip of birch bark, which he slid beneath the little pyramid of wood he had built; it smoked blackly before bursting into flame. She was as exhausted as if she had spent the entire day moving furniture. Jean-Louis's sweaty T-shirt clung to his belly. Bernard went about his work without haste. Sure of yourself, aren't you, my lovely? she thought. That's because you're in your element here. But I'd like to see you in the city. Jean-Louis began struggling with the mess tins, while Bernard opened a can of stew with the point of his hunting-knife.

"Just like the good old days," she said, getting to her feet, but neither of the men reacted. "Shall I look after the vegetables?"

"What vegetables?" asked Jean-Louis. "We'll do without them for once."

Bernard approached the fire with the coffee pot and set it on a flat stone.

"There must be some edible plants around," she said.

"Or some roots." Jean-Louis gave her a scornful look and she added quickly, "What do we do about the mosquitoes?"

"We put up with them," muttered Bernard, without shifting his gaze from the fire. Was he angry? It was hard to say. He was so good at hiding his feelings, he was so virile.

V

The horses were invisible in the darkness, but their eyes glowed briefly when Bernard threw a fir branch onto the fire. Jean-Louis had been asleep for ten or fifteen minutes, stupefied by all the brandy he'd consumed. Bernard had taken no more than a swig or two, showing little interest in his friend's stories. He had just sat there, appearing to listen, as indifferent as if he had been in the company of a perfect stranger. He had said nothing, content to sit there and gaze at the fire. And she had done the same, driven by some irritating need to follow his example. There was no moon; but for the glow of the fire, the night would have been pitch black. Jean-Louis was snoring more loudly than usual. Bernard got up to cover him with a blanket. As he was about to turn back to the fire, she asked him to pass her one. He unrolled the blanket and draped it over her shoulders. Just as he was about to move away, she reached up and seized his arm, though she'd sworn to let him sweat a little before making a move in his direction. Her curiosity had simply gotten the better of her. She was thinking of no one but herself, no need but her own, as she drew close to him beneath the blanket. A strange sort of hero, she thought, to tremble like that, like a cornered beast. She looked up at him. He was gazing at the fire, his hands clasped over his knees, his teeth clamped about the stem of his pipe. It had been a long time since he had experienced the marvellous power of her feminine allure. He seemed to be barely breathing. When she passed an arm around his waist, she felt him shudder. "It's nice here like this, isn't it?" she seemed to say as she pressed her body to his. He lay his hand on her naked shoulder. It was warm and slightly moist.

She thought he might be working up the courage to take the initiative, but he just sat there, with one hand on her shoulder, almost like a big brother. She waited a moment, then blew gently into his ear, causing him to shiver and tighten his grip on her shoulder. Then she rolled over and pulled him down on top of her. His lips tasted of tobacco. He let her unbutton his shirt and unfasten his belt. The metal buckle burned her belly when she hitched up her dress. He was breathing heavily now. But it was she who took him, impaling herself on him, then riding him, quickly, voraciously, oblivious to his muffled moans. At the moment of climax, she fell forward onto him, her body shaken with spasms. It seemed to her that her pleasure had never been so keen.

Later, when the fire had gone out and the night had swallowed them up, he caressed her breasts with the tips of his fingers and she mounted him again, with the impression this time that her possession of him was complete, as if it were she who was penetrating him. He pressed his body tightly to hers and she pulled the blanket over them.

VI

She could hear crackling sounds. Her left shoulder blade was aching. The smell of burning wood reminded her where she was. When she raised the blanket, the cold air struck her like ice water. He was crouched before the fire, his head lowered, as if he were studying something between his knees.

"Good morning."

He merely nodded.

"Where's Jean-Louis?"

"Gone for a walk," he replied, gesturing towards the woods. The trees were barely visible through the fog. She pulled her shawl from beneath her and covered her shoulders with it, then approached the fire. The horses were grazing nearby. Jean-Louis returned with an aluminum cup filled with dew-soaked strawberries. He passed them, first to Bernard, then to her. When he asked how they had slept, Bernard merely replied that the coffee was ready. She noticed at that moment that one of the three blankets was still rolled up behind the saddle. For breakfast, they had a box of rusks and cheese. Then Bernard made more coffee. Only Jean-Louis continued to labour under the illusion that they were back in the good old days. Why in God's name couldn't he be still? Why couldn't he enjoy the silence whose absence he was always lamenting in the city? But he couldn't contain his enthusiasm for this foggy morning, which reminded him of so many others.

"Bernard, do you remember the time we . . .?"

But Bernard was busy gathering the mess tins together.

They didn't speak on the return trip. Jean-Louis must have guessed from their silence that neither of them shared his exuberance. Besides, he had taken the lead. She wished he would just disappear, as if by magic, so she could have Bernard all to herself. It was absurd to part like this, when things had only begun. At one point, she almost turned in the saddle to tell him she would return at the first possible opportunity. Perhaps he was thinking the same thing, who could say?

VII

They had been driving now for about ten minutes. Neither of them had said a word. The sky was a flat, unbroken grey, the sort of sky that heralded rain, a slow, grey, monotonous drizzle. Bernard had made no move to detain them when, following the meal, she had said they must be on their way.

"Would you have preferred to stay a little longer?" she asked.

"Why ask that now?"

"Bernard looked tired."

"Bernard, tired?"

"I think he was."

Jean-Louis forced a laugh. "Is that why you wanted to leave?"

"I didn't force you to go."

"You couldn't sit still, not even at the table."

"The truth is that I was tired of hearing about all your exploits," she said after a moment. "You could have been quiet for a bit and let us breathe."

"Oh, go to hell!"

"Listen, Jean-Louis . . ." She took a breath. "Bernard and I made love together."

"What are you saying?"

"Not just once. Twice. While you were sleeping off your brandy."

"I hardly drank a drop."

"Is that what you call ten ounces?"

"The bottle was half empty."

They fell silent. A fine rain began to mist the windshield. Jean-Louis switched on the wipers.

"If there's one person you women will never have, it's Bernard."

"You're wrong there, my friend. I had him."

He broke into laughter. "You'll say anything."

"Your hero let himself be seduced by his buddy's girl."

"Shut up!"

She closed her eyes, trying to recapture the experience, recalling only isolated details, like the burning sensation of his belt buckle against her belly.

"It's true," she said. "I swear it."

"Swear all you like, I'll never believe you," he said. She thought she could detect a note of desperate faith in his voice. "With anyone else, perhaps, but not with him."

She kept her eyes closed, paying no further attention to him, tormented by the frustrating suspicion that she had lost something precious, something that had happened to her and that would never happen again, not in quite the same way. She wondered if Bernard were struggling with the same memory lapse. But no, she thought, not him. And in her mind's eye, she saw him seated in front of the window, smoking his corn-cob pipe, happy with the rain that was falling on his garden.

Gaétan Brulotte
Translated by Matt Cohen

THE SECRET VOICE

Gaétan Brulotte was born in Lauzon on April 8, 1945, and studied at the Université de Paris under Roland Barthes, receiving his Ph.D. in modern literature in 1978. He has since taught in several universities, including Université du Québec à Montréal, Laval, California, and New Mexico. He currently lives in Trois-Rivières, where he teaches French language and literature.

Brulotte's first novel, *L'Emprise* (*Double Exposure*) was published in 1978 and won the Prix Robert-Cliche. A book of short stories, *Le Surveillant*, followed in 1982; it was awarded the Prix Adrienne-Choquette as well as the Prix France-Québec. A second collection of stories, *Ce qui nous tient*, appeared in 1988.

Le Surveillant was translated in 1990 as *The Secret Voice* by Matt Cohen, and it is from this collection that the title story has been taken. "The Secret Voice" exemplifies Brulotte's fascination with the juxtaposition of the formal and the fantastic, as well as his recurring subject—contemporary humanity in the grip of a hostile, strange, yet alluring universe. Brulotte's work has been compared to that of the American writer John Hawkes. "While reading Brulotte we sometimes laugh," Gilles Marcotte has written, "but it is never a frank laugh, because even the most fantastic situations in which he places his characters are too similar to those in which we live."

∽

"The Secret Voice" is reproduced from *The Secret Voice* (Erin: Porcupine's Quill, 1990) and was originally published under the title "La voix secrète" in *Le Surveillant* (Montreal: Les Quinze, Éditeurs, 1982).

A VOICE. Which shattered language. Deliciously. A foreign voice, which said: "Touch me. I am the skin of time. And I never think. Thought, knowledge, meditation—there are many people still struggling at this level. Let's leave them to it. You and I—we go beyond. There is nothing to understand, my sweet. It is enough to experience. Yes—in feeling everything. To feel the orifice of the planet open against my mouth. To hold the beauty of our thrilling words and let ourselves reach across the night, with nothing to separate us, SWALK..."

The voice always whispered this magic syllable, SWALK. Prolonging it. Nonchalantly. Sensually. SWALK: sealed with a loving kiss, is what it meant. The voice taught us to repeat this term. SWALK. Orgasmic provocation of an echo, mutual fulfilment in the same euphoric chaos. It was such an exquisite pleasure to hear that warm intonation. Which seized us, again and again, reconnecting us to life. We girls who had been overeducated, overprotected. SWALK. SWALK. Rare spring of deep emotion to succeed in touching us. We cherished the voice for all the doors it made yield within us.

That voice talked to us over the telephone. It talked to us when we dialed its mysterious number, discovered by one of us. Dream figures, over which we brooded, jealously: our deep secret. The number gave us free access to the forbidden kingdom of that disturbing male voice. Always the same: deep, soft, sweet, sympathetic. A silky evening murmur. Or Sunday afternoon. Waiting at the tips of our fingers. To fill our adolescent emptiness.

That unknown voice hid itself under the name of Albert.

What damp and longing looks, what liberating confessions, what electronic body-to-body, what paradise close to home did Albert offer us?

Should we call him all together? Then, all excited, we would talk to him in turn, amuse ourselves with him by confessing everything and nothing. Some of us innocent, others provocative, we told him about our problems of the moment—mostly imaginary—our loves—in fact nonexistent—or our desires—a mixture of pretence and dreams.

Always the same unfailing welcome. His patience. His politeness. Also his curiosity. His indiscreet questions were encouraged by our confidences. His playful insistence made us important. Albert was interested in the colour of our hair, of our eyes, in the shape of our lips. He solicited precise physical descriptions, the better to construct images around the anonymous voices he was hearing. He murmured our names, invented affectionate surnames for us, decorated them with charming diminutives. Often, with one of us, an intimacy developed, a closeness explicitly sensual. And this was indeed the most titillating. Blushing exchanges, temperatures rising. His man's words sought us out, quietly, never sliding into vulgarity—that would have put us off—and ended, in their distance, by having marvellous effects on us. To us, Albert was a consoling prince. He was giving us therapy through words and making possible our small transgressions. Transgressions that were reassuring because they were without consequence, yet essential because they were our release.

"Let's get excited, just a little," he would murmur when, in secret, I could call him alone.

Deeds. Words. Silences. Hypnosis. SWALK. It was better than in books. My body knew itself. The ear no longer paid attention to the understanding of the words: hearing lost its head, its normal intelligence went to sleep, the wild talk had no more meaning. It became a kind of probe slid into me, exquisite penetration that left me paralyzed with pleasure.

Strong, honest male presence—tender and captivating—it insinuated itself into my silence, numbed me like a venom, caught me in the mesh of its desire. Sugared state of being. Space saturated with exquisite delight. The whole body abandoned to the sensuous pleasure of language, to the languor of sensual pleasure. That sorcerer's voice, carrying me away.

"Sail with me, my little boat, into the wind, come to my smile . . ."

And always his desire, tuned perfectly to mine, half-whispered. Sweet murmured invocations of desire.

Memories of drunkenness in his company. Time for serenity and for passion. Time to taste the slow rise of pleasure. SWALK. The long, complex awakening of the senses with him, breathless, in the night on the telephone, the glow of darkness. Slipping sensually through surrounding mists. Floating in the stream of his voice, of my own. Mad explosion of flesh in the throat, agonies of separation.

I wasn't playing my role. I was sixteen years old and in love with this voice. I had no idea whose it was. The strongest feeling of my life had only a wire to hang on to. That's how it was.

In time it evaporated, that so soft voice. But it came back much later, thirty years later, one evening when I discovered by chance, while leafing through an old box of letters, that so exciting number: Albert's.

There it was, the misty sound of love conserved, numbered, among the essential mementoes of my past. SWALK. Sealed with a loving kiss. Explosive fetish still adored for the return of those first thrills that it evoked. And when I told the whole story to my husband, the voice, overwhelming wave, came back more strongly. But did I really remember it, with its whole range of sights, its carefully modulated army of joyous moments, its throatful of secret emotions? The more I repeated the number to myself, the more the old voice notes were reborn and came together again to replay the harmonies of that scenario of the past.

The inner ear heats up, becomes aroused, hallucinates. The ear knows what it wants, and goes to find it, back there where the old full orchestral score of love is being performed anew. The ear knows and wants that voice with its power to surround softly, its lulling tones that make the world fall away, and all the erotic vistas that lie beyond.

The temptation was irresistible. My hands fumbled nervously with the telephone. Memory of actions so often repeated. No answer. Relief? Disappointment.

By this event my husband and I were plunged into an unprecedented state of excitement. Because, in this random number, my husband recognized that of one of his childhood friends, Henri, whom he sometimes still saw.

Various theories occurred to us. Might I have been mistaken about the number? That would seem to be impossible, the memory of it was anchored in my flesh itself. Might someone different now have that number? But no, it was in fact the number of Henri's mother, he had always lived there because his father died just after Henri married. Might Henri have played the role of Albert? Unlikely. He would have been too young, because he was the same age as us. While the voice of the unknown man had, in its timbre, the undeniable weight of time. Then who wore the mask of Albert? Lacking any clues, the riddle remained entire and we were left without a solution.

Finally, tired of analyzing, interpreting, uselessly examining and re-examining, we lost interest in the story.

Then, one summer evening, something happened: we received an invitation that we could not politely refuse—I had to accompany my husband to Henri's house. The story of Albert hardly crossed our minds. Instead we had our appearance to worry about. The occasion was supposed to be formal: the men in black tie, the women in evening gowns.

It was crowded. Most people were standing. Everyone stiffened by the varnish of manners and the cramp of etiquette.

Introductions. Kissing of hands. Meeting of eyes. Disconnected cocktail conversation. Trays heavy with glasses and bottles. Petits fours. The classic display of the total emptiness of fashionable parties.

At a certain moment during the evening, having talked too much, I became aware of an overwhelming thirst (I never take alcohol). I went to the kitchen to get something to drink. Sitting there was Henri's mother, whom I had already met. Beside her, standing, was her maid, a corpulent woman in uniform complete with cap. I asked the hostess if I might have a glass of water. She immediately relayed my desire to her domestic who said, simply: "Yes, of course, Madame."

Those four words, however insignificant and natural in their context, stunned me: they had been uttered in a voice abnormally low and I stood there, stupefied, because I was absolutely certain I had just heard the voice of Albert! In a state of shock I accepted my glass of water, trembling, and ran back to my husband. I pushed him out to the terrace, away from everyone else, and told him what had happened. I had been so totally stricken that I was unable to control myself and couldn't even speak without stammering. We had to leave.

Afterwards I spent long hours shut up in my apartment, in the circle of a candle's light listening to my favourite operas and my foreign voices, my voices of men. Away from the world.

My husband says I seem like the image of a Madonna, a virgin who has lost her will, contemplating the eternal.

There is nothing to understand, my sweet. Feeling is all. I am the skin of time. And I never think. SWALK.

Monique Proulx
Translated by Sheila Fischman

Beach Blues

Monique Proulx was born in Quebec City in 1952. She has written numerous radio and television plays, as well as film scripts and stage plays. In 1983, she published her first book of short stories, *Sans cœur et sans reproche*, the title story of which has been translated by Sheila Fischman as "Feint of Heart." The book was an immediate success, winning both the Prix Adrienne-Choquette and the Grand Prix Littéraire du Journal de Montréal. Proulx's first novel, *L'Homme invisible à la fenêtre* (1993), was translated in 1994 by Matt Cohen (*Invisible Man at the Window*), who has also translated her most recent novel, *Le Sexe des étoiles*, which was also made into a successful feature film for which Proulx wrote the script.

"Beach Blues," translated here by Sheila Fischman, is another of the linked stories that make up *Sans cœur et sans reproche*, which follows the lives of two young people from childhood to maturity. In this story, the female narrator and her husband, Claude, are on holiday in California. She is "surfing towards her fortieth birthday" and not liking it: "When is it exactly," she asks, "that we see our lives distinctly cut in two, with the greater part behind us . . ." In many ways, Proulx's work is reminiscent of Alice Munro's *Lives of Girls and Women*. Both writers portray characters—or rather the characters portray themselves—with grim humour and relentless honesty.

∽

"Beach Blues" is a translation of "Beach Blues" published in *Sans cœur et sans reproche: nouvelles* (Montreal: Québec-Amérique, 1983).

Monday, March 2

The sea. Violet, violent, the scent of liquid guts and viscera drifting windward, perfectly casual, dreadfully colossal beneath the cape of light that sets it afire so that it sizzles to the very depths of space, to infinity; it lies there before me, rushes to meet me, and I shrink back, I let myself fall to the ground, terrified, subjugated, overwhelmed, shuddering from head to toe. You got me again, you slut, it's the same thing every time we get together, you swallow my heart, you make me howl with confusion and amazement, you bring me to my hands and knees, I'm paralyzed in your presence and I can stay that way for hours, watching you, absolutely drunk, obsessively persuaded that at last I am touching whatever is magic and holy in the universe.

Arrived in San Diego last night after an exhausting six-hour delay due to some problem or other with a motor that kept the plane at the Toronto airport. "*Better if it happens down here than up there*," as the Californian—fiftyish and already tanned—seated next to Claude in the DC-8 said, laughing. Throughout the entire flight he kept holding out conversational perches that Claude (falling back on his fatigue and his very Nordic coolness) persisted in not taking hold of. The bachelor apartment in La Jolla Claude had reserved two weeks earlier had been rented by somebody else. It was dark, a liquid darkness because of the humidity. Claude fulminated, rummaging desperately in his stock of addresses until he finally unearthed a room for us in Pacific Beach, while I just let him get tangled up in his manly role as guide, laughing to myself as I savoured with delight the youthful glow of the sunburnt faces, the white teeth, the clean T-shirts crowding all around us, I breathed in the scents of hibiscus and wild magnolia that seemed to ripple on all sides in the dark, like ghosts. O, the seductive ease of lands that have known neither ice ages nor mammoths; O, the insidious fascination exerted by anything that is warm, soft, and scented on my poor, white, ill-adapted, Inuit skin . . .

All at once the sun emerges from the yellow smog to consummate its dying on the horizon, then starts to rebound off the cliffs of Ellen Scripps Peak and Alligator Head, and I watch it with something like anxiety, I see it going full tilt, setting fire to the rocky arms of La Jolla Cove, then it throws itself at me in a flood of volcanic heat. Bliss. I swoon. Rolling slowly onto my belly I let out little squeals like a cat in heat, let myself be filled to the marrow of my bones by an obscene sense of well-being that falls like manna from on high. I am alone. No one to witness my lust, no one to see me stagnate on the sand like a cataleptic nymphomaniac. Before me water, space, and white pelicans nonchalantly indulging in fishing and flight—pelicans! To think that back home we have neurasthenic sparrows, sparrows on welfare that frolic in the air . . . Don't think about home. (Don't think about the snow back home and far away, of the Belmont cemetery covered by snow, of Max G's wan face, of the pale little eyes of Dr. No, of my mother's snowy face. Don't think about mama, dear little mama, dear old little mama, who sleeps now buried in the snow. It's all over now for mama, finished, kaput. Ssshh.)

Small, black, shiny dots are moving on the water, far away on my left, and in spite of the distance it's easy enough to identify them as surfers pitting themselves against the waves, looking like seals in their skintight suits of gleaming rubber and, I swear, invariably blonde, tanned, and muscular. To be quite certain I take a long look at myself in my pocket mirror. What I see there is not what you would call pretty and is as un-Californian as can be. A bone-coloured face marbled with sweat and angry red blotches, straight black hair with improbable white streaks at the temples that I haven't yet quite made up my mind to dye. The tired mask of a white witch who is surfing painfully, leaning backwards, towards her fortieth birthday. Old. I am aging, you are aging, we are aging. Old age. (Ssshh.)

And while I blissfully mineralize on the sand, lulled by the scents of sea and wind, by the sun's ingratiating warmth, it suddenly strikes me that I've seen hardly anyone older than twenty-five since I arrived in San Diego. What do they do with their old people here? Hide them deep in the closets of their pink stucco houses? Throw them into the sea? I pull myself up on one elbow and silently laugh as I scrutinize the foamy line of the horizon for the bleached bones that should be drifting across the water, swollen by the surf: the backbones, shoulderblades, femurs of all those poor old people who have perhaps been jettisoned into the sea, the open sea off La Jolla Cove . . .

There is nothing, needless to say, nothing but gulls and pelicans, big white pelicans that let themselves be lazily carried by the waves, wailing ironically in my direction.

Tuesday, March 3

It came back last night, the nightmare I thought I'd finally got over, whose sinister vapours I thought I'd extricated from my unconscious forever. How little we know one another and how fragile we are . . . What made it germinate again like a bad seed, what could have given birth to it after such a beautiful day when I felt in a state of such total plenitude, at peace with life, with others, for the first time in months?

Such a glorious day . . . Sea, sun, tropical flowers, the persistent stench of the old Eden, at once lost and regained . . . Claude came and joined me around six at Pannikin's, where I was drinking coffee and entertaining myself by reading the classified ads in the *Reader*, where the solid American pragmatism bursting out on all sides seemed to me to conceal ludicrous discordances, chronically incompatible in their way with the beauty and luxuriance of the natural settings that still permeated me: *Will do anything for $1500; Make hundreds weekly, at home; Stop! Need money? Sell your own time; Let me show you the easy way to earn $500.*

We talked, very little, he thought I seemed to be doing all right, he said so, I thought he looked tired and pale, I didn't say so, we decided to go for seafood at T.D. Hay's, just a few feet from our hotel room. There, seated next to the vast tinted window, we savoured crab and Chablis while we looked out at the Pacific, so breathtakingly beautiful with its ochre and white and stretching all the way to our table, or so it seemed, beneath the milky crust formed by the blend of glimmers from the setting sun and the myriad pelicans spiraling down to its surface. Claude took my hand under the table and I remember very clearly, I suddenly felt like another person, a young and radiant stranger, lifted up by something almost stifling—by happiness no doubt. And then we made love the minute we got home, hastily, as if we were very young and eager never to leave each other, never to die. That beautiful, beautiful day . . .

And then night. I was sleeping very deeply and I think dreamlessly when it began and part of me, floating on the surface of awareness, began to moan: "Oh no . . . not again . . ." It was indeed the same atmosphere, uneasy, oppressive, the same darkness—everything is happening in black and white, as in an old period film—and presently, the identical unfolding of a morbid scenario that must be imprinted on some of the opaque cells of my brain.

I am sitting in a dark place—which is neither known to me nor particularly hostile *a priori*. Actually, it's a kind of waiting room, with old wooden benches, the kind you see in European railway stations but with no window or door. I KNOW that something terrible is going to happen to me any minute now, but I don't feel sad or panicky, instead I'm overwhelmed by a kind of gloomy, glacial indifference that enfolds me like a shroud. Someone beside me says, very distinctly: "It's cancer. Yes, that's right, cancer . . ." then starts jabbering trivialities and laughing. Soon I'm surrounded by a cackling concert of voices talking among themselves, utterly indifferent to me: among the voices I recognize Claude's, then my mother's, and even that of my next-door neighbour, Claire, with whom I'm on very friendly terms in "real" life. At the same time the room I am in is quietly being transformed, the walls seem to be moving together, then they dissolve, and all at once I'm horrified to discover that the place where I'm now lying full-length is a coffin, which hugs the dimensions of my body more and more closely. On the right, emerging furtively from the darkness, something horrible is gliding towards me, something I must avoid watching at all costs, on pain of some hideous chastisement. I can't help catching a glimpse of two vague spots, shiny as the eyes of an animal, that are approaching me, and I say, horrified: "That's Death, Death is coming towards me . . ." and I clench my jaws, I squeeze my eyes shut, and I repeat to myself like a litany, while clutching desperately at this possible way out: "It's a dream. It's just a dream. Hurry, I have to wake up. Hurry, hurry . . ."

Usually at this stage of the nightmare my dread is so acute that I wake up, but only partially: I can distinguish the outlines of the furniture in the room I'm in—last night I could SEE the curtains blowing at the window we'd left open—and at the same time the nightmare has taken on a palpable density and continues ineluctably, the eyes keep coming closer to me ten times more realistically, and it is only after endless seconds of the most intense panic that I wake up completely, shrieking.

It all strikes me as so banal, and the childish symbolism sticks out like a sore thumb: it most likely means that I'm lonely here and that I'm afraid of death. Fine. Knowing it, with the certainty of an analyst, does not take away, alas, the terrifying feelings I experience every time, nor does it explain the unhealthy recurrence of the nightmare. Claude was kind, as he always is, he instinctively did what you do when a small child is frightened: he hugged me and cuddled me and kissed me, and of course this morning he couldn't help looking terribly tired, so that I can nevertheless sense the degree to which my neurotic terrors ruined his sleep and messed up his day's work at the university.

Today again the sun is triumphant. I gathered mussels just now with a little French boy whose family has settled in La Jolla—there is an entire French colony living here, in fact, the only ones who consume the mussels, needless to say, in this world of burger-eaters.

The little French boy, whose name is Maxime, comes galloping back to me and gives me a big plastic bag for the mussels, which are beginning to feel the effects of the heat. I'd say he's about ten years old. His short, short hair stands up on his skull—his father is probably in the military—and he has an oddly turned-up nose that gives him the appearance of an inquisitive little insect. With a knowing look he asks if what I'm writing is a novel, and when I tell him no he seems disappointed. But still he takes the trouble to give me, in a learned and protective tone of voice, an exhaustive lesson on the best way to prepare *moules marinières*.

I feel tired and neurasthenic all at once. Even the sea can't chase away all the gloom that is filling me, like the threat of a downpour. Tonight, after the mussels, I take a hot bath to soothe the burning sensation I'm beginning to suffer on account of the sun, and on the sly I swallow two Librium, to be sure that I'll sleep. Without dreaming.

Wednesday, March 4

Here and there, in the crevices of the rocks, the ebb-tide has left little artificial lakes that teem with terribly vulnerable miniature animal lives: I just have to set down my foot there and a whole commotion is created, instantaneously, a general panic that sends scampering in every direction baby crabs, tadpoles, a swarm of sea creatures to whom I must appear as some enormous and apocalyptic monster. It's reassuring in the end to think that nearby there are creatures smaller than we are, and even more insignificant and destitute, who are struggling fiercely to survive. It helps, I don't know how much, but it helps you to confront the staggering immensity of the universe, of space, of the sea ...

I am watching the pelicans that have taken up residence on a rocky ridge a few hundred metres from shore. So much grace and skill is brought together in these great mythical birds, such serenity in the way they move, feed, travel through centuries, through millennia of life on earth, you might say, and apparently so smoothly... I stopped by the University of San Diego Library this morning after I'd dropped off Claude at his meeting, and there I read a few lines in an encyclopedia that was lying on a table. The *Pelecanus onocrotalis* is a species of the family *Pelecanidae* in the order *Totipalmate*, and is remarkable for the form of its beak, in which the upper mandible is flattened and terminates in a hook, while the lower one consists of two bony branches that support a large naked pouch which is capable of great distention. (Aha.) They have, moreover, a featherless face and throat, pointed wingtips, a V-shaped tail, short, reticulated tarsus, and four toes joined by a single large membrane (they're MUCH better than that!!!). They like to live in groups, on the shores of the sea, lakes, rivers. They feed on fish with which they fill their pouch and later swallow as digestion is completed (clever little beasts!). Females lay their eggs—between two and five, perfectly white—on rocks near the water. According to popular belief, the pelican tears open its own sides so the brood can drink its blood. This belief, which arose from the pelican's habit of pressing its pouch against its breast to release the food intended for its young, has earned it a reputation as the emblem of maternal love ...

I slammed the book shut. Encyclopedias are full of all kinds of garbage.

Who said that memory—or oblivion—could provide comfort at certain moments? Who claimed that somewhere in the world there exists a measure of comfort for every pain that besets us?

I lost whatever lightness and insouciance I had all at once when Mama died. When she died the child within me died as well, and all that was left me was my own aging carcass, which I cannot even recognize as mine. Mothers come, mothers go. They smile, they're affectionate, they can make you believe they're eternal. Mine had sparkling eyes that were incredibly youthful. She radiated a fierce and timeless energy I couldn't measure myself against. She loved me. She gave me so much affection, always, so much affection. "Dear little Franny. My baby angel . . ." Who will ever call me by such ridiculous pet names, as meltingly tender as caramel? Who will ever love me so much, love me as I am, savagely, with so much indulgence and lack of restraint? Who will trust me the way she did, viscerally, despite myself? No one. There is no one else. How can I remember I was once a child? She has been dead since last fall. I can't get used to it. I swear, I'll never get used to it. What I am mourning now, inconsolably, along with my mother, the only mother I'll ever have, is the little girl within me, the little girl who has gone forever, with her skipping rope under her arm.

Requiescat in pace.

I am watching the pelicans. Maxime is pretending to play with some seaweed but is discreetly watching me from a distance. He's bored. He comes up to me and proudly shows off a crab he has caught, holding it by the lower abdomen like a pro. Intrigued, he asks me why I'm crying and I begin by saying I'm not, but then, encouraged by confidence—after all, if there's anyone who is understanding, it's a child—I let myself go altogether, I tell him that my Mama, my dear little Mama, my one and only Mama, is dead, buried, finished . . . For a brief moment he stares at me, perplexed. "Mine too, my mother died a long time ago!" he exclaims triumphantly as he moves away towards the rocks. And he laughs.

There are no children any more.

Thursday, March 5

It is two-thirty a.m. in Quebec. Here, the night is just beginning, with the continuous roar of the wind and the muted pallor that comes from the belvederes and grudgingly pierces the dark. As soon as the sun has set there's nothing outside here, not even insects or moths: it is dark, that's all. Claude is fast asleep, as if it were two-thirty in the morning. It's the jet lag: Claude is still carrying his jet lag on his shoulders, grimacing with pain and fatigue. (Fifth station: Jesus falls asleep on his feet.)

The day was wasted, lost. So much for Thursday, March fifth. There was a break at the university today, for Claude and the flock of communicologists who have been meeting for three days to discuss with suitable gravity the future of microwaves and high-tech satellites. Claude had the brilliant idea of introducing me to Marsh—a charming colleague, sensitive and brilliant, *dixit* Claude—and Marsh's delightful wife, Beverley. All Californians have delightful wives, and all delightful individuals get on my nerves. I like only the anxious, the tormented, the intolerable, who shatter in your hands at the first opportunity—from frantic joy or hilarious despair. We spent the afternoon and early evening by the sea, at Pacific Beach, drinking beer, chatting, eating Bar-B-Q chips and dips, American-style. The sun was beating down, Beverley was shading her delightful little nose under a huge straw hat and every now and then she took my hand to show me how much she adored me. Californians adore everyone, with no distinction of character or sex. The men were talking together, brilliantly re-creating remarks from the interrupted meeting as though their lives and ours suddenly depended on it, satellites kept crisscrossing in the air and deploying their mobile antennae on their geo-stationary orbits thousands and millions of light years from me. While Beverley tried to lure me into impenetrable discussions about conjugal love and relationships that are so difficult to live despite and because of the artificiality of the partners' roles, the eternal question remaining always, alas and goddammit, who, I mean *who*, is going to wash the dishes . . .

And it became unbearable: at one point I felt hideously feminine, an emotional little thing who talks bravely about "genuine" individuals and "genuine" passions, a delightful, sensitive knickknack who indulges in erudite introspection while at her side her man is once again directing the universe from the heights of his cosmogonic learning. I went for a swim, alone, even though the water was glacial. Through what mysterious spell do we always find ourselves, no matter what our degree of advancement and maturity, in the same unvarying ghettos, separated by the same barriers, males and females travelling along parallel, desperately parallel roads? I looked surreptitiously at Claude. He had so much confidence—in himself, in his Aristotelian logic, he took himself so seriously while everything around him exploded in light and fabulous colours, the space, the wind, the clouds, the sky, the sun, the sea: LIFE.

That was not the end of it, unfortunately. The air turned chilly and we went to Marsh and Beverley's where we drank some syrupy vodka. I tried to slip away, claiming a headache, but Claude gave me a look filled with such pleading, it all seemed to be so important to him, that I abdicated. I let her show me around the apartment (big, luxurious, flashy) and offered my oohs and aahs at the appropriate moments, I summoned up my most motherly solicitude as I bent over the cradle of Marsh Jr., their little two-year-old angel, while next door the men were still navigating in deep space. In the middle of the party Marsh brought out a cigar-sized Colombian joint and passed it around. I thought to myself, That's it, finally, surely, something is going to HAPPEN, we'll laugh like lunatics, idiotically, break plates, do the belly-dance, start an orgy...

Nothing.

Apparently they all got acclimatized to the devastating effect of the grass very quickly, all but Claude, who simply reconstructed Cape Canaveral, with the help of Marsh—while I, I took my share and gobbled every sour-cream chip in the house, listening sadly while Beverley recounted the story of her blossoming maternitude. One day or another every liberated woman ends up talking about her curtains and the little angel's diapers.

And now Claude is asleep. Claude, the strange man with whom I've been sharing for ten years now my relatively intimate private life. I watch him sleep. I hate him for sleeping the bland and monotonous sleep of the just, I hate him for being a communicologist, for being forty-two years old, for looking it, and for no longer being able to give me palpitations when he looks at me.

Sleep is impossible. A Librium for the lady?

No. I don't want Librium, I don't want sleep, I want LIFE: life and its glittering procession, its carnival floats, its pomps and its vanities and its triumphant works, its balsmusettes, its frenzied dances, its monstrous binges, its dazzling and savage sex, I want life, goddammit, before it's too late!

Friday, March 6

"And there I am, standing in what after all is nothing more than what was . . . I shall be nothing more than what I am. Never shall I have been what I was. Nothing more. Alone. Needlessly alone and severed from my dream. Oh, if only a dream could bleed in the place where the laceration occurred . . ."

Good old Aragon, who could bring forth words as ripe and beautiful as a tree, a fruit, words that come back to haunt you when you least expect it . . .

This afternoon I walked all the way to Seal Rock to get a better look at what exactly the surfer-seals were playing at on their frail boards of laminated wood, in their sexy black rubber outfits. Their game consists of keeping their balance on the waves as if they really were seals and not long-limbed bodies—inevitably blond, tanned, and muscular. There's one in particular I've been watching for a while now, who is phenomenally good at it. Each time, he appears to be swallowed up forever in the undertow, but the next wave lifts him up again into the light, like an elf, and he dances on the water, with the water, the sea accompanies him and guides him in a heartbreakingly beautiful pas de deux. He finally washes up on the shore a few feet from me, gives me a brief, vacant look, and then takes off again, running towards the water with his surfboard under his arm: every object, every being around him must seem so drab and mediocre compared to her, Big Blue, who accepts him as a partner only long enough for an intensely sensual fusion . . .

When is it exactly that we see our lives distinctly cut in two, with the greater part behind us, farther and farther behind us? It seems to me that now the dice have been thrown and I, too, no longer will be what I once was. Which is unbearably little. I still remember my dreams and my ambitions, no longer as great blazing things that have the power to oppress and to exalt, but as scraps of yellowed paper made dry and outmoded by time. A person would need an inner alarm bell that makes us jump and saves our lives when the first important compromise is made, the one that will lead to all the others. Soon we'll live only on compromises; and perhaps we've heard that disturbing alarm bell quite clearly after all and quickly blocked our ears with tons of cotton batting and Quies ear plugs to be sure we'll never hear it again . . . (Please God, let me live a sullen little life, don't let my heartbeat change too much, don't let me know the anxiety that undermines, the freedom that leads to insecurity, the exaltation that infuriates, I beg you, let me live like a rock, like a calf . . .)

Where are all the beautiful books I'll never write, whose titles I'd already imagined when I was twenty, blazing in the darkness like guiding stars? Where are my follies of yesteryear?

I'm raving. It's the sun. Good old Françoise. You don't quit your job at forty, a good, well-paid job as professional scribbler, bureaucratic scriptwriter, sterile woman of letters in the pay of the state and of Max G., her immediate boss. It's when they turn forty that women are beautiful and blablabla and dubadubdub goodbye.

I see his face again, the kindly round face of Renault, of Doctor Renault, of the man I've called for years, for a laugh and because of friendship, Doctor No. Just think: he gave me my first IUD, was the first to show me the colour of the neck of my uterus and treated me to every emotion in the book. We even had a brief fling, long, long ago, something thrilling and madly sexual that lasted for two weeks.

Mysterious matters were going on inside my organism, inexplicable menstrual delays that gave me a glimpse of the possible shadow, at once undesirable and stirring, of an embryo gone astray in my belly like a little birdy fallen from a nest. "Tell me, Doctor, yes or no: am I pregnant?" "This may sound funny, Françoise, but I believe it's the beginning of menopause . . ." He laughed. We had a good laugh, especially me. "Are you out of your mind, Doctor No? I'm thirty-nine years old. I'll be forty next week. I'm too YOUNG!" "It happens, it happens all the time, it's not serious, you didn't want children, did you?"

No, Doctor No. I didn't want children, but even more I didn't want anyone to tell me I couldn't—the irrevocable absence of the POSSIBILITY of creating, the water dried up, the taps rusty, the plumbing falling apart, broken-down, out of commission . . . at the barely nascent dawn of my forties . . .

Menopause. Drought. Old age. Death. Happy birthday, Françoise, little Franny, little baby angel.

Good old Doctor No.

This is a good place for me. The wind thinks I'm a reef and slaps my face, quite mercilessly. There's just one pelican, wheeling very high in the air, or so it seems, above my head. I feel good because I know this is all temporary, it's a vacation, a rare and precious moment I must hold onto like a dried violet in a padded place inside my memory.

Next week we'll leave here. Go back home to the snow where there awaits, huddled into itself like a slug, like a canker, my two-fold sterility.

Sunday, March 8

Now I know why I hate Sunday so much. It's the day when the beasts, mindless with fatigue, are let loose in the arena, where, lumbering stiff-legged, their eyes squinting in the overly bright light of idleness, they stumble upon blades of grass, they spread everywhere like bad news, and nibble patiently at your living space. There's a smell of family and religion. A smell of organized holidays stamped and arranged by the book with timetables and a proper education: at ten o'clock we-get-up, at eleven o'clock we-wash-our-bottoms, at noon we-go-to-Mama's-for-lunch, at two o'clock we-go-to-the-beach, at five o'clock we-come-home-and-wash-our-bottoms-again, at six we-go-to-a-restaurant-for-supper, at eight we-watch-TV, and at ten o'clock it's-beddy-bye . . . (We mustn't overexert ourselves, mustn't overindulge in good things: it's on Saturday night of course that we can use our bottoms for something besides being washed.)

The troop has taken over Pacific Beach. Dozens of them are preening themselves by the seaside, maintaining their impeccable condition, caring for their ridged muscles, abetted by jogging, push-ups, sit-ups, Frisbees, surfing, twists of torso, shoulders, and buttocks previously anointed with coconut oil, needless to say. The beach looks like a gigantic gymnasium teeming with healthy and virile occupations: Ben Weider would be thrilled. There's no fat here, no cellulite, no soft, white, pendant flesh (anyone here who is obese must go into hiding with the old people, in the darkest depths of the closets of their little pink stucco houses). The tanned young men lope like tigers along the seashore, their soft blonde curls stirring agreeably in the wind; as they pass by they cast appreciative glances at the tanned young girls loping along the seashore in the opposite direction, their ravishing hair like a Vogue cover photo rippling aesthetically over their shoulders. From high on the balcony of my hotel room—from which they'd have to pay me a lot to pry me loose—I cast my own appreciative gaze on all that splendid loping youth, mentally addressing the appropriate wishes to the gazelle-like damsels. Today, March 8, is also double-X chromosome day. The Ys will have to look out for themselves.

During the entire weekend Claude and I had "had words" to use a politely constipated expression. In honest, intelligible language it means we ripped each other's guts out, we inflicted on one another wounds so deep and cruel I can't envisage any possible scarring, not now, not later. I don't really know how it started, and deep down it doesn't even matter. What matters for the moment, what I am applying myself to doing—conscientiously and with overwhelming fervour—is to drink myself into oblivion with Coors beer, a difficult undertaking if ever there was one, since Coors beer has more effect on my bladder than on my soul.

Tristan and Isolde. Lancelot and Guinevere. Bonnie and Clyde. Claude and me. We're such a long way from the heroic couple, from the glorious couple running hand-in-hand along the ocean's luminous shore—while the gulls emit a melancholy kee-ow, kee-ow, while the blazing sun kindles the horizon and the director yells: "Cut!" Such a long way from being a couple, period. We met at an age when people already have their own vision of the world, one that's irreversible, at an age when each of us sails along by herself on her own personal iceberg. And it continues like that, getting worse and worse or better and better—depending on your view of life as a couple. Our respective icebergs occasionally brush against each other, move apart inordinately, collide with a great crash and roar on days when the wind is strong. I'm going through a bad period, unquestionably. Claude may be going through one as well—who knows what hides beneath the shimmering surface of his iceberg? His own anguish is discreet, as are his joys and his orgasms, he takes pains not to make waves around him. His discretion is of no help to me, nor is anything else about him for that matter; he is simply there, he persists in continuing to resemble someone I once loved very much, passionately. A long, long time ago.

Time. Filthy time. Time passes. There is no such thing as wild, passionate love, there's no youthfulness or prologues possible. I've always loved prologues. No more Coors beer.

We cannot imagine we're so stingy: give me more, more of everything, more love, more time, I want more, it cannot end stupidly, just like that, with nothing in my hands, nothing in my pockets, crows' feet next to my eyes and a lump of clay where there is supposed to be a heart.

The nightmare returned last night, and the night before. There's nothing more to do, nothing but settle as comfortably as I can into the horror. Yesterday, while I was still lying in my "coffin" and the terrifying lights were coming nearer, I convinced myself, oddly, and for the first time, that I MUST look to my right, that the solution would come when I confronted those pupils that frighten me so badly. I was unable to turn my head, so paralyzed was I by panic.

Claude has gone out for a walk, alone. We are all very much alone in this goddamn galley-ship that's heading God knows where. He is probably trying to defuse the harsh words I said to him—exactly what words I can't remember, I only know they were scathing and effective. I excel at nasty verbal sparring matches. If those matches were an Olympic event I'd win the gold medal, hands down.

I lean back. I look up. I'm drunk. I see a big pelican tracing concentric circles overhead, again and again, as if he were taking me for a fish out of water and wanted to swallow me alive. Here birdy, birdy, nice birdy . . . Is that how you tame a pelican? Would he agree to live in a cage beside a desk, to inspire a lonely, aging woman who is struggling with the world?

Monday, March 9

I cannot make myself feel guilty. Though I search assiduously in all the nooks and crannies of my mind, I find nothing there but a kind of stupid, unbroken snicker, a mute wave of exhilaration that needed only a word from me and then it sprang like a panther. Claude's voice on the telephone asking if I've had a good day. I say yes, quickly, holding back with great difficulty the snicker that—

whoops!—nearly escaped from my mouth. Claude's voice informs me that he'll be eating out with colleagues, but if I want to come it's all right, I mean, really, no problem . . . No, no, I thank him, smoothly. I was well aware of the reluctance in his invitation, but it's about as important to me as my first brassiere. Nothing could be better in the best of all possible worlds. Me and my stupid snicker, we'll be able to let loose a little, have our own little gourmet feast, just the two of us. Claude's voice is ceremonial and lukewarm as it is when he's suffering from a toothache, or from chronic rancour.

Horrible woman. Not the faintest sense of guilt. In its place, that fatuous, disdainful giggle and two fine bruises on the backside where the bumps on the rock prodded me.

It was grey and cold today, but that didn't stop me from walking along the La Jolla coast, sitting down every now and then to breathe in the salty odour of seaweed and to watch the sea furiously shaking its gigantic mane as far as the eye could see. It was beautiful, it was wild. At Cold Fish Point I suddenly spotted a surfer clinging intrepidly to his board as he was tossed about between sea and sky like a shipwreck in distress. I sat in a corner of a rock, sheltered from the wind, and watched him. He was doing fine, even though the enormous waves were threatening to throw him off balance at any moment. In the end he let himself glide to shore in a broad supple movement like a snake, and I recognized him as the seal from Seal Point. The one who stood out from all the others last Friday because of his ethereal grace.

We were close enough to hear each other's voices. He didn't see me right away. He was busy getting out of his black rubber suit when I yelled at him, something appallingly idiotic like "Great!" or "Very nice!" He looked in my direction, took the time to shed his suit completely—why he's naked as a worm, for goodness sake—except for a tiny little miniature RED thing by way of briefs, to towel off torso and thighs, to toss a woollen jacket over his shoulders, before heading in my direction with long peaceful strides: "What did you say?" And that's it. We're off to the races.

The Blessed Virgin knows to what degree my intentions were not libidinous—not consciously at any rate—when that admiring exclamation got away from me, at which point I could only, in a sense, applaud morally, chastely encourage his high-voltage, aesthetic prowess.

The seal sat down beside me; he was around twenty-four, with candid eyes and a charming smile as fresh and appetizing as the flesh of an apple. We launched into a deaf-mute conversation, shouting into one another's ears in an attempt to dominate the combined clamour of wind and sea. Where was I from, with my so un-Californian looks and my so un-American accent? How did he manage to keep from falling and wasn't the water terribly cold? Soon we simply laughed, because for one reason or another conversation was totally impossible. He asked if he could squeeze into the hollow of the rock, next to me, for better shelter from the wind, then he lit up a joint which I began, philosophically, to share with him despite the unpropitious place and time—when in Rome I always do as the Romans do, even if it means pasta for breakfast.

We were silent. It was comfortable like that, with shoulder touching shoulder, we communicated through our respective warmth, without the slightest embarrassment. We looked at the sea and toked on the joint. He loved the sea at least as much as I did, you could tell from the tenderly respectful way he watched it. At one point a wave even more gigantic than the others came rushing at us, tossing its foam high into the air, and at exactly the same moment we both gave an admiring whistle. It made us laugh, we became very jovial all of a sudden, we started to touch each other's hands for no reason, and his skin began to burn very warmly through my clothes. He was handsome and young and incredibly sexy, he made me think of a jar of honey, fragrant and sweet, into which you just can't help sticking your finger. That's the way it happened, Father—I am confessing to all-powerful God—suddenly, unexpectedly, I felt I had the soul of a famished she-wolf—yum, yum, come a little closer

Little Surf-Riding Hood, let me nibble at your lower belly, this way little Romulus, little Remus, let me suckle you at the nipples of my experience—while he had the soul of a consenting sheep, or so it seemed, since we laughed like psychopaths as we slid onto the dried seaweed and began to make love.

When I left he couldn't get over it. I'm probably the first elderly forty-year-old he's got it on with in this land of mumbling and wailing youngsters, possibly the last, poor waif. While I, I walked, alone, to the car and drove straight back to the hotel, while shudders of hilarity ran through me to the tips of my toes.

I sit here facing the window, night is falling, and I'm still laughing as I hold a parsley-tomato-capers-and-cheese omelet on my lap . . .

Tuesday, March 10

"What's your name? . . . Where are you from? . . . Do you skate? . . . Have you been to the Zoo? . . . Bazaar del Mundo? . . . Balboa Park? . . . Man you've GOT to go!"

He tracked me down here at the La Jolla Cove, and now he's inundating me with questions, he's erecting plans, he's still unsatisfied. Things are different this morning: the sun has come back in force, the sea lulls herself, sluggishly, and I look at him with surprise, disconcerted at having had something in common with him. Who is he? What did he do with his surfboard? He left it back at Seal Rock, he felt like walking for a while and then he spotted me—what a wonderful coincidence! What a marvelous coincidence! Out of the corner of my eye I watch him talk. His skin is definitely the colour of ripe apricots—the taste too, if I remember correctly—skin that cries out for anthropophagous bites. I'm not sure what to do with him this morning. Finally I graze his shoulder with my fingertip, to brush away some grains of sand. He gets down on his knees beside me, studies me with inordinately serious eyes: "You turn me on . . . You really turn me on . . ."

Could we not have left it there, finally, and simply kept a memory of our strange embrace on the rock, of the odours of grass and dried seaweed? Apparently not. Apparently our every deed follows us in the most microscopic detail, apparently anyone can turn up out of the blue, asking for explanations, demanding logic. (What did you do with the necklace I gave you twenty years ago that you claimed you'd always wear? We said hello on the street five years ago, why didn't you say hello today?) I suppose in this case logic would mean reviving to the point of saturation, of mutual disgust, what had been an exciting and full experience.

We lapse into generalities, trivialities. My sign. His sign. His job. My job. No doubt for my benefit, he had traded in his little red briefs for little black ones: he's just as cute, just as munchable as yesterday, but can I help it if my head and my sex don't have their heart in it today? Because time is passing, because he's so incredibly young and I'm so deplorably fortyish, I agree to see him again, I promise to give him the whole day and the whole evening tomorrow. (What have you done with your heart that you PROMISED would be mine forever?) He kisses me on the lips before he goes, skipping away over the rocks. There is something acutely overwhelming about the power of joy that we sometimes hold over others, and no doubt it is the certainty that we must put an end to it.

The pelicans were flapping their wings on the rocky crest a hundred metres into the sea. I was observing their graceful comings and goings when all at once an enormous pelican loomed up behind me and started tracing a circle around my head, then touched down in the middle of the crest among the others. What happened next was strange, was indescribably agonizing: after a few wavering hesitations, a few flutterings of wings, all the pelicans, with the biggest one in the middle, seemed to merge into perfect alignment and come to a standstill, their heads turned uniformly in my direction. I had the unsettling sensation that there was some sign I couldn't decipher, some kind of long-distance hypnosis accomplished by their calm and multiple gazes. Maxime came up and stood beside me, startling me. I turned towards him and the spell was broken. When I looked at the rocky crest again the pelicans had scattered untidily onto the sea. Anyway, it was probably just a fleeting hallucination brought on by the abuses the sun had made me commit.

Oh, the painful meal we ate together tonight, Claude and I, in a dimly lit restaurant designed unequivocally to make non-lovers feel as out of place as polar bears in the desert... We exchanged only a few words, absolutely neutral words, that managed nonetheless to give me the haunting impression that we were both walking on quail's eggs. I told him I'd be home late Wednesday night, told him to keep the car after he dropped me off at La Jolla. He didn't ask any questions. Told me he had to go to Phoenix Thursday morning, for a last-minute two-day meeting with some researchers. I didn't ask any questions. Once our divergent schedules were on the table we had nothing else to say to one another. The lines on his brow, more deeply incised than usual, cried out to me that he was in as much pain as I was, from everything: from our clumsiness, from the words lurking behind our silences that we couldn't say aloud, and most of all from the spectre of a break-up suddenly looming between us like a brutally obvious fact, like an abyss.

Wednesday, March 11

The room is big and it smells of humidity. I slowly lift the sheets to watch the bubbles move and the wavelets undulate whenever I make the slightest movement. Sleeping in a water-bed doesn't seem to me like a rest cure: among other things, how can you be sure some sea monster won't come and bite your backside when you're sleeping? It doesn't seem though to be an immediate concern of my surfer-lover, who breathes with steadfast serenity. It seems that I'm condemned for all eternity to watch other people sleep. What is it that makes sleep come so easily to men, makes them so easily submersible in the void, while I seem to be a permanent insomniac? It can only mean some other void, one that is firmly rooted in their brains and protects them from quibbling and from nocturnal anxiety. Or else a flagrant injustice is being done to me, one that must be denounced at all costs, and for which Fate must be dragged into court.

His name is Mike, he's twenty-three and a half, he works on construction sites when there is any work. His sleep delivers him up to my inspection: he's as bereft of defences as a newborn puppy. A few drops of saliva stand out delicately on his pouting lip. He is more motionless than a thing, more touching than a holy picture . . . Everything inside his head must be clean, smooth and pink, with no unnecessary twists and turns. I give myself another hour's respite at his side before I take a taxi to Pacific Beach and my hotel.

When he joined me on the beach this morning he wanted to take me everywhere, he had concocted a tourist menu so indigestible that I nearly changed my mind, contenting myself with lying there and dozing all day long. Bazaar del Mundo? (Tourist trap.) Old Town? (Ditto.) Black Beach? (Too far, too steep, too . . . too nudist.) The Zoo? (For the moment, *Homo californianus* is the only weird species I need.) The races at Del Mar? (Are you kidding?) Roller-skating in Balboa Park? (ARE YOU CRAZY?) Still he doesn't grow disheartened. Hunched up in the 1967 Volkswagen he'd borrowed from one of his friends we slowly combed the streets of his neighbourhood, Ocean Beach, vaguely derelict, faintly-decrepit-flower-power-holdovers falling apart beneath the dazzling luminosity, with flowers everywhere, purple cliffs, the triumphant presence of the sea and sun sidling deep into the narrowest alleys. He wanted to take me home right away, to start "that" again; while for me, "that" was becoming something remote, watered-down, a soft and pinkish proposition that definitely no longer attracted me. Turning him down, unfortunately, was out of the question: it would have been false representation, it would have required from me an energy I didn't have. (Where's that juicy sex you PROMISED me??) I made him wait: by insisting we watch the sun set over the ocean, by smoking a joint, by wolfing down three incredible meals in one at an "All-you-can-eat-special-restaurant," by desperately flailing about in an attempt to feel at least something, some emotion, some warmth, some sort of complicity . . . Nothing. He was handsome and kind, his most deeply felt desire was to be able one day to afford a Jacuzzi and a trip to Hawaii, his most immediate desire was to go to bed with me. Finally, when I went with him to his favourite bar and tried to drink a little madness from my scotch, there seemed to me to appear—floating like a banner above the country music, the dance floor, the ping-pong tables, the popcorn machines, the overcharged bodies—the true image of America: young, reckless, narcissistic, implacably drawn to trivia, to tawdry things, to fleeting glimmers, to the wind . . .

We made love. Just like that, starting cold; without the stimulus of adventure and chance it all seemed to me deadly dull. There's no solution: I am too old for love and too old for sex without it. He was full of good will, but clearly more gifted on the sea than on a waterbed. "I like you, you're so different," he told me by way of conclusion, before sinking into sleep. You bet I'm different. The others are young and beautiful, they have marmoreal hair, the bodies of goddesses, and heads as light as nutshells. I'll never see him again.

What I am looking for cannot be found here. What I am looking for can undoubtedly be found behind me, in my past, in the time before my mother's grave, before the betrayal of my body and the manifold betrayal of my mind. What has become of the tunnel that brought me here, I want to take it again, right now.

Thursday, March 12

Nine a.m., San Diego airport. Our voices, mechanical, reel off words devoid of surprise, like recorded messages. "You'll be back tomorrow? All right." "Wait for me before you pay the hotel bill . . ." "It's clouding over." "Yes, looks like rain . . ."

Nothing. The impression of tearing up just for the fun of it, for want of anything better to do, a beautiful book with gold illuminations, an ancient, precious manuscript you were once very fond of. And now do I kiss him? Why doesn't he kiss me? Marsh's hand in the distance waves warmly in our direction. Just one thought, absurd, obsessive, strikes the inside of my skull like a gong: do we kiss now? Marsh arrives at our side, throws himself at me enthusiastically, hugs me as if we'd once sown our wild oats together in the mad days of our youth. Chill out, man. Get a grip. I look at Claude. Claude is looking elsewhere. His face is white, tired, his brow furrowed, there is something abrupt and veiled in his gaze that makes him clash with everything moving around him, that makes him look like nothing and no one. I suddenly see in him a craggy, poignant beauty that breaks my heart, that makes my knees tremble convulsively. Do I kiss him now?

Finally he looks at me. He picks up his brown leather briefcase (the same case I stuffed three-quarters full one wild night with blue writing paper on which were written at least two hundred times I love you-I love you-I love you; why must memory butt in and throw its heartrending nostalgia in our faces?), he intones a few words in a voice he tries to keep neutral—"So long, Françoise, see you soon . . ." and suddenly the ice breaks, a torrent of savage and crystalline water submerges us, wrenches us from the shore and from our precarious roots, it crushes our shoulders, our lips fuse together, we cling to one another like atoms of a single molecule . . . O my brother, my accomplice, my other self, my love whom I am fleeing because you resemble me too closely . . . Marsh jingles a forced little laugh, makes as if he is walking away: "C'mon . . . He's only leaving for two days . . ." Get lost, man.

I'm not crazy. The pelicans are lined up on the rocky crest opposite me and they don't take their eyes off me. When I move away on one side of the shore or the other, they go on observing me, they move their heads very perceptibly in my direction. The biggest one in the middle suddenly spreads his wings: with a great rustling of feathers, the others copy him and it's as if a snowy avalanche is unfolding beneath my gaze, a kind of pathetic ballet that I watch reverently because I know it's intended for me. I'm beginning to understand certain things.

The dream. It came back this morning, when dawn was just beginning to colour the window. I am sitting in my waiting room. Familiar voices, apathetic, surround me, but I am gliding, gliding towards my destiny, towards the coffin that all at once clasps me like a jewel-case. I know the spots of light are coming closer to me, on my right, I turn towards them calmly, I look at them, and at once a great calm sweeps over me like a warm wind. There was nothing to be afraid of, it was just that, two big bright eyes, gaping like windows, two gigantic irises, a bird's perhaps, but no, they are openings, openings onto infinity, onto eternity, towards which I am sucked up, through which I weave my way with tremendous serenity. And it is a dazzle of light, a sensation of lightness such as I've never known, I am floating, floating above a glittering expanse I know is the sea, my voice is welling up from deep inside me and informing me I've passed, I've finally succeeding in getting through . . .

Friday the thirteenth

She stands there before me, she has always been there, stirring up inexplicable things in her inner upheaval, rubbing shoulders, superbly indifferent, with the movements of small, earthly beings, so childlike in their hoary acts, their limited desires, she will be there afterwards when there is nothing else, when everything will have been silenced beneath the corrosion. How can I not see that it's she who is looking at me, gesturing at me through the unpolished white of her feathers, that she is calling to me, offering to show me the unfathomable, to touch the key to all the mysteries, who is dozing deep down, like a weapon? Wait for me, wait for me before you close upon yourself forever, O Sea, O great immutable changing eternal old Sea ...

I walk into the cold of the water, into the belly of the water, the water closes around me and all the rest is petty, pointless—gone now the muffled terror from watching to see what the faces mean, from trying to grab some love, some happiness, like winning numbers ... A little more time, just a little more and once again I shall become an Other, I swear I will, I'll be able to distinguish the Essential from that which lies painfully beneath brilliant surfaces ... Wait for me, you too, you great white bird out there towards whom I'm swimming, wait for me before you undergo your final metamorphosis, the one that will deliver you to the altar of the sun where you will be set alight, there to be reborn from your ashes, purple and gold, delivered at last from death ...

Voices. Familiar, nonchalant voices chattering around me, piled one on top of the others. Mama? Is it you, Mama, who is stroking my forehead with such a cool, light hand? I open my eyes abruptly.

Above me stand little Maxime, with his oddly turned-up nose, a tall man with straight shoulders, close-cropped hair—an army man no doubt—and Claude, his face ravaged by anxiety. They are all looking at me. The army man's voice launches into a litany: "It was the boy ... the boy who spotted her ... who notified me ... pulled her out of the water right away ... unconscious ... mouth-to-mouth resuscitation ... the waves ... swim out so far, madness ... utter madness ..." I smile at Claude. I smile at them all, I stand up despite their exhortations, I take a few steps in the room— a big, bright room, decorated European-style. I feel good. As I walk past a mirror I stop for a few moments to observe the stunning reflection the mirror sends back to me: a narrow, tanned face, bright eyes, straight hair, very black, with no white streaks at the temples. I thank them, all of them. I feel marvellously well.

This is just the beginning.

Suzanne Jacob
Translated by Wayne Grady

POMME DOULY AND THE INSTANT OF ETERNITY

Suzanne Jacob was born near Abitibi and enrolled at the Collège Notre-Dame-de-l'Assomption de Nicolet in 1965, where she was introduced to the worlds of theatre and music. She taught French as a second language from 1967 to 1972; during this period, she began writing songs and stories, some of which appeared in the journals *Liberté*, *Possibles*, and *La Nouvelle Barre du jour*. In 1970 she was named best author-composer-performer at the Patriote de Montréal, and since then she has followed the dual careers of chansonniere and writer. She divides her time between Paris and Montreal.

Her first book of poems, *Flore Cocon*, was published by Parti pris in 1978, and a second collection, *Poèmes I: Gémellaires, le Chemin de Damas*, appeared in 1980. Her first collection of short stories, *La Survie*, was published in 1979 by the publishing house Le Biocreux, which she and the writer Paul Paré (author of the "quasi-novels" *L'Improbable Autopsie* and *Ils: essai-fiction*) founded in 1978. She has also written two television dramas: *Exercice pour comparution* and *Le Mur*.

Jacob's most recent book, *Les Aventures de Pomme Douly* (1988), is a collection of linked short stories depicting the somewhat chaotic life of a beautiful, intelligent, but directionless woman living in Montreal. The story reprinted here, "Pomme Douly et l'instant d'éternité," translated by Wayne Grady as "Pomme Douly and the Instant of Eternity," picks up her life between adventures, as it were—while she is making ends meet by working as a grocery-store check-out clerk.

∽

"Pomme Douly and the Instant of Eternity" is a translation of "Pomme Douly et l'instant d'éternité" published in *Les Aventures de Pomme Douly* (Montreal: Éditions du Boréal Express, 1988).

Always getting by. There is always someone at hand to murmur the right phrase into Pomme Douly's ear. At the moment, she is getting by by working as a clerk at a Steinberg's supermarket, the one near the corner of Côte-des-Neiges and Queen Mary Road. The northwest corner. Not right at the corner, but almost. It looks out under its heavy awnings like a prostitute with too much mascara, peering across the street into the window of the Renaud-Bray bookstore. Pomme makes this depressing observation to the parasite who is currently inhabiting her refrigerator and her Corée comforter, and when his eyes don't light up with interest she figures his batteries are dead and she throws him out. It is one more act of cruelty added to a long list of atrocities, seeing that it is the middle of February and the parasite doesn't have any winter clothes to wear while searching for his next free meal. But Pomme doesn't waste time worrying about him, being well aware of the inexhaustible capacity of parasites to find new hosts, especially parasites whose specialized habitat is other people's beds.

The fact that she never allows herself to muse out loud, for the benefit of her sisters-in-bondage, on the vast number of semi-naked bodies that are, at this particular time of year, stretched out along the beaches of Florida, visions of which flash through her mind every time a bag of oranges rolls by on her conveyor belt—the conveyor belt itself constantly reminding her of the intense pleasure of watching her suitcase disappear through those little flappy curtains at the airport—doesn't mean that she doesn't complain about other things. She complains about being assigned to a different check-out counter every day, which not only makes her feel insecure herself but, along with her, all the old pensioners who come to Steinberg's under the pretext of wanting a container of plain yogurt or fifty grams of lean ground beef, but who really come out of a need to have some regularity in their lives, which Pomme feels obliged to offer but can't if she is at a different cash register every time they come in. Then there are those awful, heavy awnings that cover the store front like the mascaraed eyelashes of a cheap whore (she still likes that image), and which keeps what little sunlight that trickles down to street level from creeping in through the supermarket windows as far as the check-out counters. A losing battle, Pomme tells herself, her remarks to the effect that keeping the sunlight outside and preventing aged customers from forming lasting friendships with cashiers is in effect a form of apartheid being invariably met, during a course of multiple verbal transactions with the store manager, with nervous laughter, much shoulder shrugging, elbow flapping and knee flexing, but no action. A losing battle. But the part about excluding sunlight does seem to have unsettled the manager, a man who, because of his strong personality, gathers unto himself the several roles of father-mother, older brother, psychological counsellor and father-confessor, for his entire bevy of cashiers. He never speaks of the supermarket or of the employees of the supermarket except in the possessive. In view of which, Pomme tells herself, I come to work with my hair tied up in two ponytails sticking straight out of my head above my ears: who then, she wonders, will speak to me of losing battles?

"You shouldn't complain, my dear. We all get what we deserve out of life, all things come to those who wait." That is what Pomme's parents told her.

Pomme's parents have been dead for years, cut off in the prime of their lives, but they continue to use their direct trunk line to communicate with her about important things. When they were alive, from the time she was old enough to nurse they had told her that before she pitched her tent she should know where the sun was going to rise. "Everyone knows that souls choose their mothers before being born. My child, you should have chosen a better Steinberg's." Would her mother be touched by an iota of uncertainty about the way things work in the world, a world in which she had obstinately behaved as though she possessed absolute knowledge? She didn't live long enough to see her bedrock of convictions shaken by the rumbling of vast oceanic fault lines. "My child, you should, my child, you should have . . ." These words were the foundation stones upon which her parents built Pomme's personality. They didn't live long enough to see the lengths Pomme has to go to in order to separate that pedestal from her real life, but they didn't need the pedestal any more, now that they can speak directly into her brain via their trunk line.

"Well, Pomme, you've been very quiet these past two days. We're getting bored. No one to denounce today? No complaints? What's going on?"

Pomme's only response is to punch in her cash register. She is busy thinking about the instant of eternity. Everything happens in an instant, in that flash of lightning that welds two beings together, solders them into a single entity, sets things up so that among the thousands and millions of people who rub shoulders every day in every city, one person is suddenly, miraculously, fused to another, maybe for a few months in the flesh but really for all eternity in each other's memory. Pomme is trying desperately to seize that moment, to isolate it, to control it, but without success. Thunderbolts, love philtres, MDA capsules, would they prolong the moment? Pomme thinks about it. If she can find that instant, she will be saved. Because she has decided to live alone for at least fifteen days a year. In the fifteen days since the last person to whom she was fused by one of those instants of eternity moved out of her apartment, Pomme has been unmistakably smitten by a new instant of eternity. But she has been alone now for ten days, ten days today. She is enamored of her solitude. She cleaned up her apartment after the departure of the last parasite, but as the days pass she feels more and more weighed down by the threat of a new instant of eternity, an instant that will throw her into a new eternity.

"Forty dollars and fifty-six cents. Do you have the penny? No? Never mind, I'll put one in myself."

What's a penny? What's a bus token? What's a straight pin, she asks herself. She watches yet another can of ready-to-heat tomato sauce come toward her on the belt. Hunt's Tomato Sauce, in a red can, this week's special. You idiot,

Pomme thinks, can't you do one thing at a time? How can you find the answer to one question when you drown it under a thousand others? Why don't you try to figure out how many two-hundred-gram packages of spaghetti this customer has to go through in order to use up all these cans of Hunt's Tomato Sauce, and then calculate how many weeks it will take her to eat all that spaghetti, so that you'll know when to put Hunt's Tomato Sauce on special again in your stupid supermarket.

"It isn't *my* stupid supermarket," Pomme says aloud.

"I beg your pardon?" says the customer.

"I was speaking to my mother," Pomme replies without displaying any of the signs of a stable friendship that she usually shows to the midriffs of every customer that has passed the age of being considered a person who needs direct human warmth in order to go on living.

"You're crazy," the customer states, backing away.

"Thirty-two fourteen, fifteen, twenty-five, fifty, seventy-five, thirty-three, thirty-four, thirty-five, thank you, Ma'am, next please."

Pomme closes the cash drawer and crosses her arms over her chest. "You're crazy" keeps echoing in her head. A fresh line of Hunt's Tomato Sauce is waiting for her at the end of the conveyor belt. In front of it four chicken breasts glare at her through their cellophane wrapper.

Am I crazy? she groans. Her gaze sweeps along the row of maple branches that line Queen Mary Road until they reach the gates of the Côtes-des-Neiges cemetery, where it follows the trunks up, above the trees to the sky, which looks a lot like rice pudding, and then up past the rice pudding to emerge into the clear blue sky, a blue bluer than the veins in chicken breasts, from where her gaze transcends, encircles the globe, encompasses the Pacific Ocean, the island of Japan, continental China, flies over Tibetan monks and the Mediterranean without getting snagged on the minarets, envelops the statue of the Virgin in Biarritz, leaps across the Atlantic and descends the St. Lawrence past the coast of Charlevoix and comes to an abrupt three-point landing at check-out counter number eight, Steinberg's, and illuminates it. Pomme bestows a radiant smile upon the person in front of her, a person who is waiting for her to punch through a dozen cans of Hunt's Tomato Sauce and four chicken breasts. Pomme takes a closer look at this person. She is a young woman with golden skin and lips made orange by the blubber of whales, the very whales people are trying to save, yes, the very same ones, who cannot cry out because they are on the lips of this woman and she won't let them, case closed.

Three and three. Pomme closes her cash. It's time for lunch. But who can eat when she feels threatened by the instant of eternity on one hand, and endless rows of Hunt's Tomato Sauce on the other, and when her mind is filled with the fate of a whale whose blubber rests on the lips of a human being with golden, luminous skin? Pomme is of two minds. Shall she or shall she not depart from her usual custom of munching almonds and raisins in front of the bestseller rack in the Renaud-Bray bookstore, and whether she does or not the instant of eternity will descend upon her just the same, she is certain of it. She is a young, married woman, this golden-skinned youth. Why shouldn't she be? Only a young, married woman could light up a supermarket with her skin in the middle of February. Why is that? I will go to the Italian café, says Pomme to herself, and I will order a cappuccino. Why the Italian café? Because it's the weekly special, my darling, Pomme answers herself. She walks into the Italian café, finds a table in the enclosed and heated sidewalk section, and forgets that the instant of eternity can descend upon her because events move beyond intuition when they come sufficiently close to intuitive people. Intuition is like radar that can only detect objects when they are far away. What are you talking about? Pomme demands of her brain. We are here to order a cappuccino, and maybe, if we feel like it, a plate of ravioli in Sauce Aurore.

She orders a plate of ravioli in Sauce Aurore. She should have gone to Italy with Plume and Bull, the man from Seville, everyone told her and told her that she should have gone: still, this is a good Sauce Aurore, all things considered. It is just then that the luminous, golden woman enters the Italian café, and hence the life of Pomme for the second time. She looks around for a place to sit; the enclosed and heated sidewalk section is full, except, of course, for the chair across from Pomme. She comes over to Pomme's table. "May I join you?" she says. Pomme says: "You may." The young, married woman sits without taking off her heavy coat, or her gloves, or her scarf. She smiles.

"Do you recognize me?" she asks after a long silence. Pomme says nothing. Pomme does not respond.

"My name is Anna," says the young, married woman. "I am happy. I would like to talk to you. Does it bother you that I would like to talk to you?"

"My name is Pomme," says Pomme.

"I have just escaped from my mother's house," says the young, married woman. "I don't know where to go."

"Why were you buying all that Hunt's Tomato Sauce and four chicken breasts?" asks Pomme. "I thought you had just got married, that you were a young, married woman."

Anna laughs. Her laughter wafts through the entire room. Italian men throw themselves across their tables to kiss Anna's hand.

"I bought those things to give to whoever is going to take me home," Anna says. "I am sure to meet someone soon who will want to."

"You sound very sure of yourself," Pomme assures her.

Pomme has finished her plate of ravioli in Sauce Aurore, she has finished her cappuccino, she has listened to Anna's incredible story of gentle incarceration from which Anna has so recently escaped. None of it makes sense, and the orange on her lips has faded perceptibly as she progresses further into her unbelievable tale. Pomme notices the time. "I've got to run!" she says. "Here, take my address. There may be a time when you don't meet someone, or when you don't have a place to stay. You never know." Anna could turn up any night; Pomme no longer lives alone. There is always the chance of Anna.

"No, but the instant, don't you see? The instant—when was it? Was it at the cash when I just came back from a trip around the planet, or when I saw the orange in your lipstick, or when? Maybe it was when you told me your name: Anna. Your lips remained slightly parted for a second after you said it—maybe that was the critical second, the instant that slid by unnoticed."

"Like those lemon seeds sliding around in your salad dressing," says Anna. "What if it was your smile between those absurd ponytails of yours?"

"Yes, my everlasting," Pomme murmurs, completely absorbed in the retrieval of the lemon seeds. "The instant may have been trapped by the weekly special. What do you think?"

Anne Dandurand
Translated by Luise Von Flotow-Evans

TO CONSOLE MYSELF, I IMAGINE THAT THE BOMBS HAVE FALLEN

Anne Dandurand was born in Montreal on November 19, 1953—"the same day television came to Montreal," as she says—the twin sister of the writer Claire Dé. She worked as a union organizer for La Fédération des travailleurs du Québec as well as for the Committee on the Status of Women from 1978 to 1981, and as a journalist from 1983 to 1987 for such magazines as *Châtelaine*, *La Vie en rose*, *Québec rock* and *Montréal ce mois-ci*. She has acted for television, cinema, and the stage.

Her first book, co-authored with Claire Dé, was *La Louve-garou*, which was published in 1982. She then appeared solo with *Voilà c'est moi: c'est rien, j'angoisse*, subtitled *journal imaginaire*, in 1987. She has published two collections of stories: *L'Assassin de l'intérieur/Diables d'espoir* (1988; *Deathly Delights*), and *Petites âmes sous ultimatum* (1991). She has also written three screenplays: *Ruel-Malenfant* (1980), *Le rêve assassin* (1981), and (again with Claire Dé) *Rachel et Réjean inc.* (1987).

The following story, translated by Luise Von Flotow-Evans, appeared in the anthology *Celebrating Canadian Women* (1989), edited by Greta Nemiroff.

∽

"To Console Myself. I Imagine That The Bombs Have Fallen" is reproduced from *Celebrating Canadian Women: Prose and Poetry by and about Canadian Women* (Markham: Fitzhenry and Whiteside, 1989) and was originally published under the title "Pour me consoler j'imagine que les bombes sont tombées" in *Voilà c'est moi: c'est rien, j'angoisse* (Montreal: Triptyque, 1987).

To console myself. I imagine that the bombs have fallen. By chance three thousand people in the Métro have been spared. I imagine the chaos, the terror and, very quickly, the organization for survival. The beginning of the women survivors' great anger, which will last three thousand years.

Establishment of a new order, an absolute matriarchy. Genetic manipulations, mutations, parthenogenesis—women have created a new race.

Men now have ten arms around their bodies. They lose their memories every evening and only get them back in the morning: this keeps them confused and in a state of servitude. We women use telepathy to keep all knowledge strictly to ourselves. We now have cold blood, and our legs are joined under a layer of fine scales.

No one has returned to the surface; in fact, no one remembers the colour of the sky.

Over the centuries our territory has grown larger, its tunnels descending always farther. We use lead panels for reinforcement, which the men painstakingly engrave all day long. The age of a passage can be determined by the mosaic design on its walls.

During the first millennium the women also developed a tree in their laboratories from which everyone draws their subsistence. It grows from the ceiling, and its fruits, at ground level, look like clusters of crystal glasses. Each one contains a liquid with a different colour and taste. Delights and poisons. Only the women can tell them apart, and we keep the secret well. A man is never sure of what a woman is offering him.

It is morning. You are still asleep: your ten hands cover your face: I don't know your name, even if I have met you before. You wake up, panic-stricken like the others. Then you see me and you feel vaguely that I have to touch you. I run my hands through your hair, and your memory returns. Every morning it's the same: the men have to be touched by a woman to recover their identity. The ones who forget too often go crazy.

But this morning, though I don't know you, you make me want to break the taboo.

What if I took you on as a partner? What if we return together towards the light, the real light? There is still a bit of daring in the depths of your eyes, and didn't I see you drawing reminiscences of words on the slabs you were engraving?

But your ancestors weren't capable of loving: so how would you have learned? And why should I risk losing the attachment I have to my sisters? After all, they're the ones who saved my life.

No, it's goodbye forever then: if I return to fresh air, I'll go alone.

Gilles Pellerin
Translated by Matt Cohen

IN MY CONDITION

Gilles Pellerin, teacher and short-story writer, was born in Shawinigan in 1954 and now lives in Quebec City, where he recently founded the publishing house L'Instant Même. In 1988 his story "Le Songe" won first prize in a short-story contest sponsored by L'Office franco-québécois, and that year his first collection of stories, *Ni le lieu ni l'heure*, won the Grand Prix Logidisque for works of science fiction and fantasy. He has published in many Quebec and international literary journals, including *XYZ, Nouvelles nouvelles, Écriture, Possibles, Solaris,* and *Nouvelles francophones d'aujourd'hui*. His most recent short-story collection, *Je reviens avec la nuit*, appeared in 1992.

"Dans mon état," the story translated here by Matt Cohen as "In My Condition," first appeared in *XYZ* in 1989. Like the stories of Claire Dé, Pellerin's blend of stream-of-consciousness and dark humour slowly elucidates a bizarre version of the world. In this story, we again come across a sudden twist at the end, in which everything we thought we understood is turned on its head; an experience not unfamiliar to anyone living in modern, urban North America.

"In My Condition" is a translation of "Dans mon état" published in *XYZ*, no. 20 (winter 1989).

Something to show me, just two minutes, promise, anyway it's easy to see that I'm tired, nothing more normal in my condition.

My condition, how could I forget it? All evening we've been talking of nothing else. I come in, everyone rushes up, it seems I'm looking well, even blooming, that is my face and my stomach. When everyone has taken a good look and assured me that it suits me marvellously, they rush to kiss my blooming face. We have always given each other generous kisses, but it seems to me the mouths are warmer, sweeter, moister than usual.

Among the women is a stranger who isn't staying long because she is not satisfied with the formal way I speak after the introductions and which I impose on those meeting me for the first time. She is called Jacinth, and moreover she says "tu." She palpates me right away, asks me the results of the ultrasound, wants to know my preference, the name, and is delighted that I refused the ultrasound; that makes it a mystery, which she proposes to solve in front of us, but not before I admit a preference. When she has to confess that, seer though she is, she can't get me to say what I want, she finally withdraws her hands, disappointed (doubtless less by the verdict than by my stubbornness): a boy.

It appears that I'm upset, she isn't surprised: I give her the impression of someone who is closed. It isn't unusual to see people fighting their own desires, doing whatever they can to get away from them. Even if it's unconscious, we all have a preference. Has she already mentioned it? She's a bit of a clairvoyant, these things don't escape her. She reassures me: a boy isn't so bad.

As a joke, Jeanne has cooked liver, but what liver: marinated in raspberry vinegar and a few secret herbs, it will transform my baby—my son—into a real genius. A genius isn't so bad, either. Did they put on this circus when it happened to the others?

It's just that I wasn't expected to have a baby, I even projected the image of a woman who had decided not to have them because of nuclear war, pollution, unemployment, my rotten character. Claudine thinks I am lucky to be having one now that I am mature—she, if she had it to do over again . . . To that I reply that Nicholas is lucky to have a mother who is so young and mine will never know anything but a mother who is wrinkled, worn out by nuclear war, pollution, and unemployment, a mother with whom everyone wonders how he's going to be able to work out his oedipal complex.

I refuse the wine, they insist, I hold firm, not out of heroism—it's just that it doesn't taste right. I am congratulated—the face Lucie would have made if I had accepted. Claudine is worried: Nicholas likes beer. One day, when she had to answer the telephone while she was having a drink before supper, he got absolutely smashed. On that question Jacinth has a story about druids, orgies, and the solstice that I don't exactly listen to but that doesn't seem to reassure Claudine, nor does Madeleine when she warns her with her customary humour, "Don't worry, in two years it'll be crack."

As always, Claudine is receiving our phobias like a parabolic antenna. (Jacinth knows about this phenomenon, she's a bit telepathic.) Through Claudine's mouth, we hear about stereotypes, chickenpox, daycare, sign language, everything that we can't quite deal with—and she adds that it is all wonderful. If she were at her house I know she'd wind herself around Nicholas like a boa, the terrible kissing constrictor. That touches me, along with everything the girls are offering me: the memories of Madeleine when she was a naughty little girl, when she stuck crayons in our backs, called us names, stole our friends; Lucie's pre-natal yoga book; the pickle-flavoured ice cream Lucie pretends I'm supposed to have for dessert.

But the best things come to an end, especially wonderful evenings (in my condition). Jacinth will drop me off, it's on her way. This evening I would have preferred that it be Claudine. Or Lucie, or Madeleine. I don't want to be difficult or, even less, to hurt the feelings of someone who has had a difficult time: in the intimacy of the car she tells me everything, from the sperms and the eggs on. Three times. All girls. I had paid so little attention to her I didn't even know she was a mother. Did it go well? Nausea, edemas, high blood pressure. But she has no regrets, on the contrary. Pain enlivens awareness. Life is a mystery—don't they talk about the mystery of life? Suffering leads to transcendence. She's in a position to know. And me?

Should I tell her I haven't had the slightest desire to bring up? That at worst I am uncomfortable when it is hot? I invent nauseas, say that I am absolutely repelled by liver, kidneys, veal heart—everything I had to consent to eat for our mutual well-being, my *son's* and mine. I quote unlikely recipes, whatever seems the least appetizing, I tell about the embarrassment I suffered from my continual need to go pee at a certain colloquium, I make myself laugh, less to cut short my fictional martyrdom than to prevent her from telling me what I presume to have been her own.

Now that we're talking about it: her teeth are floating. Something to show me, just two minutes. So I go up, not without protecting myself by the sacred need for sleep (in my condition).

In the elevator she asks me what I think of Felix. I know, we are supposed to say *tu, René, Félix*. I am prudish enough to take offence, prudent enough to reply evasively—I really like him . . . which threatens to lead us into a story about music or national ingratitude, worse: a numerology course starting with a death notice with only the number 8, the time, the day, the month, the year. As she won't take her eyes off the crystal ball she seems to see under my dress, I realize my mistake, I resent the trial of intentions to which I have been subjected by her, I repeat that I really like him, she explains to me that the name means "the good omen," or "felicity," I try to absolve myself: And yours? I ask, in the tone she's been waiting for. The eldest is Anna. To prove my good will I quickly say that it's pretty. And the other two? Olga and Liuodmila. I approve but conviction fails me.

We're there, she turns on the light, I no longer know how to speak except to say that it's pretty, the leather sofa, the halogen lamp, the laquered coffee table, the meditation rug (Armenian), and still I haven't seen anything, she puts her finger to her lips, *Shhh*, leads me into what I assume to be the boudoir until I see the furniture, the cribs, the chest of drawers on top of which are aligned, like a decrescendo, a set of three nested Russian dolls, Anna and the younger matriochki, Olga and Lioudmila, it's pretty.

∽

Claude-Emmanuelle Yance
Translated by David Homel

THE LOVE OF LIES

Claude-Emmanuelle Yance was born in Quebec City. She moved to the French island of Nouvelle-Calédonie, where she lived for nine years, and then spent two years in Paris before returning to Quebec. Although she acknowledges the influences of the South Pacific as well as of Paris in her linguistic arsenal, it is to the land and the people of Quebec that she responds most fully as a writer. "When I returned to Quebec," she has said, "I understood that what filled me up and made me the kind of writer that I am was the land here, the nature here. I might have fewer words, fewer images, fewer tools at my disposal here, but my territory as a writer, my interior landscape, was created for me in Quebec."

Yance's first collection of short stories, *Mourir comme un chat*, was published in 1987 by L'Instant même, the publishing house started by Gilles Pellerin. The book won the Prix Adrienne-Choquette and identified Yance as "one of the most promising of Quebec's young writers." The present story, "L'amour du mensonge," translated by David Homel as "The Love of Lies," was first published in *XYZ* in 1989 and is part of a second collection of linked stories called *Vous avez des nouvelles de Baudelaire? (Have You Heard from Baudelaire?)*. The new series of stories was suggested to Yance by "L'Étranger," one of the stories included in her first collection, in which a short prose poem by Charles Baudelaire haunts the central character and changes her life. "What I am looking for in these new stories," Yance stated, "is to pit the poems of Baudelaire against contemporary situations and characters, to see what the result will be."

↜

"The Love of Lies" is a translation of "L'amour du mensonge" published in *XYZ*, no. 18 (summer 1989).

> Would it not suffice that you be the appearance
> To charm a heart in flight from truth?
> Charles Beaudelaire, *Les Fleurs du Mal*

"Flowers of Evil. Some of you have already done this research. Your relevant commentary, we feel sure, will guide us through this wonderful labyrinth that may eventually lead us—or may not—to the quintessence of the poem. Yes, please, speak... You in the middle..."

... in this little restaurant. Right here, across the way, at the corner of Rue d'Assas and Vaugirard, for example. The big foggy bay windows on this rainy day. The invisible wall of warm air you push through as you go inside. The smells, sharp yet fleeting. I'll have to wait for him, I'm sure. Take a table that's not too isolated, but not too near other people. Display an attentive, preoccupied expression as I read the menu. Or, better, don't read anything at all, let your eyes wander with studied casualness. Don't let him catch you in the act of being preoccupied. Relax, give the impression of serenity and self-assurance.

And while you're at it, pay attention to what you wear that day, choose calm, discreet colours. Blue, for instance. Nothing that might make him nervous or fluster him. Turn your back to the door, don't look as though you were waiting for him, but thanks to the mirrors, you will know exactly when he comes through the door. Don't leave anything to chance, avoid the little quiver of surprise. Put all the solidity in the world on your side.

There he is. He slips into the booth, both hands on the table, leaning in my direction. A smile. His blue eyes are a little misty. Then comes the way he pulls back, as if a smile was too great a gift. He says he doesn't have much time, he grabs the menu, asks me if I've ordered.

I have to choose: either blurt out the words or slow my rhythm even further. Let him snatch me up, or drag him along behind.

Freed from the waiter, he seems to collapse upon himself. Now's the time to please him. Casually at first, open the door to questions about his work and research. Listen to him, try to ask only the right questions, those that best hide how little I know about the area, and get him going on to new explanations. A delicate moment. He could completely lose me in this forest of unknown notions through which he moves so subtly. I must hold on to what I have to say, despite the shifting sands beneath my feet, but I must not stiffen, it's important to be flexible as I play the rhythm of our conversation. Later, I'll take the upper hand again, in another field. Perhaps he'll be just a little curious about my literary studies. But don't get weighed down, simply mention a few landmarks, don't get boxed into using words that might impress him, but which mean less and less to me every day. The language of the academy, duplicitous, false, fascinating.

Just the time it takes for the waiter to disappear after bringing us our coffees.

I don't know what words I'll use, whether I'll look him in the eye, or whether I'll be able to keep my hand from toying with the lumps of sugar on the table—but I'll tell him that his wife and I are in love.

Already I imagine his eyes: they will give the impression of unmoving concentration, while in reality they will already be stealing away from me. He will clear his throat, his way of stalling for time, getting his thoughts together.

Two things I can imagine inside myself: my heart beating with fear as the emptiness of time opens up before us. How can I continue being here now? And my desire to pin him down, to cut off his escape.

> Handsome cases, devoid of jewels . . .
> Emptier that way . . .

. . . but the scene can just as well become an empty shell before my eyes. He came in so late, he was so hurried, he unknowingly exhausted my will to speak. I don't even have that old desire to seek refuge behind our usual conversation. My heart's stopped pounding, I don't want to have a pounding heart any more, I want only cowardice. I will be blind to everything.

Another empty shell. This time, tuned by fear. I want to speak, I will speak. A colleague is coming our way, he makes room for him in the booth, invites him to have a coffee. Why not?

Will I have the strength to start again another day? I'll need to avoid everything that might empty me of my decision. I don't have the luxury of several attempts. The telephone, perhaps?

I carefully chose the first sentences. I tried out their rhythm, recovered my little drawl when I needed it, polished the words. But he doesn't connect, and ends up setting the tone. Half-serious, half-joking, perhaps even open laughter. My sentences stop working together. My turn to clear my throat. Watch out for those first few moments when I might stumble. Let his silence come forward; it will come. Then slice up the space into tiny parts and put my words into each one, occupy it completely, round it out. And say: your wife and I are in love. Say it.

Imagine everything that might happen next. The silence like a bottomless pit. Who will fill it—the one who's most fragile?

His humour is the hardest thing to take. "Oh, really? Well, that's good news!" No other way out but silence. Afterwards, who knows?

A letter, perhaps? I choose the day, the paper, the words, the colour of time, my degree of decision. I sit down, I go into myself. I'm going to say something terrible.

But what makes me so sure? She said it. But then I hear other words that say the opposite. Is it the rush of her body? But doesn't she stop herself, doesn't she refuse it sometimes?

To write, even about the love of lies, is an operation of truth-telling. You must grasp the subtle means the poet uses to make the essence of Woman enter the form of Beauty, to cause the two to join together in a lie.

Appropriate his humour; choose a fine sunny day. Put this smiling sun into my letter. And say that I love her.

A timeless date, laugh the way you do when something ridiculous happens to you. Laugh and walk away. And leave him nonplussed, disarmed, burdened by this unexpected package.

So it might as well be the phone.

Don't choose the day; don't decide to call. Once, when he calls. In the midst of a serious conversation, important, technical, overflowing with highfalutin words and ideas as solid as statues. In the middle of a pure desert. Slip away on tiptoe, without him noticing, and listen to myself loving her. Then, tell him.

I dropped everything on the ground, and now I gaze peacefully upon my disaster, while he can't offer anything but silence. Then quietly hang up.

So much grey in his hair. So soon? He didn't know what to put on this morning; the way that shirt doesn't go with his sweater is touching. No use looking at the colour of his socks. His throat-clearing tells me he's intimidated. He'll make puns about the menu or the people to hide it. I'll laugh freely and the conversation will veer off into folly: a defence against tenderness. I love the way he defends himself.

When he lapses into silence, I'll have to flush him out with questions. I'll discover the path he wants to take, and follow him, awkward as I go.

When he returns to me, it will be my turn to protect myself. He's not handsome by any means, but he does inspire tenderness: the grey in his hair, his childish concern over a problem as important as choosing what to have for dessert, the way he goes looking for a coin in his little change purse.

He's going to suggest we leave. Too late now to tell him what's gotten stuck in my throat. He slides out of the booth; I could hold him back another minute. I could.

I tell myself, How lovely she is!

I don't love her. But who do I love?

André Carpentier
Translated by Wayne Grady

TRAGEDY HOUSES MY WOUND

André Carpentier was born in Montreal on October 29, 1947. He graduated from the Université du Québec à Montréal in 1973 with a masters degree in literature, and is a short-story writer and novelist. He helped edit the visual-arts magazine *L'Écran* in 1974, and the next year became the assistant director of the International Pavilion of Humour at Montreal's Man and His World, a position he held until 1980. During this time, he organized a collective of comic-strip artists called La Bande déssinée kébécoise whose work appeared in the journal *La Barre du jour*. He also published articles in *La Presse*, *Moebius*, and *Le Livre d'ici*.

Carpentier's first two novellas, *Axel et Nicholas* and *Mémoires d'Axel*, were published jointly in Montreal in 1973, and his novel, *L'aigle volera à travers le soleil*, followed in 1978. But it was with the publication of his first collection of short stories, *Rue Saint-Denis* (1978) that he first came into prominence as a writer of highly intellectual, somewhat difficult works of short fiction. One of the stories in it, "Les sept rêves et la réalité de Perrine Blanc," translated by Wayne Grady as "The Seven Dreams and the Reality of Perrine Blanc," concerned a woman undergoing a slow process of disintegration at the hands of her psychologist, who was directing her dream therapy. Carpentier's most recent collection of stories, *De ma blessure atteint et autres détresses* (1990), further explores his interest in the fantastic and the psychology of control. The story included here, translated by Grady as "Tragedy Houses My Wound," is the title story from that collection.

∽

"Tragedy Houses My Wound" is a translation of "De ma blessure atteint" published in *De ma blessure atteint et autres détresses* (Montreal: XYZ, 1990).

> One of my constant preoccupations
> is trying to understand how other
> people can exist...
> — Fernando Pessoa

> Where would I go, if I could go;
> what would I be, if I could be;
> what would I say if I had a voice:
> who is this who calls himself me?
> — Samuel Beckett

Every day lately there is this uncontrollable shaking, to the point where any sense of my own precariousness is completely shattered. Alone in my house in the Lakes region south of Rivière-du-Loup, I am slowly giving in to the contraction of light. I am ridding myself of the reality of others, I want my mind to need nothing but the symbols of self-denial, the indices of nonexistence. Little by little, my mind has lost all sense of connectedness; I am no longer capable of anything more complicated than saying whether certain randomly chosen chambers of thought are close together or far apart, and most of them are far apart. I am opening this story anywhere, with a semi-abstract scene related to me on the phone a few minutes ago by Séraphin Lange, whom I have sent to deliver a message to someone we used to call Toucheur.

In the scene, Toucheur has stopped dead in the middle of the sidewalk and is absorbed, as I'd hoped he would be, in the examination of a specimen of handwriting whose characters are harmoniously but irregularly modulated, in which the angles vary from zero to ninety degrees, a trait also seen in the model. The axis is irregular and the individual letters are crowded together. The looped ascenders all seem to lean to the left, the non-looped ones to the right. There are three curliques that appear unattached to any corresponding letters; the upstrokes and downstrokes alternate and complement one another in a way that creates a satisfying equilibrium. The connectors between letters are thin to the point of invisibility, but the ovals seem well joined at the top. The opening flourish of the first capital letter becomes a solid downstroke that loops at the bottom, swings and thickens to the right, and ends by underlining the rest of the first word; the second capital—and here aesthetics overrides the rules of grammar—begins with a similar loop that continues across the top of the final word. The preposition, isolated between these two upper-cased words by narrow spaces on either side, is written as though in a different font; more like printing—with serifs, a short, thick horizontal stroke, and a lopsided "o" that looks like a fat drop of water—which threatens to destroy the graphological unity of the whole, but somehow does not. The eye glides smoothly from beginning to end, despite a break in the alignment after the first word. The text ends with a crooked, cross-like structure, a "t" in what seems to be yet a third typeface. The italicized effect of the syntagm is provided by an overall slant of about ten degrees to the right. The sign itself appears to be a hasty imitation of the logo for Coca-Cola, and reads: "Room to Let."

A shout floats down from above his head, in fact from a high porch, but Toucheur pretends not to hear it: "Sir! Hey, sir!" The voice is that of my informant, Séraphin Lange, who recognizes Toucheur but has been instructed not to let on at first. I'll explain why later.

Since Toucheur and I had written the sign ourselves and had immediately considered it a work of considerable merit, Toucheur is in no doubt about the origin of this bizarre calligraphy, even though it has been twenty years or more since we penned it. (We produced the placard jointly, or more precisely, alternatively, in the distant past when we were both working for a property owner.) Toucheur knows exactly where this sign came from; what he is trying to figure out is how it came, two decades later, to be tacked to the porch of a rooming house two doors down from his own house at the extreme north end of Boulevard Saint-Laurent.

Lange leans over the porch rail towards Toucheur: "I am not the owner, but please allow me to inform you that there is no room to let in this house. That sign has absolutely no relationship to the availability or nonavailability of rooms in this establishment. I know: I myself am a resident of this domicile."

Toucheur studies the placard like one exploring an elusive memory. He must be thinking that beings from a distant past are best represented to us in the form of things: I, or so I would like to believe, and perhaps to some extent he, are simply impressions created by the time we spent together, and if that is not exactly what he is thinking, it must come pretty close to it. Ah, but I forgot to tell you what I should have made clear at the beginning, which would have made me the kind of writer Toucheur and Papineau are in their own books: all the things I have just described, that particular instant at that time (late afternoon) of that day, are nothing more than the products of rustling leaves and feathers, and the sighing of forgotten winds sleeping peacefully at various strata of sky.

"Whose sign is this?" Toucheur demands without taking his eyes off the square of cardboard.

"Not mine," says Lange, defensively.

"The landlord's, then?" asks Toucheur.

"No, not his . . . but what is this? You seem to be more interested in the sign than you are in the room!"

"Yes, well—it's just that I recognize the handwriting. In fact, I helped make this sign."

I'm improvising, since I know very little about how the actual conversation went; I'm trying to reconstruct it in order to understand myself better, because I was somewhere else, which is to say here, in my house in the Lakes region, but at the same time I was there, for the simple reason that it was me who planned the whole thing and sent Lange to Toucheur's house with the sign as a sign of recognition, as a kind of pledge, you might say. But let me continue to proceed by the caprices of thought . . .

Not that it matters, but I do have a postcard, hastily scrawled, that shows the area where all this rediscovery by proxy takes place. There is a small park, on the bank of the

Rivière des Prairies, frequented on hot summer evenings by adolescents with nothing better to do, on Sundays by Italians in white singlets, and the rest of the time by Hassidic Jews. From Saint-Jean-Baptiste Day to Labour Day, the park resounds with the hollow plock of racquets striking tennis balls and the athletic cries of the players in the nine courts arranged along one side, in the shelter of a row of honeysuckle bushes. The area is famous for its elm trees, which are more than a hundred years old, and whose canopies adorn the upper half of a painting by Marc-Aurèle Fortin; one of the four elms in front of the rooming house has a diameter of four feet at chest height. The house itself is of red brick, three storeys high counting the street level (below the balcony) and the attic. It is a solid structure planted squarely on its lot, which is barely four feet wider than the house itself; it has a mansard roof and several dormers.

"Oh yes," Lange is saying, "I know you recognize that sign! And not only because it is written all over your face, but also because I have come a long way with the express purpose of showing it to you."

Toucheur has always given the impression of being a rock against which all waves break, even waves originating within himself; but recently, I've been told, his emotions have been trying to leak out. Lange would add as well that Toucheur wants to live, and the more his desire to live increases, the greater the role anxiety and suspicion play in him.

"You mean to tell me that you hung this sign two steps from my house just so that I would see it, to give it to me or, what I suppose is more likely, to sell it to me . . ."

"To return it to you would be a better way of putting it."

"But I don't understand how you came to possess this placard in the first place. The last time I . . ."

The utter incomprehensibility of the thing stops Toucheur in his tracks.

The sign is none other than the very one that he and I made together while we were at Teacher's College, when

Papineau was there—Papineau was the third member of our dynamic trio. At the time, the three of us were studying with the vague intention of becoming French teachers, outside the province, if possible, or at least in the remoter reaches of it. Toucheur had wanted to study sociology or political science, but his father said he wouldn't have a Bolshevik in the family, and refused to pay for Toucheur's post-secondary education. As a result, Toucheur had had to choose a less expensive institute, and so had ended up at Teacher's College. I don't remember how Papineau had come to be there, perhaps because of a similar shortage of funds, or maybe he had felt he had an aptitude for teaching, who knows? I also can't recall a thing about myself at that time, how I got to that school or anything else.

"Don't worry, that sign doesn't belong to me, either," Lange hastens to explain. Lange's face has been ravaged by ethyl alcohol, but his expression is serene. He is one of those people who is proud and possessive of his intelligence and who, having had more than his share of rude awakenings, understands that life is nothing but a little social game. That's why I chose him as my messenger; also for his name, but I'll explain that later, too. "It is, at least for the next few minutes, the property of your friend from the Lakes region."

Toucheur searches his memory without success. "Do I know that area?" he asks.

"Well, if you don't I strongly advise you to waste no time in acquainting yourself with it. It's downriver from Quebec City, south of Rivière-du-Loup in a corner of the province between the borders of New Brunswick and Maine—a land of pure azure . . . But leave that for now, it isn't all that important."

Toucheur has regained control of himself: "But you say I know someone from there!"

"You do, the same friend with whom you wrote that sign you are holding in your hands, who has not forgotten you after all these years, even though he feels badly that he has only recently remembered you."

"You mean G.D.!"

Having read everything that Toucheur has published over the past fifteen years—short stories or prose fragments—I knew he liked to set himself up as a mere spectator of his own depths, to purge himself of his emotions and perversities by feigning to invent incoherent fictions about things that don't concern him. These filtered revelations, combined with accidental confidences I have garnered over the years, have enabled me to compile a total portrait of him, albeit from a distance. Toucheur was an apparently indifferent youth who was nonetheless agitated by suppressed rages, a passive-aggressive for whom childhood seemed an endless ordeal. School was no release for these passions; until Teacher's College, except for one half-year, he had passed himself off as a distracted student, undisciplined, inattentive. It took the seeds of freedom in the machinery of Teacher's College to change all that, and the friends he was forced to make there, especially Papineau and myself, whose secret gardens were without right angles, and who displayed similar preoccupations and behavioral characteristics to his own. But I'm rambling rather than speaking directly: at Teacher's College he was no longer treated as a sociopath just because he spent all his time reading books, and no prefect confiscated his copies of Kafka, Camus, and Koestler. He was no longer treated as though he were retarded, or a faggot, just because he preferred to spend his time with Robert Louis Stevenson or Conrad rather than go carousing with fellow students. (It must be said that, during this period of the Quiet Revolution, the word "faggot" was applied to anyone who lacked the conventional trappings of virility or who showed an indiscriminate attraction to other men.)

"The very same," says Lange. "Your old friend G.D. has sent me here to put that sign in your hands, but in such a way that you would pick it out instantly from among the everyday things of the world. So that you would not be able to pass by without recognizing not only the sign, but more importantly, what it stood for and continues to represent: a direct link between you . . ."

"But why all this stage directing? Why the mystery?"

"The delivery of the sign must be memorable, and so I couldn't just hand it over to you, could I? Your friend wanted it to reawaken in you the memory of the sign that you had created together, so that the very randomness of the delivery becomes a kind of settlement, and its deeper meaning would be transferred along with the object itself."

At Teacher's College, I hung around almost exclusively with Papineau—who was called that because his hair seemed to be in a permanent state of rebellion—and with Toucheur, whose nickname had stuck with him from childhood. His grandfather, who lived in the country and spoke only English (which in itself was remarkable), had taken to calling him Two-Shirts when he was a child because he always wore two shirts, one over top of the other. Back in the city the name had been gallicized to Touchert, then simply Toucheur—just as the English "rubbers" has become *les robeurs*, and "T-shirt" is *un ticheur*. All I know about my own nickname is that I was called G.D.—or sometimes Gideon—because I used to go around carving those initials in school desks. That's at least what I've been told; I have no recollection of it myself. You have to imagine a scrawny kid, frightened of his own shadow, fresh out of public school, hostile to all authority figures, his subconscious animated by a desire for destruction but at the same time fascinated by purity—it could have been either of them but let's say it's Toucheur, no, well, it doesn't have to be him, exactly—just imagine someone who's deaf, completely out of his element, trying hard to hear something but not knowing what it is or even what hearing means, an ecstatic lover in search of meaning, who somehow finds himself a vocation. I guess I'm talking about Papineau here but perhaps I am confused by all this distance and only think I'm describing others when in fact I am really using my memory of them to get at something important about myself—as one might draw a portrait of an anguished cynic from his own mad laughter, ignoring his actual words, even though his mind is vibrating with curiosity though he would rather die than let it show in his eyes, a liar who suddenly sees a black hole opening up in the middle of the earth; was it me, or him, or him, or all three of us? If we all threw our lots in together, one for all and all for one, it must have been because we had discovered some profound or rather some high ambition, or possibly some privation or compulsion in ourselves that demanded it.

"Have I mentioned that my name is Lange?" says Lange. At this, Toucheur sees another aspect of those years rise out of the shadows, like a challenge to the light: for a few seconds he is dazed. "I see my angelic name, combined with the ritualized return of the placard and my formal familiarity, has reminded you of something . . ."

"Why do you say that?" asks Toucheur in astonishment.

"Because it's part of the message."

"You're right. All this reminds me of a poem G.D. wrote and dedicated to me, called, in fact, 'Room to Let,' I never knew why. It was about an angel . . . wait a minute, it's coming back to me: 'Before I return to my nonexistence, I want you to know. I will put a token in the hands of a messenger; it will have the power of ultimate self-denial.' Ah . . ."

"And the angel . . . will come . . ."

"And the angel will come and expose this sign to your sight, without saying my name. When you have recognized the sign for what it is and are fully conscious of the circumstances of its creation, he will give it back to you. Then you will know that I have returned to my wound . . ."

". . . exempt . . ."

". . . exempt from tears that will not have been shed."

Even in those days we were different in many respects; for example, I hung around with lots of people, Toucheur with hardly anyone, Papineau mostly with a girl with whom he had fallen in love. Both Toucheur and Papineau thought everything belonged to them, especially things that did not belong to them, while I never had a thing, not even the things that were mine. In our eyes, a tree was an object of fascination: to Papineau it was a work of art; to Toucheur, yet another source of terror; to me, it was a cave, a call to mystery. They were more inspired than I was, and better at it; my revenge was to inspire them. I may not have been an artist, but I was a deft model. They watched me, I showed them how to live. They stuffed their minds like suitcases—with facts, with thoughts, with models; I on the other hand had no time to plan ahead, I was always pressing forward, saving nothing for later, in a hurry. My body was my suitcase, rounded at the corners as it was. They herded their minds toward a future; I bashed mine against a barricade. Life pressed down on them like a burden, while for me it was a kind of day trip. I ran under the sky with those who demanded paradise on earth . . . and right away! I was locked into it as though into the most confining virtue.

"Imagine remembering the whole poem by heart!" Toucheur marvels. "It's true I helped get it published in the school magazine, but even so . . . What a memory I have!"

"With a little prompting from me," interrupts Lange.

"A word here and there."

"Hah! Let's hear you recite it again, then."

"Ahem . . . 'Before I go, I . . . I'll send you a messenger,' ah . . . Christ, I've forgotten it already! I don't get it, I had it right on the tip of my tongue a minute ago!" He feels swamped by so many mysteries hitting him at once. "It was you who made me . . . who . . ."

"Yes . . ."

"How is it that you know that poem? Who the hell are you," asks Toucheur, shakily.

Let us dwell on this image of us as we approached our twenties: at school we would each withdraw from the world, each into himself, but with a shared attitude that united us. We wrote, albeit with more good intentions than talent, trenchant little poems in which we launched a holy crusade against tradition, above all against any form of seriousness. Toucheur or Papineau, a few years later, would call it "writing on the run." Our stance obviously put others' backs up, but they kept an eye on us anyway, out of curiosity, I would say, and with the secret hope of reaching, through us, the frontiers of the inaccessible, from which we continually sent dispatches during the initial phase of our research. We also began gravitating around a small poetry magazine, attractively typed, mimeographed, and stapled in the upper left-hand corner, as we had seen done elsewhere, and which we entitled *SkyWords*. Oh, how proud we were of that little conceit! Our teachers thought it was all nonsense, which was precisely the point; our own audacity shielded us from their reproaches.

"Who am I? I am Lange, as I've already told you, a humble bearer of tidings. And I know the poem for the very simple reason that it is pasted on the back of the very sign you are holding, in the top corner. I can read it from here. You were my prompt."

"You've come here to tell me that the prophecy in that poem has come to pass?"

"You're very quick, aren't you. I have come here to deliver a certain sign, on one side of which appear the words 'Room to Let,' written by you and your erstwhile friend, and on the other side, the poem that gives side A, so to speak, its meaning. I am only a simple delivery boy, don't forget, an exiled cab driver who, after they closed the mine at Gagnon, had to trade his past for a future in the Lakes region. When the company closed the mine, Gagnon became a ghost town. I'd spent twenty years of my life in a kind of sealed beaker, never travelling farther than the outskirts of Gagnon, two-dollar fares to the airport, to the hospital, to the trailer court, back downtown; when the town disappeared, I had to find another cab stand. Since then, I have been criss-crossing the province, little brown parcels jiggling on the passenger seat . . ."

"Why are you telling me all this?"

"So you'll know I exist."

I wish I could remember how it was we fell apart, the three of us! Not that it would change anything, I suppose . . . Until recently the thoughts of Toucheur and Papineau that crossed my mind were mostly muddled up with confused and, in some strange way, guilty feelings. (I don't know how to explain this anxiety; I do note, however, that, contrary to appearances, they have remained more in touch with each other than with me.) Now, one fact has just come to light that changes the scenario. I have been told recently that Toucheur put me in one of his unpublished stories, in the guise of an enigmatic character who is not particularly important to the plot. I interpret this as a desire to hold on to what we had shared during the short but very intense period of our friendship. Here's what he wrote: "His bearing and his gestures were part of a choreographic work by Béjart, his voice was an incantatory wail from Coltrane's sax. His words were like a poem by Prévert, or perhaps Benjamin Péret. Taken together he was a Modigliani painting, someone wearing a suit, sitting straight up on a hard chair, head down, a heavy shadow hiding the length of his face, his eyes so intense you could fall through them into the void." Of course I could hardly recognize my own poor figure behind these words—who would?—but I was grateful to Toucheur for having identified in me what it was that had fed our best times together, a time when a whole new universe of art and thought was opening up to us. I wanted, how shall I put this?—I didn't want to return to nothingness without honouring the announcement I'd made in "Room to Let." I got out the sign and the poem, whose central image has never left me.

"How was it that you made me remember the poem?"

"Human memory is infinite. It is enough to shine a small light into the caverns of the cranium to illuminate any detail. In truth, we never forget anything unless we need to chase it out of our consciousness in order to maintain some degree of equilibrium."

"And so my inability to remember the poem a second time, if I understand you, signifies that I now wish to wipe my memories of G.D. out of my mind?"

"Or memories that are somehow associated with G.D., perhaps."

Toucheur seems to have a certain amount of trouble with the heaviness of that idea; he becomes sombre, and the traits of a whole new person begin to assemble in him, pushing him to the end of the scene. "Am I to understand from the delivery of this sign that G.D. . . . that is, that he is already . . . that he must . . ."

"Would you like me to prompt you again?"

"Is he?"

"How should I know? I repeat, I am a simple porter: I deliver messages, I don't interpret them. If you want the answer to your question, you'll have to find it yourself. Who knows? The whole point of this bizarre transaction might be to lure you into visiting your friend in person, for . . ."

"For what, a final meeting?"

"That depends."

The rest of the story can only be written in the future conditional, because I can only guess what Toucheur does next; as for my own actions, the future tense will do. Toucheur would drive to Rivière-du-Loup that same night. I won't know if, like me, he will have lost that former resilience that allowed us to stay up all night hitting the books. He would want to speak to me about his uneasiness. He would arrive just as the light was spreading over the lake, a little later in the village and my house. He would eat before coming to knock on my door. I won't answer. I'll pretend I'm not there, that I've already gone. He would assume I had cleared out, collapsed, passed away, kicked the bucket, but I will be there lurking behind the window. I will have left two bundles of stapled sheets of paper on the doorstep, one addressed to Papineau, whom I will have informed by some other means, the other to Toucheur. The dozen pages directed at Toucheur will have the last page on top, and in the bottom left-hand margin there will be a drawing of a blue dog, the colour of azure, a sort of guide dog whose muzzle will be in the form of a death's head. Above the dog, in a large, round balloon that is lifting the dog skywords, I will have rewritten the four words rendered illegible by the edges of the drawing, each word printed above the last three lines of the text: "tragedy" "houses" "my wound." Toucheur would be thinking of a plane, or a boat, or a taxi, anything that could be chartered to take him to the extreme end of all roads, where there would be nothing but the world behind and another world ahead. But he would not go any farther than to Papineau's; they would eat raw turnips and drink Cuban rum to my good health. Life would seem to them to have been a long and precarious affair. They would exhaust their repertoire of anecdotes about the three of us, and drink themselves blind in order to see me once again with them, with my howevers and my therefores. They would call me Gideon, interrupting their mad laughter with sentences like: "How little control we exercise over our own lives!" I will let them have their little verbal triumphs. They would speak in such a way about me while I, in the meantime, will be slipping silently off the planet, which will continue to turn on its axis as it always has. I will have arrived at my terminus, which they would call a **tragedy**. By the time darkness invades the village and the **houses**, I will have escaped from the world and returned to **my wound**, exempt from tears that will not have been shed.

Claire Dé
Translated by Matt Cohen

CONSUMING LOVE

Claire Dé was born in Montreal on November 19, 1953, the twin sister of Anne Dandurand. She divided her time between Montreal and Paris for many years, and now lives permanently in Paris.

Her first book, co-authored with her sister, was *La Louve-garou* (1982), a feminist version of the Quebec folkloric tales of the *loup-garou*, or werewolf. *Le Désir comme catastrophe naturelle*, a collection of short fiction published in 1989, won the Prix Stendhal. Her most recent work is the novel *Sourdes amours*, which came out in 1993.

"Un amour dévorant," translated here as "Consuming Love" by Matt Cohen, first appeared in the Montreal literary magazine *XYZ* in 1990. It is a sly tale with a delicious twist at the end, typical of what Dé refers to as her "dry and restrained sense of humour," but it also contains undercurrents that propel it into the realm of the serious.

∽

"Consuming Love" is a translation of "Un amour dévorant" from *XYZ*, no. 24 (winter 1990).

loved him right away. As soon as I entered into his service. I was still very young, an orphan. His wife had just died unexpectedly, there were no children. He was lonely. He needed company. He needed to feel cared for.

Perhaps that was why I loved him: his solitude. He sweated solitude, and I have a strong sense of smell. It had the fragrance of mimosa honey laid over a base of bitterness gone slightly sour. He wasn't so bad, just a bit withdrawn.

As the years went by I grew very attached to him. I didn't so much have to serve him as to be always attentive, present. I put some order back into his life. For example, I am very strict about schedules. There is a time for everything: a time to satisfy one's hunger, a time to act, a time to relax. A certain discipline leads to peace of mind.

Our life together quickly became organized and unchanging. In the morning he went to work; from what I could understand, his job consisted of filling pieces of paper with numbers. I waited for him at the house, which I took care of. In the evening he returned, we would eat, then a walk for the digestion, television, bed.

"Pierre Elliott, take five," is what he always said while limply shaking my fingers before retiring to his room. I was very grateful that he would allow me to be the one to take off his socks, for me it was a kind of privileged intimacy. I slept in the adjoining room, but always with one eye open: ready to respond instantly should he call. Because I am of the race of grand factotums and other top level domestics: loyal, faithful, zealous, well-trained, conciliatory—all this tempered by a dry and restrained sense of humour. Add to this that I am almost always modest.

At night I would dream of Egyptian cats and archaeological digs where I would discover giant dinosaur bones. At sunrise I would stretch my limbs, meticulously clean my black uniform, then I would wake him up with a brief greeting and wash his hands and face.

I loved him. In my way. Never beyond the proprieties! I wouldn't have allowed myself that. I know how to stay in my place, I'm not one of those bad-tempered lapdogs who make effusive displays of emotion, as noisy as they are misplaced. He was the Master and I was Pierre Elliott; he gave the orders and I obeyed. For a decade that's how it was. Thanks to him I lived in perfect happiness. But nothing is more fragile than happiness, especially perfect happiness.

Until he was forced into retirement, he often repeated to me afterwards. He was never again the same. He turned bad. He went out every day, as before. But to drink. And earlier and earlier.

Then he started beating me. Kicks in the shins. Hard slaps to the back of the head. Virulent punches in the ribs. And always at the least expected moments. He no longer talked, he shouted his orders out harshly. And he would jump on me, accusing me of trivial mistakes and errors.

Then he shut me up. Literally sequestered me. No way of even getting a breath of fresh air. I no longer had the right to go out, except to the back yard, like a prisoner. Me, so proud of my appearance, so well cared-for. Gradually I became dirty and repellent.

Even alone with me in the house he would carefully lock the windows and doors to be sure I didn't escape. But I made no effort to get away; I still loved him. I only hoped he would assume his responsibilities, remake his life.

My martyrdom went on and on, for years. I started to feel old, my joints stiffened, but my devotion and innate good health allowed me, despite meagre and irregular meals, to resist his inflictions. Like all those who are abused, I sank with painful delectation into guilt and masochism.

At that time I believed I would die from the beatings of the man I had served and adored all my adult life. Then, one evening, the first warm evening of a chilly spring, he returned home, his step even heavier than usual, his approach so hesitant that I was afraid and, for the first time, hid myself in a closet.

Searching for me he became agitated. "Pierre Elliott! Pierre Elliott!" he bellowed, but I stayed where I was. I heard him banging against the furniture, then the crash of a fall. Then nothing.

I slept where I was. Curled up in a ball. Right on the ground, in the midst of the worn-out shoes of his dead wife.

The Master had grown cold and hard as a stone. Cardiac arrest, probably. He was stretched out on his stomach, I cautiously turned him onto his back. What sorrow I felt then, in spite of the ways he had wounded me. I felt such pain that for a week I couldn't eat, drink, sleep.

For a long time I resisted . . . But then an unbearable craving took hold of me, began to drive me crazy. I tried to proceed as neatly as possible. I began with the ears. They were nice and plump. Delicious.

I had loved him alive. Dead I loved him twice as much. I kept up this diet for a good month. At the end he was unrecognizable. It was a neighbour who sniffed out something and contacted the authorities. Now the police do not know what to do with me, an aging and placid Labrador, seventeen years old: having tasted human flesh I can no longer stomach dog food.

Marie José Thériault
Translated by David Homel

PORTRAITS OF ELSA

Marie José Thériault was born in Montreal on March 21, 1945, the daughter of Yves Thériault. She attended the Collège Marie de France until 1961; after leaving school she worked as a salesperson, an interpreter, a proofreader, and, from 1964 to 1973, a professional dancer. In 1973 she became an editor and translator for the performing arts magazine *Entr'acte*, and in 1975 she began working for the publishing house Éditions Hurtubuise HMH, of which she became literary director in 1978. She has served on the editorial boards of many literary magazines, including *XYZ*, *Vice Versa*, and *Liberté*. In 1987, she founded Les Éditions Sans Nom, a publishing house devoted to art books.

Her first book of poems, *Poèmes*, was published in 1972. It was followed by *Notre royaume est de promesses* (1974), *Pourtant le sud...* (1976), and *Lettera Amorosa* (1978). *La Cérémonie*, her first collection of short stories, appeared in 1979 (and was translated in 1980 as *The Ceremony* by David Lobdell). It was hailed as the brilliant investigation of "a mysterious world where men and women, sometimes disguised as animals or mythical beasts, engage one another in a ruthless struggle for survival." Her second short-story collection, *Agnès et le singulier bestiaire*, was published in 1982; *L'Envoleur de chevaux et autres contes* was published in 1986; and then came *Portraits d'Elsa et autres histoires* in 1990. Thériault has also written a novel, *Les Demoiselles de Numidie* (1984), and has translated works by Julia Sorel and Robert Kroetsch.

The story included here is the title story of *Portraits d'Elsa et autres histoires*, translated by David Homel. A remarkably subtle yet powerful story about the disappearance of the self, its effect is created by the gradual accumulation of images "of childhood and memory and dreams dug up."

"Portraits of Elsa" is a translation of "Portraits d'Elsa" published in *Portraits d'Elsa et autres histoires* (Montreal: Les Quinze, Éditeur, 1990).

First Portrait

When she removes her stockings, Elsa does not roll them down to her ankle, then slide them over her foot. When she removes her stockings, Elsa pulls them off by the toes.

To take them off, she has established a strict routine that gives the lie to her unfocused look as she sits on the edge of the bed, as though everything, the room itself, the particular time of day, the suspicious presence of a witness, as though all that, as I was saying, meant absolutely nothing at all.

She sits and places her bag on the floor. She displays neither modesty nor passion as she unbuttons her blouse. The edges of it fall over her breasts that are no more impressive naked than clothed. Her eyes have no expression, her face no movement. Only the watcher's desire, his interest, could turn Elsa's careful way of taking off her stockings by the toes into something glorious.

Observe her: first she lowers her head, then contemplates her feet, side by side on the floor. Then, gently, she slips one foot out of the prison of her shoe. Her leg is already half raised, and now she brings it up to her breast, widening the slit of her skirt and revealing the fleshy folds of her sex, while her other hand runs over her lower leg a time or two. Like a child making a discovery, Elsa's mouth opens half way; carefully, she examines her leg, as if seeking in a crystal ball some secret indication of her future. Once she has completed her curious caress, Elsa delicately takes hold of the amber nylon that cowls her toes. She pulls a little; the stocking resists. A light flares in Elsa's eyes—a light so discreet you'd have to be an intimate of hers to see it. Her right hand begins a series of movements under the elasticized top of her stocking, as she methodically loosens the nylon's hold on her thigh. In an astonishing suspension of balance—as though she were about to execute a kind of seated, impossible pirouette—she performs three simultaneous movements designed to complete the denuding of her leg. She presses down on the fabric with her palm, she pulls on the end with the other hand, and she describes a circle with her ankle. Her foot turns and twists and pivots and finally frees itself from the stranglehold of the stocking. Then Elsa, who still appears unreachable, in meticulous concentration, slowly strips her leg, the colour of ripe fruit, then drops the stocking on the floor, in a soft little pile, next to her bag.

Symmetry reaches perfection when Elsa performs the same rite to remove her other stocking.

When it is all over, when both Elsa's legs are naked, only then does she recover her neutral expression and the perfect emptiness of her eyes. She lifts her skirt around her waist and lies back, at my disposal.

To tell the truth, Elsa's little ritual doesn't interest me. I gaze around the room and smoke a cigarette while it runs its course. But don't think I rush in, oh no. I hold my position a few more seconds. My own patience excites me.

That's enough. Now's the time. I drop a few bills on the floor, on Elsa's stockings. I spread the edges of her blouse and her dark thighs with my elbows. I put my hands on her insignificant breasts and take my pleasure in her. Quickly. With my clothes on. Without taking the time to imagine that, at each of my thrusts, she might let out the little yelp of a bitch.

Second Portrait

First, her legs. Wrapped in black fishnet stockings. Seated woman (detail), as in a painting. Just her legs. The rest of her is beyond vision, made opaque by N's need to first capture the arrogance of her ankles (ankles Elsa has crossed, one over the other, the way elegant ladies do when they sit in an armchair), then the oblique line that runs to her knees, and finally her knees themselves, superbly present, though almost too pointed.

Elsa keeps her legs still as the eye of N's camera frames and extracts their scandalous beauty. But, in Elsa's mind, they suddenly become prostheses, artificially sliced off at the thighs by the stirring desire of a man whose only pleasure is in fragments. For a moment she imagines herself outside herself, observing and judging, free of the caprice to which she has agreed; before she can stop it, a melancholy smile pulls at her lips, a smile so fleeting that the consent written on her face is scarcely altered.

N has changed the camera angle. In the view-finder, Elsa's thighs appear, sliced off in the middle—like two crosses standing together—by the hem of her stockings pinched into place by her garter belt. Nothing else. The field of vision stops just below and just above. N lingers over that piece of Elsa where her pale skin contrasts with the fabric, then continues his stubborn exploration of her seated body, stopping at each station like a penitent: the naked, depilated, obscene pubis; the belly barely covered by a scanty undergarment; the perfect navel that can accommodate an ounce of musk; her adolescent breasts with their reddish nipples; her nonchalant arms and passive hands in long buckskin gloves; her neck, chin, face . . . N's artificial eye dissolves in contemplation, but for Elsa, his act of worship is a diligent, clinical examination of her perverted innocence.

N has imprisoned Elsa's features in his view-finder. He extends his arm; there are banknotes in his hand. Elsa takes them and slides them under her stocking, against her skin.

"Do your job," N tells Elsa.

N's camera fastens onto Elsa's face and stays there, its eye steady as N tries to capture the full cycle of changes that will torment Elsa over the next minutes. Her neck thrown slightly back; this wrinkle that appears between her eyes; the almost imperceptible swelling of her lower lip as she opens her teeth to breathe more easily; the quivering of her nostrils; the rolling of her voluptuous head; the circle her mouth makes as she cries out. Everything but her body. Everything but her arms and legs, none of their lascivious movements. Everything but the labour itself.

Only afterwards will N be able to fulfil his desire. When the screen brings back each of the fragments of Elsa frozen in their magazine pose, N will anchor them in his memory. With them, he will travel up to the actress's fluid face whose bliss he will imitate. For only there, in the solitary deciphering of the whole through the part, will N's pleasure approach its final limits.

Third Portrait

Elsa in an excessively violet dress, surrounded by the heavy perfume of lilacs that fills the room. Elsa in a little girl's dress. A flower among flowers. The rounded shape of the crinoline, petals from which her forearms seem to hang. Her small breasts imprisoned in bees' nests and her fragile throat wrapped in linen complement her posture, the stiffness of a stamen, and that hint of spitefulness in her face.

Sitting cross-legged in the little armchair, she displays the perfect socks in which her ankles are swathed and her white shoes, held on by double straps fastened by buttons that cut crosswise into her insteps. Now and again she sighs in a strangely impatient manner and lifts the layered flounces of her skirt, then lowers them quickly, allowing the man to see—if he's alert, and not distracted by something else—her little lace panties she pretends not to want to show. So light, in her stirrings and rustlings of tulle and nylon, Elsa conjures up one of those sideshow dolls whose stiff dresses glitter with industrial colours.

While she nibbles on her thumb and listens to him, the man tells her the detailed story of a little girl who's just like her, the story of a little Elsa full of knowing complicity, always ready for the performances of the dumb-show and the acting out of fables told by a grandfather eager to explore his personal fictions. The story he tells Elsa is so astonishingly light and gracefully innocent it seems out of place coming from a man so wrinkled on the outside, so faded on the inside. He must truly have a great nostalgia for virtue, though its hold upon him is rather frivolously expressed; no doubt he takes great pleasure in reliving its whims and paradoxes.

Does he want to be listened to? Probably not. Little does it matter to him that Elsa seems lost in her own thoughts, and that boredom or interest—he could not say which—has given her face an expression that is neither wholly alert nor completely absent. He speaks, recites, tells his story. Perhaps his words, as long as they remain readable, lead Elsa to discreetly recover the subtle bonds that marry vice and innocence within her. Yer her supposed clairvoyance is annulled by Elsa's sudden, childish, impatient way of letting out a great sigh while lifting and lowering her skirt over her crossed legs.

Yet soon his story is broken by gasps of quick breath. It becomes steadily less coherent, its punctuation consisting of ever more specific and obscene actions. Then Elsa rises from her armchair and kneels down between the old gentleman's legs. There, wholly submissive, she respects his instructions to the letter to diligently reveal what he keeps secret. The excess of violet flounces and lace and favours, little Elsa's docile ingenuousness, such perfect obedience to his every whim, will soon turn grandpa into a man completely overwhelmed by pleasure.

But, if struck by ecstasy (the way we say *struck by lightning*), were he to murmur the name of Elsa and cry the name of Elsa and whimper the name of Elsa, it would be out of pain. For—how could we not know?—suddenly he *saw*: the mouth, the fingers that laboured him, Elsa's mouth, Elsa's fingers and fingernails, her acerated, sharp-edged nails, her red mouth, her nails painted a vulgar, vibrant scarlet colour . . . Elsa . . . my Elsa . . .

He saw.

A real mouth. And a real whore's fingernails.

Fourth Portrait

"For you," Elsa tells him, "I am a paradise you will lose. Childhood and memory and dream dug up, divulged in the moistness between the legs, obliterated in a groan. For you, I will always be the shimmering horizon, where all deaths come together—ecstasy yet degradation yet madness yet forgetfulness shivering under my painted flesh (mask, veil, shroud, according to the depth of desire). My task is to appease, as it is to destroy. I will always be your victory and your ruin. The echo of what once was. The void."

Elsa uses the same words each time. The same or very similar words. Sometimes, she alters the order of the words, however, or changes the sequence of the phrases.

"For you," Elsa will tell him, "I am all deaths disguised, satisfaction in whore's paint, madness. Moist flesh moaning, mingled; beneath ecstasy, there is nothing. Excavated, degraded, shrouded paradise (for you, victory or ruin, both consequences of a childhood you need to shake off). My task is flesh and memory, the uneasy dream, the broken horizon. The echo still shivers, for what was, was. The veil hides it. Then comes forgetfulness, then the void."

She talks, she tells him that—did he ask for that particular recitation?—or something else, but all the while Elsa's eyes are impenetrable, as if under the influence of some strange unconsciousness (we couldn't call it ingenuousness any more), or pain that makes her a stranger to, in discontinuity with, detached from—everything. From everything. Except his fingers, aerial fingers, tapering fingers, burning and gently stripping Elsa of her materiality.

She talks, she says this or that or something else, a woman droning through a text she's learned but sometimes upsetting its logical order (although . . .). She's all but motionless, standing, arms hanging, entirely prey to the hands that delicately reveal her body. He, through the access of her open blouse (he has already undone the buttons while we related her words), brushes her small breasts with his tongue and teases her nipples into erection.

She talks, she says this and that. The man has begun to drive speech out of her head.

Elsa—made immune to pleasure by her commerce, or is it to savour pleasure more fully?—slowly shudders as the man's mouth brands her.

Then he—quickly quickly suddenly we don't know why—pulls down and casts away the skirt that was restraining Elsa. Without her skirt, Elsa is naked.

No. *Almost naked.*

A pause. The man's eyes. His elfin musician's fingers return and caress her skin, everywhere, Elsa's white skin, and make it sing.

Then he slips to his knees in the intimacy of the black net that stretches across her legs, and one after the other, unhurriedly, he strips them bare with both hands. He inserts his index fingers between nylon and flesh, he pulls and unrolls Elsa's stocking down to Elsa's knee, then from her calf to Elsa's ankle, then onto Elsa's foot, then.

Then nothing is left but her naked leg, two naked legs. He nips at them. He licks them. He *torments* them—as if they were martyrs for the burning.

Elsa has ceased her recitation; she could not go on. Now she moans, "For you, I will be," being all manner of things, "my task is moistness," incoherently, "dreams divulged," words either dictated or from her own storehouse, and she has no idea (not that it matters) to whom, him or her, she sends them.

Then—too soon, it seems to her—he takes (he loves?) Elsa. Half naked and half reclining, with the eagerness of a man afraid to lag behind her—or himself. But he is good. He is soothing. When their pleasure takes place, it is neither weak nor silent; it resounds with all that was.

Then, nothingness.

He slips the rolled banknotes (not without tenderness, though a bit mechanically) between the swollen lips of Elsa's sex.

Elsa cries. She does every time.

Now she knows: for him, she is all women. Never will she be that single one.

Fifth Portrait

Elsa's expression is at the edge of hatred, just inside it; call it contempt. As if she were ready to issue an order or spit out an insult, but for the time being, she keeps her silence. First she must make him submit, in silence. Strip the crawling man of his voice and make him beg her for it; refuse to issue the command that would fulfil him.

Elsa's eyes are trained to recognize the slightest hint of pleasure, so she can swiftly extirpate it and snuff out its progress. Her eyes are trained for disrespect and disgust, for the mute demands that debase the man at her feet, before her, first disobeys, then obeys with extraordinary fervour. Elsa's eyes are trained to detect the paradoxes of this relationship, and play upon them, and clarify its *very confused hierarchy*.

Elsa's eyes are trained to train.

As are her movements. Her words.

With one hand, with one arm sheathed in a glove that covers it to the shoulder, Elsa slowly produces the cat-o'-nine-tails that nestles against her skin, inside her boot. Do not be surprised if Elsa's act brings the beginnings of a low moan from the man, fashioned from fear and desire, a lament that is part sob, part song. The sight of the little whip—which she has not yet used, which she consents only to *exhibit*—elicits fleeting, secret, forbidden thoughts that leave him excited and, anticipating Elsa's command, for which he will atone (or so it seems) himself.

Elsa will not tolerate such impatience. Spoken or wordless, she issues orders that will keep him in an infinite state of abjection, as if suspended above ecstasy, until the rest of his dignity has been consumed.

It would be useless to try to describe in words, without prostituting them, everything that happens next; to represent it to ourselves is enough. The interior of this flower-filled room with its delicate furniture—a setting whose pleasantness is marked by the actors and their props—will be the theatre of perversions of such perfect intensity, such absolute vulgarity, that at the end they will leave a kind of splendorous glow.

Afterwards, when everything has been consumed (because Elsa has permitted it to be so), crawling on his hands and knees (the final humiliation), he will place the banknotes he is holding in his mouth between her booted thighs—like a dog.

This scenario (which is his) that Elsa has rigorously respected down to the last didascalia will end the moment he leaves her. When Elsa raises her eyes and sees her own reflection in the mirror, her look is not part of the script.

Let us say (it is the author's prerogative) that, at first, Elsa smiles ironically, wearily to herself. But let us also say that her smile does not last, and that a sudden desire overtakes her—one she did not foresee, one that was not written—to spit in her own face. And let us have her do just that.

Final Portrait

I, Elsa, flee him. He would reconstitute me; he asks, "Tell me about yourself." He notes it down. In fine, elegantly negligent handwriting, he records the words I pronounce and sometimes, thinking I don't see, replaces one with another.

Elaborate tales run through me with their beauty and misery. No matter where they come from, I receive them with urgency, as though they are doomed to disappear, but my transcription takes place in cool equilibrium. There are times when I understand that a certain secret will reduce neither the power nor the effect of my words, for brief is their trace through space, suspended like the momentum you break just before it propels you into the void. When I must, without my scribe knowing, I remove these shoots whose survival might weaken my words.

The space between us grows or shrinks, depending on whether the working words carry pleasure or signs of pain (that, we share with ordinary couples—but I think the comparison stops there because for us, breakups are as absurd as our bond is inevitable; our symbiosis is perfect, down to what is missing).

When we are close to each other, I increase my surveillance of his pen. Is he taking too many liberties? I modify what comes next "in accordance." I correct a detail or two. I add balance. But I make sure he knows nothing of this. Most of the time, I confess, his *ductility*—which is admirable—is like that of a calligrapher of whom a poet (which one?) once said that his hand "must be empty" in order to be inspired. He becomes a line of ink that never breaks and never ends, even in its breaches (its arched entryways?), forever inhabited by breath primeval.

Other times (is it out of fear of disorder?), we keep our distances. Whether by purposeful decision, it is hard to say. When I can't be sure that he truly respects my suggestions, I ElsaElsa, come to doubt *the reality we are inventing for me*. I begin to lose sight of my register, my tempos are no longer my own, my melody escapes my influence (here, I won't bring up the question of *authority*); in other words, I lose myself. You might come to believe—and you wouldn't be wrong—in the supremacy of my copyist (my creator?). And when you see how, with varying degrees of comfort, I slip into the roles he assigns me without my approval, could you not also suspect me of happily granting him—at least a little bit, at least now and again—the pre-emimence he enjoys?

Where lies truth?

Who is truth?

No doubt we always end up using infinitely organizable strategies to weave these very Penelopean bonds. Yet despite them, in the end, I, ElsaElsaElsa, multiplied among all selves, don't really know the preferences of he who transcribes me.

Neither do I know (a glaring lack of knowledge) which of us is the *other* in this singular conversation in which we find ourselves alone, together.

The Canadian Short Story Library Series

The Canadian Short Story Library series undertakes to publish fiction of importance to a fuller appreciation of Canadian literary history and the developing Canadian tradition. Work by major writers that has fallen into obscurity is restored to canonical significance, and short stories by writers of lapsed renown are gathered in collections or appropriate anthologies.

Selected Stories of Robert Barr
Edited by John Parr

Selected Stories of Isabella Valancy Crawford
Edited by Penny Petrone

Selected Stories of Mazo de la Roche
Edited by Douglas Daymond

Selected Stories of Norman Duncan
Edited by John Coldwell Adams

Voyages: Short Narratives of Susanna Moodie
Edited by John Thurston

Short Stories by Thomas Murtha
Edited by William Murtha

Waken, Lords and Ladies Gay: Selected Stories of
Desmond Pacey
Edited by Frank M. Tierney

The Race and Other Stories by Sinclair Ross
Edited by Lorraine McMullen

Selected Stories of Duncan Campbell Scott
Edited by Glenn Clever

Selected Stories of Ernest Thompson Seton
Edited by Patricia Morley

The Lady and the Travelling Salesman:
Stories by Leo Simpson
Edited by Henry Imbleau

Many Mansions: Selected Stories of Douglas O. Spettigue
Edited by Leo Simpson

Selected Stories of E.W. Thomson
Edited by Lorraine McMullen

Forest and Other Gleanings: The Fugitive Writings of
Catharine Parr Traill
Edited by Michael A. Peterman and Carl Ballstadt

Pioneering Women: Short Stories by Canadian Women,
Beginnings to 1880
Edited by Lorraine McMullen and Sandra Campbell

Aspiring Women: Short Stories by Canadian Women,
1880–1900
Edited by Lorraine McMullen and Sandra Campbell

New Women: Short Stories by Canadian Women,
1900–1920
Edited by Sandra Campbell and Lorraine McMullen

The paper used in this publication meets the minimum requirements
of American National Standard for Information Sciences -
Permanence of Paper for Printed Library Materials, ANSI Z39.48-1992.

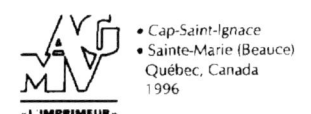

- Cap-Saint-Ignace
- Sainte-Marie (Beauce)
Québec, Canada
1996